The Prairie Flower
A Tale Of The Indian Border

By

Gustave Aimard

The Prairie Flower
A Tale Of The Indian Border
by Gustave Aimard

Copyright © 2024

All Rights reserved.

ISBN: 978-93-62204-76-9

Published by

DOUBLE 9 BOOKS

2/13-B, Ansari Road
Daryaganj, New Delhi – 110002
info@double9books.com
www.double9books.com
Tel. 011-40042856

ABOUT THE AUTHOR

Gustave Aimard wrote multiple volumes about Latin America and the American frontier. Oliver Aimard was born in Paris. As he previously stated, he was the offspring of two married individuals, "but not to each other". His father, François Sébastiani de la Porta (1775-1851), was a commander in Napoleon's army and a representative of the Louis Philippe government. Sebastiani was married to the Duchess of Coigny. In 1806, the couple had a daughter, Alatrice-Rosalba Fanny. The mother died shortly after she was born. Fanny was reared by her grandmother, Duchess of Coigny. Aimard was placed as a baby with a family that were paid to raise him. By the age of nine or twelve, he was sent off on a herring boat. Later, about 1838, he served briefly with the French Navy. After one more trip to America (when he claims he was adopted into a Comanche tribe), Aimard returned to Paris in 1847, the same year his half-sister, Duchess de Choiseul-Pralin, was cruelly killed by her noble husband. Reconciliation or acknowledgement by his biological family did not occur. After serving briefly in the Garde Mobil, Aimard returned to the Americas.

CONTENTS

CHAPTER I
A HUNTING ENCAMPMENT

America is the land of prodigies! Everything there assumes gigantic proportions, which startle the imagination and confound the reason. Mountains, rivers, lakes and streams, all are carved on a sublime pattern.

There is a river of North America—not like the Danube, Rhine, or Rhone, whose banks are covered with towns, plantations, and time-worn castles: whose sources and tributaries are magnificent streams, the waters of which, confined in a narrow bed, rush onwards as if impatient to lose themselves in the ocean—but deep and silent, wide as an arm of the sea, calm and severe in its grandeur, it pours majestically onwards, its waters augmented by innumerable streams, and lazily bathes the banks of a thousand isles, which it has formed of its own sediment.

These isles, covered with tall thickets, exhale a sharp or delicious perfume which the breeze bears far away. Nothing disturbs their solitude, save the gentle and plaintive appeal of the dove, or the hoarse and strident voice of the tiger, as it sports beneath the shade.

At certain spots, trees that have fallen through old age, or have been uprooted by the hurricane, collect on its waters; then, attached by creepers and concealed by mud, these fragments of forests become floating islands. Young shrubs take root upon them: the petunia and nenuphar expand here and there their yellow roses; serpents, birds, and caimans come to sport and rest on these verdurous rafts, and are with them swallowed up in the ocean.

This river has no name! Others in the same zone are called Nebraska, Platte, Missouri; but this is simply the *Mecha-Chebe* the old father of waters, *the* river before all! the Mississippi in a word!

Vast and incomprehensible as is infinity, full of secret terrors, like the Ganges and Irrawaddy, it is the type of fecundity, immensity, and eternity to the numerous Indian nations that inhabit its banks.

Three men were seated on the bank of the river, a little below its confluence with the Missouri, and were breakfasting on a slice of roast elk, while gaily chatting together.

The spot where they were seated was remarkably picturesque. The bank of the river was formed of small mounds, enamelled with flowers. The strangers had selected for their halt the top of the highest mound, whence the eye embraced a magnificent panorama. In the foreground, dense curtains of verdure which undulated with each breath of air: on the islands innumerable flocks of dark-winged flamingos, perched on their long legs, plovers and cardinals fluttering from bough to bough, while numerous alligators lazily wallowed in the mud. Between the islands, the silvery patches of water reflected the sunbeams. In the midst of these masses of coruscating light, fishes of every description sported on the surface of the water, and traced sparkling furrows. Further back, as far as the eye could reach, the tops of the trees that bordered the prairie, and whose dark green scarcely showed upon the horizon.

But the three men we have mentioned seemed to trouble themselves very slightly about the natural beauties that surrounded them, as they were fully engaged in appeasing a true hunter's appetite. Their meal, however, only lasted a few minutes, and when the last fragments had been devoured, one lighted his Indian pipe, the other took a cigar from his pocket. They then stretched themselves on the grass, and began digesting with that beatitude which characterizes smokers, while following with a languid eye the clouds of bluish smoke that rose in long spirals with each mouthful they puffed forth. As for the third man, he leant his back against a tree, crossed his arms, on his chest, and went to sleep most prosaically.

We will profit by this momentary repose to present these persons to our readers, and make them better acquainted with each other. The first was a Canadian half-breed, of about fifty years of age, and known by the name of "Bright-eye." His life had been entirely spent on the prairie among the Indians, all of whose tricks he was thoroughly acquainted with.

Like the majority of his countrymen he was very tall, more than six feet in height: his body was thin and angular; his limbs were knotty, but covered with muscles, hard as ropes; his bony and yellow face had a remarkable expression of frankness and joviality, and his little grey eyes sparkled with intelligence; his prominent cheekbones, his nose bent down over a wide mouth supplied with long white teeth, and his rounded chin, made up a face which was the most singular, and, at the same time, the most attractive that could be imagined.

His dress differed in no respect from that of the other wood rangers; that is to say, it was a strange medley of European and Indian fashions, generally adopted by all the white prairie hunters and trappers. His weapons consisted of a knife, a pair of pistols, and an American rifle, now lying on the grass, but within reach of his hand.

His companion was a man of thirty to thirty-two years of age at the most, but who appeared scarce twenty-five, tall, and well made. His blue eyes, limpid as a woman's, the long light curls that escaped beneath the edge of his Panama hat, and floated in disorder on his shoulders, the whiteness of his skin, which contrasted with the olive and brown complexion of the hunter, were sufficient evidence that he was not born in the hot climate of America.

In fact, this young man was a Frenchman, Charles Edward de Beaulieu, and was descended from one of the oldest families in Brittany. But, under this slightly effeminate appearance, he concealed a lion's courage which nothing could startle or even surprise. Skilled in all bodily exercises, he was also endowed with prodigious strength, and the delicate skin of his white and unstained hands, with their rosy nails, covered nerves of steel.

The Count's dress would reasonably have appeared extraordinary in a country remote from civilization to anyone who had leisure to examine it. He wore a hunting jacket of green cloth, of a French cut, and buttoned over his chest; yellow doeskin breeches, fastened by a waist belt of varnished leather; a cartouche box, and a hunting knife in a bronzed steel sheath, and with an admirably chiselled hilt: while his legs were covered by long riding boots, coming up over the knee. Like his companion, he had laid his rifle on the grass: this weapon, richly damascened, must have cost an enormous sum.

The Count de Beaulieu, whose father followed the princes into exile and served them actively, first in Condé's army and then in all the Royalist plots that were incessantly formed during the Empire, was an ultra-Royalist. Left an orphan at an early age, and possessed of an immense fortune, he was nominated a lieutenant in the Gardes du Corps. After the fall of Charles X., the Count, whose career was broken up, was assailed by a fearful despondency, and an unenviable disregard for life filled his heart. Europe became hateful to him, and he resolved to bid it an eternal farewell. After intrusting the management of his fortune to a confidential agent, the Count embarked for the United States.

But American life, narrow, paltry, and egotistic, was not made for him; for the young man understood the Americans no better than they did him. His heart was ulcerated by the meanness and trickery he saw daily committed by the descendants of the Plymouth Brethren, so he one day resolved to bury himself in the depths of the country, and visit those immense prairies whence the first lords of the soil had been driven by the cunning and treachery of their crafty despoilers.

The Count had brought with him from France an old servant of the family, whose progenitors, for many generations, had uninterruptedly served the Beaulieus. Before embarking, the Count imparted his plans to Ivon Kergollec, leaving him at liberty to remain behind or follow; the servant's choice was not long, he simply replied that his master had the right to do what he pleased without consulting him, and as it was his duty to follow his master everywhere, he should do so. Even when the Count formed the resolve of visiting the prairies, and thought it right to tell his servant his resolution, the answer was still the same. Ivon was about forty-five years of age, and was a true type of the hardy, simple, and withal crafty Breton peasant; he was short and stumpy, but his well-knit limbs and wide chest denoted immense strength. His brick-coloured face was illumined by two small eyes, which sparkled with cleverness and flashed like carbuncles.

Ivon, whose life had been spent calmly and lazily in the gilded halls of Beaulieu House, had gradually assumed the regular habits of a nobleman's lackey; having had no occasion to prove his courage, he was completely ignorant of the possession of that quality, and, although during the last few months he had been placed in many dangerous circumstances while following his master, he was still at the same point, that is to say, he completely doubted himself, and had the innate conviction that he was as cowardly as a hare; so nothing was more curious after a meeting with the Indians than to hear Ivon, who had been fighting like a lion and performing prodigies of valour, excuse himself humbly to his master for having behaved so badly, as he was not used to fighting.

It is needless to say that the Count excused him, while laughing heartily, and telling him as a consolation—for the poor fellow was very unhappy at this supposed cowardice—that the next time he would probably do better, and that he would gradually grow accustomed to this life, which was so different from that he had hitherto led. At this consolation the worthy man-servant would nod his head sorrowfully, and reply, with an accent of thorough conviction:—

"No, sir, I can never have any courage. I feel sure of it; it is a sad truth, but I am a poltroon. I am only too well aware of it."

Ivon was dressed in a complete suit of livery, though, in regard to present circumstances, he was, like his companions, armed to the teeth, and his rifle leant against the tree by his side.

Three magnificent horses, full of fire and blood, hobbled a few paces from the hunters, were carelessly browsing on the climbing peas and young tree shoots.

We have omitted to mention two peculiarities of the Count. The first was, he always carried in his right eye a gold eyeglass, fastened round his neck by means of a black ribbon; the second, that he continually wore kid gloves, which we confess, greatly to his annoyance, had now grown very dirty and torn.

And now, by what strange combination of chance were these three men, so differing in birth, habits, and education, met together some five or six hundred leagues from any civilized abode, on the banks of a river, if not unknown, at any rate hitherto unexplored, seated amicably on the grass, and sharing a breakfast which was more than frugal? We can explain this in a few words to the reader by cursorily describing a scene that occurred in the prairie about six months prior to the beginning of our narrative.

Bright-eye was a determined man, who, with the exception of the time he served the Hudson's Bay Company, had always hunted and trapped alone, despising the Indians too much to fear them, and finding in braving them that delight which the courageous man experiences, when, alone and beneath the eye of Heaven, he struggles, confiding in his own resources, against a terrible and unknown danger. The Indians knew and feared him for many a long year. Many times they had come into collision with him, and they had nearly always been compelled to retreat, leaving several of their men on the field. Hence they had sworn against the hunter one of those hearty Indian hatreds which nothing can satiate save the punishment of the man who is the object of it.

But as they knew with what sort of man they had to deal, and did not care to increase the number of the victims he had already sacrificed, they resolved to await, with the peculiar patience characteristic of their race, the propitious moment for seizing their foe, and till then confine themselves to carefully watching all his movements, so as not to lose the favourable opportunity when it presented itself.

Bright-eye at this moment was hunting on the banks of the Missouri. Knowing himself watched, and instinctively suspecting a trap, he took all the precautions suggested to him by his inventive mind and the deep knowledge he possessed of Indian tricks. One day, while exploring the banks of the river, he fancied he noticed, a slight distance ahead of him, an almost imperceptible movement in the thick brushwood. He stopped, lay down, and began crawling gently in the direction of the thicket. Suddenly the forest seemed agitated to its most unexplored depths, A swarm of

Indians rose from the earth, leaped from the trees, or rushed from behind rocks; the hunter, literally buried beneath the mass of his enemies, was reduced to a state of powerlessness, before he could even make an attempt to defend himself.

Bright-eye was disarmed in a twinkling; then a chief walked up to him, and holding out his hand, said coldly —

"Let my brother rise; the Redskin warriors are waiting for him."

"Good, good," the hunter growled; "all is not over yet, Indian, and I shall have my revenge."

The chief smiled.

"My brother is like the mockingbird," he said ironically; "he speaks too much."

Bright-eye bit his lips to keep back the insult that rose to them; he got up and followed his victors. He was a prisoner to the Piékanns, the most warlike tribe of the Blackfeet; and the chief who had taken him was his personal enemy. The chief's name was *Natah Otann* (the Grizzly Bear). He was a man of five-and-twenty at the most, with a fine intelligent face, bearing the imprint of honesty. His tall figure, well-proportioned limbs, the grace of his movements, and his martial aspect, rendered him a remarkable man. His long black hair, carefully parted, fell in disorder on his shoulders; like all the renowned warriors of his tribe, he wore on the back of his head an ermine skin, and round his neck bears' claws mingled with buffalo teeth, a very dear and highly-honoured ornament among the Indians. His shirt of buffalo hide, with short sleeves, was decorated round the neck with a species of collar of red cloth, ornamented with fringe and porcupine quills; the seams of the garment were embroidered with hair taken from scalps, the whole relieved by small bands of ermine skin. His moccasins of different colours, were loaded with very elegant embroidery, while his buffalo hide robe was quilted inside with a number of clumsy designs, intended to depict the young warrior's achievements.

Natah Otann held in his right hand a fan made of a single eagle's wing, and, suspended round the wrist from the same hand by a thong, the short-handled long-lashed whip peculiar to the prairie Indians; on his back hung his bow and arrows in a quiver of a jaguar's skin; at his waist a bullet bag, his powder flask, his long hunting knife, and his club. His shield hung on his left hip, while his gun lay across the neck of his horse, which wore a magnificent panther skin for a saddle. The appearance of this savage child of the woods, whose cloak and long plumes fluttered in the wind, curveting, on a steed as untamed as himself, had something about it striking, and, at the same time, grand.

Natah Otann was the first sachem of his tribe. He made the hunter a sign to mount a horse one of the warriors held by the bridle, and the whole party proceeded at a gallop towards the camp of the tribe. They rode onward in silence, and the chief seemed to pay no attention to his prisoner. The latter, free in appearance, and mounted on an excellent horse, made not the slightest attempt to escape; at a glance he had judged the position, saw that the Indians did not lose sight of him, and that he should be immediately recaptured if he attempted flight. The Piékanns had formed their camp on the slope of a wooded hill. For two days they seemed to have forgotten their prisoner, to whom they never once spoke. On the evening of the second day, Bright-eye was carelessly walking about and smoking his pipe, when Natah Otann approached him.

"Is my brother ready?" he asked him.

"For what?" the hunter said, stopping and pouring forth a volume of smoke.

"To die," the chief continued, laconically.

"Quite."

"Good; my brother will die tomorrow."

"You think so," the hunter replied with great coolness.

The Indian looked at him for a moment in amazement; then he repeated, "My brother will die tomorrow."

"I heard you perfectly well, chief," the Canadian said, with a smile; "and I repeat again, do you believe it?"

"Let my brother look," the sachem said, with a significant gesture.

The hunter raised his head.

"Bah!" he said, carelessly; "I see that all the preparations are made, and conscientiously so, but what does that prove? I am not dead yet, I suppose."

"No, but my brother will soon be so."

"We shall see tomorrow," Bright-eye answered, shrugging his shoulders.

And leaving the astonished chief, he lay down at the foot of a tree and fell asleep. His sleep was so real, that the Indians were obliged to wake him next morning at daybreak. The Canadian opened his eyes, yawned two or three times, as if going to put his jaw out, and got up. The Redskins led him to the post of torture, to which he was firmly fastened.

"Well!" Natah Otann said, with a grin, "what does my brother think at present?"

"Eh!" Bright-eye answered, with that magnificent coolness which never deserted him, "do you fancy that I am already dead?"

"No, but my brother will be so in an hour."

"Bah!" the Canadian said, carelessly; "many things can happen within an hour."

Natah Otann withdrew, secretly admiring the intrepid countenance of his prisoner; but, after taking a few steps, he reflected, and returned to Bright-eye's side.

"Let my brother listen," he said, "a friend speaks to him."

"Go on, chief, I am all ears."

"My brother is a strong man; his heart is great," Natah Otann said; "he is a terrible warrior."

"You know something of that, chief, I fancy," the Canadian replied.

The sachem repressed a movement of anger.

"My brother's eye is infallible, his arm is sure," he went on.

"Tell me at once what you want to come to, chief, and don't waste your time in your Indian beating round the bush."

The chief smiled as he said, in a gentler voice, "Bright-eye is alone; his lodge is solitary. Why has not so great a warrior a companion?"

The hunter fixed a searching glance on the speaker.

"What does that concern you?" he said.

Natah Otann continued, —

"The nation of the Blackfeet is powerful; the young women of the Piekann tribe are fair."

The Canadian quickly interrupted him.

"Enough, chief," he said; "in spite of all your shiftings to reach your point, I have guessed your meaning; but I will never take an Indian girl to be my wife; so you can refrain from further offers, which will not have a satisfactory result."

Natah Otann frowned.

"Dog of the palefaces," he cried, stamping his foot angrily, "this night my young men will make war whistles of thy bones, and will drink the firewater out of thy skull."

With this terrible threat, the chief finally quitted the hunter, who regarded him depart with a shrug, and muttered, "The last word is not spoken yet; this is not the first time I have found myself in a desperate position, but I have escaped; there are no reasons why I should be less lucky today. Hum! this will serve me as a lesson: another time I will be more prudent."

In the meantime the chief had given orders to begin the punishment, and the preparations were rapidly made. Bright-eye followed all the movements of the Indians with a curious eye, as if he were a perfectly unconcerned witness.

"Yes, yes," he went on, "my fine fellows, I see you; you are preparing all the instruments for my torture; there is the green wood intended to smoke me like a ham; you are cutting the spikes you mean to run up under my nails. Eh, eh!" he added, with a perfect air of satisfaction; "you are going to begin with firing; let's see how skilful you are. Ah, what fun it is for you to have a white hunter to torture. The Lord knows what strange ideas may be passing through your Indian noddles; but I recommend you to make haste, or it is very possible I may escape."

During this monologue, twenty warriors, the most skilful of the tribe, had ranged themselves about one hundred yards from the prisoner; the firing commenced; the balls all struck within an inch of the hunter's head, who, at each shot, shook his head like a drowned sparrow, to the great delight of the spectators. This amusement had gone on for some twenty minutes, and would probably have continued much longer, so great was the fun it afforded the Blackfeet; when suddenly a horseman bounded into the centre of the clearing, dispersed the Indians in his way by heavy blows of his whip, and profiting by the stupor occasioned by his unexpected appearance, galloped up to the prisoner, got down, quickly cut the thongs that bound him, thrust a brace of pistols in his hand, and remounted. All this was done in less time than it has taken us to write it.

"By Tobias!" Bright-eye joyfully exclaimed, "I was quite sure I wasn't going to die this time."

The Indians are not the men to allow themselves to be long subdued by any feeling; the first moment of surprise past, they surrounded the horseman, shouting, gesticulating, and brandishing their weapons furiously.

"Come, make way there, you scoundrels," the newcomer shouted in a commanding voice, lashing violently at those who had the imprudence to come too near him. "Let us be off," he added, turning to the hunter.

"I wish for nothing better," the latter made answer; "but it does not seem easy."

"Bah! let us try it, at any rate," the stranger continued, carefully affixing his glass in his eye.

"We will," Bright-eye said cheerfully.

The stranger who had so providentially arrived, was the Count de Beaulieu, as our readers will probably have conjectured.

"Hilloh!" the Count shouted loudly, "come here, Ivon."

"Here I am, my lord," a voice answered from the forest; and a second horseman, leaping into the clearing, coolly ranged himself by the side of the first.

There was something strange in the group formed by these three stoical men in the midst of the hundreds of Indians yelling around them. The Count, with his glass in his eye, his haughty glance, and disdainful lip, was setting the hammer of his rifle. Bright-eye, with a pistol in each hand, was preparing to sell his life dearly, while the servant calmly awaited the order to charge the savages. The Indians, furious at the audacity of the white men, were preparing, with multitudinous yells and gestures, to take a prompt vengeance on the men who had so imprudently placed themselves in their power.

"These Indians are very ugly," the Count said; "now that you are free, my friend, we have nothing more to do here, so let us be off."

And he made a sign, as if to force a passage. The Blackfeet moved forward.

"Take care," Bright-eye shouted.

"Nonsense," the Count said, shrugging his shoulders, "can these scamps intend to bar the way?"

The hunter looked at him with the air of a man who does not know exactly if he has to do with a madman or a being endowed with reason, so extraordinary did this remark seem to him. The Count dug his spurs into his horse.

"Well," Bright-eye muttered, "he will be killed, but for all that he is a fine fellow: I will not leave him."

In truth it was a critical moment: the Indians, formed in close column, were preparing to make a desperate charge on the three men—a charge which would, probably, be decisive, for the Europeans, without shelter, and entirely exposed to the shots of their enemies, could not hope to escape.

Still, that was not the Count's conviction. Not noticing the gestures and hostile cries of the Redskins, he advanced towards them, with his glass still in his eye. Since the Count's apparition, the Indian sachem, as if struck with stupor at the sight, had not made a move, but stood with his eyes fixed upon him, under the influence of extraordinary emotion. Suddenly, at the moment when the Blackfeet warriors were shouldering their guns, or fitting their arrows to the bows, Natah Otann seemed to form a resolution: he rushed forward, and raising his buffalo robe,—

"Stop!" he shouted, in a loud voice.

The Indians, obedient to their chiefs voice, immediately halted. The sachem took three steps, bowed respectfully before the Count, and said in a submissive voice:—

"My father must pardon his children, they did not know him: but my father is great, his power is immense, his goodness infinite: he will forget anything offensive in their conduct toward him."

Bright-eye, astonished at this harangue, translated it to the Count, honestly confessing that he did not understand what it meant.

"By Jove!" the Count replied, with a smile, "they are afraid."

"Hum!" the hunter muttered, "that is not so clear: it is something else; but no matter, it will be diamond cut diamond."

Then he turned to Natah Otann.

"The great pale chief," he said, "is satisfied with the respect his red children feel for him: he pardons them." Natah Otann made a movement of joy. The three men passed through the ranks of the Indians, and buried themselves in the forest, their retreat being in no way impeded.

"Ouf!" Bright-eye said, as soon as he found himself in safety, "I'm well out of that; but," he added shaking his head, "there is something extraordinary about the matter, which I cannot fathom."

"Now, my friend," the Count said to him, "you are free to go whither you please."

The hunter thought for an instant. "Bah!" he replied, after a few moments had passed, "I owe you my life. Although I do not know you, you strike me as a good fellow."

"You flatter me," the Count remarked, smiling.

"My faith, no; I say what I think. If you are agreeable we will stay together, at any rate until I have acquitted the debt I owe you by saving your life in my turn."

The Count offered him his hand.

"Thanks, my friend," he said, much moved; "I accept your offer."

"That is settled, then," the hunter joyfully exclaimed, as he pressed the offered hand.

Bright-eye, at first attached to the Count by gratitude, soon felt quite a paternal affection for him. But he understood no more than the first day the young man's behaviour, for he acted under all circumstances as if he were in France, and, by his rashness, universally foiled the hunter's Indian experience. This was carried so far, that the Canadian, superstitious like all primitive natures, soon grew into the persuasion that the Count's life was protected by a charm, so many times had he seen him emerge victoriously from positions in which anyone else would have infallibly succumbed.

At length, nothing appeared to him impossible with such a companion, and the most extraordinary propositions the Count made him seemed perfectly feasible, the more so as success crowned all their enterprises by some incomprehensible charm, and in a way contrary to all foresight. The Indians, by a strict agreement, had given up all contests with them, and even avoided any contact: if they perceived them at any time, all the Redskins, whatever tribe they might belong to, treated the Count with the utmost deference, and addressed him with an expression of terror mingled with love, the explanation of which the hunter sought in vain, for none of the Indians could or would give it.

This state of things had lasted for six months up to the moment when we saw the three men breakfasting on the banks of the Mississippi. We will now take up our story again at the point where we left it, terminating our explanation, which was indispensable for the right comprehension of what follows.

CHAPTER II
A TRAIL DISCOVERED

Our friends would probably have remained for a long time plunged in their present state of beatitude had not a slight sound in the river suddenly recalled them to the exigencies of their position.

"What's that?" the Count said, flipping off the ash from his cigar.

Bright-eye glided among the shrubs, looked for a moment, and then calmly returned to his seat.

"Nothing," he said; "two alligators sporting in the mud."

"Ah!" the Count said. There was a moment's silence, during which the hunter mentally calculated the length of the shadow of the trees on the ground.

"It is past midday," he said.

"You think so," the young man remarked.

"No; I am sure of it, sir Count."

"Confound you! you are at it again," the young man said with a smile. "I have told you to call me by my Christian name; but if you do not like that, call me like the Indians."

"Nay!" the hunter objected.

"What is the name they gave me, Bright-eye? I have forgotten."

"Oh! I should not like, sir—"

"Eh?"

"Edward, I meant to say."

"Come, that is better," the young man remarked laughingly; "but I must beg of you to repeat the nickname."

"They call you 'Glass-eye.'"

"Oh, yes! that's it;" the Count continued his laugh. "Only Indians could have such an idea as that."

"Oh," Bright-eye went on, "the Indians are not what you suppose them; they are as crafty as the demon."

"Come, stop that, Bright-eye; I always suspected you of having a weakness for the Redskins."

"How can you say that, when I am their obstinate enemy, and have been fighting them for the last forty years?"

"That is the very reason that makes you defend them."

"How so?" the hunter said, astonished at this conclusion, which he was far from expecting.

"For a very simple reason. No one likes to contend with enemies unworthy of him, and it is quite natural you should try to elevate those against whom you have been fighting for forty years."

The hunter shook his head.

"Mr. Edward," he said, with a thoughtful air, "the Redskins are people whom it takes many a long year to know. They possess at once the craft of the opossum, the prudence of the serpent, and the courage of the cougar. A few years hence you will not despise them as you do now."

"My good fellow," the Count objected, "I hope I shall have left the prairies within a year. I am yearning for a civilized life. I want Paris, with its opera and balls. No, no; the desert does not suit me."

The hunter shook his head a second time. Then he continued, with a mournful accent, which struck the young man, and, as if rather speaking to himself, than replying to the Count's remarks—

"Yes, yes; that is the way with Europeans: when they arrive on the prairies, they regret civilized life, and the desert is only gradually appreciated; but when a man has breathed the odours of the savannah, when during long nights he has listened to the rustling of the wind in the trees, and the howling of the wild beasts in the virgin forests—when he has admired that proud landscape which owes nothing to art, where the hand of God is imprinted at each step in ineffaceable characters: when he has gazed on the glorious scenes that rise in succession before him—then he begins by degrees to love this unknown world, so full of mysteries and strange incidents; his eyes are opened to the truth, and he repudiates the falsehoods of civilization. At such a a moment he experiences emotions full of secret charms, and recognizing no other master save that God, in whose presence he feels himself so small, he forgets everything to lead a nomadic life, and remains in the desert, because there alone he feels free, happy—a man, in a word! Ah, sir, whatever you may say, whatever you may do, the desert now holds you: you have tasted its joys and its griefs; it will not allow you to depart so easily—you will not see France again so speedily—the desert will retain you in spite of yourself."

The young man had listened with an emotion for which he could not account, to this long harangue. In his heart he recognized, through the hunter's exaggeration, the justice of his reasoning, and felt startled at being compelled to allow him to be in the right. Not knowing what to reply, or feeling that he was beaten, the Count suddenly turned the conversation.

"Hum!" he began, "I think you said it was past twelve?"

"About a quarter past," the hunter answered.

The Count consulted, his watch.

"Quite right," he said.

"Oh!" the hunter continued, pointing to the sun, "that is the only true clock; it never goes too fast or too slow, for Heaven regulates it."

The young man bowed his head affirmatively.

"We will start," he said.

"For what good at this moment?" the Canadian asked. "We have nothing pressing before us."

"That is true; but are you sure we have not lost our way?"

."Lost our way!" the hunter exclaimed, with a start of surprise, almost of anger; "no, no, it is impossible. I guarantee that within a week we shall be on Lake Itasca."

"The Mississippi really runs from that lake?"

"Yes; for, in spite of what is asserted, the Missouri is only the principal branch of that river: the savants would have done better to assure themselves of the fact, ere they declared that the Mississippi and Missouri are two separate rivers."

"What would you have, Bright-eye?" the Count said, laughingly. "Savants are the same in all countries; being naturally indolent, they rely on one another, and hence the infinity of absurdities they put in circulation with the most astounding coolness."

"The Indians are never mistaken."

"That is true; but then the Indians are not savants."

"No; they see for themselves, and only assert what they are sure of."

"That is what I meant," the Count replied.

"If you will listen to me, Mr. Edward, we will remain here a few hours longer to let the great heat pass off, and when the sun is going down we will start again."

"Very good; let us rest then. Ivon appears to be thoroughly of our opinion, for he has not stirred."

The Count had risen; before sitting down, he mechanically cast a glance on the immense plain which lay so calmly and majestically at his feet.

"Eh!" he suddenly exclaimed, "what is that down there?—look, Bright-eye."

The hunter rose and looked in the direction indicated by the Count.

"Well—do you see nothing?" the young man remarked.

Bright-eye, with his hand over his eyes to shield them from the glare of the sun, looked attentively without replying.

"Well?" the Count said, at the expiration of a moment.

"We are no longer alone," the hunter answered; "there are men down there."

"How men? We have seen no Indian trail."

"I did not say they were Indians."

"Hum! I suppose at this distance it would be rather difficult to decide who they are."

Bright-eye smiled.

"You always judge from your knowledge obtained in the civilized world, Mr. Edward," he answered.

"Which means—?" the young man said, intensely piqued at the observation.

"That you are always wrong."

"Hang it, my friend! You will allow me to observe, all individuality apart, that it is impossible at this distance to recognize anybody. Especially when nothing can be distinguished, save a little white smoke."

"Is not that enough? Do you believe that all smoke is alike?"

"That is rather a subtle distinction; and I confess that to me all smoke is alike."

"That's where the error is," the Canadian continued, with great coolness, "and when you have spent a few years in the prairie you will not be deceived."

The Count looked at him attentively, convinced that he was laughing at him; but the other continued, with the utmost calmness—

"What we notice down there is neither the fire of Indians nor of hunters, but is kindled by white men, not yet accustomed to a desert life."

"Perhaps you will have the goodness to explain."

"I will do so, and you will soon allow that I am correct. Listen, Mr. Edward, for this is important to know."

"I am listening, my good fellow."

"You are not ignorant," the hunter continued imperturbably, "that what is conventionally called the desert is largely populated."

"Quite true," the young man said, smiling.

"Good; but the enemies most to be feared in the prairies are not wild beasts so much as men; the Indians and hunters are so well aware of this fact that they try as much as possible to destroy all traces of their passage and hide their presence."

"I admit that."

"Very good; when the Redskins or the hunters are obliged to light a fire, either to prepare their food or ward off the cold, they select most carefully the wood they intend to burn, and never employ any but dry wood."

"Hum! I do not see the use of that."

"You will soon understand me," the hunter continued; "dry wood only produces a bluish smoke, which is difficult to detect from the sky, and this renders it invisible at a short distance; while on the other hand, green wood, through its dampness, produces a white dense smoke, which reveals for a long distance the presence of those who kindle it. This is the reason why, by a mere inspection of that smoke, I told you just now that the people down there were white men, and strangers, moreover, to the prairie, else they would have employed dry wood."

"By Jove," the young man exclaimed, "that is curious, and I should like to convince myself."

"What do you intend doing?"

"Why, go and see who are the people that have lighted the fire."

"Why disturb yourself, since I have told you?"

"That is possible; but what I propose doing is for my personal satisfaction; since we have been living together you have told me such extraordinary things, that I should like, once in a way, to know what faith to place in them."

And not listening to the Canadian's observations, the young man aroused his servant.

"What do you want, my lord?" the latter said, rubbing his eyes.

"The horses, and quickly too, Ivon."

The Breton rose and bridled the horses; the Count leaped into the saddle; the hunter imitated him, though shaking his head; and the three trotted down the hill.

"You will see Mr. Edward," Bright-eye said, "that I was in the right."

"I am certain of it; still I should like to judge for myself."

"If that is the case, allow me to go in front; for, as we do not know with what people we may have to deal, it is as well to be on our guard."

The Canadian headed the party. The fire the Count had seen from the top of the hill was not so near as he supposed, the hunter was incessantly compelled to get out of the way of dense thickets which barred the way, and this lengthened the distance; so that they took nearly two hours in reaching the spot they were steering for. When they had at length arrived within a short distance of the fire which had so perplexed M. de Beaulieu, the Canadian stopped, making his companions a sign to imitate him. When they had done so, Bright-eye got down, gave his horse's bridle to Ivon, and taking his rifle in his hand, said, "I am going on a voyage of discovery."

"Go," the young man replied, laconically.

The Count was a man of tried courage; but since he had been in the prairie he had learned one thing, that courage without prudence is madness in the presence of enemies who never act without calling craft and treachery to their aid; hence, gradually renouncing his chivalrous ideas, he was beginning to adopt the habits of the desert, knowing very well that in an ambuscade the advantage nearly always remains with the man who first discovers the enemies whom chance may bring in his way. The Count, therefore, patiently awaited the hunter's return, who had silently glided among the trees, and disappeared in the direction of the fire. At the end of about an hour the shrubs shook, and Bright-eye reappeared at a point opposite to that where he had started. The old wood ranger had been considerably bothered by the apparition of the distant fire which the Count pointed out to him from the top of the hill. So soon as he was alone, putting in practice the axiom, that the shortest road from one point to another is a curved line, the truth of which is proved in the prairie, he had taken a wide circuit, in order to come, if it were possible, on the trail of the men he wished to observe, and from it discover who they really were.

In the desert, the meeting most feared is that with man. Every stranger is at first an enemy, and hence persons generally accost each other at a distance, with the barrel of the gun advanced, and the finger on the trigger. With that infallible glance the experience of the savannahs had given him, Bright-eye had noticed from a distance a place where the grass was laid, and the strangers must have passed along that road. The hunter, still bent down to escape observation, soon found himself on the edge of a track about four feet wide, the end of which was lost in a virgin forest a short distance ahead. After stopping a minute, to recover his breath, the Canadian placed the butt of his rifle on the ground, and began carefully studying the traces so deeply imprinted on the plain. His investigation did not last ten minutes; then he raised his head with a smile, threw his rifle on his shoulder, and quietly returned to the spot where he had left his companions, not even taking the trouble to go to the fire. This brief examination had told him all he wished to know.

"Well, Bright-eye, any news?" the Count asked, on noticing him.

"The people, whose fire we perceived," the hunter replied, "are American emigrants, pioneers who wish to set up their tent in the desert. The family is composed of six persons—four men and two women; they have a waggon to carry their baggage, and have with them a large number of beasts."

"Mount your horse, Bright-eye, and let us go and welcome these worthy people to the desert."

The hunter remained motionless and thoughtful, leaning on his rifle.

"Well," the Count said, "did you not hear me, my friend?"

"Yes, Mr. Edward, I perfectly understood you; but among the traces left by the emigrants I discovered others which appeared to me suspicious, and I should like, before venturing into their camp, to beat up the neighbourhood."

"What traces do you allude to?" the young man asked, quickly.

"Well," the hunter went on, "you know that, rightly or wrongly, the Redskins claim to be kings of the prairies, and will not endure there the presence of white men."

"I consider that they are perfectly right in doing so; since the discovery of America, the white men have gradually dispossessed them of their territory, and driven them back on the desert; they are defending their last refuge, and are justified in doing so."

"I am perfectly of your opinion, Mr. Edward; the desert ought to belong to the hunters and the Indians; unfortunately the Americans do not think so, and they daily quit their cities and proceed into the interior, establishing themselves here and there, and confiscating to their benefit the most fertile countries, and those richest in game."

"What can we do, my good friend?" the Count answered, with a smile; "it is an irremediable evil, which we must put up with; but I cannot yet see where you wish to arrive with these reflections, which, though extremely just, do not appear to me exactly suited to the occasion; so pray have the goodness to explain your meaning."

"I will do so. Well, I noticed, by certain signs, that the emigrants are closely followed by a party of Indians, who probably only await a favourable moment to attack and massacre them."

"The deuce!" the young man said; "that is serious of course you warned these worthy people of the danger that threatens them."

"I—not at all. I have not spoken to them, nor even seen them."

"What! you have not seen them?"

"No; so soon as I recognized the Indian sign, I hurried back to consult with you."

"Very good; but as you did not go to their camp, how were you able to give me such precise information about them and their number?"

"Oh, very easily," the hunter answered simply; "the desert is a book entirely written by the hand of God, and it cannot hide its secrets from a man accustomed to read it. I needed only to look at the trail for a few minutes to divine everything."

The Count fixed on the hunter a glance of surprise. Though he had been living in the prairie for more than six months, he could not yet understand the species of divination with which the hunter seemed gifted, with reference to facts that were to himself as a dead letter.

"Perhaps, though," he said, "the Indians whose trail you detected are harmless hunters."

Bright-eye shook his head.

"There are no harmless hunters among the Indians, especially when they are on the trail of white men. These Indians belong to three plundering tribes which I am surprised to see united; they doubtlessly meditate some extraordinary expedition, in which the massacre of these emigrants will be one of the least interesting episodes."

"Who are these Indians? Do you think they are numerous?"

The hunter reflected for a moment.

"The party I discovered is probably only the vanguard of a more numerous band," he answered; "as far as I could judge, there were not more than forty; but the Redskin warriors march with the speed of the antelope, and they can hardly ever be counted; the party is composed of Comanches, Blackfeet, and Sioux; that is to say, the three most warlike tribes in the prairie."

"Hum!" the Count remarked, after a moment's reflection, "if these demons really mean to attack the Americans, as everything leads us to suppose, the poor fellows appear to be in an awkward position."

"Unless a miracle occur, they are lost," the hunter said, concisely.

"What is to be done—how to warn them?"

"Mr. Edward, take care what you are going to do."

"Still we cannot allow men of our own colour to be murdered almost in our presence; that would be cowardly."

"Yes; but it would be astounding folly to join them; reflect that there are only three of us."

"I know it," the young man said, thoughtfully; "still I would never consent to abandon these poor people without trying to defend them."

"Stay, there is only one thing to be done, and perhaps Heaven will come to our aid."

"Come, be brief, my friend, time presses."

"In all probability, the Indians have not yet discovered our trail, although they must be a short distance from us. Let us, then, return to the spot where we breakfasted, and which commands the entire prairie. The Indians never attack their enemy before four in the morning; as soon as they attempt their attack on the emigrants, we will fall on their rear; surprised by the sudden aid given the Americans, it is possible they will fly, for the darkness will prevent them counting us, and they will never suppose that three men were so mad as to make such an attack upon them."

"By Jove!" the Count said, laughing, "that is a good idea of yours, Bright-eye, and such as I expected from so brave a hunter as yourself; let us hurry back to our observatory, so as to be ready for every event."

The Canadian leaped on his horse, and the three men retraced their steps. But, according to his custom, Bright-eye, who was apparently a sworn foe to a straight line, made them describe an infinite number of turnings, to throw out any person whom accident brought on their track.

They arrived at the top of the hill just at the moment the sun was disappearing beneath the horizon. The evening breeze was rising, and beginning to agitate the tops of the great trees with mysterious murmurs. The howling of the tigers and cougars was already mingled with the lowing of the elks and buffaloes, and the sharp yelping of the red wolves, whose dusky outlines appeared here and there on the river bank. The sky grew more and more gloomy, and the stars began dotting the vault of heaven.

The three hunters sat down carelessly on the top of the hill, at the same spot they had left a few hours previously with the intention of never returning, and made preparations for supper,—preparations which did not take long, for prudence imperiously ordered them not to light a fire, which would have at once revealed their presence to the unseen eyes which were, at the moment, probably surveying the desert in every direction. While eating a few mouthfuls of pemmican, they kept their eyes fixed on the camp of the emigrants, whose fire was perfectly visible in the night.

"Oh Lord!" Bright-eye said, "those people are ignorant of the first law of the desert, else they would guard against lighting a fire which the Indians can see for ten leagues round."

"Bah! that beacon will guide us where to go to their aid," the Count said.

"Heaven grant that it be not in vain."

The meal over, the hunter invited the Count and his servant to sleep for a few hours.

"For the present," he said, "we have nothing to fear; let me keep watch for all, as my eyes are accustomed to see in the darkness."

The Count did not allow the invitation to be repeated; he rolled himself in his cloak, and lay down on the ground. Two minutes later, himself and Ivon were sleeping the sleep of the righteous. Bright-eye took his seat against the trunk of a tree, and lit a pipe to soothe the weariness of his night watch. All at once, he bent his body forward, placed his ear to the ground, and seemed to be listening attentively. His practised ear had heard a sound at first imperceptible, but which seemed to be gradually drawing nearer.

The hunter silently cocked his rifle, and waited. At the expiration of about a quarter of an hour there was a slight rustling in the thicket, the branches parted, and a man made his appearance.

This man was Natah Otann, the sachem of the Piékanns.

CHAPTER III
THE EMIGRANTS

When he went out on the trail, the hunter's old experience did not deceive him; and the traces he had followed up were really those of an emigrant family. As it is destined to play a certain part in our story, we will introduce it to the reader, and explain, as briefly as possible, by what chain of events it was at this moment encamped on the prairies of the Upper Mississippi, or, to speak like the learned, on the banks of the Missouri.

The history of one emigrant is that of the mass. All are people who, burdened by a numerous family, find a difficulty in rendering their children independent, either through the bad quality of the land they cultivate, or because, in proportion as the population increases, the land, in the course of a few years, gains an excessive value.

The Mississippi has become during the last few years the highway of the world. Every vessel that enters on its waters brings the new establishments the means of supplying themselves, either by barter or for money, with the chief commodities of existence. Thus the explorers have spread along both banks of the river, which have become the highways of emigration, by the prospect they offer the pioneers of possessing fine estates, and holding them a number of years, without the troublesome process of paying rent.

The word "country," in the sense we attach to it in Europe, does not exist for the North American. He is not, like our rustics, attached, from father to son, to the soil which has been the cradle of his family. He is only attached to the land by what it may bring him in; but when it is exhausted by too large a crop, and the colonist has tried in vain to restore its primitive fertility, his mind is speedily made up. He disposes of things too troublesome or expensive to transport; only keeps what is absolutely necessary, as servants, horses, and domestic utensils; says good-bye to his neighbours, who press his hand as if the journey he is about to undertake is the simplest matter in the world, and at daybreak, on a fine spring morning, he gaily sets out, turning a parting and careless glance at that country where he and his family have lived so long. His thoughts are already directed forward; the past no longer exists for him, the future alone smiles on him and sustains his courage.

Nothing is so simple, primitive, and at the same time picturesque, as the departure of a family of pioneers. The horses are attached to the wagons, already laden with the bed furniture and the younger children, while on the other side are fastened the spinning wheels, and swaying behind, a skin filled with tallow and pitch. The axes are laid in the bottom of the cart, and cauldrons and pots roll about pell-mell in the horses' trough; the tents and provisions are securely fastened under the vehicle, suspended by ropes. Such is the moveable estate of the emigrant. The eldest son, or a servant, bestrides the first horse, the pioneer's wife sits on the other. The emigrant and his sons, with shouldered rifles, walk round the wagon, sometimes in front, sometimes behind, followed by their dogs, touching up the oxen and watching over the common safety.

Thus they set out, travelling by short stages through unexplored countries and along frightful roads, which they are generally compelled themselves to make: braving cold and heat, rain and snow, striving against Indians and wild beasts, seeing at each spot almost insurmountable difficulties rising before them: but nothing, stops the emigrants, no peril can check them, no impossibility discourage them. They march on thus for whole months, keeping intact in their hearts that faith in their luck which nothing shakes, until they at length reach a site which offers them those conditions of comfort which they have sought so long.

But, alas! how many families that have left the cities of America full of hope and courage have disappeared, leaving no other trace of their passage of the prairie than their whitened bones and scattered furniture. The Indians, ever on the watch at the entrance of the desert, attack the caravans, mercilessly massacre the pioneers, and carry off into slavery their wives and daughters, avenging themselves on the emigrants for the atrocities to which they have been victims during so many centuries, and continuing, to their own profit, that war of extermination which the white men inaugurated on their landing in America, and which, since that period, has gone on uninterruptedly.

John Black belonged to the class of emigrants we have just described. One day, about four months previously, he quitted his house, which was falling to ruins, and loading the little he possessed on a cart, he set out, followed by his family, consisting of his wife, his daughter, his son, and two menservants who had consented to follow his fortunes. Since that period they had not stopped. They had marched boldly forward, cutting their way by the help of their axes through the virgin forests, and determined on traversing the desert, until they found a spot favourable for the establishment of a new household.

At the period when our story takes place, emigration was much rarer than it is at present, when, owing to the recent discovery of auriferous strata in California and on the Fraser River, an emigration fever has seized on the masses with such intensity, that the old world is growing more and more depopulated, to the profit of the new. Gold is a magnet whose strength attracts, without distinction, young or old, men or women, by the hope, too often deceived, of acquiring in a little time, at the cost of some slight fatigue, a fortune; which, however, rarely compensates for the labour undergone in its collection.

It was, therefore, unusual boldness on the part of John Black thus to venture, without any possible aid, into a country hitherto utterly unexplored, and of which the Indians were masters. Mr. Black was born in Virginia: he was a man of about fifty, of middle height, but strongly built, and gifted with uncommon vigour; and, although his features were very ordinary, his face had a rare expression of firmness and resolution.

His wife, ten years younger than himself, was a gentle and holy creature, on whose brow fatigue and alarm had long before formed deep furrows, beneath which, however, a keen observer could have still detected traces of no ordinary beauty.

William Black, the emigrant's son, was a species of giant of more than six feet in height, aged two-and-twenty, of Herculean build, and whose jolly, plump face, surrounded by thick tufts of hair of a more than sandy hue, breathed frankness and joviality.

Diana, his sister, formed a complete contrast with him. She was a little creature, scarce sixteen years of age, with eyes of a deep blue like the sky, apparently frail and delicate, with a dreamy brow and laughing mouth, which belonged both to woman and angel; and whose strange beauty seduced at the first glance and subjugated at the first word that fell from her rosy lips. Diana was the idol of the family—the cherished idol, that everyone adored, and who, by a word or a glance, could command the obedience of the rude natures that surrounded her, and who only seemed to live that they might satisfy her slightest caprices.

Sam and James, the two labourers, were worthy Kentucky rustics, of extraordinary strength, and who concealed a great amount of cunning beneath their simple and even slightly silly aspect. These two young fellows, one of whom was twenty-six, the other hardly thirty, had grown up in John Black's house, and had vowed to him an unbounded devotion, of which they had furnished proofs several times since the journey began.

When John left his house to go in search of a more fertile country, he proposed to these two men to leave him, not wishing to expose them to the dangers of the precarious life which was about to begin for himself; but both shook their heads negatively, replying to all that was said to them, that it was their duty to follow their master, no matter whither he went, and they were ready to accompany him to the end of the world. The emigrant had been obliged to yield to a determination so clearly expressed, and replied, that as matters were so, they might follow him. Hence these two honest labourers were not regarded as servants, but as friends, and treated in accordance. In truth, there is nothing like a common danger to draw people together; and during the last four months John Black's family had been exposed to dangers innumerable.

The emigrant took with him a rather large number of beasts, which caused the caravan, despite all the precautions taken, to leave such a wide trail, as rendered an Indian attack possible at any moment. Still, up to the present moment, when we pay them a visit, no serious danger had really menaced them. At times they were exposed to rather smart alarms; but the Indians had always kept at a respectable distance, and limited themselves to demonstrations, hostile it is true, but never followed by any results.

During the first week of their march, the emigrants, but little versed in the mode of life of the Redskins, who incessantly prowled round the party, had been afflicted with the most exaggerated fears, expecting every moment to be attacked by those ferocious enemies, about whom they had heard stories which might make the bravest tremble; but, as so frequently happens, they had grown used to this perpetual threat of the Indians, and, while taking the strictest precautions for their safety, they had learned almost to deride the dangers which they had so much feared at the outset, and felt convinced that their calm and resolute attitude had produced an effect on the Redskins, and that the latter would not venture to come into collision with them.

Still, on this day a vague restlessness had seized on the party: they had a sort of secret foreboding that a great danger menaced them. The Indians, who, as we have said, usually accompanied them out of reach of gunshot, had all at once become invisible. Since their start from their last camping ground, they had not seen a single one, though they instinctively suspected that, if the Indians were invisible, they were not the less present, and possibly in larger numbers than before. Thus the day passed, sorrowfully and silently for the emigrants: they marched side by side, eye and ear on the watch, with their fingers on the trigger, not daring to impart their mutual fears, but (to use a Spanish expression) having their beards on their shoulders, like men expecting to be attacked at any moment. Still, the day passed without the slightest incident occurring to corroborate their apprehensions.

At sunset, the caravan was at the foot of one of those numerous mounds to which we have already alluded, and so large a number of which border the banks of the river at this spot. John Black made a sign to his son, who drove the cart, to stop, get down, and join him: while the two females looked around them restlessly, the four men, assembled a few paces in the rear, were engaged in a whispered conversation.

"Boys," Mr. Black said to his attentive companions, "the day is ended, the sun is descending behind the mountains over there, it is time to think about the night's rest. Our beasts are fatigued; we ourselves need to collect our strength for tomorrow's labour; I think, though open to correction, that we should do well to profit by the short time left us to establish our camp."

"Yes," James answered, "we have in front of us a hillock, on the top of which it would be easy for us to take up our quarters."

"And which," William interrupted him, "we could convert into an almost impregnable fortress in a few hours."

"We should have a hard job in getting the wagon up the hill," the father said, shaking his head.

"Nonsense," Sam objected, "not so much as you suppose, Master Black; a little trouble, and we can manage it."

"How so?"

"Why," the servant replied, "we need only unload the wagon."

"That's true; when it's empty, it will be easy to get it to the top of the hill."

"Stay," William observed, "do you think, father, that it is really necessary to take all that trouble? A night is soon spent, and I fancy we should do well to remain where we are: the position is an excellent one; it is only a few paces to the river bank, and we can lead our oxen to water."

"No; we must not remain here, the place is too open, and we should have no shelter if the Indians attacked us."

"The Indians!" the young man said, with a laugh; "why, we have not seen a single one the whole day."

"Yes; what you say, William, is correct, the Redskins have disappeared; but shall I tell you my real thoughts? It is really this disappearance, which I do not understand, that troubles me."

"Why so, father?"

"Because, if they are hiding, they are preparing some ambuscade, and do not wish us to know the direction where they are."

"Come, father, do you really believe that?" the young man remarked in a light tone.

"I am convinced of it," the emigrant said earnestly. The two servants bowed their heads in affirmation.

"You will pardon me, father, if I do not share your opinion," the young man continued. "For my own part, on the other hand, I feel certain that these red devils, who have been following us so long, have eventually understood that they could gain nothing from us but bullets, and, like prudent men, have given up following us further."

"No, no; you are mistaken, my son, it is not so."

"Look ye, father," the young man continued, with a certain amount of excitement, "allow me to make an observation which, I think, will bring you over to my way of thinking."

"Do so, my son; we are here to exchange our opinions freely, and select the best: the common interest is at stake, and we have to act for the safety of all: under circumstances so grave as the present, I should never forgive myself for neglecting good advice, no matter from whom it came; speak, therefore, without timidity."

"You know, father," the young man went on, "that the Indians understand honour differently from ourselves; that is to say, when the success of an expedition is not clearly proved to them, they have no shame about resigning it, because what they seek in the first place is profit."

"I know all that, my son; but I do not see yet what you are driving at."

"You will soon understand me. For nearly two months, from sunrise, the moment we set out, to sunset, which is generally the time of our halt, the Redskins have been following us step by step, and we have been unable to escape for a single moment these most troublesome neighbours, who have watched our every movement."

"That is true," John Black said, "but what do you conclude from that?"

"A very simple thing: they have seen that we were continually on our guard, and that if they attempted to attack us, they would be beaten; hence they have retired, that is all."

"Unfortunately, William, you have forgotten one thing."

"What is it?"

"This: the Indians, generally not so well armed as the white men, are afraid to attack them, especially when they suppose they shall have to deal with persons almost as numerous as themselves, and in the bargain, sheltered behind wagons and bales of merchandise; but that is not at all the case here: since they have been watching us, the Indians have had many opportunities of counting us, and have done so long ago."

"Yes," Sam said.

"Well, they know that we are only four—they are at least fifty, if they are not more numerous. What can four men, in spite of all their courage, effect against such a considerable number of enemies? Nothing, The Redskins know it, and they will act in accordance; that is, when the opportunity offers, they will not fail to seize it."

"But—"—the young man objected.

"Another consideration to which you have not paid attention," John Black quietly continued, "is that the Indians, whatever the number of their enemies may be, never quit them without having attempted, at least once, to surprise them."

"In truth," William answered, "that astonishes me on their part: however, I am of your opinion, father; even if the precautions we propose taking only serve to reassure my mother and sister, it would be well not to neglect them."

"Well spoken, William," the emigrant remarked, "let us therefore set to work without delay."

The party broke up, and the four men, throwing their rifles on their shoulders, began making active preparations for the encampment. Sam collected the oxen by the aid of the dogs, and led them down to the river to drink. John, in the meanwhile, went up to the wagon.

"Well, my love," his wife asked him, "why this halt, and this long discussion? Has any accident occurred?"

"Nothing that need at all alarm you, Lucy," the emigrant answered; "we are going to camp, that is all."

"Oh, gracious me! I do not know why, but I was afraid lest some misfortune had happened."

"On the contrary; we are quieter than we have been for a long time."

"How so, father?" Diana asked, thrusting her charming face from under the canvas which concealed her.

"Those rascally Indians, who frightened us so much, my darling Diana, have at length made up their minds to leave us; we have not seen a single one during the whole day."

"Oh, all the better!" the girl said quickly, as she clapped her dainty palms together; "I confess that I am not brave, and those frightful Red men caused me terrible alarm."

"Well, you will not see them again, I hope," John Black said, gaily; though while giving his daughter this assurance to appease her fears, he did not believe a word he uttered. "Now," he added, "have, the goodness to get down, so that we may unload the wagon."

"Unload the wagon," the old lady remarked, "why so?

"It is just possible," the husband answered, anxious not to reveal the real reason, "that we may remain here a few days, in order to rest the cattle."

"Ah, very good," she said; and she got out, followed by her daughter.

The two ladies had scarce set foot on ground, ere the men began unloading the wagon. This task lasted nearly an hour. Sam had time enough to lead the cattle to water, and collect them on the top of the hill.

"Are we going to camp, then?" Mrs. Black asked.

"Yes," her husband answered.

"Come, Diana," the old lady said.

The two women packed up some kitchen utensils, and clomb the hill, where, after lighting the fire, they began preparing supper. So soon as the cart was unloaded, the two labouring men, aided by William, pushed it behind, while John Black, at the head of the team, began flogging the horses. The incline was rather steep, but owing to the vigour of the horses and the impatience of the men, who at each step laid rollers behind the wheels, the wagon at last reached the top. The rest was as nothing, and within an hour the camp was arranged as follows.

The emigrants formed, with the bales and trees they felled, a large circle, in the midst of which the cattle were tied up, and then put up a tent for the two women. When this was effected, John Black cast a glance of satisfaction around. His family were temporarily protected from a coup de main—thanks to the manner in which the bales and trees were arranged, and the party were enabled to fire from under cover on any enemy that might attack them, and defend themselves a long time successfully.

The sun had set for more than an hour before these various preparations were completed, and supper was ready. The Americans seated themselves in a circle round the fire, and ate with the appetite of men accustomed to danger—an appetite which the greatest alarm cannot deprive them of. After the meal, John Black offered up a prayer, as he did every evening before going to rest; the others standing, with uncovered heads, listened attentively to the prayer, and when it was completed, the two ladies entered the hut prepared for them.

"And now," Black said, "let us keep a careful watch the night is dark, the moon rises late, and you are aware that the Indians choose the morning, the moment when sleep is deepest, to attack their enemies."

The fire was covered, so that its light should not reveal the exact position of the camp; and the two servants lay down side by side on the grass, where they soon fell asleep: while father and son, standing at either extremity of the camp, watched over the common safety.

CHAPTER IV
THE GRIZZLY BEAR

All was calm in the prairie; not a sound disturbed the silence of the desert. On the sudden appearance of the Indian, whatever the emotion Bright-eye might feel, it was impossible for Natah Otann to perceive anything: the hunter's face remained calm, and not a muscle moved.

"Ah!" he said, "the sachem of the Piékanns is welcome: does he come as a friend or an enemy?"

"Natah Otann comes to sit by the fire of the palefaces, and smoke the calumet with them," the chief replied, casting a searching glance around him.

"Good: if the chief will wait a moment, I will light the fire."

"Bright-eye can light it, the chief will wait: he has come to talk with the palefaces, and the conversation will be long."

The Canadian looked fixedly at the Redskin; but the Indian was impassive like himself, and it was impossible to read anything on his features. The hunter collected a few handfuls of dry wood, struck a light, and soon a bright flame sprung up, and illumined the mount. The Indian drew near the fire, took his calumet from his girdle, and began grimly smoking. Bright-eye not wishing to remain in any way behindhand, imitated his every movement with perfectly feigned indifference, and the two men sat for several moments puffing clouds of smoke at each other. Natah Otann at length broke the silence.

"The pale hunter is a warrior," he said; "why does he try to hide himself like the water rat?"

Bright-eye did not consider it advisable to reply to this insinuation, and continued smoking philosophically, while casting a side-glance at his questioner.

"The Blackfeet have the eye of the eagle," Natah Otann continued, "their piercing eyes see all that happens on the prairie."

The Canadian made a sign of assent, but did not yet reply; the chief continued:—

"Natah Otann has seen the trail of his friends the palefaces, his heart quivered with pleasure in his breast, and he has come to meet them."

Bright-eye slowly removed his pipe from his lips, and turning towards the Indian, examined him carefully for an instant, and then answered—

"I repeat to my brother that he is welcome: I know that he is a great chief, and am happy to see him."

"Wah!" the Indian said, with a cunning smile: "is my brother so satisfied as he says at my presence?"

"Why not, chief?"

"My brother is angry still that the Blackfeet fastened him to the stake of torture."

The Canadian shrugged his shoulders contemptuously, and coldly answered:—

"Nonsense, chief! why do you fancy I am angry with you or your nation? war is war; I have no reproaches to make to you. You wished to kill me, I escaped; so we are quits."

"Good: does my brother speak the truth? has he really forgotten?" the chief asked with some vivacity.

"Why not?" the Canadian answered cautiously. "I have not a forked tongue, the words my mouth utters come from my heart: I have not forgotten the treatment you made me undergo, I should lie if I said so: but I have forgiven it."

"*Ochi*! my brother is a greatheart: he is generous."

"No: I am merely a man who knows Indian customs, that is all: you did no more and no less than all the Redskins do under similar circumstances: I cannot be angry with you for having acted according to your nature."

There was a silence; the two men went on smoking. The Indian was the first to interrupt it.

"Then my brother is a friend," he said.

"And you?" the hunter asked, answering one question by another.

The chief rose with a gesture full of majesty, and threw back the folds of his buffalo robe.

"Would an enemy come like this?" he asked, in a gentle voice.

The Canadian could not repress a movement of surprise; the Blackfoot was unarmed, his girdle was empty: he had not even his scalping knife,—

that weapon from which the Indians part so unwillingly. Bright-eye offered him his hand.

"Shake hands, chief," he said to him. "You are a man of heart: now speak, I am listening to you: and, in the first place, will you have a draught of firewater?"

"The firewater is an evil counsellor," the chief replied, with a smile; "it makes the Indians mad: Natah Otann does not drink it."

"Come, come, I see that I was mistaken with regard to you, chief; that pleases me: speak, my ears are open."

"What I have to say to Bright-eye other ears must not listen to."

"My friends are in a deep sleep, you can speak without fear; and even if they were awake, as you know, they do not understand your language."

The Indian shook his head.

"Glass-eye knows everything," he replied, "the Grizzly Bear will not speak before him."

"As you please, chief: still, I would remark that I have nothing to say to you: you can speak, therefore, or be silent at your ease."

Natah Otann seemed to hesitate for an instant, and then continued:—

"Bright-eye will follow his friend to the river bank, and there listen to the words of the Blackfoot chief."

"Hum!" the hunter said, "and who will watch over my companions during my absence? No, no," he added, "I cannot do that, chief. The Redskins have the cunning of the opossum: while I am near the river, my friends may be surprised. Who will respond for their safety?"

The Indian rose.

"The word of a chief," he said, in a proud voice, and with a gesture full of majesty.

The Canadian looked at him attentively. "Listen, Redskin," he said to him, "I do not doubt your honour, so do not take in ill part what I am going to say to you."

"I listen to my brother," the Indian answered.

"I must watch over my companions. Since you insist on speaking to me in secret, I consent to follow you, but on one condition, that I do not lay aside my weapons; in that way, should one of those things happen, which are too common in the prairie, and which no human foresight can prevent,

I shall be able to face the danger and sell my life dearly: if what I propose suits you, I am ready to follow you; if not, not."

"Good," the Indian said, with a smile, "my pale brother is right, a true hunter never quits his weapons. Bright-eye may follow his friend."

"Very well, then," the Canadian said, resolutely, as he threw his rifle on his shoulder.

Natah Otann began descending the hill. While gliding noiselessly through the shrubs and thickets, the Canadian walked literally in his footsteps; but though pretending the most perfect security, he did not omit carefully examining the vicinity, and lending an ear to the slightest sound, but all was calm and silent in the desert, and after some ten minutes' walk the two men reached the riverside.

The Mecha-Chebe rolled its waters majestically in a bed of golden sand, while at times a few vague shadows appeared on the bank: they were wild beasts coming to drink in the river. Two leagues from them, at the top of the hill, sparkled the last flames of an expiring fire, which appeared at intervals between the branches. Natah Otann stopped at the extremity of a species of small promontory, the point of which advanced some distance into the water. This spot was entirely free from vegetation: the eye could survey the prairie for a great distance, and detect the slightest movement in the desert.

"Does this place suit the hunter?" the chief asked.

"Capitally," Bright-eye replied, resting the butt of his rifle on the ground, and crossing his hands over the muzzle: "I am ready to hear the communication my brother wishes to make me."

The Indian walked up and down the sand with folded arms and drooping head, like a man who is reflecting deeply. The hunter followed him with his glance, waiting calmly, till he thought proper to offer an explanation. It was easy to see that Natah Otann was ripening in his brain one of those bold projects such as Indians frequently imagine, but knew not how to enter upon it. The hunter resolved to put a stop to this state of things.

"Come," he said, "my brother has made me leave my camp; he invited me to follow him; I consented to do so: now that, according to his desire, we are free from human ears, will he not speak, so that I may return to my companions?"

The Indian stopped before him.

"My brother will remain," he said; "the hour is come for an explanation between us. My brother loves Glass-eye?"

The hunter regarded his querist craftily.

"What good of that question?" he asked: "it must be a matter of indifference to the chief whether I love or not the man he pleases to call Glass-eye."

"A chief never loses his time in vain discourses," the Indian said, peremptorily; "the words his lips utter are always simple, and go straight to the point; let my brother then answer as clearly as I interrogate him."

"I see no great inconvenience in doing so. Yes, I love Glass-eye; I love him not only because he saved my life, but because he is one of the most honourable men I ever met."

"Good! for what purpose does Glass-eye traverse the prairie? My brother doubtlessly knows."

"My faith, no! I confess to you, chief, my ignorance on that head is complete. Still, I fancy that, wearied with the life of cities, he has come here with no other object than to calm his soul by the sublime aspect of nature, and the grand melodies of the desert."

The Indian shook his head; the hunter's metaphysical ideas and poetic phrases were so much Hebrew to him, and he did not understand them.

"Natah Otann," he said, "is a chief, he has not a forked tongue; the words he utters are as clear as the blood in his veins. Why does not the hunter speak his language to him?"

"I answer your questions, chief, and that is all. Do you fancy that I would go out of my way to interrogate my friend as to his intentions? They do not concern me; I have no right to seek in a man's heart for the motive of his actions."

"Good! my brother speaks well; his head is grey, and his experience long."

"That is possible, chief; at any rate you and I are not on such friendly terms that we should exchange our thoughts without some restriction, I fancy; you have kept me here for an hour without saying anything, so it is better for us to separate."

"Not yet."

"Why not? Do you imagine I am like you, and that instead of sleeping o' nights as an honest Christian should do, I amuse myself with rushing about the prairie like a jaguar in search of prey?"

The Indian began laughing.

"Wah!" he said, "my brother is very clever; nothing escapes him."

"By Jingo! there is no great cleverness in guessing what you are doing here."

"Good! then let my brother listen."

"I will do so, but on the condition that you lay aside once for all those Indian circumlocutions in which you so adroitly conceal your real thoughts."

"My brother will open his ears, the words of his friend will reach his heart."

"Come, make an end of it."

"As my brother loves Glass-eye, he will tell him from Natah Otann that a great danger threatens him."

"Ah!" the Canadian said, casting a suspicious glance at the other, "and what may the danger be?"

"I cannot explain further."

"Very good," Bright-eye remarked, with a grin, "the information is valuable, though not very explicit; and pray what must we do to escape the great danger that menaces us?"

"My brother will wake his friend, they will mount their horses, and retire at full speed, not stopping till they have crossed the river."

"Hum! and when we have done that, we shall have nought more to fear?"

"Nothing."

"Only think of that," the hunter said, ironically; "and when ought we to start?"

"At once."

"Better still." Bright-eye walked a few paces thoughtfully; then he returned, and stood before the chief, whose eyes sparkled in the gloom like those of a tiger cat, and who followed his every movement.

"Then," he said, "you cannot reveal to me the reason that forces us to depart?"

"No!"

"It is equally impossible, I suppose, for you to tell me of the nature of the danger that menaces us?" he went on.

"Yes."

"Is that your last word?"

The Indian bowed his head in affirmation.

"Very good, as it is so," Bright-eye said all at once, striking the ground with the butt of his rifle, "I will tell it you."

"You?"

"Yes, listen to me carefully; it will not be long, and will interest you I hope."

The chief smiled ironically.

"My ears are open," he said.

"All the better, for I shall fill them with news which, perhaps, will not please you."

"I listen," the impassive Indian repeated.

"As you said to me a moment back—and the confidence on your part was useless, for I have known you so long on the prairie—the Redskins have the eyes of an eagle, and they are birds of prey, whom nothing escapes."

"Go on."

"Here I am; your scouts have discovered, as was not difficult, the trail of an emigrant family; that trail you have been following a long time so as not to miss your blow; supposing that the moment had arrived to deal it, you have assembled Comanches, Sioux, and Blackfeet, all demons of the same breed, in order this very night to attack people whom you have been watching for so many days, and whose riches you covet because you suppose them so great—-eh?"

Natah Otann's face revealed no emotion. He remained calm, although internally restless and furious at having his thoughts so well guessed.

"There is truth in what the hunter says," he replied, coldly.

"It is all true," Bright-eye exclaimed.

"Perhaps; but I do not see in it for what reason I should have come here to warn my Paleface brother."

"Ah, you do not see that; very well. I will explain it to you. You came to seek me, because you are perfectly well aware that Glass-eye, as you call him, is not the man to allow the crime you meditate to be committed with impunity in his presence."

The Blackfoot shrugged his shoulders. "Can a warrior, however brave he may be, hold his ground against four hundred?" he said.

"Certainly not," Bright-eye went on; "but he can control them by his presence, and employ his ascendency over them to compel them to give up their prospects; and that is what Glass-eye will undoubtedly do, for reasons of which I am ignorant, for all of you have for him an incomprehensible respect and veneration, and as you fear lest you may see him come among you at the first shot fired, terrible as the destroying angel, you seek to remove him by a pretext, plausible with anyone else, but which will produce on him no other effect than making him engage in the affair. Come, is that really all? have I completely unmasked you? Reply."

"My brother knows all; I repeat, his wisdom is great."

"Now, I presume, you have nothing to add? Very well, good night."

"A moment."

"What more?"

"You must."

"Very well; but make haste."

"My brother has spoken in his own cause, but not in that of Glass-eye; let him wake his friend, and impart our conversation to him; mayhap he is mistaken."

"I do not believe it, chief," the hunter answered, with a shake of his head.

"That is possible," the Indian persisted; "but let my brother do as I have asked him."

"You lay great stress on it, chief!"

"Great."

"I do not wish to vex you about such a trifle. Well! you will soon allow that I was right."

"Possibly; I will await my brother's reply for half an hour."

"Very good; but where shall I bring it to you?"

"Nowhere!" the Indian exclaimed, sharply. "If I am right, my brother will imitate the cry of the magpie twice; if I am mistaken, it will be that of the owl."

"Very good, that's agreed; you shall soon hear, chief."

The Indian bowed gracefully.

"May the Wacondah be with my brother!" he said.

After this courteous salutation, the two men parted. The Canadian carelessly threw his rifle on his shoulder, and stalked back to his camp, while the Indian followed him with his glance, apparently remaining insensible;

but as soon as the hunter had disappeared, the chief lay down in the sand, glided along in the shade like a serpent, and in his turn disappeared amid the bushes, following the direction taken by Bright-eye, though at a considerable distance.

The latter did not fancy himself followed; he therefore paid no attention to what went on around him, and regained his camp without noticing anything of an extraordinary nature. Had not the Canadian been preoccupied, and his old experience lulled to sleep for the moment, he would have certainly perceived, with that penetration which distinguished him, that the desert was not in its usual state of tranquillity: he would have felt unusual tremors in the leaves, and possibly have seen eyes flashing in the shade of the tall grass. He soon reached the camp where the Count and Ivon were sleeping profoundly. Bright-eye hesitated a few seconds ere awakening the young man whose sleep was so peaceful; still, reflecting that the least imprudence might entail terrible consequences, whose result it was impossible to calculate, he bent over him, and gently touched his shoulder. Though the touch was so slight, it sufficed to wake the Count; he opened his eyes, sat up, and looking at the old hunter—

"Is there anything fresh, Bright-eye?" he asked.

"Yes, Sir Count," the Canadian replied, seriously.

"Oh, oh, how gloomy you are, my good fellow," the young man said, with a laugh. "What's the matter then?"

"Nothing, yet; but we may soon have a row with the Redskins."

"All the better, for that will warm us, as it is horribly cold," he replied, shivering. "But how do you know the fact?"

"During your sleep I received a visitor."

"Ah?"

"Yes."

"And who was the person who selected such an important moment to pay you a visit?"

"The sachem of the Blackfeet."

"Natah Otann?"

"Himself."

"Upon my word, he must be a somnambulist, to amuse himself by walking about the desert at night."

"He does not walk, he watches."

"Oh, I am in a bother; so keep me no longer in suspense; tell me what passed between you. Natah Otann is not the man to put himself out of the way without strong reasons, and I am burning to know them."

"You shall judge."

Without any further preface, the hunter described in its fullest details the conversation he had with the chief.

"By Jove! that's serious," the Count said when Bright-eye had ended his story. "This Natah Otann is a gloomy scoundrel, whose plans you fully penetrated, and you behaved splendidly in answering him so categorically. For what has this villain taken me? Does he fancy, I wonder, that I shall act as his accomplice? Let him dare to attack those poor devils of emigrants down there, and by the saints, I swear to you, Bright-eye, that blood will be shed between us, if you help me."

"Can you doubt it?"

"No, my friend, I thank you; with you and my coward of an Ivon, I shall manage to put them to flight."

"Is my lord calling me?" the Breton asked, raising his head.

"No, no, Ivon, my good fellow; I only say that we shall soon have some fighting."

The Breton emitted a sigh, and muttered, as he lay down again,—

"Ah! if I had as much courage as I possess goodwill; but alas! as you know, I am a wonderful coward, and I shall prove more harm to you than good."

"You will do all you can, my friend, and that will be sufficient."

Ivon sighed in reply. Bright-eye had listened laughingly to this colloquy. The Breton still possessed the privilege of astonishing him, for he did not at all comprehend his singular organization. The Count turned towards him.

"So it is settled?" he said.

"Settled," the hunter answered.

"Then give the signal; my friend."

"The owl, I suppose?"

"By Jove!" the Count said.

Bright-eye raised his fingers to his mouth, and, as had been agreed with Natah Otann, imitated twice the cry of the owl, with rare perfection. Hardly had the echo of the last cry died away, than a great rumour was heard in the bushes, and, before the three men had time to put themselves in a posture of defence, some twenty Indians rushed upon them, disarmed them in a twinkling, and reduced them to a state of utter defencelessness. The Count shrugged his shoulders, leant against a tree, and, thrusting his glass in his eye, said,—-

"This is very funny."

"Well, I can't see the point of the joke," muttered Ivon, in a grand aside.

Among the Indians, whom it was easy to recognize as Blackfeet, was Natah Otann! After removing the weapons of the white men, so that they could not attempt a surprise this time, he walked towards the hunter.

"I warned Bright-eye," he said.

The hunter smiled contemptuously.

"You warned us after the fashion of Redskins," he replied.

"What does my brother mean?"

"I mean that you warned us of a danger that threatened us, and not that you intended treachery."

"It is the same thing," the Indian replied, with utter calmness.

"Bright-eye, my friend, do not argue with those scoundrels," the Count said.

And turning haughtily to the chief,—

"Come! what do you want of us?" he asked.

Since his arrival on the prairie, and through his constant contact with the Indians the Count had almost unconsciously learned their language, which he spoke rather fluently.

"We do not wish to do you any hurt; we only intend to prevent your interference in our affairs," Natah Otann said respectfully; "we should be very sorry to have recourse to violent measures."

The young man burst into a laugh.

"You are humbugs! I can manage to escape, in spite of you."

"Let my brother try it."

"When the moment arrives; as for the present, it is not worth the trouble!"

While speaking in this light tone, the young man took his case from his pocket, chose a cigar, and, pulling out a lucifer match, stooped down and rubbed it on a stone. The Indians, considerably puzzled by his movements, followed them anxiously; but suddenly they uttered a yell of terror, and fell back several paces. The match had caught fire with the friction; a delicious blue flame sported about its extremity. The Count carelessly twisted the slight morsel of wood between his fingers, while waiting till all the sulphur was consumed. He did not notice the terror of the Indians.

The latter, with a movement as swift as thought, stooped down, and each picking up the first piece of wood he found at his feet, all began rubbing it against the stones. The Count, in amazement, looked at them, not yet understanding what they were about. Natah Otann seem to hesitate for a moment; a smile of strange meaning played, rapidly as lightning, over his gloomy features; but reassuming almost immediately his cold impassiveness, he took a step forward, and respectfully bowing before the Count—

"My father commands the fire of the sun," he said, with all the appearance of a mysterious terror, while pointing to the match.

The young man smiled; he had guessed the secret.

"Which of you," he said haughtily, "would dare to contend with me?"

The Indians regarded each other with amazement. These men, so intrepid and accustomed to brave the greatest dangers, were vanquished by the incomprehensible power their prisoner possessed. As, while talking to the chief, the Count had not watched his match, it had gone out before he could use it, and he threw it away. The Indians rushed upon it, to assure themselves that the flame was real. Without appearing to attach any importance to this action, the Count drew a second match from his box, and renewed his experiment. His triumph was complete; the Redskins, in their terror, fell at his feet, imploring him to pardon them. Henceforth he might dare anything. These primitive men, terrified by the two miracles he had performed, regarded him as a superior being to themselves, and were completely mastered by him. While Bright-eye laughed in his sleeve at the Indians' simplicity, the young man cleverly employed his triumph.

"You see what I can do," he said.

"We see it," Natah Otann made answer.

"When do you intend to attack the emigrants?"

"When the moon has set, the warriors of the tribe will assault their camp."

"And you?"

"Will guard our brother."

"So you now fancy that is possible," the Count said, haughtily.

The Redskins shuddered at the flash of his glance.

"Our brother will pardon us," the chief replied, submissively; "we only knew him imperfectly."

"And now?"

"Now we know that he is our master, let him command, and we will obey."

"Take care!" he said, in a tone which made them shudder, "for I am about to put your obedience to a rude trial."

"Our ears are open to receive our brother's words."

"Draw nearer."

The Blackfeet took a few hesitating steps in advance, for they were not yet completely reassured.

"And now listen to me attentively," he said, "and when you have received my orders, take care to execute them thoroughly."

CHAPTER V
THE STRANGE WOMAN

We are now obliged to return to the Americans' camp. As we have said, Black and his son were mounting guard, and the pioneer was far from easy in his mind. Although not yet possessed of all the experience required for a desert life, the four months he had spent in fatiguing marches and continued alarms had endowed him with a certain degree of vigilance, which, under existing circumstances, might prove very useful; not, perhaps, to prevent an attack, but, at least, to repulse it. The situation of his camp was, besides, excellent; for from it he surveyed the prairie for a great distance, and could easily perceive the approach of an enemy.

Father and son were seated by the fire, rising from time to time, in turn, to cast glances over the desert, and assure themselves that nothing menaced their tranquillity. Black was a man gifted with an iron will and a lion's courage; hitherto his schemes had been unsuccessful, and he had sworn to make himself an honourable position, no matter at what cost.

He was the descendant of an old family of squatters. The squatter being an individuality peculiar to America, and vainly sought elsewhere, we will describe him as he is, in a few words. On the lands belonging to the United States, not yet cleared or put up for sale, large numbers of persons have settled, with the desire of eventually *purchasing* their lots. These inhabitants are called squatters. We will not say that they are the pick of the western emigrants, but we know that, in certain districts, they have constituted themselves a regular Government, and have elected magistrates to watch over the execution of the Draconian laws they have themselves laid down to insure the tranquillity of the territories they have invaded. But by the side of these quasi-honest squatters, who bow their necks beneath a yoke that is often harsh, there is another class of squatters, who understand the possession of land in its widest sense; that is to say, whenever they discover, in their vagabond peregrinations, a tract of land that suits them, they instal themselves there without any further inquiry, and caring nothing for the rightful owner, who, when he arrives with his labourers to till his estate, is quite annoyed to find it is in the hands of an individual who, trusting to the axiom that possession is nine points of the law, refuses to give it up, and if he insist, drives him away by means of his rifle and revolver.

We know a capital story of a gentleman, who, starting from New York with two hundred labourers, to clear a virgin forest he had purchased some ten years previously, and never turned to any use, found, on arriving at his claim, a town of four thousand souls built on the site of his virgin forest, of which not a tree remained. After numberless discussions, the said gentleman esteemed himself very fortunate in being able to depart with a whole skin, and without paying damages to his despoilers, whom he had momentarily hoped to oust. But there is no more chance of ousting a squatter, than you can get a dollar out of a Yankee, when he has once pocketed it.

John Black belonged to the former of the two classes we have described. When he reached the age of twenty, his father gave him an axe, a rifle with twenty charges of powder, and a bowie knife, saying to him—

"Listen, boy. You are now tall and strong; it would be a shame for you to remain longer a burden on me. I have your two brothers to support. America is large; there is no want of land. Go in God's name, and never let me hear of you again. With the weapons I give you, and the education you have received, your fortune will soon be made, if you like: before all, avoid all disagreeable disputes, and try not to be hanged."

After this affectionate address, the father tenderly embraced his son, put him out of the cabin, and slammed the door in his face. From that moment John Black had never heard of his father—it is true that he never tried to obtain any news about him.

Life had been rough to him at the outset; but owing to his character, and a certain elasticity of principle, the sole inheritance his family had given him, he had contrived to gain a livelihood, and bring up his children without any great privations. Either through the isolation in which he had passed his youth, or for some other reason we are ignorant of, Black adored his wife and children, and would not have parted from them on any account. When fatality compelled him to give up the farm he occupied, and look for another, he set out gaily, sustained by the love of his family, no member of which was ungrateful for the sacrifices he imposed on himself; and he had resolved to go this time so far, that no one would ever come to dispossess him, for he had been obliged to surrender his farm to its legitimate proprietor, which he had done on the mere exhibition of the title deeds, without dreaming of resistance —a conduct which had been greatly blamed by all his neighbours.

Black wished to see his family happy, and watched over it with the jealous tenderness of a hen for its chicks. Thus, on this evening, an extreme alarm had preyed on him, though he could not explain the cause: the disappearance of the Indians did not seem to him natural; everything around was too calm, the silence of the desert too profound: he could not remain at any one spot, and, in spite of his son's remarks, rose every moment to take a look over the intrenchments.

William felt for his father a great affection, mingled with respect: the state in which he saw him vexed him the more, because there was nothing to account for his extraordinary restlessness.

"Good gracious, father!" he said, "do not trouble yourself so much; it really causes me pain to see you in such a state. Do you suppose that the Indians would have attacked us by such a moonlight as this? Look, objects can be distinguished as in broad day; I am certain you might even read the Bible by the silvery rays."

"You are right for the present moment, Will. The Redskins are too crafty to face our rifles during the moonshine; but in an hour the moon will have set, and the darkness will then protect them sufficiently to allow them to reach the foot of the barricade unnoticed."

"Do not imagine they will attempt it, my dear father! Those red devils have seen us sufficiently close to know that they can only expect a volley of bullets from us."

"Hum! I am not of your opinion; our beasts would be riches to them: I do not wish to abandon them, as we should then be compelled to return to the plantations to procure others, which would be most disagreeable, you will allow."

"It is true; but we shall not be reduced to that extremity."

"May Heaven grant it, my boy; but do you hear nothing?"

The young man listened attentively.

"No," he said, at the end of a moment.

The emigrant proceeded with a sigh: "I visited the river bank this morning, and I have rarely seen a spot better suited for a settlement. The virgin forest that extends behind us would supply excellent firewood, without reckoning the magnificent planks to be obtained from it: there are several hundred acres around, which, from their proximity to the water, would produce, I am certain, excellent crops."

"Would you feel inclined to settle here, then?"

"Have you any objection?"

"I—none at all! provided we can live and work together. I care little at what place we stop: this spot appears to me as good as another, and it is far enough from the settlements to prevent our being turned out, at least for a great number of years."

"That is exactly my view."

At this moment a gentle quivering ran along the tall grass.

"This time I am certain I am not mistaken," the emigrant exclaimed; "I heard something."

"And I too!" the young man said, rising quickly, and seizing his rifle.

The two men hurried to the entrenchments, but they saw nothing of a suspicious nature: the prairie was still perfectly calm.

"'Tis some wild beast going down to drink, or returning," Will said, to reassure his father.

"No, no," the latter replied, with a shake of the head; "it is not the noise made by any animal—it was the echo of a man's footfall, I am convinced."

"The simplest way is to go and see."

"Come then."

The two men resolutely climbed over the intrenchments, and with rifles outstretched, went round the camp, carefully searching the bushes, and assuring themselves that no foe lurked in them.

"Well!" they exclaimed, when they met.

"Nothing—and you?"

"Nothing."

"It is strange," John Black muttered, "and yet the noise was very distinct."

"That is true; but I repeat, father, that it was nothing but an animal leaping somewhere near. In a night so calm as this, the slightest sound is heard for a great distance; besides, we are now certain that no one is concealed near us."

"Let us go back," the emigrant said, thoughtfully. They began climbing over the entrenchments; but both stopped suddenly, by mutual agreement, hardly checking a cry of amazement, almost of terror. They had just perceived a human being, whose outline it was impossible to trace at such a distance, crouched over the fire.

"This time I will have it out," the emigrant exclaimed, taking a prodigious bound into the camp.

"And I, too," his son murmured, as he followed his example.

But when they came opposite their strange visitor, their surprise was redoubled. In spite of themselves, they stopped to gaze on the stranger, without thinking to ask how he had entered their camp, and by what right he had done so.

As far as they could form a judgment, they soon began to consider the extraordinary being before them—a woman; but years, the mode of life she led, and perchance cares, had furrowed her face with such a multitude of cross hatchings, that it was impossible to conjecture her age, or whether she had formerly been lovely. The large black eyes, surmounted by thick brows crossing her curved nose, and deep sunk, flashed with a gloomy fire; her salient and empurpled cheekbones, her large mouth studded with dazzling teeth, and her thin lips and square chin, gave her at first an appearance which was far from arousing sympathy and exciting confidence; while her long black hair, matted with leaves and grass, fell in disorder on her shoulders. She wore a costume more suited for a man than a woman. It was composed of a long robe of buffalo hide, with short sleeves, fastened on the hips by a girdle bedizened with beads. This robe had the skirt fringed with feathers, and only came down to the knee. Her *mitasses* were fastened round the ankles, and reached slightly above the knee, where they were held up by garters of buffalo hide. Her *humpis* or slippers were plain and unornamented. She wore iron rings on her wrist, two or three bead collars round her neck, and earrings. From her girdle hung on one side a powder flask, an axe, and a bowie knife; on the other, a bullet pouch and a long Indian pipe. Across her knees lay a rather handsome gun, of English manufacture.

She was crouching over the fire, which she gazed at fixedly, with her chin on the palm of her hand.

On the arrival of the Americans, she did not rise, and did not even appear to notice their presence. After examining her attentively for some time, Black walked up, and, tapping her on the shoulder, said—

"You are welcome, woman; it seems as if you were cold, and the fire does not displease you."

She slowly raised her head on feeling the touch, and, fixing on her questioner a gloomy glance, in which it was easy to perceive a slight wildness, she replied in English, in a hollow voice, and with guttural accent—

"The Palefaces are mad; they ever think themselves in their towns; they forget that in the prairie the trees have ears and the leaves eyes to see and hear all that is done. The Blackfeet Indians raise their hair very skilfully."

The two men looked at each other on hearing these words, whose meaning they were afraid to guess, though they seemed somewhat obscure.

"Are you hungry? Will you eat?" John Black continued, "or is it thirst that troubles you? I can, if you like, give you a good draught of firewater to warm you."

The woman frowned.

"Fire-water is good for Indian squaws," she said, "what good would it do me to drink it? Others will come who will soon dispose of it. Do you know how many hours you still have to live?"

The emigrant shuddered, in spite of himself at this species of menace.

"Why speak to me thus?" he asked; "have you any cause of complaint against me?"

"I care little," she continued. "I am not among the living, since my heart is dead."

She turned her head in every direction with a slow and solemn movement, while carefully examining the country.

"Stay," she continued, pointing with her lean arm to a mound of grass a short distance off, "'twas there he fell—'tis there he rests. His head was cleft asunder by an axe during his sleep—poor James! This spot is ill-omened: do you not know it? The vultures and the crows alone stay here at long intervals. Why, then, have you come here? Are you weary of life? Do you hear them? They are approaching; they will soon be here."

Father and son exchanged a glance.

"She is mad. Poor creature!" Black muttered.

"Yes; that is what they all say on the prairies," she exclaimed, with some accusation in her voice. "They call me *Ohucahauck Chiké* (the evil one of the earth), because they fear me as their evil genius. You, also, fancy me mad, eh? ah! ah! ah!"

She burst into a strident laugh, which ended in a sob; she buried her face in her hands, and wept. The two men felt awed in spite of themselves; this strange grief, these incoherent words, all aroused their interest in favour of this poor creature, who appeared so unhappy. Pity was at work in their hearts, and they regarded her silently without daring to disturb her. In a few moments she raised her head, passed the back of her hand over her eyes to dry them, and spoke again. The wild expression had disappeared; the very sound of her voice was no longer the same; as if by enchantment, a complete change had taken place in her.

"Pardon," she said mournfully, "the extravagant words I have uttered. The solitude in which I live, and the heavy burden of woe which has crushed me so long, at times trouble my reason; and then the place where we now stand reminds me of terrible scenes, whose cruel memory will never be erased from my mind."

"Madam, I assure you—," John Black continued, not knowing what he said, so great was his surprise.

"Now the fit has passed away." She interrupted him with a gentle and melancholy smile, which gave her countenance a very different expression from that the Americans had hitherto remarked; "I have been following you for the last two days to come to your help; the Redskins are preparing to attack you—"

The two men shuddered: and, forgetting all else to think only of the pressing danger, they cast a restless glance around them.

"You know it?" Black exclaimed.

"I know all," she answered; "but reassure yourselves. You have still two hours ere their horrible war cry will sound in your ears; that is more than enough to render you safe."

"Oh! we have good rifles and keen sight," said William, clutching his weapon in his nervous hands.

"What can four rifles, however good they may be, do against two or three hundred tigers thirsting for blood, like those you will have to fight? You do not know the Redskins, young man."

"That is true," he answered; "but what is to be done?"

"Seek a refuge?—where find help in these immense solitudes?" the father added, casting a despairing glance around him.

"Did I not tell you I wished to help you?" she said, sharply.

"Yes; you told us so; but I try in vain to detect of what use you can be to us."

She smiled a melancholy smile.

"It is your good angel that brought you to the spot where you now are. While I was watching you all the day, I trembled lest you might not encamp here. Come!"

The two men, surprised by the ascendancy this strange creature had gained over them in a few minutes, followed her without reply. After walking about a dozen steps, she stopped, and turned toward them.

"Look," she said, stretching out her thin arm in a north-west direction, "your enemies are there, scarce two leagues off, buried in the tall grass. I have heard their plans, and was present at their council, though they little suspected it. They are only waiting for the moon to set, ere they attack you. You have scarce an hour left."

"My poor wife!" Black murmured.

"It is impossible for me to save you all: to fancy it would be madness; but I can, if you wish it, attempt to save your wife and daughter from the fate that menaces them."

"Speak! speak!"

"This tree, at the foot of which we are now standing, although apparently possessing all the vigour of youth, is internally hollow, so that only the bark stands upright. Your wife and daughter, supplied with some provisions, will get into the tree and remain there in safety till the danger has passed away. As for ourselves—"

"As for us," Black quickly interrupted her, "we are men accustomed to danger: our fate is in the hands of God."

"Good; but do not despair: all is not lost yet."

The American shook his head.

"As you said yourself, what can four men do against a legion of demons like those who menace us? But that is not the question of the moment. I do not see the hole by which my wife and daughter can enter the tree."

"It is twenty to twenty-four feet up, hidden among the branches and leaves."

"The Lord be praised! they will be sheltered."

"Yes; but make haste and warn them, while your son and I make all the preparations."

Black, convinced of the necessity of haste, ran off, while the stranger and William constructed, with that dexterity produced by the approach of danger, a species of handy ladder, by which the two women could not merely ascend the tree, but go down into the cavity. Black waked the ladies, and called the servants; in a few words he explained to them what was passing; then, loading his wife and daughter with provisions, furs, and other indispensable objects, he led them to the spot where the stranger was expecting them.

"This is my most precious treasure," Black said; "if I save it, I shall be solely indebted to you."

The two ladies began thanking their mysterious protectress; but she imposed silence on them by a peremptory gesture.

"Presently, presently," she said; "if we escape, we shall have plenty of time for mutual congratulations; but at this moment we have something more important to do than exchange compliments. We must get into a place of safety."

The two ladies fell back, quite repulsed by this rough reception, while casting a curious and almost alarmed glance on the strange creature. But the latter, perfectly stoical, seemed to notice nothing. She explained in a few clear words the means she had found to conceal them: recommended them to remain silent in the hollow tree, and then ordered them to mount. The two ladies, after embracing Black and his son, began resolutely ascending the rungs of the improvised ladder. They reached in a few seconds an enormous branch, on which they stopped, by the orders of the stranger. Black then threw down into the interior of the tree the furs and provisions, after which the ladder was placed inside, and the ladies glided through the hole.

"We leave you the ladder, which is useless to us," the stranger then said. "But be very careful not to come out till you have seen me again; the least imprudence, under the circumstances, might cost your lives. However, keep your minds at rest. Your imprisonment will not be long, a few hours at the most: so be of good cheer."

The ladies once again tried to express their gratitude; but, without listening, the stranger made Black a sign to follow her, and rapidly descended from the tree. Aided by the Americans, she then began removing every trace that might have revealed where the ladies were bestowed. When the stranger had assured herself, by a final glance, that all was in order, and nothing could betray those who were so famously hidden, she sighed, and followed by the two men, walked to the intrenchments.

"Now," she said, "let us watch attentively around us, for these demons will probably crawl close up in the shadows. You are free and honest Americans, show these accursed Indians what you can do."

"Let them come!" Black muttered hoarsely.

"They will soon do so," she replied, and pointed to several almost imperceptible black dots, which, however, grew larger, and were evidently approaching the encampment.

CHAPTER VI
THE DEFENCE OF THE CAMP

The Redskins have a mode of fighting which foils all the methods employed by European tactics. In order to understand their system properly, we must, in the first place, bear in mind that the Indian idea of honour is different from ours. This understood, the rest may be easily admitted. The Indians, in undertaking an enterprise, have only one object—success, and all means are good to attain it. Gifted with incontestable courage, at times rash to an excess, stopping at nothing, and recoiling before no difficulty— for all that, when the success of these enterprises appears to them dubious, and that consequently the object is missed, they retire as easily as they advanced, not considering their honour compromised by a retreat, or by leaving the battlefield to an enemy more powerful than themselves, or well on his guard.

Thus, their system of fighting is most simple, and they only proceed by surprises. The Redskins will follow the enemy's trail for entire months with unequalled patience, never relaxing their watch for a moment, spying him night and day, while ever careful not to be themselves surprised: then, when the occasion at last presents itself, and they fancy the moment arrived to execute the project, all the chances for or against which they have so long calculated, they act with a vigour and fury which frequently disconcert those they attack; but if after the first onset they are repulsed—if they see that those they attack will not let themselves be intimidated, and are prepared to resist, then, on a given signal, they disappear as if by enchantment, and, without any shame, begin watching again for a more favourable moment.

Black, on the advice of the stranger, had placed himself and his party in such positions that they could survey the prairie in every direction. The stranger and himself were leaning on their rifles in the angle that faced the river. The prairie at this moment presented a singular appearance. The breeze, which at sunset had risen with a certain strength, was gently dying out, scarce bending the tops of the great trees. The moon, almost departed, only cast over the landscape an uncertain and timorous gleam, which, in lieu of dissipating the gloom, only rendered the darkness visible, through the striking contrasts between the obscurity and the pale and fugitive rays of the declining planet.

At times, a dull roar or sharp bark rose in the silence, and, like a sinister appeal, reminded the emigrant that implacable and ferocious enemies were on the watch around, although invisible. The purity of the atmosphere was so great, that the slightest sound could be heard for an immense distance, and it was easy to distinguish the enormous blocks of granite that formed black dots on the ground.

"Do you know for certain that we shall be attacked this night?" the American asked, in a low voice.

"I was present at the last council of the chiefs," the unknown replied distinctly.

The emigrant bent on her a scrutinising glance, which she recognised, and immediately understood; she shrugged her shoulders disdainfully.

"Take care," she said to him, with a certain emphasis, "let not doubt invade your mind; what interest should I have in deceiving you?"

"I know not," he replied dreamily "but I also ask myself what interest you have in defending me?"

"None; since you place the matter on that footing, what do I care whether your wealth is plundered, your wife, your daughter, and yourself scalped? it is a matter of supreme indifference to me; but must the affair be only regarded from that side? Do you imagine that material interests have a great weight with me? If that is your opinion, I shall withdraw, leaving you to get out of your present position in the best way you can."

While uttering these words, she had thrown her rifle over her shoulder, and prepared to climb over the palisade, but Black quickly checked her.

"You do not understand me," he said; "any man in my place would act as I do; my position is fearful, you allow it yourself; you entered my camp, and it is impossible for me to guess how. Still, I have hitherto put the utmost confidence in you, as you cannot deny; but I do not know who you are, or what motive causes you to act. Your words, far from explaining, plunge me, on the contrary, into greater uncertainty; the safety of my entire family and all I possess is at stake: reflect seriously on all this, and I defy you to disapprove of my not putting utter confidence in you, although you are, doubtlessly, deserving of it, so long as I do not know who you are."

"Yes," she answered, after a moment's reflection, "you are right, the world is so, people must first of all give their name and quality; egotism is so thoroughly the master over the whole surface of the globe, that even to do a person a service, you require a certificate of honesty, for no one will admit disinterestedness of heart,—that aberration of generous minds, which practical people brand as madness. Unfortunately, you must take me for what I appear, at the risk of seeing me go away, and hence any confidence on my part would be superfluous. You will judge me by my acts, the only proof I can and will give you of the purity of my intentions; you are free to accept or decline my assistance, and after all is over, you can thank or curse me at your choice."

Black was more perplexed than ever; the stranger's explanations only rendered the fog denser, instead of affording him light. Still, in spite of himself, he felt himself attracted toward her. After a few moments of serious reflection, he raised his head, struck his rifle barrel smartly with his right hand, and looking his companion well in the face, said in a firm voice,—

"Listen, I will no longer try to learn whether you come from God or the devil; if you are a spy of our enemies, or our devoted friend—events, as you said, will soon decide the question. But bear this in mind, I will carefully watch your slightest gesture, your every word. At the first suspicious word or movement, I will put a bullet through your head, even if I am killed the moment after. Is that a bargain?"

The stranger began laughing.

"I accept," she said. "I recognise the Yankee in that proposition."

After this, the conversation ceased, and their entire attention was concentrated on the prairie. The most profound calm still continued to brood over the desert; apparently, all was in the same state as at sunset. Still the stranger's piercing eyes distinguished on the river bank several wild beasts flying precipitately, and others escaping across the river, instead of continuing to drink. One of the truest axioms in the desert is:—there can be no effect without a cause. Everything has a reason in the prairie, all is analysed or commented on; a leaf does not fall from a tree, a bird fly away, without the observer knowing or guessing why it has happened.

After a few moments of profound examination, the stranger seized the emigrant's arm, and bending down to his ear, said in a weak voice, like the sighing of the breeze, one word which made him tremble, as she stretched out her arm in the direction of the plain.

"Look!"

Black bent forward.

"Oh!" he said a minute after, "what is the meaning of this?"

The prairie, as we have already mentioned, was covered in several places by blocks of granite and dead trees; singularly enough, these black dots, at first a considerable distance from the camp, seemed approaching insensibly, and now were only a short way from it. As it was physically impossible for rocks and trees to move of their own accord, there must be a cause for this, which the worthy emigrant, whose mind was anything but subtle, cudgelled his brains in vain to guess. This new Birnam Wood, which moved all alone, made him excessively uncomfortable; his son and servants had also noticed the same fact, though equally unable to account for it. Black remarked specially that a tree he remembered perfectly well seeing that same evening more than one hundred and fifty feet from the mound, had suddenly come so close, that it was hardly thirty paces off. The stranger, without evincing any emotion, whispered—

"They are the Indians!"

"The Indians?" he said, "impossible!"

She knelt behind the palisade, shouldered her rifle, and after taking a careful aim, pulled the trigger. A flash traversed the darkness, and at the same moment the pretended tree bounded like a deer. A terrible yell was raised, and the Redskins appeared, rushing toward the camp like a herd of wolves, brandishing their weapons, and howling like demons. The Americans, very superstitious people, reassured by seeing that they had only to deal with men, when they feared some spell, received their enemies bravely with a rolling and well-directed fire. Still, the Indians, probably knowing the small number of white men, did not recoil, but pushed on boldly. The Redskins were hardly a few yards off, and were preparing to carry the barricades, when a shot, fired by the stranger, tolled over an Indian ahead of the rest, at the instant he turned to his comrades to encourage them to follow him.

The fall of this man produced an effect which the Americans, who fancied themselves lost, were far from anticipating. As if by enchantment, the Indians disappeared, the yells ceased, and the deepest silence prevailed again. It might be supposed that all that had passed was a dream. The Americans regarded each other with amazement, not knowing to what they should attribute this sudden retreat.

"That is incomprehensible," Black said, after assuring himself by a hasty glance that none of his party were wounded; "can you explain that, mistress, you, who seem to be our guardian angel, for it is to your last shot we owe the rest we at present enjoy?"

"Ah!" she said, with a sarcastic smile, "you are beginning to do me justice, then."

"Do not speak about that," the emigrant said, with an angry voice; "I am a fool; pardon me, and forget my suspicions."

"I have forgotten them," she replied. "As for that which astounds you, it is very simple. The man I killed, or, at any rate, wounded, was an Indian chief of great reputation; on seeing him fall, his warriors were discouraged, and they ran to carry him off the field, lest his scalp should fall into your hands."

"Oh, oh!" Black said, with a gesture of disgust; "do these Pagans fancy we are like themselves? No, no! I would kill them to the last man, in self-defence, and no one could blame me for it; but as for scalping, that is a different matter. I am an honest Virginian, without a drop of red blood in my veins. My father's son does not commit such infamy."

"I approve your remarks," the stranger said, in a sorrowful voice; "scalping is a frightful torture; unfortunately, many white men on the prairies do not think like you; they have adopted Indian fashions, and scalp, without ceremony, the enemies they kill."

"They are wrong."

"Possibly; I am far from justifying them."

"So that," the emigrant joyfully exclaimed, "we are free from these red devils."

"Do not rejoice yet; you will soon see them return."

"What, again?"

"They have only suspended their attack to carry off their killed and wounded, and probably to invent some other plan, to get the better of you."

"Oh, that will not be difficult; in spite of all our efforts, it will be impossible for us to resist that flock of birds of prey, who rush on us from all sides, as on a carcass. What can five rifles effect against that legion of demons?"

"Much, if you do not despair."

"Oh, as for that, you may be easy, we will not yield an inch; we are resolved to die at our posts."

"Your bravery pleases me," the stranger said, "perhaps all will end better than you suppose."

"May Heaven hear you, my worthy woman."

"Let us lose no time; the Indians may return to the charge at any moment, so let us try to be as successful this time as the first."

"I will."

"Good! Are you a man of resolution?"

"I fancy I have proved it."

"That is true. How many days' provisions have you here?"

"Four, at the least."

"That is to say, eight, if necessary."

"Pretty nearly."

"Good! Now, if you like, I will get rid of your enemies for a long time."

"I ask nothing better."

Suddenly the war cry of the Redskins was again heard, but this time more strident and unearthly than the first.

"It is too late!" the stranger said, sorrowfully, "All that is left is to die bravely."

"Let us die, then; but first kill as many of these Pagans as we can," John Black answered. "Hurrah! my boys, for Uncle Sam!"

"Hurrah!" his comrades shouted, brandishing their weapons.

The Indians responded to this challenge by yells of rage, and the combat recommenced, though this time it was more serious. After rising to utter their formidable war cry, the Indians scattered, and advanced slowly toward the camp, by crawling on the ground. When they found in their road the stump of a tree or a bush capable of offering them shelter, they stopped to fire an arrow or a bullet. The new tactics adopted by their enemies disconcerted the Americans, whose bullets were too often wasted; for, unluckily, the Indians were almost invisible in the gloom, and, with that cunning so characteristic of them, shook the grass so cleverly, that the deceived emigrants did not know where to aim.

"We are lost," Black exclaimed despondingly.

"The position is indeed becoming critical; but we must not despair yet," the stranger remarked; "one chance is left us; a very poor one, I grant; but which I shall employ when the moment arrives. Try to hold out in a hand-to-hand fight."

"Come," the emigrant said, shouldering his rifle, "there is one of the devils who will not get any further."

A Blackfoot warrior, whose head rose at this moment above the grass, had his skull fractured by the American's bullet. The Redskins suddenly rose, and rushed, howling, on the barricade, where the emigrants awaited them firmly. A point-blank discharge received the Indians, and a hand-to-hand fight began. The Americans, standing on the barricades and clubbing their rifles, dashed down every one who came within their reach. Suddenly, at the moment when the emigrants, overpowered by numbers, fell back a step, the stranger rushed up the barricade, with a torch in her hand, and uttering such a savage yell, that the combatants stopped, with a shudder. The flame of the torch was reflected on the stranger's face, and imparted to it a demoniac expression. She held her head high, and stretched out her arm, with a magnificent gesture of authority.

"Back!" she shrieked. "Back, devils!"

At this extraordinary apparition, the Redskins remained for a moment motionless, as if petrified, but then they rushed headlong down the slope, flying, with the utmost terror. The Americans, interested witnesses of this incomprehensible scene, gave a sigh of relief. They were saved! Saved by a miracle! They then rushed toward the stranger, to express their gratitude to her.

She had disappeared!

In vain did the Americans look for her everywhere; they could not imagine whither she was gone: she seemed to have suddenly become invisible. The torch she held in her hand, when addressing the Indians, lay on the ground, where it still smoked; it was the only trace she left of her presence in the emigrants' camp.

John Black and his companions lost themselves in conjectures on her account, while dressing, as well as they could, the wounds they had received in the engagement, when his wife and daughter suddenly appeared in the camp. Black rushed toward them.

"How imprudent of you!" he exclaimed. "Why have you left your hiding place, in spite of the warnings given you?"

His wife looked at him in amazement.

"We left it," she replied, "by the directions of the strange woman to whom we are all so deeply indebted this night."

"What! have you seen her again?"

"Certainly; a few moments back she came to us; we were half dead with terror, for the sounds of the fighting reached us, and we were completely ignorant of what was occurring. After reassuring us, she told us that all was over, that we had nothing more to fear, and that, if we liked, we could rejoin you."

"But she—what did she do?"

"She led us to this spot; then, in spite of our entreaties, she went away, saying that as we no longer needed her, her presence was useless, while important reasons compelled her departure."

The emigrant then told the ladies all about the events of the night, and the obligations they owed to this extraordinary female. They listened to the narrative with the utmost attention, not knowing to what they should attribute her strange conduct, and feeling their curiosity aroused to the utmost pitch. Unfortunately, the peculiar way in which the stranger had retired, did not appear to evince any great desire on her part to establish more intimate relations with the emigrants.

In the desert, however, there is but little time to be given to reflections and comments; action is before all; men must live and defend themselves. Hence Black, without losing further time in trying to solve the riddle, occupied himself actively in repairing the breaches made in his entrenchments, and fortifying his camp more strongly, were that possible, by piling up on the barricades all the articles within reach. When these first duties for the common safety were accomplished, the emigrant thought of his cattle. He had placed them at a spot where the bullets could not reach them, close to the tent, into which his wife and daughter had again withdrawn, and had surrounded them by a quantity of interlaced branches. On entering this corral, Black uttered a cry of amazement, which was soon changed into, a yell of fury. His son and the men ran up; the horses and one-half the cattle had disappeared. During the fight the Indians had carried them off, and the noise had prevented their flight being heard. It seemed probable that the stranger's interference, by striking the Indians with terror, had alone prevented the robbery being completed, and the whole of the cattle carried off.

The loss was enormous to the emigrant; although all his cattle had not disappeared, enough had been carried off to render further progress impossible. His resolution was formed with that promptitude so characteristic of the Northern Americans.

"Our beasts are stolen," he said; "I must have them back."

"Quite right," William answered; "at daybreak we will go on their track."

"I, but not you, my son," the emigrant said. "Sam will go with me."

"What shall I do then?"

"Stay in the camp, to guard your mother and sister. I will leave James with you."

The young man made no reply.

"I will not let the Pagans boast of having eaten my oxen," Black said, wrathfully. "By my father's soul, I will get them back, or lose my scalp!"

The night had passed away while the camp was being fortified. The sun, though still invisible, was beginning to tinge the horizon with a purple light.

"Ah, look!" Black continued, "here's day; let us lose no time, but set off. I recommend your mother and sister to your care, Will, as well as all that is here."

"You can go, father," the young man said. "I will keep good watch during your absence; you may be easy."

The emigrant pressed his son's hand, threw his rifle, over his shoulder, made a sign to Sam to follow him, and walked towards the entrenchment.

"It is useless to wake your mother," he said, as he walked on; "when she comes out of the tent, you will tell her what has occurred, and what I have done; I am certain she will approve of it. So, good-bye, my boy, and mind you are on the watch."

"And you, father—good luck!"

"May Heaven grant it, boy," the emigrant said, sorrowfully. "Such splendid cattle!"

"Stay!" the young man exclaimed, holding his father back, at the moment the latter was preparing to climb over the barricades. "What is that I see down there?"

The emigrant turned quickly.

"Do you see anything, Will—-whereabouts?"

"Look, father, in that direction. But what is the meaning of it? It must be our cattle."

The emigrant looked in the direction his son indicated.

"What!" he exclaimed joyfully; "why, those are our cattle. Where on earth do they come from? And who is bringing them back?"

In fact, at a great distance on the prairie, the American's cattle were visible, galloping rapidly in the direction of the camp, and raising a cloud of dust behind them.

CHAPTER VII
THE INDIAN CHIEF

The Count de Beaulieu was far from suspecting, as he carelessly prepared to light a cigar, that the lucifer match he employed would at once render him so important in the sight of the Indians. But, so soon as he recognized the power of the weapon chance placed in his hands, he resolved to employ it, and turn to his own profit the superstitious ignorance of the Redskins. Enjoying, in his heart, the triumph he had obtained, the Count frowned, and employing the language and emphatic gestures of the Indians, when he saw they were sufficiently recovered to listen to him, he addressed them with that commanding tone which always imposes on the masses.

"Let my brothers open their ears; the words my lips utter must be heard and understood by all. My brothers are simple men, prone to error; truth must enter their hearts like an iron wedge. My goodness is great, because I am powerful; instead of chastising them when they dared to lay hands on me, I am satisfied with displaying my power before their eyes. I am a great physician of the pale faces; I possess all the secrets of the most famous medicines. If I pleased, the birds of the air and the fish of the river would come to do me homage, because the Master of Life is within me, and has given me his medicine rod. Listen to this, Redskins, and remember it: when the first man was born, he walked on the banks of the Mecha-Chebe; there he met the Master of Life: the Master of Life saluted him, and said to him, 'Thou art my son.' 'No,' the first man made answer, 'thou art my son, and I will prove it to thee, if thou dost not believe me; we will sit down and plant in the earth the medicine rod we hold in our hands; the one who rises first will be the younger, and the son of the other.' They sat down then, and looked at each other for a long time, until at length the Master of Life turned pale, and the flesh left his bones; on which the first man exclaimed, joyfully, 'At length thou art assuredly dead.' And they regarded each other thus during ten times ten moons, and ten times more; and as at the end of that time the bones of the Master of Life were completely bleached, the first man rose and said, 'Yes, now there is no more doubt; he is certainly dead.' He then took the medicine stick of the Master of Life, and drew it from the earth. But then the Master of Life rose, and taking the stick from him, said to him, 'Stop! here I am; I am thy father, and thou art my son.' And the first man recognized him as his father. But the Master of Life then added, 'Thou art my son, first man; thou can'st not die; take my medicine staff; when I have to communicate with my Redskin sons, I will send thee.' This is the medicine staff. Are you ready to execute my orders?"

These words were uttered with so profound an accent of truth, the legend related by the Count was so true and so well known by all, that the Indians, whom the miracle of the match had already disposed to credulity, put complete faith in it, and answered respectfully—

"Let my father speak: what he wishes we wish. Are we not his children?"

"Hence," the Count continued, "I wish to speak with you, chief, alone."

Natah Otann had listened to the Count's discourse with the deepest attention: at times, an observer might have noticed a flash of joy cross his features, immediately followed, however, by a feeling of pleasure, which lit up his intelligent eyes: he applauded, like his warriors, perhaps more warmly than they, when the young man ceased speaking; on hearing him say that he would speak with the sachem alone, a smile played on his lips: he made the Indians a sign to retire, and walked towards the Count with an ease and grace which the other could not refrain from noticing. There was a native nobility in this young chief, which pleased at the first glance, and attracted sympathy.

After bowing respectfully, the Blackfeet warriors went down the hill, and collected about one hundred yards from the camping place.

There were two men whom the Count's eloquence had surprised quite as much as the Indian warriors. These were Bright-eye and Ivon; neither of them understood a syllable, and the young man's Indian science completely threw them out; they awaited in the utmost anxiety the denouement of this scene, whose meaning they could not decipher.

When left alone (for the hunter and Ivon soon also withdrew), the Frenchman and the Indian examined each other with extreme attention. But whatever efforts the white man made to read the sentiments of the man he had before him, he was obliged to allow that he had to deal with one of those superior natives, on whose faces it is impossible to read anything, and who, under all circumstances, are ever masters of their impressions; furthermore, the fixity and metallic lustre of the Indian's eye caused him to feel a secret uneasiness, which he hastened to remove by speaking, as if that would break the charm.

"Chief," he said, "now that your warriors have retired—"

Natah Otann interrupted him by a sign, and bowed courteously.

"Pardon me, Monsieur le Comte," he said, with an accent which a native of the banks of the Seine would have envied: "I think the slight practice you have had in speaking our language is wearisome to you; if you would please to express yourself in French, I fancy I understand that language well enough to follow you."

"Eh?" the Count exclaimed, with a start of surprise, "what is that you say?"

Had a thunderbolt fallen at the Count's feet he would not have been more surprised and terrified than on hearing this savage, who wore the complete costume of the Blackfeet, and whose face was painted of four different colours, express himself so purely in French. Natah Otann did not seem to notice his companion's agitation, but continued coldly—

"Deign to pardon me, Monsieur le Comte, for employing terms which must certainly have offended you by their triviality; but the few occasions I have for speaking French in this desert must serve as an excuse."

M. de Beaulieu was a prey to one of those surprises which grow gradually greater. He no longer knew were he awake, or suffering from a nightmare; what he heard seemed to him so incredible and incomprehensible, that he could not find words to express his feelings.

"Who on earth are you?" he exclaimed, when sufficiently master of himself to speak.

"I!" Natah Otann remarked carelessly; "why, you see I am a poor Indian, and nothing more."

"'Tis impossible," the young man said.

"I assure you, sir, that I have told you the exact truth. Hang it," he added with charming frankness, "if you find me a little less—what shall I say?— coarse, you must not consider it a crime; that results from considerations entirely independent of my will, which I will tell you some day, if you wish to hear them."

The Count, as we think we have said, was a man of great courage, whom but few things could disturb; the first impression passed, he bravely took his part; perfectly master of himself henceforth, he frankly accepted the position which accident had so singularly made for him.

"By Jove!" he said, with a laugh, "the meeting is a strange one, and may reasonably surprise me; you will therefore pardon, my dear sir, that astonishment—in extreme bad taste, I grant—which I at first evidenced on hearing you address me as you did. I was so far from expecting to meet, six hundred leagues from civilised countries, a man so well bred as yourself, that I confess I at first hardly knew what Saint to invoke."

"You flatter me, sir; believe me that I feel highly grateful for the good opinion you are good enough to have of me; now, if you permit, we will go back to our business."

"On my faith, I am so staggered by all that has happened, that I really do not know what I am about."

"Nonsense, that is nothing; I will lead you back to the right track; after the charming address you made us, you seem to desire speech with me alone."

"Hum!" the Count said, with a smile, "I am afraid that I must have appeared to you supremely ridiculous with my legend, especially my remarks, but then I could not suspect that I had an auditor of your stamp."

Natah Otann shook his head sadly; a melancholy expression for a moment darkened his face.

"No," he said, "you acted as you were bound to do; but while you were speaking, I was thinking of those poor Indians sunk so deeply in error, and asking myself whether there was any hope of their regeneration before the white men succeed in utterly destroying them."

The chief uttered these words with such a marked accent of grief and hatred, that the Count was moved by the thought how this man, with a soul of fire, must suffer at the brutalization of his race.

"Courage!" he said, holding out his hand to him.

"Courage!" the Indian repeated, bitterly, though clasping the proffered hand; "after each defeat I experienced in the struggle I have undertaken, the man who has served as my father, and unfortunately made me what I am, never ceases to say that to me."

There was a moment of silence; each was busied with his own thoughts; at length Natah Otann proceeded:—

"Listen, Monsieur le Comte; between men of a certain stamp there is a species of undefinable feeling, which attaches them to each other in spite of themselves; for the six months your have been traversing the desert in every direction, I have never once lost sight of you; you would have been dead long ere this, but I spread a secret ægis over you. Oh, do not thank me," he said, quickly, as the young man made a sign, "I have acted rather in my own interest than yours. What I say surprises you, I daresay, but it is so. Allow me to tell you, that I have views with reference to yourself, whose secrets I will unfold to you in a few days, when we know each other better; as for the present, I will obey you in whatever you wish; in the eyes of my countrymen, I will keep up that miraculous halo which surrounds your brow. You wish these American emigrants to be left at peace, very good; for your sake I pardon this race of vipers; but I ask you one favour in return."

"Speak!"

"When you are certain the people you wish to save are in security, accompany me to my village,—that is all I desire. That will not cost you much, especially as my tribe is encamped not more than a day's march from the spot where you now are."

"I accept your proposition, chief. I will accompany you wherever you please, though not till I am certain that my *protégés* no longer require my aid."

"That is agreed. Stay, one word more."

"Say it."

"It is well understood that I am only an Indian like the rest, even to the two white men who accompany you!"

"You demand it?"

"For our common welfare: a word spoken thoughtlessly, any indiscretion, how trifling soever, would destroy us both. Ah! you do not know the Redskins yet," he added, with that melancholy smile which had already given the Count so much subject for thought.

"Very good," he answered; "you may be easy; I am warned."

"Now, if you think proper, I will recall my warriors; a longer conference between us might arouse their jealousy."

"Do so; I trust entirely to you."

"You will have no reason to repent it," Natah Otann replied, graciously.

While the chief went to join his companions, the Count walked up to the two white men.

"Well?" Bright-eye asked him, "have you obtained what you wanted from that man?"

"Perfectly," he answered; "I only wished to say a few words to him."

The hunter looked at him cunningly.

"I did not think him so easy," he said.

"Why so, my friend?"

"His reputation is great in the desert; I have known him for a very long period."

"Ah!" the young man said, not at all sorry to obtain some information about the man who perplexed him so greatly; "what reputation has he then?"

Bright-eye seemed to hesitate for a moment.

"Are you afraid to explain yourself clearly on that head?" the Count asked.

"I have no reason for that; on the contrary, with the exception of that day on which he wished to flay me alive—a slight mistake, which I pardon with my whole heart,—our relations have always been excellent."

"The more so," the Count said, with a laugh, "because you never met again, to my knowledge, till this day."

"That is what I meant to say. Look you—Natah Otann, between ourselves, is one of those Indians whom it is far more advantageous not to see: he is like the owl—his presence always forebodes evil."

"The deuce! You trouble me greatly by speaking so, Bright-eye."

"Suppose I had said nothing, then," he answered, quickly; "for my part, I should prefer to be silent."

"That is possible; but the little you have allowed to escape has, I confess, so awakened my curiosity, that I should not be sorry to learn more."

"Unfortunately, I know nothing."

"Still you spoke of his reputation—is that bad?"

"I did not say so," Bright-eye answered, with reserve. "You know, Mr. Edward, that Indian manners are very different from ours: what is bad to us is regarded very differently by Indians; and so—"

"So, I suppose," the Count interrupted, "Natah Otann has an execrable reputation."

"No, I assure you; that depends upon the way in which you look at matters."

"Good; and what is your personal opinion?"

"Oh, I, as you are aware, am only a poor fellow; still it seems to me as if this demon of an Indian is more crafty than his whole tribe; between ourselves, he is regarded as a sorcerer by his countrymen, who are frightfully afraid of him."

"Is that all?"

"Nearly."

"After that," the Count said, lightly, "as he has asked me to accompany him to his village, the few days we spend with him will enable us to study him at our ease."

The hunter gave a start of surprise.

"You will not do so, I trust, Sir?"

"I do not see what can prevent me."

"Yourself, Sir; who, I hope, will not walk, with your eyes open, into the lion's jaws."

"Will you explain—yes, or no?" the Count exclaimed with rising impatience.

"Oh, what is the use of explaining?—will what I say stop you? No, I am persuaded of that. You see, therefore, it is useless for me to say more; besides, it is too late—the chief is returning."

The Count made a movement of ill-humour, at once suppressed; but this movement did not escape Natah Otann, who at this moment appeared on the plateau. The young man walked toward him.

"Well?" he asked eagerly.

"My young men consent to do what our Paleface father desires; if he will mount his horse and follow us, he can convince himself that our intentions are loyal."

"I follow you, chief," the Count replied, making Ivon a sign to bring up his horse.

The Blackfeet welcomed the three hunters with unequivocal signs of joy.

"Forward!" the young man said.

Natah Otann raised his arm. At this signal the warriors drove in their knees, and the horses started like a hurricane. No one, who has not witnessed it, can form an idea of an Indian chase: nothing stops the Redskins—no obstacle is powerful enough to make them deviate from their course; they go in a straight line, rolling like a human whirlwind across the prairie crossing gulleys, ravines, and rocks, with dizzy rapidity. Natah Otann, the Count, and his two companions, were at the head of the cavalcade, closely followed by the warriors. All at once the chief checked his horse, shouting at the top of his voice—

"Halt!"

All obeyed, as if by enchantment: the horses stopped dead, and remained motionless, as if their feet were planted in the ground.

"Why stop?" the Count asked; "we had better push on."

"It is useless," the chief said, calmly; "let my Pale brother look before him."

The Count bent on his horse's neck.

"I can see nothing," he said.

"That is true," the Indian said; "I forgot that my brother has the eyes of the Palefaces; in a few minutes he will see."

The Blackfeet anxiously collected round their chief, whom they questioned with their glances. The latter, apparently impassive, looked straight ahead, distinguishing in the darkness objects invisible to all but himself. The Indians, however, had not long to wait, for some horsemen soon came up at full speed. When they arrived near Natah Otann's party, they stopped.

"What has happened?" the chief asked, sternly; "why are my sons running away thus? They are not warriors I see, but timid women."

The Indians bowed their heads with humility at this reproach, but made no answer. The chief continued—"Will no one inform us of what has happened—why my chosen warriors are flying like scattered antelopes—where is Long Horn?"

A warrior emerged from the ranks.

"Long Horn is dead," he said, sorrowfully.

"He was a wise and renowned warrior; he has gone to the happy hunting grounds to hunt with the upright warriors. As he is dead, why did not the Blackbird take the totem in his hand in his place?"

"Because the Blackbird is dead," the warrior answered, in the same tone.

Natah Otann frowned, and his brow was contracted by the effort he made to suppress his passion.

"Oh!" he said, bitterly, "the greathearts of the east have fought well; their rifles carry truly. The two best chiefs of the nation have fallen, but the Red Wolf still remained—why did he not avenge his brothers?"

"Because he has also fallen," the warrior said, in a mournful voice.

A shudder of anger ran through the ranks.

"Wah!" Natah Otann exclaimed, with grief, "what is he also dead?"

"No; but he is dangerously wounded."

After these words there was a silence. The chief looked around him, and then said —

"So; four Palefaces have held at bay two hundred Blackfeet warriors; killed and wounded their bravest chiefs, and those warriors have not taken their revenge. Ah! ah! what will the White Buffalo say when he hears that? He will give petticoats to my sons, and make them prepare food for the more courageous warriors, instead of sending them on the warpath."

"The camp of the Long Knives was in our power," the Indian replied, who had hitherto spoken for his comrades, "we already had them down with our knees on their chests, a portion of their cattle was carried off, and the scalps of the Palefaces were about to be attached to our girdles, when the Evil Genius suddenly appeared in their midst, and, by her mere appearance, changed the face of the combat."

The chief's face became still severer at this news, which his warriors received with unequivocal marks of terror.

"The 'Evil Genius!'" he said; "of whom is my brother speaking?"

"Of whom else can I speak to my father, save the *Lying She-wolf of the Prairies??*" the Indian said, in a low voice.

"Oh! oh!" Natah Otann answered, "did my brother see the She-wolf?"

"Yes; we assure our father," the Blackfeet shouted altogether, happy to clear themselves from the accusation of cowardice that weighed on them.

Natah Otann seemed to reflect for a moment.

"At what place are the cattle my brothers carried off from the Long Knives?" he asked.

"We have brought them with us," a warrior answered, "they are here."

"Good," Natah Otann continued, "let my brothers open their ears to hear the words the Great Spirit breathes unto me:—the Long Knives are protected by the She-wolf: our efforts would be useless, and my sons would not succeed in conquering them; I will make a great medicine to break the charm of the She-wolf when we return to our village, but till then we must be very cunning to deceive the She-wolf, and prevent her being on her guard. Will my sons follow the advice of an experienced chief?"

"Let my father utter his thoughts," a warrior answered, in the name of all, "he is very wise: we will do what he wishes: he will deceive the She-wolf better than we can."

"Good; my sons have spoken well. This is what we will do:—We will return to the camp of the Palefaces, and will restore them their beasts; the Palefaces, deceived by this friendly conduct, will no longer suspect us; when we have made the great medicine, we will then seize their camp and all it contains, and the Lying She-wolf will be unable to defend them. I have spoken; what do my sons think?"

"My father is very crafty," the warrior replied; "what he has said is very good, his sons will perform it."

Natah Otann cast a glance of triumph at the Count de Beaulieu, who admired the skill with which the chief, while appearing to reprimand the Indians for the ill success of their enterprise, and evincing the greatest wrath against the Americans, had succeeded in a few minutes in inducing them to carry out his secret wishes.

"Oh! oh!" the Count murmured, aside, "this Indian is no common man, he deserves studying."

Still, a moment of tumult had followed the chief's words. The Blackfeet, recovered from the panic and terror which had made them fly with the feet of gazelles, to escape speedily from the ruined camp, where they had experienced so rude a defeat, had got off their horses, and were engaged, some in laying on their wounds chewed leaves of the oregano, others in collecting the cattle and horses which they had stolen from the Palefaces, and which were scattered about.

"Who is this Lying She-wolf of the Prairies, who inspires such horror in these men?" the Count asked Bright-eye.

"No one knows her," the hunter answered, in a low voice, "she is a woman whose mysterious life has hitherto foiled the most careful attempts at investigation: she does no harm to any but the Indians, whose implacable foe she appears to be: the Redskins affirm that she is invulnerable, that bullets and arrows rebound from her without doing her any injury. I have often seen her, though I have had no opportunity of speaking with her. I believe her to be mad, for I have seen her perform some of the wildest freaks at some moments, though at others she appears in full possession of her senses: in a word, she is an incomprehensible being, who leads an extraordinary life in the heart of the prairies."

"Is she alone?"

"Always."

"You excite my curiosity to the highest degree," the Count said; "no one, I suppose, could give me any information about this woman?"

"One person could do so, if he cared to speak."

"Who's that?"

"Natah Otann," the hunter said, in a low voice.

"That is strange," the Count muttered; "what can there be in common between him and this woman?"

Bright-eye only answered by a significant glance.

The conversation was broken off, and at the chief's order the Blackfeet remounted their horses.

"Forwards!" Natah Otann said, taking the head of the column again with the Count and his companions.

The whole troop set out at a gallop in the direction of the American camp, taking the cattle in their midst.

CHAPTER VIII
THE EXILE

We are compelled, for the proper comprehension of the facts that will follow, to break off our story for a moment, in order to describe a strange adventure which happened on the Western Prairies some thirty odd years before our story opens.

The Indians, whom people insist so wrongly, in our opinion, in regarding as savages, have certain customs which display a thorough knowledge of the human heart. The Comanches, who appear to remember that in old times they enjoyed a far advanced civilization, have retained the largest amount of those customs which are, certainly, stamped with originality.

One day in the month of February, which they call *the Moon of the Arriving Eagles,* and in the year 1795 or 1796, a village of the Red Cow tribe was in a state of extraordinary agitation. The hachesto, or public speaker, mounted on the roof of a lodge, summoned the warriors for the seventh hour of the day to the village square, near the ark of the first man, where a grand council would be held. The warriors asked each other in vain the purport of this unforeseen meeting, but no one could tell them: the hachesto himself was ignorant, and they were obliged to await the hour of assembling, although the comments and suppositions still went on to a great extent.

The Redskins, whom badly-informed authors represent to us as cold, silent men, are, on the contrary, very gay, and remarkable gossips when together. What has caused the contrary supposition is, that in their relations with white men the Indians are, in the first place, checked by the difficulties of the language—equally insurmountable, by the way, for both parties—and next by the distrust which every American native feels towards Europeans, whoever they may be, owing to the inveterate hatred that separates the two races.

During our lengthened residence among Indian tribes we often had opportunities for noticing what mistakes are made with respect to the Redskins. During their long evening gossips in the villages, or the hunting expeditions, there was a rolling fire of jokes and witticisms, often lasting whole hours, to the great delight of the audience, who laughed that hearty Indian laugh, without care or afterthought, which cleaves the mouth to the ears, and draws tears of delight,—a laugh which, for metallic resonance, can only be compared with that of negroes, though the former is far more spiritual than the latter, whose notes have ever something bestial about them.

Toward the decline of day, the hour selected for the meeting, the village square presented a most animated appearance. The warriors, women, children, and dogs, those inseparable guests of the Redskins, pressed round a large circle left empty in the centre for the council fire, near which the principal chiefs of the nation crouched ceremoniously. At a sign from an old sachem whose hair, white as silver, fell in a cloud on his shoulders, the pipe bearer brought in the great calumet, the stem of which he presented to each chief in turn, while holding the bowl in the palm of his hand. When all the chiefs had smoked, the pipe bearer turned the calumet to the four cardinal points, while murmuring mysterious words which no one heard; then he emptied the ash into the fire, saying aloud,—

"Chiefs, warriors, women, and children of the Red Cow, your sachems are assembled to judge a very grave question; pray to the Master of Life to inspire them with wise words."

Then the pipe bearer, after bowing respectfully to the chiefs, withdrew, taking the calumet with him. The council began, and, at a sign from the aged sachem, a chief rose, and bowing, took the word:—

"Venerated sachems, chiefs, and warriors of my nation," he said, in a loud voice, "the mission with which I am entrusted is painful to my heart: listen to me indulgently, be not governed by passion; but let justice alone preside over the severe decree which you will, perhaps, be compelled to pronounce. The mission which I am entrusted with is painful, I repeat; it fills my heart with sadness: I am compelled to accuse before you two renowned chiefs belonging to two illustrious families, who have, with equal claims, deserved well of the nation on many occasions by rendering it signal services; these chiefs, as I must name them before you, are the Bounding Panther, and the Sparrow Hawk."

On hearing these names, so well known and justly esteemed, pronounced, a shudder of astonishment and pain ran though the crowd. But, at a sign from the oldest chief, silence was almost immediately re-established, and the chief continued—

"How is it that a cloud has suddenly passed over the mind of these two warriors, and tarnished their intellect to such an extent, that these two men, who so long loved one another as brothers, whose friendship was cited among the nation, have suddenly become implacable enemies, so that, when they see each other, their eyes flash lightning, and their hands seek their weapons to commit murder? No one can say; no one knows it; these chiefs, when interrogated by the sachems, maintained an obstinate silence, instead of revealing the causes of their cruel enmity, which brings trouble and desolation on the tribe. Such a scandal must not last longer; tolerating it would be giving a pernicious example to our children! Sachems, chiefs, and warriors, in the name of justice, I demand that these irreconcilable enemies should be eternally banished from the tribe this very evening at sunset. I have spoken. Have I said well, powerful men?"

The chief sat down amid a mournful silence in this assembly of nearly two thousand people; the beating of their sorrow-laden hearts might almost be heard, such sustained attention did each one give to the words pronounced in the council.

"Has any chief any observation to offer on the accusation which has just been brought?" the old sachem said, in a weak voice, which was, however, perfectly heard in every part of the square. A member of the council rose.

"I take the word," he said, "not to refute Tiger Cat's accusation, for unfortunately all he has said is most scrupulously correct; far from exaggerating facts, he has, with that goodness and wisdom which reside in him, weakened the odiousness of that hatred; I only wish to offer a remark to my brothers. The chiefs are guilty, that is only too fully proved; a longer discussion on that point would be tedious; but, as Tiger Cat himself told us, with that loyalty which distinguishes him, these two men are renowned chiefs, chosen warriors, and they have rendered the nation signal services; we all love and cherish them for different reasons; let us be severe, but not cruel; let us not drive them from among us as unclean creatures; before striking, let us make one more attempt to reconcile them; this last step, taken in the presence of the whole nation, will, doubtlessly, touch their hearts, and we shall have the happiness of keeping two illustrious chiefs. If they remain deaf to our prayers, if our observations do not obtain the success we desire, then, as the case will be without a remedy, let us be implacable; put an end to this scandal which has lasted too long, and, as Tiger Cat asked, drive them for ever from our nation, which they dishonour. I have spoken. Have I said well, powerful men?"

After bowing to the sachems, the chief resumed his seat in the midst of a murmur of satisfaction, produced by his hearty language. Although these two speeches were contained in the programme of the ceremony, and everyone knew what the result of the meeting would be, the unreconciled chiefs had so much sympathy among the nation, that many persons still hoped they would be reconciled at the last moment, when they saw themselves on the point of being banished. The strangest thing connected with the hatred between the two men was, that the reason of it was completely unknown, and no one knew how to account for it. When silence was restored, the oldest sachem, after a consultation with his colleagues in a low voice, took the word.

"Let the Bounding Panther and the Sparrowhawk be introduced to our presence."

At the two opposite corners of the square, the crowd parted like overripe fruit, and left a passage for a small band of warriors, in the centre of which the two accused men walked. When they met, they remained perfectly calm, a slight arching of the eyebrows being the only sign of emotion they displayed. They were each about twenty-five years of age, well built, and active, and of martial aspect. They wore their grand costume and war paint, but their weapons were carried by their respective friends. They presented themselves before the council with great respect and modesty, which the assembly approved of heartily. After looking at them with a glance at once sorrowful and benevolent, the eldest sachem rose with an effort, and, supported by two of his colleagues, who held him under the arms, he at length spoke in a weak voice.

"Warriors, my beloved children," he said, "from the spot where you stood you heard the accusation brought against you; what have you to say in your defence?—are those words true? do you really entertain this irreconcilable hatred to each other? Speak."

The two chiefs bowed their heads silently. The sachem continued—

"My cherished children, I was already very old, when your mother, a child, whose birth I also saw, brought you into the world. I was the first to teach you the use of those weapons, which later became so terrible in your vigorous hands. Now that I am about to sleep the eternal sleep, only to wake again in the happy hunting grounds, give me a supreme consolation which will make me the happiest of men, and repay me for all the sorrow you have caused me. Come, children, you are young and adventurous, love alone ought to find a place in your hearts; hatred is a passion belonging to a ripe age, it does not become youth; offer one another those honest hands, embrace, like the two brothers you are, and let all be eternally forgotten between you. I implore you, my children; you cannot resist the prayers of an old man so near the tomb as I am."

There was a moment of supreme anxiety in the crowd; all waited with panting hearts for what was about to happen. The two chiefs directed a tender glance at the old sachem, who regarded them with tears in his eyes, then turned towards each other; their lips trembled, as if they wished to speak; a nervous tremor agitated their bodies, but no sound passed their lips; their arms remained inert by their sides.

"Answer," the old man continued, "yes or no. You must; I command it."

"No," they replied together, in a hoarse though firm voice.

The sachem drew himself up.

"It is well," he said. "As no generous feeling remains in your hearts, as hatred has eaten them up entirely, and you are no longer men but monsters, listen to the irrevocable sentence which your sachems, your equals, your relations, and friends pronounce upon you. The nation rejects you from its bosom; you are no longer children of our tribe. Fire and water are refused you on the hunting ground of your nation, we no longer know you. Chiefs who answer for you with their heads will lead you twenty-five leagues from the village; you, Bounding Panther, in a southern, and you, Sparrowhawk, in a northern direction; you are forbidden, under penalty of death, ever to set your foot again on the territory of your nation; each of you will take one of these arrows, painted of diverse colours, which will serve as a passport with the tribes through which you pass. Seek a nation to adopt you, for henceforth you have neither country nor family. Go, accursed ones! these arrows are the last presents you will receive from your brothers. Go, and may the Master of Life soften your tiger hearts! As for us, we know you no more. I have spoken. Have I said well, powerful men?"

The old man sat down again in the midst of general emotion; he veiled his face with the skirt of his buffalo robe, and wept. The two chiefs tottered away like drunken men, led to opposite corners of the square by their friends. They passed through the ranks of their countrymen, bowed down by the maledictions showered on them as they passed.

At the extremity of the village, horses were awaiting them. They galloped off, still followed by their escort. When each arrived at the spot where he was to be left, the warriors dismounted, threw their arms on the ground, and went off at full speed. Not a word had been uttered during the long ride, which lasted fourteen hours.

We will follow the Sparrowhawk: as for the Bounding Panther, no one ever knew what became of him; his traces were so completely lost, that it was impossible to find them again. The Sparrowhawk was a man of tried courage and energy; still, finding himself alone, abandoned by all those he had loved, a momentary feeling of discouragement and cold rage almost turned him mad. But his pride soon revolted, he wrestled with his sorrow, and after allowing his horse to take its necessary rest, he set out boldly.

He wandered about at hazard for many a month, following no precise direction, living by the chase, caring very little where he stopped, or the people with whom chance might bring him in contact. One day, after a long and perilous chase after an elk, which by a species of fatality he could not catch up, he suddenly found himself before a dead horse. He looked around him: no great distance off lay a sword, near which was a corpse, easily recognizable as that of a European by the dress.

Sparrowhawk felt his curiosity excited; with that sagacity peculiar to the Indians, he began ferreting about in every direction. His search was almost immediately crowned with success; he saw, at the foot of a tree, an old man with greyish hair and wild beard, dressed in tattered clothes, and lying motionless. The Indian quickly went up to examine the condition of the stranger, and try to restore him, if he were not dead. The first thing Sparrowhawk did was to lay his hand on the heart of the man he wished to succour. The heart beat, but so feebly, it seemed as if it must soon stop. All the Indians are to a certain extent doctors, that is to say, they possess a knowledge of certain plants, by means of which they often effect really wonderful cures.

While trying to restore the stranger, the Indian examined him attentively. Though his hair was beginning to turn grey, the man was still young, not more than forty to forty-five; he was tall and well-built; his forehead was wide and high; his nose aquiline; his mouth large, and his chin square. His clothes, though in rags, were well cut and made of fine cloth, which plainly showed that he must belong to a better class of society—the reader will understand that these delicate distinctions escaped the notice of the Indian— he only saw a man of intelligent appearance, and on the point of death; and though he belonged to the white race, a race which, like all his countrymen, he detested, and for good reasons—at the sight of such distress, he forgot his antipathy, and only thought of helping him.

Near the stranger there lay, in confusion on the grass, a surgeon's pocketbook, a brace of pistols, a gun, a sabre, and an open book. For a long time Sparrowhawk's efforts met with no success, and he was despairing whether he could raise the dying man to life, when a transient glow suffused his face, and his heart began beating more quickly and strongly. Sparrowhawk made a gesture of delight at this unexpected success. It was almost incredible! This warrior, whose whole life had been hitherto spent in waging war of ambushes and surprises with the whites, and committing the most refined cruelties on the unhappy Spaniards who fell into his hands, now rejoiced at recalling to life this individual, who, to him, was a natural enemy.

In a few minutes the stranger slowly opened his eyes, but he closed them again at once, as the light probably dazzled them. Sparrowhawk did not lose heart, and resolved to carry out a good work so well begun. His expectations were not deceived: the stranger presently opened his eyes again; he made an effort to rise, but was too weak, his strength failed him, and he fell back again. The Indian then gently supported him, and seated him against the trunk of the catalpa, at whose foot he had been hitherto lying. The stranger thanked him by a sign, muttering one word, *beber* (drink).

The Comanches, whose life is passed in periodical excursions into the Spanish territory, know a few words of that language. Sparrowhawk spoke it rather fluently. He seized the gourd hanging to his saddle bow, and which he had filled two hours before, and put it to the stranger's lips; so soon as he had tasted the water, he began swallowing it in heavy gulps. But the Indian, fearing an accident, soon took the gourd from his lips. The stranger wished to drink again.

"No," he said, "my father is too weak, he must eat something first."

The patient smiled, and pressed his hand. The Indian rose joyfully; took from his provision bag some fruit, and handed it to the man. Through these attentions the stranger was sufficiently recovered, within an hour, to get up. He then explained to Sparrowhawk, in bad Spanish, that he and one of his friends were travelling together, that their horses died of fatigue, while themselves could procure nothing to eat or drink in the desert. The result was, that his friend died in his arms only the previous day, after frightful suffering, and he should have probably shared the same fate, had not his lucky star, or rather Providence, sent him help.

"Good," the Indian replied, when the stranger ended his narrative, "my father is now strong, I will lasso a horse, and lead him to the first habitation of the men of his own colour."

At this proposition the stranger frowned; a look of hatred and haughty contempt was legible on his face.

"No," he said; "I will not return to the men of my colour, they have rejected and persecuted me, I hate them; I wish to live henceforward in the desert."

"Wah!" the Indian exclaimed, in surprise, "has my father no nation?"

"No," he answered, "I am alone, without country, relatives, or friends; the sight of a man of my colour excites me to hatred and contempt; all are ungrateful, I will live far from them."

"Good," the Indian said; "I, too, am rejected by my nation; I, too, am alone; I will remain with my father—I will be his son."

"What?" the stranger ejaculated, fancying he had misunderstood him, "Is it possible? Does banishment also exist among your wandering tribes? You, like myself, are abandoned by those of your race and blood, and condemned to remain alone—alone for ever?"

"Yes," Sparrowhawk said, sorrowfully, bowing his head.

"Oh!" the stranger said, directing a glance of strange meaning toward heaven, "oh, men! they are the same everywhere, cruel, unnatural, and heartless!"

He walked about for a few moments, muttering certain words in a language the Indian did not understand; then he returned quickly to him, and pressing his hand, said, with feverish energy:—

"Well, then, I accept your proposition; our fate is the same, and we ought not to separate again. Victims both of the spite of man, we will live together; you have saved my life, Redskin; at the first impulse I was vexed at it, but now I thank Providence, as I can still do good, and force men to blush at their ingratitude."

This speech was far too full of philosophic precepts for Sparrowhawk thoroughly to understand it; still, he caught its sense, that was enough for him, as he was too glad to find in his companion a man afflicted by similar misfortunes to his own.

"Let my father open his ears," he said; "he will remain here while I go and find a horse for him; there are many manadas in the neighbourhood, and I shall soon have what we want; my father will be patient during Sparrowhawk's absence. I will leave him food and drink."

"Go," the stranger said; and two hours later the Indian returned with a magnificent steed.

Several days were then spent in vagabond marches, though each took them deeper into the desert. The stranger seemed afraid of meeting white men; but with the exception of the story he had told of his narrow escape from death, he maintained an obstinate silence as to his past life. The Indian knew not then who he was, nor why he had ventured so far into the desert at the risk of perishing. Each time Sparrowhawk asked him any details about his life he turned the conversation, and that so adroitly, that the Indian could never bring him back to the starting point. One day, as they were rambling along side by side, talking, Sparrowhawk, who was rather vexed at the slight confidence the stranger placed in him, asked categorically—

"My father was a great chief in his nation?"

The stranger smiled sorrowfully.

"Perhaps," he answered; "but now I am nothing."

"My father is mistaken," the Indian said, seriously; "the warriors of his nation may not have valued him, but he still remains the same."

"All that is smoke," the stranger replied. "The love of country is the greatest and noblest passion the Master of Life has placed in the heart of man—my father had a revered name among his people."

The stranger frowned, and his face assumed an expression the Indian had never seen before.

"My name is a curse," he said, "no one will hear it uttered again; it has been like a brand seared on my forehead by the partisans of the man whom I, humble as I am, helped to overthrow."

Sparrowhawk made a gesture of supreme disdain.

"The chief of the nation must return to his warriors: if he betrays them, they are masters of his scalp," he said, in a firm voice.

The stranger, surprised at being so well understood by this primitive man, smiled proudly.

"In demanding his head," he said, "I staked my own; I wished to save my country. Who can blame me?"

"No one," Sparrowhawk replied, quickly; "every warrior must die."

There was a lengthened silence; Sparrowhawk was the first to break it.

"We are destined," he said; "to live long days together, my father wishes his name to remain unknown, and I will not insist on knowing it; still, we cannot wander about at hazard, we must find a tribe to adopt us, men to recognize us as brothers."

"For what purpose?"

"To be strong and everywhere respected: we owe it to our brothers, as they owe it to us; life is only a loan which the Master of Life makes us, on the condition that it is profitable to those who surround us. By what name shall I present my father to the men from whom we may ask asylum and protection?"

"By any you please, my son; as I am no longer to hear my own, any other is a matter of indifference to me."

Sparrowhawk reflected for an instant.

"My father is strong," he said, "his scalp is beginning to resemble the snows of winter, he will henceforth be called the White Buffalo."

"The White Buffalo; be it so," the stranger answered, with a sigh; "that name is as good as another; perhaps I shall thus escape the weapons of those who have sworn my death."

The Indian, charmed at knowing how henceforth to call his friend, then said to him, joyfully—

"In a few days we shall reach a village of Blood Indians or Kenhas, where we shall be received as if we were sons of the nation; my father is wise, I am strong, the Kenhas will be happy to receive us; courage, old father! this country of adoption will be, perhaps, worth your own."

"France, farewell!" the stranger uttered, in a choking voice.

Four days later they reached the village of the Kenhas, where a friendly reception was given them.

"Well," Sparrowhawk said to his companion, after they had been adopted according to all the Indian rites, "what does my father think? Is he happy?"

"I fancy," the other said, with a melancholy air, "that nothing can restore the exile the country he has lost."

CHAPTER IX
THE MASSACRE

Days, months, years, passed away: the White Buffalo seemed to have completely renounced that country which he was forbidden ever to see again. He had completely adopted Indian customs, and, through his wisdom, had so thoroughly acquired the esteem and respect of the Kenha nation, that he was counted among the most revered sachems.

Sparrowhawk, after giving on many occasions undeniable proofs of his courage and military talents, had gained also a firm and honourable place in the nation. If an experienced chief were required for a dangerous expedition, he was ever selected by the council of the sachems, for they knew that success constantly crowned his enterprises. Sparrowhawk was a man of clear mind, who at once understood the intellectual value of his European friend; obedient to the old man's lessons, he never acted under any circumstances without having taken his advice, and always followed his counsels: hence he speedily began reaping the advantage of his skilful conduct. Thus, when he two years later married a Kenha girl, and when his wife made him father of a boy, he took him in his arms, and presented him to the old man, saying, with great emotion:

"The White Buffalo sees this warrior, he is his son, my father will make a man of him."

"I swear it," the old man replied, firmly.

When the child was weaned, the father kept the promise he had made his friend, and gave him his son, leaving him at liberty to educate the boy as he thought fit. The old man, rejuvenated by the hope of this education, which gave him the chance of making a man after his own heart of this frail creature, joyfully accepted the difficult task. The child received from its parents the name of Natah Otann, a significant name, for it is that borne by the most dangerous animal of Northern America, the grizzly bear.

Natah Otann made rapid progress under the guidance of the White Buffalo. The latter had a few books by him, which enabled him to give his pupil a very extensive education, and make him very learned. Thence resulted the strange circumstance of an Indian, who, while following exactly the customs of his fathers, hunting and fighting like them, and who was now leading his tribe, being at the same time a distinguished man, who would not have been out of place in any European drawing room, and whose great intellect had understood and appreciated everything.

Singularly enough, Natah Otann, on attaining manhood, far from despising his countrymen, brutalized and ignorant as they were, felt an ardent love for them, and a violent desire to regenerate them. From that moment his life had an object, which was the constant preoccupation of his existence—to restore the Indians to the rank from which they had fallen, by combining them into a great and powerful nation. The White Buffalo, the confidant of all the young chief's thoughts, at first accepted these projects with the sceptical smile of old men, who, having grown weary of everything, have retained no hope in the depths of their heart: he fancied that Natah Otann, under the impression of youthful ardour, let himself be carried away by an unreflecting movement, whose folly he would soon recognize. But when able to appreciate how deeply these ideas were rooted in the young man's heart, when he saw him set resolutely to work, the old man trembled, and was afraid of his handiwork. He asked himself if he had done well in acting as he had done, in developing so fully this chosen intellect, which alone, and with no other support than its will, was about to undertake a struggle in which it must inevitably succumb.

He then sought to destroy with his own hands the edifice he had built with so much labour: he wished to turn in another direction the ardour that devoured his pupil, and give another object to his life, by changing his plan. It was too late. The evil was irremediable. Natah Otann, on seeing his master thus contradict himself, defeated him with his own weapons, and obliged him to bow his head before the merciless blows of that logic he had himself taught his pupil.

Natah Otann was a strange composite of good and evil; in him all was in extreme. At times, the most noble feelings seemed to reside in him; he was good and generous; then, suddenly, his ferocity and cruelty attained gigantic proportions, which terrified the Indians themselves. Still, he was generally good and gentle toward his countrymen, who, unaware of the cause, but subject to his influences, feared him, and trembled at a word that fell from his lips, or a simple frown.

The white men, and especially the Spaniards and Americans, were Natah Otann's implacable enemies; he waged a merciless war on them, attacking them wherever he could surprise them, and killing, under the most horrible tortures, those who were so unhappy as to fall into his hands. Hence his reputation on the prairies was great; the terror he inspired was extreme; several times already the United States had tried to get rid of this terrible and implacable foe; but all their plans failed, and the Indian chief, bolder and more cruel than ever, drew nearer to the American frontier, reigned uncontrolled in the desert, of which he was absolute lord, and at times went, fire and sword in hand, to the very cities of the Union to demand that tribute which he claimed even from white men.

We must not be taxed with exaggeration. All we here narrate is scrupulously exact; and if we now and then alter facts, it is only to weaken them. If we uncovered the incognito that veils our characters, many of our readers would recognize them at the first glance, and certify to the truth of our statements.

A terrible scene of massacre, of which Natah Otann was the originator, had aroused general indignation against him. The facts are as follow:—

An American family, consisting of father, mother, two sons of about twelve, a little girl between three and four years of age, and five servants, left the Western States with the intention of working a claim they had bought on the Upper Mississippi. At the period we are writing of, white men rarely traversed these districts, which were entirely left to the Indians, who wandered over them in every direction, and, with a few half-bred and Canadian hunters and trappers, were the sole masters of these vast solitudes. On leaving the clearings, their friends warned the emigrants to be on their guard. They had been advised not to enter into the desert in so small a body, but await other emigrants, who would soon proceed to the same spot; for a caravan of fifty to sixty determined men might pass safe and sound through the Indians.

The head of the American family was an old soldier of the war of independence, gifted with heroic courage, and thorough British obstinacy. He answered coldly, to those who gave him this advice, that his servants and himself could hold their own against all the Prairie Indians; for they had good rifles and firm hearts, and would reach their claim in the face of all opposition. Then he made his preparations like a man whose mind, being made up, admits of no delay, and he started against the judgment of his friends, who predicted numberless misfortunes. The first few days, however, passed quietly enough, and nothing happened to confirm these predictions. The Americans advanced peacefully through a delicious country, and no sign revealed the approach of the Indians, who seemed to have become invisible.

The Americans are men who pass most easily from extreme prudence to the most foolish and rash confidence, and on this occasion were true to their character. When they saw that all was quiet around them, and no obstacle checked their progress, they began to laugh and deride the apprehensions of their friends; they gradually relaxed in their vigilance; neglected the precautions usual on the prairie; and at last almost wished to be attacked by Indians, to make them feel the weight of their arms. Things went on thus for nearly two months; the emigrants were not more than ten days' march from their claim; they no longer thought of the Indians: if at times they alluded to them in the evening, before going to sleep, it was only to laugh at the absurd fears of their friends, who fancied it impossible to take a step in the desert without falling into an ambuscade of the Redskins.

One night, after a fatiguing day, the emigrants went to bed, after placing sentries round the camp, rather to keep wild beasts off than through any other motive; the sentinels, accustomed not to be troubled, and fatigued by their day's labours, watched for a few moments, then their eyelids gradually sank, and they fell asleep. Their awakening was destined to be terrible.

About midnight, fifty Blackfeet, led by Natah Otann, glided like demons in the darkness, clambered into the encampment, and ere the Americans could seize their weapons, or even dream of defence, they were bound. Then a horrible scene took place, the frightful interludes of which the pen is impotent to describe. Natah Otann organised the massacre, if we may be allowed to employ the term, with unexampled coolness and cruelty. The chief of the party and his five servants were stripped and attached to trees, flogged, and martyrized, while the two lads were literally roasted alive in their presence. The mother, half mad with terror, escaped, carrying off her little girl in her arms: but, after running a long distance, her strength failed her, and she fell senseless. The Indians caught her up; imagining her to be dead, they disdained to scalp her; but they carried off the child, which she pressed to her bosom with almost herculean strength. The child was taken back to Natah Otann.

"What shall we do with it?" the warrior asked, who presented it to him.

"Into the fire!" he replied, laconically.

The Blackfoot calmly prepared to execute the pitiless order he had received.

"Stop!" the father cried with a piercing shriek. "Do not kill an innocent creature in that horrible manner. Are not the atrocious tortures you inflict on us enough?"

The Blackfoot hesitated, and looked at his chief; the latter reflected.

"Stay," he said, raising his hand, and addressing the emigrant; "you wish your child to live?"

"Yes!" the father answered.

"Good!" he answered, "I will sell you her life."

The American shuddered at this proposition. "On what terms?" he asked.

"Listen!" he said, laying a stress on every word, and darting at him a glance which made him tremble to the marrow. "My conditions are these. I am master of all your lives; they belong to me; I can prolong or cut them short without the slightest opposition from you; but, I hardly know why," he added, with a sardonic smile, "I feel merciful today; your child shall live. Still, remember this; whatever the nature of the torture I inflict on you, at the first cry you utter, your child shall be strangled. You have it in your power to save her if you will."

"I accept," the other answered. "What do I care for the most atrocious torture, so long as my child lives?"

A sinister smile played round the chief's lips. "It is well," he said.

"One word more."

"Speak."

"Grant me a single favour; let me give a last kiss to this poor creature."

"Give him his child," the chief commanded. ·

An Indian presented the little girl to the wretched man. The innocent, as if comprehending what was taking place, put her arms round her father's neck, and burst into tears. The latter, frightfully bound as he was, could only bestow kisses on her, into which his whole soul passed. The scene had something hideous about it; it resembled a witches' Sabbath. The five men fastened naked to trees, the children twisting on the burning charcoal, and uttering piercing cries, and these stoical Indians, illumined by the ruddy glow of the fire, completed the most fearful picture that the wildest imagination could have invented.

"Enough," Natah Otann said.

"A last gift, a last remembrance."

The chief shrugged his shoulders. "For what good?" he said.

"To render the death you intend for me less cruel."

"What is it you want?"

"Hang round my daughter's neck this earring, suspended by a lock of my hair."

"Is that really all?"

"It is."

"Very good."

The chief came up, took from the emigrant's ear a ring he wore in it, and cut off with a scalping knife a lock of his hair; then, turning to him with a sardonic laugh, he said—

"Listen carefully. Your companions and yourself are going to be flayed alive; of a strip of your skin I will make a bag to hold the lock of hair and ring. You see that I am generous, for I grant you more than you ask; but remember the conditions."

The emigrant looked at him disdainfully.

"Keep your promises as well as I shall mine: and now begin the torture— you will see a man die."

Things were done as had been arranged; the emigrant and his servants were flayed alive. The emigrant endured the torture with a courage which even the chief admired. Not a cry, not a groan, issued from his bleeding chest; he was made of granite. When his skin was entirely stripped off, Natah Otann went up to him; the unhappy wretch was not yet dead.

"Thou art a man," he said to him. "Die satisfied. I will keep the promise I made thee."

And moved doubtlessly by a feeling of pity for so much firmness, he blew out his brains.

This horrible punishment lasted four hours. The Indians plundered all the Americans possessed, and what they could not carry off they burned. Natah Otann rigidly kept the oath he had made to his victim: as he said, from a strip of his skin, imperfectly tanned, he made a bag, in which he placed the lock of hair, and hung it round the child's neck by a cord also made of his skin. On the homeward road to his village, Natah Otann paid the most assiduous attention to the poor little creature; and, on rejoining the tribe, the chief declared before all that he adopted the girl, and gave her the name of Prairie Flower.

At the period our story begins, Prairie Flower was fourteen years of age; she was a charming creature, gentle and simple, lovely as the princess of a fairy tale. Her large blue eyes, veiled by long brown lashes, reflected the azure of the heaven, and she ran about, careless and wild, through the forests and over the prairie, dreaming at times beneath the shady recesses of the giant trees, living as the birds live, forgetting the past, which was to her as yesterday, caring nothing for the future, which to her had no existence, and only thinking of the present to be happy.

The charming girl had unconsciously become the idol of the tribe. The old White Buffalo more especially felt an unbounded affection for her; but the experiment he had made with Natah Otann disgusted him with a second trial at education. He only watched over her with truly paternal care, correcting any fault he might notice in her with a patience and kindness nothing could weary. This old tribune, like all energetic and implacable men, had the heart of a lamb; having entirely renounced the world which mistook him, he had refreshed his soul in the desert, and recovered the illusions and generous impulses of his youth.

Prairie Flower had retained no remembrance of her early years; as no one ever alluded in her presence to the terrible scenes which introduced her to the tribe, fresher impressions had completely effaced them. Loved and petted by all, Prairie Flower fancied herself a child of the tribe. Her long tresses of light hair, gilded like ripe corn, and the dazzling whiteness of her skin, could not enlighten her, for in many Indian nations these anomalies are found; the Mandans, among others, have many women and warriors who, if they put on European clothes, might easily pass for whites.

The Blackfeet, seduced by the charms of this gentle young creature, attached the destinies of the tribe to her. They considered her their tutelary genius, their palladium: their faith in her was deep, serene, and simple. Prairie Flower was truly the Queen of the Blackfeet; a sign from her rosy fingers, a word from her dainty lips, was obeyed with unbounded promptitude and devotion. She could do anything, say everything, demand everything, without fearing even a second's hesitation to her will. She exercised this despotic authority unsuspectingly; she alone was unaware of the immense power she possessed over these brutal natives, who in her presence became gentle and devoted.

Natah Otann was attached to his adopted daughter, so far as organizations like his are capable of yielding to any feeling. At first he sported with the girl as with an unimportant plaything; but gradually, as the child was transformed and became a woman, these sports became more serious, and his heart was attracted. For the first time in his life, this man, with his indomitable soul, felt a feeling stir in him which he could not analyze, but which, through its force and violence, astonished and terrified him.

Then, a dumb struggle began between the chiefs head and heart. He revolted against this influence which subjugated him: he, hitherto accustomed to break through every obstacle, was now powerless before a child, who disarmed him with a smile, when he tried to overpower her. This struggle lasted a long time; at length, the terrible Indian confessed himself vanquished, that is to say, he allowed the current to carry him away, and without attempting a resistance, which he felt to be useless, he began to love the young maiden madly. But this love at times caused him sufferings so terrible, when he thought of the manner in which Prairie Flower had become his adopted daughter, that he asked himself with terror, whether this deep love which had seized on his brain, and mastered him, was not a chastisement imposed by Heaven.

Then, he fell back in his usual state of fury, redoubled his ferocity with those unhappy beings whose plantations he surprised, and, all reeking with blood, his girdle hung with scalps, he returned to the village, and displayed the hideous trophies before the girl. Prairie Flower, astonished at the state in which she saw a man whom she believed to be—not her father, for he was too young—but a relative, lavished on him all the consolations and simple caresses which her attachment to him suggested to her: unfortunately, these caresses heightened his suffering, and he would rush away half mad with grief, leaving her sad and almost terrified by this conduct, which was so incomprehensible to her.

Matters reached such a pitch, that the White Buffalo, whose vigilant eye was constantly fixed on his pupil, considered that he must, at all risks, cut away the evil at the root, and withdraw the son of his friend from the deadly fascination exercised over him by this innocent enchantress. When he felt convinced of the chiefs love for Prairie Flower, the old sachem asked for a private interview with his pupil: the latter granted it, quite unsuspecting the reason which urged the White Buffalo to take this step.

One morning the chief presented himself at the entrance of his friend's lodge. The White Buffalo was reading by the side of a fire kindled in the middle of the hut.

"You are welcome, my son," he said to the young man. "I have only a few words to say to you, but I consider them sufficiently serious for you to hear them without delay; sit down by my side."

The young man obeyed. The White Buffalo then carefully changed his tactics: he, who had so long combated the chief's views as to the regeneration of the Indian race, entered completely into his views, with an ardour and conviction carried so far, that the young man was astonished, and could not refrain from asking what produced this sudden change in his opinion?

"The cause is very simple," the old man answered. "So long as I considered that these views were only suggested by the impetuosity of youth, I merely regarded them as the dreams of a generous heart, which was deceiving itself, and not taking the trouble to weigh the chances of success."

"What now?" the young man asked, quickly.

"Now, I recognize all the earnestness, nobility, and grandeur, contained in your plans; and not only admit their possibility, but I wish to aid you, so as to ensure success."

"Is what you say quite true, my father?" the young man asked, with exultation.

"I swear it: still we must set to work immediately." The chief examined him for a moment carefully, but the old man remained impassive.

"I understand you," he at length said, slowly, and in a deep voice; "you offer me your hand on the verge of an abyss. Thanks, my father, I will not be unworthy of you; I swear to you by the Wacondah."

"Good; believe me, my son, I recognize you," the old man said, shaking his head mournfully. "One's country is often an ungrateful mistress; but it is the only one which gives us true enjoyment of mind, if we serve her disinterestedly for herself alone."

The two men shook hands affectionately; the compact was sealed. We shall soon see whether Natah Otann had really conquered his love as he imagined.

CHAPTER X
THE GREAT COUNCIL

Natah Otann set to work immediately, with that feverish ardour that distinguished him. He sent emissaries in every direction to the principal chiefs of the western prairies, and convoked them to a great plain in the valley of the Missouri, at a spot called "The Tree of the Master of Life," on the fourth day of the moon of the hardened snow. This spot was held in great veneration by the Missouri Indians, who went there constantly to hang up presents. It was an immense sandy plain, completely denuded of vegetation; in the centre of the desert rose a gigantic tree, an oak, twenty feet in circumference at least, the trunk being hollow, and the tufted branches covering an enormous superficies. This tree, which was a hundred and twenty feet in height, and which grew there by accident, necessarily was regarded by the Indians as something miraculous; hence the name they gave it.

On the appointed day, the Indians arrived from all sides, marching in good order, and camping at a short distance from the spot selected for the council. An immense fire had been kindled at the foot of the tree, and at a signal given by the drummers, or *Chichikouès*, the chiefs collected around it, a few paces behind the sachems. The Blackfeet, Nez Percés, Assiniboins, Mandans, and other horsemen, formed a tremendous cordon round the council fire; while scouts traversed the desert in every direction, to keep off intruders, and insure the secrecy of the deliberations.

In the east the sun was pouring forth its beams; the desert, parched and naked, was mingled with the boundless horizon; to the south, the Rocky Mountains displayed the eternal snow of the summits; while in the north-west, a silvery ribbon indicated the course of the old Missouri. Such was the landscape, if we may call it so, where the barbarous warriors, clothed in their strange costumes, were assembled near the symbolic tree. This majestic sight involuntarily reminded the observer of other times and climes, when, by the light of the incendiary fires they kindled, the ferocious comrades of Attila rushed to conquer and rejuvenate the Roman Empire.

Generally the natives of America have a Divinity, or more correctly, a Genius, at times beneficent, but more frequently hostile. The worship of the savage is less veneration than fear. The Master of Life is an evil genius, rather than kind; hence the Indians give his name to the tree to which they attribute the same powers. Indian religions, being all primitive, make no account of the moral being, and only dwell on the accidents of nature, which they make into gods. These different tribes strive to secure the favour of the deserts, where fatigue and thirst entail death, and of the rivers, which may swallow them up.

The chiefs, as we have said, were crouching round the fire, in a state of contemplative immobility, from which it might be inferred that they were preparing for an important ceremony of their worship. Presently Natah Otann raised to his lips the long war pipe, made of a human thighbone, which he wore hanging round his neck, and produced a piercing and prolonged sound. At this signal, for it was one, the chiefs rose, and forming in Indian file, marched twice round the tree, singing, in a low voice, a hymn, to implore its assistance for the success of their plans. At the third time of marching round, Natah Otann took off a magnificent collar of grizzly bears' claws from his neck, and hung it to the branches of the tree, saying,—

"Master of Life, look on us with a favourable eye. I offer thee this present."

The other chiefs imitated his example each in turn; then they resumed their seats round the council fire. The pipe bearer then entered the circle, and after the customary ceremonies, offered the calumet to the chiefs, and when each had smoked, the oldest sachem invited Natah Otann to take the word.

The Indian chief's plan was probably the most daring ever formed against the whites, and, as the White Buffalo said, mockingly, must offer chances of success through its improbability, because it flattered the superstitious ideas of the Indians, who, like all primitive nations, place great faith in the marvellous. It is besides, the quality of oppressed nations, to whom reality never offers aught but disillusions and suffering, to take refuge in the supernatural, which alone offers them consolation. Natah Otann had drawn the first idea of his plan from one of the oldest and most inveterate traditions of the Comanches, his ancestors. This tradition, by reciting which his father often lulled him to sleep in his childhood, pleased his adventurous mind; and when the hour arrived to put in execution the projects which he had so long revolved, he invoked it, and resolved to employ it, in order to collect the other Indian nations around him in one common whole.

When Motecuhzoma (whom Spanish writers improperly call Montezuma, a name which has no meaning, while the first signifies the *stern lord*) found himself imprisoned in his palace by that talented adventurer,

Cortez, who, a few days later, tore his kingdom from him, the Emperor, who preferred to confide in greedy strangers than take refuge in the midst of his people, had a presentiment of the fate reserved for him. A few days prior to his death, he assembled the principal Mexican chiefs who shared his prison, and addressed them thus:—

"Listen! My father, the Sun, has warned me that I shall soon return to him. I know not how or when I am destined to die, but I am certain that my last hour is close at hand."

As the chiefs burst into tears at these words, for they held him in great veneration, he consoled them by saying—

"My last hour is near on this earth, but I shall not die, as I am returning to my father, the Sun, where I shall enjoy a felicity unknown in this world; weep not, therefore, my faithful friends, but, on the contrary, rejoice at the happiness which awaits me. The bearded white men have treacherously seized the greater portion of my empire, and they will soon be masters of the remainder. Who can stop them? Their weapons render them invulnerable, and they dispose at their will of the fire from heaven; but their power will end one day; they, too, will be the victims of treachery; the penalty of retaliation will be inflicted on them in all its rigour. Listen, then, attentively, to what I am about to ask of you; the safety of our country depends on the fidelity with which you execute my last orders. Each of you take a title of the sacred fire which was formerly kindled by the Sun himself, and on which the white men have not yet dared to lay a sacrilegious hand to extinguish it. This fire burns before you in this golden censer; take it unto you, not letting your enemies know what has become of it. You will divide the fire among you, so that each may have a sufficiency; preserve it religiously, ant never let it go out. Each morning, alter adoring it mount on the roof of your house, at sunrise, and look toward the east; one day you will see me appear, giving my right hand to my father, the Sun; then you will rejoice, for the moment of your deliverance will be at hand. My father and I will come to restore you to liberty, and deliver you for ever from these enemies, who have come from a perverse world, that rejected them from its bosom."

The Mexican chiefs obeyed the orders of their well-beloved Emperor on the spot, for time pressed. A few days later, Motecuhzoma mounted on the roof of his palace, and prepared to address his mutinous people, when he was struck by an arrow, it was never known by whom, and fell into the arms of the Spanish soldiery who accompanied him. Before breathing his last sigh, the Emperor sat up, and raising his hands to heaven, said, with a supreme effort, to his friends assembled round him—"The fire! the fire! think of the fire."

These were his last words: ten minutes later he had ceased to breathe. In vain did the Spaniards, whose curiosity was strongly aroused by this mysterious recommendation, try by all the means in their power to penetrate its meaning; but they did not succeed in making one of the Mexicans they interrogated speak. All religiously preserved their secret, and several, indeed, died of torture, rather than reveal it.

The Comanches, and nearly all the nations of the Far West, have kept this belief intact. In all the Indian villages, the fire of Motecuhzoma, which burns eternally is guarded by two warriors, who remain by it for twenty-four hours without eating or drinking, when they are relieved by two others. Formerly the guardians remained forty-eight hours instead of twenty-four. It frequently happened that they were found dead when the reliefs came, either through the mephitic gases of the fire, which had great effect on them, owing to their long fast, or for some other reason. The bodies were taken away, and placed in a cavern, where, as the Comanches say, a serpent devoured them.

This belief is so general, that it is not only found among the Red Indians, but also among the Manzos. Many men, considered to be well educated, keep up, in hidden corners, the fire of Motecuhzoma, visit it every day, and do not fail at sunrise to mount on the roof of their houses and look towards the east, in the hope of seeing their well-beloved emperor coming to restore them that liberty for which they have sighed during so many ages, and which the Mexican Republic is far from having granted them.

Natah Otann's idea was this:—To tell the Indians, after narrating the legend to them, that the time had arrived when Motecuhzoma would appear and act as their chief; to form a powerful band of warriors, whom he would spread along the whole American frontier, so as to attack his enemies at every point simultaneously, and not give them the time to look about them. This project, mad as it was, especially in having to be executed by Indians, or men the least capable of forming alliances, which have ever caused them defeats; this project, we say, was deficient neither in boldness nor in nobility, and Natah Otann was really the only man capable of carrying it out, could he but find, among the persons he wished to arouse, two or three docile and intelligent instruments, that would understand his idea, and heartily cooperate with him.

The Comanches, Pawnees, and Sioux were of great utility to the chief, as well as the majority of the Indians of the Far West, for they shared in the belief on which Natah Otann based his plans, and not only did not need to be persuaded, but would help him in persuading the Missouri Indians by their assent to his assertions. But in so large an assembly of nations, divided by a multitude of interests, speaking different languages, generally hostile to each other, how would it be possible to establish a tie sufficiently strong to attach them in an indissoluble manner? How convince them to march together without jealousy? Lastly, was it reasonable to suppose that there would not be a traitor to sell his brothers, and reveal their plans to the Yankees, whoever have an eye on the movements of the Indians, for they are so anxious to be rid of them?

Still, Natah Otann did not recoil; he did not conceal from himself the difficulties which he should have to overcome; but his courage grew with obstacles. His resolution was strengthened, if we may use the term, in proportion to the responsibilities which must every moment rise before him. When the sachems made him the signal to rise; Natah Otann saw that the moment had arrived to begin the difficult game he wished to play. He took the word resolutely, certain that, with the men he had before him, all depended on the manner in which he handled the question, and that, the first impression once made, success was almost certain.

"Chiefs of the Comanches, Osages, Sioux, Pawnees, Mandans, Assiniboins, Missouris, and all you that listen to me. Redskin brothers," he said, in a firm and deeply accentuated voice, "for many moons my spirit has been sad. I see, with sorrow, our hunting grounds, invaded by the white men, grow smaller every day. We, whose innumerable peoples covered, scarce four centuries back, the immense extent of territory compassed between the two seas, are now reduced to a small party of warriors who, timid as antelopes, fly before our despoilers. Our sacred cities, the last refuge of the civilization of our fathers, the Incas, will become the prey of those monsters with human faces who have no other god but gold. Our dispersed race will possibly soon disappear from that world which it has so long possessed and governed alone. Tracked like wild animals; brutalized by firewater, that corrosive poison invented by the white men for our ruin; decimated by the sword and white diseases, our wandering tribes are now but the shadow of a people. Our conquerors despise our religion, and wish to bow us beneath the laws of the crucified One. They outrage our wives; kill our children; burn our villages; and will reduce us, if they can, to the state of wild beasts, under the pretext of civilizing us. Indians, all you who hear me, is our blood so impoverished in our veins, and have you all renounced your independence! Reply, will you die as slaves, or live free?"

At these words, pronounced in aloud tone, and heightened by an energetic gesture, a tremor ran through the assembly; brows were bent firmly, all eyes sparkled.

"Speak, speak again, sachem of the Blackfeet," all the chiefs shouted unanimously.

Natah Otann smiled proudly, his power over the masses was revealed to him. He continued:—

"The hour has at length arrived, after so many hesitations, to shake off the shameful yoke that presses on us. Within a few days, if you please, we will drive the whites far from our frontiers, and repay them all the evil they have done us. For a long time I have watched the Americans and Spaniards. I know their tactics, their resources: to utterly destroy them, what do we need, my well-beloved brothers? two things alone—skill and courage!"

The Indians interrupted him with shouts of joy.

"You shall be free," Natah Otann continued. "I will restore to you the valleys of your ancestors, the fields where their bones are buried, and which the sacrilegious plough disperses in every direction. This project, ever since I became a man, has fermented in my heart, and become my life. Far from me and from you the thought that I intend to force myself on you as chief, especially since the prodigy of which I have been witness, in the appearance of the great emperor! No; after that supreme chief, who must guide you to liberty, you are free to choose the man who will execute his orders, and communicate them to you. When you have chosen him, you will obey him; follow him everywhere; and pass with him through the most insurmountable dangers, for he will be the elect of the Sun; the lieutenant of Motecuhzoma! Do not deceive yourselves, warriors; our enemy is powerful, numerous, well disciplined, warlike, and has, before all, the habit of conquering us, which is a great advantage to him. Name, then, this lieutenant; let his election be free; take the most worthy, and I will joyfully march under his orders!"

And, after saluting the sachems, Natah Otann disappeared in a crowd of warriors, with calm brow, but with a heart devoured by restlessness. His eloquence, so novel to the Indians, had seduced them, and thrown them into a species of frenzy. They considered the daring Blackfoot chief a genius superior to themselves, and almost bowed the knee to him in adoration, so cleverly had he struck the chord which must touch their hearts. For a long time the council gave way to a sort of madness, and all spoke at once; when this emotion was calmed, the wisest of the sachems discussed the opportunity for taking up arms, and the chances of success. It was now that the tribes of the Far West, who believed in the legend of the sacred fire, became so useful; at length, after a protracted discussion, opinions were unanimous for a general uprising. The ranks, momentarily broken, were reformed, and the White Buffalo, invited by the chiefs to express the opinions of the council, spoke as follows:—

"Chiefs of the allied Indian tribes, listen! This day it has been resolved by the following chiefs:—Little Panther, Spotted Dog, White Buffalo, Grizzly Bear, Red Wolf, White Fox, Tawny Vulture, Glistening Snake, and others, each representing a nation and a tribe, that war has been declared against the white men, our plunderers; and as this war is holy, and has liberty for its object, all men, women, and children must take part in it, each according to their strength. This very day the *wampums* will be sent by the chiefs to all the Indian tribes that, owing to the distance of these hunting grounds, were unable to be present at this great council, in spite of their great desire to be so. I have spoken."

A long cry of enthusiasm interrupted the White Buffalo, who continued, soon after:—

"The chiefs, after ripe deliberation, assenting to the request made to the council by Natah Otann, the first sachem of the Blackfeet, that they should appoint a lieutenant to the Emperor Motecuhzoma, sovereign-chief of the Indian warriors, have chosen, as supreme leader under the sole orders of the said Emperor, the wisest, most prudent, and most worthy to command us. That warrior is the sachem of the Blackfoot Indians, of the tribe of the Kenhas, whose race is so ancient, Natah Otann, the cousin of the Sun, that dazzling planet which illumines us."

A thunder of applause greeted the last words. Natah Otann saluted the sachems, walked into the circle, and said, in a haughty voice,—

"I accept, sachems, my brothers; we agree, I shall be dead, or you will be free."

"May the Grizzly Bear live for ever!" the crowd shouted.

"War to the white men!" Natah Otann continued, "a war without truce or mercy. A slaughter of wild beasts, as they are accustomed to treat us. Remember the law of the prairies:—eye for eye, tooth for tooth. Let each chief send the wampum of war to his nation, for at the end of this moon we will arouse our enemies by a thunderbolt. At the seventh hour of this night we will meet again, to select the subaltern chiefs, number our warriors, and choose the day and hour of attack."

The chiefs bowed without replying, rejoined their escorts, and soon disappeared in a cloud of dust. Natah Otann and the White Buffalo remained alone, a detachment of Blackfeet warriors watching over them at a distance. Natah Otann, with his arms crossed and head bowed, seemed plunged in profound reflection.

"Well," the old Indian said, with an almost imperceptible shade of irony in his voice, "you have succeeded, my son; you are happy. Your plans will, at length, be accomplished."

"Yes," he replied, without noticing the sarcastic tone of voice; "war is declared; my plans have succeeded; but now, friend, I tremble at such a heavy task. Will these peculiar men thoroughly comprehend me? Will they be able to read, in my heart, all the love and adoration I feel for them? Are they ripe for liberty? perhaps they have not suffered enough yet? Father, father, whose heart is so powerful and soul so great: whose life was used up in numerous contests, counsel me! help me! I am young and weak, and I only have a strong will and a boundless devotion to support me."

The old man smiled mournfully, and muttered, answering his own thoughts more than his friend: —

"Yes; my life was used up in supreme struggles: the work I helped to raise has been overthrown, but not destroyed; for a new society, full of vitality, has risen from the ruins of a decrepit society; by our efforts the furrow was ploughed too deeply for it ever to be filled up again: progress marching onward, nothing can check or stop it! Do not halt on the road you have chosen; it is the greatest and most noble a great heart can follow."

In uttering these words, the old man had allowed his enthusiasm to carry him away; his head was raised; his brow glistened; the expiring sun played on his face, and imparted to it an expression which Natah Otann had never seen before, and which filled him with respect. But the old man shook his head sorrowfully, and continued: —

"Child, how will you keep your promise? where will you find Motecuhzoma?"

Natah Otann smiled.

"You will soon see, my father," he said.

At the same moment, an Indian, whose panting horse seemed to breathe fire through its nostrils, came up to the chiefs, where he stopped suddenly, as if converted into marble; without dismounting, he bent down to Natah Otann's ear.

"Already!" the latter exclaimed, "Oh! heaven must be on my side! There is not a moment to lose. My horse! quick."

"What is the matter?" the White Buffalo asked.

"Nothing that relates to you at present, my father; but you shall soon know all."

"You are going alone, then?"

"I must for a short period. Farewell!"

Natah Otann's horse uttered a snort of pain, and started at full gallop. Ten minutes later all the Indians had disappeared, and solitude and silence prevailed round the tree of the Master of Life.

CHAPTER XI
AMERICAN HOSPITALITY

Matters had reached this point at the moment when the story we have undertaken to tell, begins: now that we have supplied these indispensable explanations, we will take up our narrative again at the point where we broke it off.

John Black and his family, posted behind the barricade that surrounded the camp, regarded with joy, mingled with alarm, the cavalcade coming toward them like a tornado, raising clouds of dust in its passage.

"Attention, boys!" the American said to his son and servants, with his hand on his trigger. "You know the diabolical trickery of these apes of the prairie; we must not let them surprise us a second time; at the least suspicious sign, a bullet! We shall thus prove to them that we are on our guard."

The emigrant's wife and daughter, with their eyes fixed on the prairie, attentively followed the movements of the Indians.

"You are mistaken, my love," Mrs. Black said; "these men have no hostile designs. The Indians rarely attack by day; when they do so, they never come so openly as this."

"The more so," the young lady added, "as, if I am not mistaken, I can see Europeans galloping at the head of the party."

"Oh!" Black said, "that really has no significance, my child. The prairies swarm with scoundrels who join those demons of Redskins when honest travellers are to be plundered. Who knows, indeed, whether white men were not the instigators of last night's attack?"

"Oh, father, I never could believe such a thing as that," Diana remarked.

Miss Black, of whom we have hitherto said but little, was a girl of about seventeen, tall and slender; her large black eyes, bordered with velvety lashes; the thick bandeaux of brown hair; her little mouth, with its rosy lips and pearly teeth, made her a charming creature, who would have been an ornament anywhere; but in the desert must naturally attract attention. Religiously educated by her mother, a good and pious Presbyterian, Diana still retained all the candour and innocence of youth, combined with that experience of everyday life imparted by the rude life of the clearings, where people begin early to think and act for themselves. In the meanwhile the cavalcade rapidly approached, and was now no great distance off.

"Those are really our animals galloping down there," Will said; "I recognise Sultan, my good horse."

"And Dolly, my poor milch cow," Mrs. Black said, with a sigh.

"Console yourselves," Diana said, "I'll answer for it these people are bringing back our cattle."

The emigrant shook his head in agitation.

"The Indians never give up what they have once seized; but, by my soul, I'll have it out with them, and not let myself be robbed without a trial for it."

"Wait a minute, father," said Will, stopping him, for the emigrant was about to leap over the intrenchments, "we shall soon know what their intentions are."

"Hum! they are very clear, in my idea. The demons want to propose to us some disgusting bargain."

"Perhaps, father, you are mistaken," Diana said, quickly; "and see, they are stopping, and apparently consulting."

In fact, on arriving within gunshot, the Indians halted, and began talking together.

"Why shall we not go on?" the Count asked Bright-eye.

"H'm, you don't know the Yankees, Mr. Edward. I am sure that, if we were to go ten paces further, we should be saluted by a shower of bullets."

"Nonsense!" the young man said, with a shrug of his shoulder; "they are not so mad as to act in that way."

"It's possible; but they would do as I tell you. Look attentively, and you will see from this spot the barrels of their rifles glistening between the stakes of the barricades."

"By Jove! it's true; then they want to be massacred."

"They would have been so long ago, had not my brother interceded in their favour," Natah Otann said, joining in the conversation.

"And I thank you, chief. The desert is large; what harm can those poor devils do you?"

"They, none; but presently others will come and settle by their side, and so on; so that in six months my brother would see a city at a spot where there is now nothing but nature as it left the omnipotent hands of the Master of Life."

"That is true," Bright-eye said, "the Yankees respect nothing; the rage for building cities renders them dangerous madmen."

"Why have we stopped, chief?" the Count said, recurring to his first question.

"To negotiate."

"Will you do me a kindness? Leave this business to me. I am curious to see how these people understand the laws of war, and how they will receive me."

"My brother is free."

"Wait for me here, then, and do not make a move during my absence."

The young man took off his weapons, which he handed to his servant.

"What?" Ivon remarked. "Are you going, my lord, in this state among those heretics?"

"How else should I go? You know very well that a flag of truce has nothing to fear."

"That is possible," the Breton said, very slightly convinced; "but if your lordship will believe me, you will, at least, keep your pistols in your belt; for an accident happens so easily, and you do not know among what sort of people you are going."

"You are mad!" the Count said, shrugging his shoulders.

"Well, then, as you are going unarmed to speak with people who do not inspire me with the slightest confidence, I must ask your lordship to permit me to accompany you."

"You, nonsense!" the young man said, laughing. "You know very well that you are a wonderful coward; that's agreed on."

"Perfectly true; but I feel capable of anything to defend my master."

"There we have it; your cowardice need only come on you suddenly, and, in your alarm, you will be ready to kill everybody. No, no, none of that; I do not wish to get into trouble through you."

And dismounting, he walked in the direction of the barricades. On arriving a short distance from them, he took out a white handkerchief, and waved it in the air. Black, still ready to fire, carefully watched the Count's every movement, and when he saw his amicable demonstration, he rose, and made him a signal to come on. The young man quietly returned his handkerchief to his pocket, lit a cigar, stuck his glass in his eye, and after drawing on his gloves, walked resolutely on. On reaching the intrenchments, he found himself in front of Black, who was waiting for him, leaning on his rifle.

"What do you want of me?" the American said, roughly. "Make haste! I have no time to lose in conversation."

The Count surveyed him haughtily, assumed the most insolent posture he could select, and puffing a cloud of smoke into his face, said dryly—

"You are not polite, my dear fellow."

"Halloa!" the other said. "Have you come here to insult me?"

"I have come to do you a service; and if you continue in that tone, I am afraid I shall be obliged not to do it."

"We'll see to that—do me a service! And what may it be?" the American asked with a grin.

"You are a low fellow," the Count remarked, "with whom it is offensive to talk. I prefer to withdraw."

"Withdraw—oh, nonsense! You are too valuable a hostage. I shall keep you, my gentleman, and only give you up at a good figure,", the American continued.

"What! Is that the way you comprehend the law of nations? That's curious," the Count said, still sarcastic.

"There is no law of nations with bandits."

"Thanks for your compliment, master. And what would you do to keep me, if I did not think proper?"

"Like this," the American said, laying his hand roughly on his shoulder.

"What!" the Count said. "I really believe, Heaven forgive me! that you dared to lay a hand on me!"

And ere the emigrant had time to prevent it, he seized him round the waist, lifted him from the ground, and hurled him over the barricade. The giant fell all bruised in the middle of his camp. Instead of withdrawing, as any other might have done in his place, the young man crossed his arms, and waited, smoking peacefully. The emigrant, stunned by his rough fall, rose, shaking himself like a wet dog, and feeling his ribs, to assure himself that there was nothing broken. The ladies uttered a cry of terror on seeing him re-enter the camp in such a peculiar way, while his son and servants looked toward him, ready to fire at the first signal.

"Lower your guns," he said to them; and leaping once more over the barricade, he walked towards the Count. The latter awaited him with perfect calmness.

"Ah! there you are," he said, "Well, how did you like that?"

"Come, come," the American replied, holding out his hand; "I was in the wrong; I am a brute beast; forgive me."

"Very good; I like you better like that; we only need to understand each other. You are now prepared to listen to me, I fancy?"

"Quite."

There are certain men, like John Black, with whom it is necessary to employ extreme measures, and prove your superiority to them. With such persons you do not argue, but smash them; after which it always happens that these men, before so intractable, become gentle as lambs, and do all you want. The American, possessed of great strength, and confiding in it, thought he had a right to be insolent with a slight and weak looking man; but so soon as this man had proved to him, in a peremptory manner, that he was the more powerful of the two, the bull drew in his horns, and recoiled all the distance he had advanced.

"This night," the Count then said, "you were attacked by the Blackfeet; I wished to come to your aid, but it was impossible, and, besides, I should have arrived too late. As, however, for some reason or other; the men who attacked you feel a certain amount of consideration for me, I have profited by my influence to make them restore the cattle they stole from you."

"Thanks; believe that I sincerely regret what has passed between us; but I was so annoyed by the loss I had experienced."

"I understand all that, and willingly pardon you, the more so as I, perhaps, gave you rather too rude a shock just now."

"Oh, do not mention it, I beg."

"As you please; it is all the same to me."

"And my cattle?"

"Are at your disposal. Will you have them at once?"

"I will not conceal from you that—"

"Very good," the Count interrupted him; "wait a minute, I will tell them to bring them up."

"Do you think I have nothing to fear from the Indians?"

"Not if you know how to manage them."

"Well, then, shall I wait for you?"

"Only a few minutes."

The Count went down the hill again with the same calm step he had gone up it. So soon as he rejoined the Indians, his friends surrounded him; they had seen all that passed, and were delighted at the way in which he had ended the discussion.

"Good heavens! how coarse those Americans are," the young man said. "Pray give him his cattle, chief, and let us have done with him. The animal all but put me in a passion."

"He is coming toward us," Natah Otann replied, with an undefinable smile. Black, indeed, soon came up. The worthy emigrant, having been duly scolded by his wife and daughter, had recognized the full extent of his stupidity, and was most anxious to repair it.

"Really, gentlemen," he said, "we cannot part in this way. I owe you great obligations, and am desirous to prove to you that I am not such a brute as I probably seem to be. Be kind enough to stay with us, if only for an hour, to show us that you bear no malice."

This invitation was given in a hearty, but, at the same time, cordial manner, and it was so evident that the good man was confused, that the Count had not the heart to refuse him. The Indians camped where they were. The chief and the three hunters followed the American into his camp, where the cattle had already been restored. The reception was as it should be in the desert; the ladies had hastily prepared refreshments under the tent, while William and the two serving men made a breach in the barricade, to give passage to his father's guests. Lucy Black and Diana awaited the newcomers at the entrance of the camp.

"You are welcome, gentlemen," the Americans wife said, with a graceful bow; "we are all so much indebted to you, that we are only too happy to receive you."

The chief and the Count bowed politely to the lady, who was doing all in her power to repair the clumsy brutality of her husband. The Count, at the sight of Diana, felt an emotion which he could not, at the first blush, understand; his heart beat on regarding this charming creature, who was exposed to so many dangers through the life to which she was condemned. Diana blushed at the ardent glance of the young man, and timidly drew nearer her mother, with that instinct of modesty innate in woman's heart, which makes her ever seek protection from her to whom she owes existence.

After the first compliments, Natah Otann, the Count, and Bright-eye, entered the tent where Black and his son were awaiting them. When the ice was broken, which does not take long among people accustomed to prairie life, the conversation became more animated and intimate.

"So," the Count asked, "you have left the clearings with the intention of never returning?"

"Oh, yes," the emigrant answered; "for a man having a family, everything is becoming so dear on the frontier, that he must make up his mind to enter the desert."

"I can understand your doing so as a man, for you can always manage to get out of difficulties; but your wife and daughter—you condemn them to a very sorrowful and dangerous life."

"It is a wife's duty to follow her husband," Mrs. Black said with a slight accent of reproach. "I am happy wherever he is, provided I am by his side."

"Good, madam; I admire such sentiments; but permit me an observation."

"Certainly, sir."

"Was it necessary to come so far to find a suitable farm?"

"Certainly not; but we should have run the risk of being someday expelled from the new clearing by the owners of the land, and compelled to begin a new plantation further away," she said.

"While now," Black continued, "at the place where we are, we have nothing of that sort to fear, as the land belongs to nobody."

"My brother is mistaken," the chief said, who had not yet spoken a word; "the country, for ten days' march in every direction, belongs to me and my tribe; the Paleface is here on the hunting grounds of the Kenhas."

Black regarded Natah Otann with an air of embarrassment.

"Well," he said, after a moment's pause, as if speaking against the grain; "we will go further, wife."

"Where can the Palefaces go to find land that belongs to nobody?" the chief continued, severely.

This time the American had not a word to say. Diana, who had never before seen an Indian so close, regarded the chief with a mingled feeling of curiosity and terror. The Count smiled.

"The chief is right," Bright-eye said, "the prairies belong to the Red men."

Black had bowed his head on his chest, in perplexity.

"What is to be done?" he muttered.

Natah Otann laid his hand on his shoulder.

"Let my brother open his ears," he said to him; "a chief is about to speak."

The American fixed an inquiring glance on him.

"Does this country suit my brother then?" the Indian continued.

"Why should I deny it? This country is the finest I ever saw; close to me I have the river, behind me, immense virgin forests. Oh yes, it is a fine country, and I should have made a magnificent plantation."

"I have told my Paleface brother," the chief went on, "that this country belonged to me."

"Yes, you told me so, chief, and it is true; I cannot deny it."

"Well, if the Paleface desires it, he can obtain so much ground as he wishes," Natah Otann said, concisely.

At this proposition, which the American was far from suspecting, he pricked up his ears; the squatter's nature was aroused in him.

"How can I buy the land when I possess nothing?" he said.

"That is of no consequence," the chief replied.

The astonishment now became general; each looked at the Indian curiously: for the conversation had suddenly acquired a grave importance which no one expected. Black, however, was not deceived by this apparent facility.

"The chief has doubtless not understood me," he said.

The Indian shook his head.

"The Paleface cannot buy the land, because he has not wherewith to pay for it; those were his words."

"True; and the chief answered that it was of little matter."

"I said so."

There was no mistake, the two men had clearly understood one another.

"There is some devilry behind that," Bright-eye muttered in his moustache; "an Indian does not give an egg, unless he expects an ox in return."

"What do you want to arrive at, chief?" the Count asked Natah Otann, frankly.

"I will explain myself," the latter said; "my brother interests himself in this family, I believe?"

"I do," the young man answered, with some surprise, "and you know my reasons."

"Good; let my brother pledge himself to accompany me during two moons, without asking any explanation of my actions, and give me his aid whenever I require it, and I will give this man as much ground as he needs to found a settlement, and he need never fear being annoyed by the Redskins, or dispossessed by the Whites, for I am really the owner of the land, and no other can lay claim to it."

"A moment," Bright-eye said, as he rose; "in my presence, Mr. Edward will not accept such a bargain; no one buys a pig in a poke, and it would be madness to submit his will to the caprices of another man."

Natah Otann frowned, his eye flashed fire, and he rose.

"Dog of the Palefaces," he shouted, "take care of thy words—I have once spared thy life."

"Your menaces do not frighten me, Redskin," the Canadian replied, resolutely; "you lie if you say that you were master of my life; it only depends from the will of God; you cannot cause a hair of my head to fall without His consent."

Natah Otann laid his hand on his knife, a movement immediately imitated by the hunter, and they stood opposite each other, ready for action. The ladies uttered a shriek of terror, William and his father stood before them, ready to interfere in the quarrel, if it were necessary. But the Count had already, quick as thought, thrown himself between the two men, shouting loudly—

"Stop! I insist on it!"

Yielding to the ascendency of the speaker, the Blackfoot and the Canadian each fell back a step, returned their knives to their girdles, and waited. The Count looked at them for a moment, then, holding out his hand to Bright-eye, said, affectionately—

"Thank you, my friend, but for the present I do not require your aid."

"Good, good," the hunter said; "you know I am yours, body and soul. Mr. Edward, it is only deferred." And the worthy Canadian sat down again quietly.

"As for you, chief," the young man continued, "the proposals are unacceptable. I should be mad to agree to them, and I hope I am not quite in that state yet. I wish to teach you this, that I have only come on the prairie to hunt for a short time; that time has passed; pressing business requires my presence in the United States, and dispels my desire to be useful to these good people; so soon as I have accompanied you to the village, according to my promise, I shall say good-bye to you, and probably never return."

"Which will be extremely agreeable to me," Bright-eye said, in confirmation.

The Indian did not stir.

"Still," the Count went on, "there is, perhaps, a way of settling the matter to the satisfaction of all parties; land is not so dear here; tell me your price, and I will pay you at once, either in dollars, or in bills on a New York banker."

"All right," the hunter said; "there is still that way open."

"Oh! I thank you, sir," Mrs. Black exclaimed, "but my husband cannot and ought not to accept such a proposal."

"Why not, my dear lady, if it suits me, and the chief accepts my offer?"

Black, we must do him the justice to say, satisfied himself by signifying his approval by a gesture; but the worthy squatter, like a true American, was very careful not to say a word. As for Diana, fascinated by such disinterestedness, she gazed on the Count with eyes sparkling with gratitude, not daring to express aloud what her secret thoughts were about this noble and generous gentleman. Natah Otann raised his head.

"I will prove to my brother," he said, in a gentle voice, and bowing courteously, "that the Red men are as generous as the Palefaces. I sell him eight hundred acres of land, to be chosen where he pleases along the river, for one dollar."

"A dollar?" the young man exclaimed, in surprise.

"Yes," the chief said, smiling, "in that way I shall be paid, my brother will owe me nothing; and if he consents to stay a little while with me, it will be of his own accord, and because he likes to be with a true friend."

This unforeseen result to a scene which had for a moment threatened to end in blood, filled all persons with surprise. Bright-eye alone was not duped by the chief's courtesy.

"There's something behind it," he muttered to himself, "but I will watch, and that demon must be very cunning to cheat me."

The Count was affected by this generosity, which he was far from expecting.

"There, chief," he said, handing him the stipulated dollar, "now we are quits; but be assured that I will not be outdone by you."

Natah Otann bowed courteously.

"Now," the Count continued, "a last favour."

"Let my brother speak, he has the right to ask everything of me."

"Make peace with my old Bright-eye,"

"As my brother desires it," the chief said, "I will do so willingly; and, as a sign of reconciliation, I beg him to accept the dollar you have given me."

The hunter's first impulse was to decline it; but he thought better of it, took the dollar, and carefully placed it in his belt. Black knew not how to express his gratitude to the Count, who had really made him a landed proprietor; and the same day the American and his son chose the land on which the plantation should be established. The Count drew up on a leaf of his pocketbook a regular deed of sale, which was signed by himself, Bright-eye, and Ivon, as witnesses, by Black as purchaser, and at the foot of which Natah Otann drew the totem of his tribe, and an animal intended to represent a bear, which formed his speaking but most emblematical signature. The chief, had he pleased, could have signed like the rest, but he wished to hide from all the instruction he owed to the White Buffalo. Black preciously placed the deed between the leaves of his family bible, and said to the Count, while squeezing his hand hard enough to smash it—

"Remember that you have in John Black a man who will let his bones be broken for you, whenever you think proper."

Diana said nothing, but she gave the young man a look which paid him amply for what he had done for the family.

"Attention," Bright-eye said, in a whisper, the first time he found himself alone with Ivon; "from this day watch carefully over your master, for a terrible danger threatens him."

CHAPTER XII
THE SHE-WOLF OF THE PRAIRIES

About four or five hours after the various events we have described in the previous chapters, a horseman, mounted on a powerful steed, caparisoned in the Indian fashion, that is to say, bedizened with feathers, and painted of glaring colours, crossed a streamlet, and galloped over the prairies, proceeding in the direction of the Virgin forest, to which we have several times alluded. The rider, dressed in the war costume of the Blackfoot Indians, and whom it was easy to recognize as a chief by the eagle feather fastened over his right ear, incessantly bent over his horse's neck, and urged it to increased speed.

It was night, but an American night, full of sharp odours and mysterious sounds, with a dark blue sky, studded with an infinite number of dazzling stars; the moon profusely spread her silvery rays over the landscape, casting a deceitful brightness, which imparted a fantastic appearance to objects. All seemed to sleep on the prairies; the wind even hardly shook the umbrageous tops of the trees; the wild beasts, after drinking at the river, had returned to their hidden dens. The horseman alone moved on, gliding silently through the darkness; at times he raised his head, as if consulting the sky, then, after a seconds rest, he galloped onwards.

Many hours passed ere the horseman thought of stopping. At length he reached a spot where the trees were so interlaced by creepers which enfolded them, that a species of insurmountable wall suddenly prevented the rider's progress. After a moment's hesitation, and looking attentively around to discover a hole by which he could pass, seeing clearly that all attempts would be useless, he dismounted. He saw that he had arrived at a canebrake, or spot where a passage can only be made by fire or axe. The Indian chief fastened his horse to the trunk of a tree; left within its reach a stock of grass and climbing peas; then, certain that his horse would want for nothing during this long night, he began thinking of himself.

First he cut down with his bowie knife the bushes and plants which interfered with the encampment he wished to form; then he prepared, with all the stoicism of a prairie denizen, a fire of dry wood, in order to cook his supper, and keep off wild beasts, if anyone took it into his head to pay him a visit during his sleep. Among the wood he collected was a large quantity of what the Mexicans call *palo mulato*, or stinking wood; this he was careful to remove, for the pestiferous smell of that tree would have denounced his presence for miles round, and the Indian, judging from the precautions he took, seemed afraid of being discovered; in fact, the care with which he had placed sand-bags round his horse's hoofs, to dull the sound, sufficiently proved this.

When the fire, so placed as not to be visible ten yards off, poured its pleasant column of flame into the air, the Indian took from his elk-skin pouch a little Indian wheat and pemmican, which he ate with considerable appetite, looking round continually in the surrounding gloom, and stopping to listen attentively to those noiseless sounds which by night trouble the imposing calmness of the desert, without any apparent cause. When his scanty meal was ended, the Indian filled his pipe with kinne-kinnick, and began smoking.

Still, in spite of his apparent calmness, the man was not easy; at times he took the pipe from his lips, looked up, and anxiously consulted the sky, through a break in the foliage above his head. At length he appeared to form an energetic resolution, and raising his fingers to his lips, imitated thrice, with rare perfection, the cry of the blue jay, that privileged bird that sings in the night; then he bent his body forward and listened, but nothing proved to him that his signal had been heard.

"Wait a while," he muttered.

And crouching again before the fire, into which he threw a handful of dry branches, he began smoking again. Several hours passed thus: at length the moon disappeared from the horizon, the cold became sharper, and the sky, in which the stars expired one after the other, was tinted with a rosy hue. The Indian, who had been slumbering for a while, suddenly shook himself, turned a suspicious glance around, and muttered hoarsely,—

"She cannot be far off."

And he again gave the signal. The last cry had scarce died out in the distance, when a roar was heard close by. The Indian, instead of being alarmed by this ill-omened sound, smiled, and said in a loud and firm voice,—

"You are welcome, She-wolf; you know it is I who am awaiting you here."

"Ah! you are there, then!" a voice answered.

A rustling of leaves was now heard in the bushes opposite the spot where the Indian was seated; the reeds and creepers were pulled back by a vigorous hand, and a woman appeared in the space left free. Before advancing, she thrust her head forward cautiously, and looked.

"I am alone," the Indian said; "you can approach without fear."

A smile played over the newcomer's lips at this answer, which she did not expect.

"I fear nothing," she said.

Before going further, we will give some indispensable details about this woman—vague, it is true, as we can only supply what the Indians said about her, but which will be useful to the reader in comprehending the facts that will follow. No one knew who she was, or whence she came. The period when she was first seen on the prairie was equally unknown. All was an inexplicable mystery connected with her. Though she spoke fluently, and with extreme purity, most of the prairie idioms, still certain words she at times used, and the colour of her skin, not so brown as that of the natives, caused the supposition that she belonged to another race from theirs. It was only a supposition, however, for her hatred of the Indians was too well known for the bravest among them ever to venture to see her sufficiently closely to render themselves certain on that head.

At times she disappeared for weeks, even for months, and it was impossible to discover her trail. Then she was suddenly seen again wandering about, talking to herself, marching nearly always by night, frequently accompanied by an idiotic and dumb dwarf, who followed her like a dog, and whom the Indians, in their credulous superstition, suspected strongly of being her familiar. This woman, ever gloomy and melancholy, with her wild looks and startling gestures, could not be accused of doing anyone harm, in spite of the general terror she inspired. Still, owing to the strange life she led, all the misfortunes that happened to the Indians, in war or hunting, were imputed to her. The Redskins considered her a wicked genius, and had given her the name of the *Spirit of Evil*. Hence the man who had come so far to see her must necessarily have been gifted with extraordinary courage, or some powerful reason impelled him to act as he was doing.

As this Blackfoot chief is destined to play a great part in this narrative, we will give his portrait in a few words. He was a man who had reached middle life, or about forty-five years. He was tall, well built, and admirably proportioned. His muscles, standing out like whipcord, denoted extraordinary vigour. He had an intelligent face; his features expressed cunning, while his eyes were rarely fixed on any object, but gave him an expression of craft and brutal cruelty, which inspired an unenviable repugnance towards him, if you took the trouble to study him carefully: but observers are rare in the desert, and with the Indians this chief enjoyed a great reputation, and was equally beloved for his tried courage and inexhaustible powers of speech, qualities highly esteemed by the Redskins.

"The night is still gloomy; my mother can approach," the Indian chief said.

"I am coming," the woman said, drily, as she advanced.

"I have been waiting a long while."

"I know it, but no matter."

"The road was long to come."

"I am here; speak!"

And she leaned against the stem of a tree, crossing her arms on her chest.

"What can I say, if my mother does not first question me?"

"That is true. Answer me then."

There was a silence, only troubled by the wind sighing in the leaves; after a few moments' reflection, the woman at length began, —

"Have you done what I ordered?"

"I have."

"Well?"

"My mother guessed rightly."

"Is it so?"

"All is preparing for action,"

"You are sure?"

"I was present at the council."

She smiled triumphantly.

"Where was the meeting place?"

"At the tree of life."

"Long ago?"

"The sun has set eight hours since."

"Good! What was resolved?"

"What you already know."

"The destruction of the whites?"

"Yes."

"When will the war signal be given?"

"The day is not yet fixed."

"Ah!" she said in a tone of regret.

"But it cannot be long," he added quickly.

"What makes you think so?"

"The Grizzly Bear is eager to finish."

"And I, too," the woman muttered in a low voice.

The conversation was again broken off. The woman paced up and down the clearing in thought. The chief followed her with his eyes, carefully examining her. All at once she stopped before him, and looked him In the face.

"You are devoted to me, chief?" she said.

"Do you doubt it?"

"Perhaps."

"Still, only a few hours ago, I gave you a decided proof of my devotion."

"What?"

"This!" he said, pointing to his left arm, which was wrapped in strips of bark.

"I do not understand you."

"You see I am wounded?"

"Well! what then?"

"The Redskins attacked the Palefaces some hours ago; they were scaling the barricade which protected their camp, when they suddenly retired on your appearance, by order of their chief, who was wounded, and thirsting for revenge."

"It is true."

"Good. And the chief who commanded the Redskins—does my mother know him?"

"No."

"It was I, the Red Wolf: does my mother still doubt?"

"The path on which I am walking is so gloomy," she replied sorrowfully; "the work I am accomplishing is so serious, and of such import to me, that at times I feel fear enter my heart, and doubt contract my chest, when I think I am alone, a poor weak woman, to wrestle with a giant. For long years I have been ripening the plan I wish to accomplish today; I have occupied my whole life to obtain the result I desire, and I fear failure at the moment of succeeding. Then, if I have no longer confidence in myself, can I trust a man whom self-interest may urge to betray, or at any rate abandon me at a moment."

The chief drew himself up on hearing these words; his eye flashed fire, and, with a gesture of wounded pride, he said,—

"Silence! my mother must not add a word. She insults at this moment a man who is most anxious to prove his truth to her: ingratitude is a white vice, gratitude a red virtue. My mother was ever kind to me; Red Wolf cannot count the occasions on which he owes his life to her. My mother's heart is ulcered by misfortune; solitude is an evil counsellor: my mother listens too much to the voices which whisper in her ear through the silence of night; she forgets the services she has rendered, only to remember the ingratitude she has sowed on her road. Red Wolf is devoted to her, he loves her; the She-wolf can place entire confidence in him, he is worthy of it."

"Dare I believe in these protestations? Can I put faith in these promises?" she muttered.

The chief continued passionately,—

"If the gratitude I have vowed to my mother is not enough, another and stronger tie attaches us, which must convince her of my sincerity."

"What is it?" she asked, looking fixedly at him.

"Hatred," he answered.

"That is true," she said, with a sinister burst of laughter. "You hate him too?"

"Yes; I hate him with all the strength of my soul: I hate him, because he has robbed me of the two things I held most to on earth,—the love of the woman I adored, and the power I coveted."

"But are you not a chief?" she said significantly.

"Yes!" he exclaimed proudly, "I am a chief, but my father was a sachem of the Kenhas; his son is brave, he is crafty, the scalps of numberless Palefaces dry before his lodge. Why then is Red Wolf only an inferior chief, instead of leading his men to battle as his father did?"

The woman seemed to take a delight in exciting the anger of the Indian, instead of calming it.

"Because doubtlessly," she said, "a wiser man than the Red Wolf has gained the votes of his brothers."

"Let my mother say that a greater rogue stole them from him, and her words will be true," he exclaimed violently. "Grizzly Bear is a Comanche dog, the son of an exile, received through favour into my tribe; his scalp will soon dry on the girdle of the Red Wolf."

"Patience!" the woman said in a hoarse voice. "Vengeance is a fruit which is only eaten ripe: the Red Wolf is a warrior; he can wait."

"Let my mother order," the Indian said, suddenly calmed; "her son will obey."

"Has the Red Wolf succeeded in obtaining the medicine which Prairie-Flower wears round her neck?"

The Indian bowed his head in confusion.

"No," he said hoarsely. "Prairie-Flower never leaves the White Buffalo; it is impossible to approach her."

The woman smiled ironically.

"What! did Red Wolf ever keep a promise?"

The Blackfoot shuddered with rage.

"I will have it," he cried, "even if I must use force in obtaining it."

"No," she replied; "cunning alone must be employed."

"I will have it," he repeated. "Before two days I will give it to my mother."

"No," she said quickly; "in two days is too soon. Let my son give it me on the fifth day of the new moon, which will begin within three days."

"Good; I swear it! My mother shall have the great medicine of Prairie-Flower."

"My son will bring it to me at the tree of the bear, near the great lodge of the Palefaces, two hours after sunset. I will await him there, and give him my final instructions."

"Red Wolf will be there."

"Till then, my son will carefully watch every movement of the Grizzly Bear; if he learns anything new, which appears to him important, my son will form on this very spot a pyramid of seven buffalo heads, and come back two hours after to wait for me. I shall have understood his signal, and will reply to his summons."

"*Oche*, my mother is powerful; it shall be done as she desires."

"My son has quite understood?"

"The words of my mother have fallen on the ears of a chief; his mind has received them."

"The sky on the horizon is covered with red bands, the sun will soon appear: let my brother return to his tribe; he must not arouse the suspicions of his enemy by his absence."

"I go; but before leaving my mother, whose wisdom has discovered all the schemes of the Palefaces, has she not made a great medicine to know if our enterprise will succeed, and if we shall conquer our enemy?"

At this moment a loud noise was heard in the canebrake, and a shrill whistle traversed the air; the Indian's horse laid hack its ears, made violent efforts to break the rope that fastened it, and trembled all over. The woman seized the chiefs arm firmly, and said in a gloomy voice,—

"Let my brother look!"

Red Wolf stifled a cry of surprise, and gazed, motionless and terrified, at the strange sight before him. A few paces off, a tiger cat and a rattlesnake were preparing for a contest. Their metallic eyeballs flashed, and seemed to emit flames. The tiger cat, crouching on a branch, with hair erect, was meowing and spitting, while closely following every move of its dangerous enemy, and awaiting the moment to attack it advantageously. The Crotalus, coiled up, and forming an enormous spiral, with its hideous head thrown back, whistled, as it balanced itself to the right and left, with a movement full of suppleness and grace, apparently trying to fascinate its enemy. But the latter did not allow it a long rest; it suddenly bounded on the serpent, which, however, moved nimbly on one side, and when the cat, after missing its leap, returned to the charge, gave it a fearful sting on the face.

The tiger cat uttered a yell of rage, and buried its long and sharp claws in the eyes of the serpent, which, however, wound round its enemy with a convulsive movement. Then the two rolled on the ground, hissing and howling, but unable to loose their hold. The struggle was long; they fought with extraordinary fury; but at length, the rings of the snake became unloosened, and its flaccid body lay motionless on the ground. The tiger cat escaped, with a meow of triumph, from the monster's terrible embrace, and bounded on a tree; but its strength was unequal to its will, and it could not reach the branch on which it wished to climb, but fell back exhausted on the ground. Then the ferocious animal, struggling with death and overcoming its agony, crouched back to the body of its enemy, and stood upon it. It then uttered a final yell of triumph, and fell, itself a corpse, by the side of the snake. The Indian had followed all the moving incidents of this cruel contest with ever-increasing interest.

"Well," he asked the unknown, "what does my mother say?"

She shook her head.

"Our triumph will cost us our life," she replied.

"What matters," the Red Wolf said, "so long as we conquer our enemies?"

And, drawing his knife, he began skinning the catamount. The woman looked at his operations for a while; then making him a parting sign, she re-entered the canebrake, where she was speedily lost to view. An hour later, the Indian chief, laden with the cat's head and the snake's skin, started off toward his village at full gallop. An ironical smile played around his lips; he needed no excuse to explain his absence, for the spoils he brought with him proved that he had spent the night in hunting.

CHAPTER XIII
THE INDIAN VILLAGE

Now that the exigencies of our story compel us to enter into closer relations with the Prairie Indians, we will introduce to the reader the primitive population of that territory, generally called Blackfoot Indians. The Blackfeet formed, at the period when this history occurred, a powerful nation, divided into three tribes, speaking the same language. First, the tribe of the Siksekai, or Blackfeet proper; next, the Kenhas, or Blood Indians; and lastly, the Piékanns. This nation, when the three tribes were united, could bring under arms nearly eight thousand warriors, which enables us to estimate the population at twenty-five thousand souls. But, at the present day, smallpox has decimated these Indians, and reduced them to a very much smaller number. The Blackfeet traverse the prairies adjoining the Rocky Mountains, sometimes even scaling those mountains between the three forks of the Missouri, called Gallatin, Jefferson, and Madison rivers. The Piékanns, however, go as far as Marine river, to trade with the American Fur Company; they also barter with the Hudson's Bay Society, and even with the Mexicans of Santa Fé. This nation, continually at war with the whites, whom they attack whenever they have the chance, are very little known, but greatly feared, especially for their skill in stealing horses, and, more than that, for their notorious cruelty and bad faith. As we have to deal principally with the Kenhas, we will occupy ourselves more particularly with that tribe. The following is the origin of the name "Blood Indians," given to the Kenhas:—

Before the Blackfeet were divided, they happened one day to be encamped a short distance from seven or eight tents of the Sassi Indians. A quarrel arose between them about a woman carried off by the Sassis, in spite of the opposition of the Piékanns, and the Kenhas resolved to kill all their neighbours, a project which they carried out with extraordinary ferocity and cruelty. In the middle of the night they attacked the tents of the Sassis, and massacred them all during their sleep, without sparing even women, children, or old men; they scalped their victims, and regained their tents, after daubing their faces and hands with blood.

The Piékanns reproached them for this act of barbarity; a quarrel ensued, which speedily degenerated into a combat, in consequence of which the three Blackfoot tribes separated. The Kenhas then received the name of Blood Indians, which they still retain, and feel a pride in it, saying that no one insults them with impunity. The Kenhas are the most active and indomitable of the Blackfeet: they have always displayed more sanguinary and rapacious instincts than the other members of their nation, especially than the Piékanns, who are justly regarded as comparatively gentle and humane.

As the three Blackfoot tribes generally live far apart, Natah Otann must have acted with great skill, and displayed great patience, ere he succeeded in making them join, and consent to march under the same banner. At every moment he was constrained to employ all the resources suggested by his fertile mind, and evince great diplomacy, in order to prevent a rupture, which was always imminent between these men, whom no tie attached, and whose pride revolted at the least appearance of humiliation.

After the events which occurred at the pioneer's camp, Natah Otann resolved to lead the Count de Beaulieu and his comrades to the chief summer village of the Kenhas, situated at no great distance from Fort Mackenzie, one of the principal depôts of the American Fur Company. The Kenhas had constructed this village only a year previously, and their vicinity at first alarmed the Americans; but the conduct of the Indians had ever been so loyal—apparently, at least, in their transactions with the white men—that the latter, at length, did not trouble themselves about their Redskin neighbours, except to buy their furs, sell them whisky, and visit their village when they wanted some amusement.

After selling Black an immense territory for a dollar, Natah Otann reminded the young man of his promise to visit his tribe, and the Count, though secretly vexed at the obligation he Was under of accepting an invitation which bore a great likeness to a command, still yielded, and followed the chief, after bidding farewell to the pioneers. Black, with his hand resting on the trigger of his rifle, looked after the Kenha horsemen, who, according to their custom, galloped across the prairie, when a rider turned back, and came up to the American's camp. The pioneer recognised, with some surprise, Bright-eye, who stopped before him.

"Have you forgotten anything?" the pioneer asked him.

"Yes," the hunter answered.

"What?"

"To say a word to you."

"Ah!" the other said, in surprise. "Go ahead, then."

"I have no time to lose; answer me as plainly as I question you."

"Very good! speak."

"Are you grateful for what the Count has done for you?"

"More than I can express."

"In case of need, what would you do for him?"

"Everything."

"Hum! that is a heavy pledge."

"It is even less than I would do; my family, my servants, all I possess, are at his disposal."

"Then you are devoted to him?"

"For life and death! Under any circumstances, by day or night; whatever may happen, at a word from him I am ready."

"You swear it?"

"I swear it."

"I hold your promise."

"I will keep it."

"I expect so. Good bye."

"Are you off already?"

"I must rejoin my companions."

"Then you have some suspicions about your Red friend?"

"You must always be on your guard with Indians," the hunter said, sententiously.

"Then you are taking a precaution?"

"Perhaps."

"In any event, count on me."

"Thanks, and good bye."

"Good bye."

The two men parted; they understood each other.

"By heaven!" the pioneer muttered, as he threw his rifle over his shoulder, and returned to the camp; "I would not be the Indian to touch a hair of the head of a man to whom I owe so much."

The Indians had stopped on the bank of a stream, which they were about to ford, when Bright-eye rejoined them. Natah Otann, busy talking with the Count, threw a side glance at the hunter, but did not say a word to him.

"Yes," the latter muttered, with a crafty smile, "my absence has bothered you, my fine fellow; you would like to know why I turned back so suddenly; but, unluckily, I am not disposed to satisfy your curiosity."

When the ford was crossed, the Canadian took his post by the Frenchman's side, and, by his presence, prevented the Indian chief renewing his conversation with the Count. An hour passed, and not a word was exchanged. Natah Otann, wearied with the hunter's obstinacy, and not knowing how to make him retire, resolved at last to give up to him: and, digging his spurs into his horse's flank, galloped forward, leaving the two white men together. The hunter watched him depart, with that caustic laugh which was one of the characteristics of his face.

"Poor horse!" he said, sarcastically, "he must suffer for his master's ill temper."

"What ill temper do you mean?" the Count said, absently.

"Why, the chief's, who is flying along over there in a cloud of dust."

"You do not seem to have any sympathy for each other."

"Indeed, we are as friendly as the grizzly bear and the jaguar."

"Which means?—"

"That we have measured our claws; and, as we find them at present of the same strength and length, so we stand on the defensive."

"Do you feel any malice against him?"

"I? not the least in the world. I do not fear him more than he does me; we are only distrustful because we know each other."

"Oh, oh!" the young man said, with a laugh; "that conceals, I can see, something serious."

Bright-eye frowned, and took a scrutinizing glance around. The Indians were galloping on about twenty paces in the rear; Ivon alone, though keeping at a respectful distance, could hear the conversation between the two men. Bright-eye leant over to the Count, laid his hand on the pommel of his saddle, and said, in a low voice—"I do not like tigers covered with a fox's skin; each ought to follow the instincts of his nature, and not try to assume others that are fictitious."

"I must confess, my good fellow," the young man replied, "that you are speaking in enigmas, and I cannot understand you at all."

"Patience!" the hunter said, tossing his head; "I will be clear."

"My faith! that will delight me, Bright-eye," the young man said, with a smile; "for ever since we have again met the Indian chief, you have affected an air of mystery, which bothers me so, that I should be charmed to comprehend you for once."

"Good! What do you think of Natah Otann

"Ah! that is where you are galled still!"

"Yes."

"Well, I will reply that this man appears to me extraordinary; there is something strange about him, which I cannot understand. In the first place, is he an Indian?"

"Yes."

"But he has travelled; he has been in white society; he has been in the interior of the United States?"

The hunter shook his head. "No," he said, "he has never left his tribe."

"Yet—"

"Yet," Bright-eye quickly interrupted him, "he speaks English, French and Spanish, as well as yourself, and perhaps better than I do, eh? Before his warriors he feigns profound ignorance; like them, he trembles at the sight of one of the results of civilization—a watch, a musical box, or even a lucifer match, eh?"

"It is true."

"Then, when he finds himself with certain persons, like yourself, for instance, sir, the Indian suddenly disappears, the savage vanishes, and you find yourself in the presence of a man whose acquirements are almost equal to your own, and who confounds you by his thorough knowledge."

"That is true."

"Ah, ah! Well, as you consider that extraordinary as I do, you will take your precautions, Mr. Edward."

"What have I to fear from him?"

"I do not know yet; but be at your ease; I shall soon know. He is sharp, but I am not such a fool as he fancies, and am watching him. For a long time this man has been playing a game, about which I have hitherto troubled myself but little; now that he has drawn us into it, he must be on his guard."

"But where did he learn all he knows?"

"Ah! that is a story too long to tell you at present; but you shall hear it someday; suffice it to say, that in his tribe there is an old chief called the White Buffalo; he is a European, and he it was who educated the Grizzly Bear."

"Ah!"

"Is not that singular! a European of immense learning; a man who, in his own country, must have held a high rank, and who thus becomes, of his own accord, chief of the savages?"

"Indeed, it is most extraordinary. Do you know this man?"

"I have often seen him; he is very aged now; his beard and hair are white; he is tall and majestic; his face is fine, his look profound; there is something about him grand and imposing, which attracts you against your will. Grizzly Bear holds him in great veneration, and obeys him as if he were his son."

"Who can this man be?"

"No one knows. I am convinced that the Grizzly Bear shares the general ignorance on this head."

"But how did he join the tribe?"

"It is not known."

"He must have been long with it."

"I told you so; he educated the Grizzly Bear, and made a European of him instead of an Indian."

"All that is really strange," the Count murmured, having suddenly grown pensive.

"Is it not so? But that is not all yet; you are entering a world you do not know, accident throws you among interests you are unacquainted with; take care; weigh well your words, calculate your slightest gesture, Mr. Edward; for the Indians are very clever; the man you have to deal with is cleverer than all of them, as he combines with Redskin craft that European intelligence and corruption with which his teacher has inculcated him. Natah Otann is a man with an incalculable depth of calculation; his thoughts are an abyss; he must be revolving sinister schemes; take care; his pressing you to promise a visit to his village; his generosity to the American squatter, the secret protection with which he surrounds you, while being the first to pretend to take you for a superior being; all this makes me believe that he wishes to lead you unconsciously into some dark enterprise, which will prove your destruction. Believe me, Mr. Edward, beware of this man."

"Thanks, my friend, I will watch," the Count said, pressing the Canadian's honest hand.

"You will watch," the latter said; "but do you know the way to do it?"

"I confess—"

"Listen to me," the hunter interrupted him; "you must first—"

"Here is the chief," the young man exclaimed.

"Confusion!" Bright-eye growled. "Why could he not stop a few minutes longer? I am sure that red devil has some familiar spirit to warn him; but no matter, I have told you enough to prevent your being trapped by false friendliness; besides, I shall be there to support you."

"Thanks. When the time comes—"

"I will warn you; but it is urgent that you should now compose your countenance, and pretend to know nothing."

"Good; that's settled; here is our man. Silence."

"On the contrary, let us talk; silence is ever interpreted either well or ill, but generally in the latter sense. Be careful to reply in the sense of my questions."

"I will try."

"Here is our man. Let us cheat the cheater."

After casting a cunning glance at the chief, who was only a few paces off at the moment, he continued aloud, and changing his tone,—

"What you ask, Mr. Edward, is most simple. I am certain that the chief will be happy to procure you that pleasure."

"Do you think so?" the young man asked, not knowing what the hunter was alluding to.

Bright-eye turned to Natah Otann, who arrived at the moment, and rode silently by their side, though he had heard the two men's last remarks.

"My companion," he said to the chief, "has heard a great deal of, and longs to see, a caribou hunt. I have offered him in your name, chief, one of those magnificent battues, of which you Redskins have reserved the scent."

"Natah Otann will be happy to satisfy his guest," the sachem replied, bowing with Indian gravity.

The Count thanked him.

"We are approaching the village of my tribe," the chief continued; "we shall be there in an hour; the Palefaces will see how I receive my friends."

The Blackfeet, who had hitherto galloped without order, gradually grew together, and formed a compact squadron round their chief. The little party continued to advance, approaching more and more the Missouri, which rolled on majestically between two high banks, covered with osier beds, whence, on the approach of the horsemen, startled flocks of pink flamingoes rose in alarm. On reaching a spot where the path formed a bend, the Indians stopped, and prepared their weapons as if for a fight; some taking their guns out of their leathern cases, and loading them; others preparing their bows and javelins.

"Are the fellows afraid of an attack?" the Count asked Bright-eye.

"Not the least in the world," the latter answered; "they are only a few minutes' ride from their village, into which they wish to enter in triumph, in order to do you honour."

"Come, come!" the young man said; "all this is charming; I did not expect, on coming to the prairies, to be present at such singular scenes."

"You have seen nothing yet," the hunter said, ironically: "wait, we are only at the beginning."

"All the better," the Count answered, joyfully.

Natah Otann made a sign, and the warriors closed up again at the same moment; although no one was visible, a noise of conchs, drums, and chichikouès was heard a short distance off. The warriors uttered their war yell, and replied by raising to their lips their war whistles. Natah Otann then placed himself at the head of the party, having the Count on his right, the hunter and Ivon on his left; and, turning towards his men, he brandished his weapon several times over his head, uttering two or three shrill whistles. At this signal the whole troop rushed forward, and turned the corner like an avalanche.

The Frenchman then witnessed a strange scene, which was not without a certain amount of savage grandeur, A troop of warriors from the village came up, like a tornado, to meet the newcomers, shouting, howling, brandishing their arms, and firing their guns. The two parties charged each other with extraordinary fury and at full speed; but when scarce ten yards apart, the horses stopped, as if of their own impulse, and began dancing, curvetting, and performing all the most difficult tricks of the riding school. After these manoeuvres had lasted a few moments, the two bands formed a semicircle opposite each other, leaving a free space between them, in which the chiefs collected. The presentations then began. Natah Otann made a long harangue to the chiefs, in which he gave them an account of his expedition, and the result he had obtained. The sachems listened to it with thorough Indian decorum. When he spoke to them of his meeting with the white men, and what had occurred, they bowed silently, without replying; but one chief, of venerable aspect, who seemed older than the rest, and appeared to be treated with great consideration by his companions, turned a profound and inquiring glance at the Count, when Natah Otann spoke of him. The young man, troubled, in spite of himself, by the fixed glance, stooped down to Bright-eye's ear, and asked him, in a low voice, who the man was.

"That is White Buffalo," the hunter answered, "the European I spoke to you about."

"Ah, ah!" the Count said, regarding him, in his turn, attentively; "I do not know why, but I believe I shall have a serious row with that gentleman before I have done."

The White Buffalo then took the word.

"My brothers are welcome," he said; "their return to the tribe is a festival; they are intrepid warriors; we are happy at hearing the way in which they have performed the duties entrusted to them." Then he turned to the white men, and, after bowing to them, continued,—"The Kenhas are poor, but strangers are always well received by them: the Palefaces are our guests, all we possess belongs to them."

The Count and his companions thanked the chief, who so gracefully did the honours of his tribe; then the two parties joined, and galloped toward the village, which was built some five hundred paces from the spot where they were, and at the entrance of which a multitude of women and children could be seen assembled.

CHAPTER XIV
THE RECEPTION

Like all the centres of Indian population near the American clearings, the Kenha village was more like a fort than an open town. As we said before, the Kenhas had only a short time previously established themselves there, by the advice of Natah Otann. The spot was magnificently selected, and owing to the precautions taken, the hill was completely protected from a sudden attack. The wigwams were built without any order, on both sides a stream, and the fortifications consisted of a sort of intrenchment formed of dead trees. These fortifications formed an inclosure, having several angles, and the gorge or open part rested on the spot where the stream fell into the Missouri. A parapet of tree stems and piled up branches, built up on the edge of a deep ditch, completed a very respectable defensive system, which few would have expected to find in the heart of the prairies.

In the centre of the village, a wide, vacant spot served as the meeting place for the chiefs. In the centre there was a wigwam of wood, in the shape of a sugar loaf. On either side of the building, maize, wheat, and other cereals kept for winter consumption were drying. A little in advance of the village were two block houses, formed of arrow-shaped intrenchments, covered with wickerwork, provided with loopholes, and surrounded by an enclosure of palisades. They were intended for the defence of the village, with which they communicated by a covered way, and to command the river and the plain. To leeward of these block houses, and about a mile to the east, might be seen a number of *Machotlé*, or scaffoldings, on which the Blood Indians lay their dead. At regular distances on the road leading to the village, long poles were planted in the ground, from which hung skins, scalps, and other objects offered by the Indians to the Master of Life and the first man.

The Indians made their entrance into the village amid the cheers of the women and children, the barking of dogs, and the deafening clamour of drums, shells, chichikouès, and war whistles. On reaching the square, at a signal from Natah Otann, the band halted, and the noise ceased. An immense fire had been prepared, before which stood an aged chief, still robust and upright. A shade of melancholy was spread over his face. He was in mourning, as was easily to be seen by the ragged clothes that covered him, and his hair cut short and mingled with clay. He held in his hand a Dacotah pipe, the stem of which was long and adorned with yellow glistening beads. This man was Cloven Foot, the first and most renowned sachem of the Kenhas. So soon as the band had halted, he advanced two paces, and with a majestic gesture invited the chiefs to dismount.

"My sons are at home," he said, "let them take their seats on the buffalo robes around the council fire."

Each obeyed silently, and sat down, after bowing respectfully to the sachem. Cloven Foot then allowed each to take a few puffs from his pipe, still holding it in his hand. When it was returned to him, he emptied the burning ash into the fire, and turning with a kind of smile to the strangers, said:—

"The Palefaces are our guests. There are fire and water here."

After these words, which ended the ceremony, all rose and retired without uttering a word, according to the Indian custom. Natah Otann then went up to the Count.

"Let my brother follow me," he said.

"Where to?" the young man asked.

"To the cabin I have had prepared for him."

"And my companions?"

"Other wigwams await them."

Bright-eye made a sign, immediately checked by the Count.

"Pardon, chief," he said, "but with your permission my comrades will live with me."

The hunter smiled, as a shade of dissatisfaction crossed the Indian's face.

"The young Pale chief will be uncomfortable, for he is accustomed to the immense huts of the whites."

"That is possible; but I shall be more uncomfortable if my comrades do not remain with me, in order to keep me company."

"The hospitality of the Kenhas is great. They are rich, and could give each a private cabin, even if their guests were more numerous."

"I am convinced of it, and thank them for their attention, by which, however, I decline to profit. Solitude frightens me. I should be worried to death had I not with me someone to talk with."

"Be it then as the young Pale chief desires. Guests have a right to command. Their requests are orders."

"I thank you for your condescension, and am ready to follow you."

"Come."

With that rapidity of resolution which the Indians possess in so eminent a degree, Natah Otann shut up his vexation in his heart, and not a trace of emotion again appeared on his stoical countenance. The three men followed him, after exchanging a meaning glance. A handsome, lofty cabin had been built in the square itself, near the hut of the first man, a species of cylinder formed in the earth, and surrounded with creeping plants. To this cabin the chief now led his guests. A woman was standing silently in the doorway, fixing on the newcomers a glance in which admiration and astonishment were blended. But was it a woman? this angelic creature, with her vague outline, whose delicious face, blushing with modesty and simple curiosity, turned towards the Count with anxious timidity. The young man asked himself this very question on contemplating this charming apparition, which resembled one of those divine virgins in the mythology of the ancient Sclavons. On seeing her, Natah Otann paused.

"What is my sister doing here?" he asked her, roughly.

The girl, startled from her silent contemplation by this brusque address, shuddered, and let her eyes fall.

"Prairie-Flower wishes to welcome her adopted father," she replied gently, in a sweet melodious voice.

"Prairie-Flower's place is not here, I will speak with her presently: let her go and rejoin her companions, the young maidens of the tribe."

Prairie-Flower blushed still deeper, her rosy lips pouted, and after shaking her head petulantly twice, she flew away like a bird, casting at the Count, as she fled, a parting glance, which caused him an incomprehensible emotion.

The young man laid his hand on his heart, to suppress its beating, and followed the girl with his eyes till she disappeared behind a cabin.

"Oh!" the chief muttered aside, "can she have suddenly recognized a being of that accursed race to which she belongs?"

Then turning to the white men, whose eyes he felt instinctively were fixed on him,—

"Enter," he said, raising the buffalo skin, which served as a door to the cabin.

They went in. By Natah Otann's care the cabin had been cleaned, and every comfort it was possible to find placed in it, that is to say—piles of furs to serve as a bed, a rickety table, some wooden clumsy benches, and a species of reed easy chair, with a large back.

"The Paleface will excuse the poor Indians if they have not done more to welcome him as he deserves," the chief said, with a mixture of irony and humility.

"It is all famous," the young man answered with a smile; "I certainly did not expect so much; besides, I have been on the prairie long enough to satisfy myself with what is strictly necessary."

"Now I ask the Pale chiefs permission to retire."

"Yes, go, my worthy host; do so: do not put yourself out of the way. Attend to your business. For my part I intend taking that rest I need so sadly."

Natah Otann bowed in reply, and withdrew. So soon as he was gone, Bright-eye made his comrades a sign to remain motionless, and began inspecting the place, peering into every corner. When he had ended this inspection, which produced no farther result than proving to him they were really alone, and that no spy was on the watch, he returned to the centre of the hut, and calling the Count and Ivon toward him, said in a low voice:—

"Listen: we are now in the wolfs throat by our own fault, and we must be prudent; in the prairies the leaves have eyes and the trees ears. Natah Otann is a demon, who is planning some treachery, of which he intends to make us the victims."

"Bah!" the Count said, lightly. "How do you know it, Bright-eye?"

"I do not know it, yet I feel sure of it; my instinct never deceives me, Mr. Edward. I have known the Kenhas a long time; we must get out of this as adroitly as we can."

"Eh! what use are such suspicions, my friend? The poor devils, I am convinced, only think of treating us properly; all this appears to me admirable."

The Canadian shook his head.

"I should like to know the cause of the strange respect the Indians pay you; that conceals something, I repeat."

"Bah! they are afraid of me; that's all."

"Hum! Natah Otann does not fear much in this world."

"Why, Bright-eye, I never saw you in this state before. Did I not know you so thoroughly, I should say you were afraid."

"Hang me! if I'll try to conceal it," the hunter replied, quickly. "I am afraid, and terribly so."

"You?"

"Yes; but not for myself; you know that during the time I have journeyed on the prairies, if the Redskins could have killed me, they would have done so. Hence, I am perfectly calm on my own account, and were there only myself—"

"Well?"

"I should not be at all embarrassed."

"Whom are you afraid for, then?"

"For you."

"Me!" the Count exclaimed, as he reclined carelessly in the easy chair. "You do these scamps a deal of honour. With my whip I would put all these hideous people to flight."

The hunter shook his head.

"You will not, Mr. Edward, persuade yourself thoroughly of one thing."

"What?"

"That the Indians are different men from the Europeans with whom you have hitherto had dealings."

"Nonsense, were a man to listen to you wood rangers, he would be, at every two steps, in danger of death, and it would be impossible to move, except by crawling on all fours, like the wild beasts; that is all trash, my good fellow. I fancy I have already twenty times proved to you that such precautions are useless, and that a man, who boldly meets danger, will always get the best of the most warlike Redskins."

"It is exactly the reason that makes them act toward you in that way, I wish to discover."

"You would do better to try and discover something else."

"What is it?"

"Who that charming girl is, of whom I only had a glance, and whom the chief sent away so brutally."

"Good! then I suppose you have fallen in love now; that's the last thing wanting."

"Why not? She is a charming girl."

. "Yes; she is charming, sir; but, believe me, do not trouble yourself about her."

"And why so, if you please?"

"Because she is not what she seems to be."

"Why, it's a perfect romance of the Anne Radcliffe school; we have been advancing from mystery to mystery during the last few days."

"Yes, and the further we go, the more gloomy matters will become around us."

"Bah, bah! I do not believe a word. Ivon, take off my boots."

The man-servant obeyed. Since his entry into the village, the worthy Breton had been in one continued trance, and trembled in all his limbs. All he saw seemed to him so extraordinary and horrible, that he expected every moment to be massacred.

"Well," the Count asked him, "what do you think of it all, Ivon?"

"Your lordship knows that I am a great coward," the Breton stammered.

"Yes, yes, that is agreed; go on."

"I am terribly afraid."

"Naturally."

"And if your lordship will allow me, I will carry my furs over there, and sleep across the doorway."

"Why so?"

"Because, as I am very frightened, I shall not sleep soundly; and if anyone comes in the night, with ill intentions, he will be obliged to step over me; I shall hear him, and, in that way, be able to warn you, which will give you time to defend yourself."

The young man threw himself back, and burst into a Homeric laugh, in which Bright-eye joined, in spite of his thoughtfulness.

"By Jove!" the Count exclaimed, looking at his servant, who was in amazement at this gaiety, which seemed to him unsuitable at so grave a moment—"I must confess, Ivon, that you are the most extraordinary poltroon I ever saw."

"Ah, sir," he answered with contrition, "it is not my fault; for I do all I can to gain courage, but it is impossible."

"Good, good!" the young man went on, still laughing. "I am not angry with you, my poor fellow; as it is stronger than yourself, you must put up with it."

"Alas!" the Breton said, uttering an enormous sigh.

"Well, you can sleep how and where you like, Ivon; I leave it entirely to you."

The Breton, without further reply, began transferring the furs to the place he had selected, while the Count went on talking with the hunter.

"As for you, Bright-eye," he said, "I leave you at liberty to watch over our safety as you may think proper, promising not to disarrange your plans in any way, and even to promote them, if necessary—but on one condition."

"What?"

"That you will arrange so that I may meet again that charming creature, of whom I have already spoken to you."

"Take care, Mr. Edward!"

"I want to see her again, I tell you, even if I am obliged to go and look for her myself."

"You will not do so, Mr. Edward."

"I will do so, on my soul! and at once, if you continue in that tone."

"You will reflect."

"I now reflect, and find it the best plan."

"But do you know who that girl is?"

"By Jove! you have just said it; she is a girl, and a charming one in the bargain."

"Granted; but I repeat, she is loved by Natah Otann."

"What do I care?"

"Take care!"

"I will not: I must see her again."

"At any risk?"

"At all."

"Well, listen to me, then."

"I will, but be brief."

"I will tell you this girl's history."

"You know her then?"

"I do."

"Go on; I am all attention."

Bright-eye drew up a bench, eat down with an air of dissatisfaction, and, after a moment's reflection, began.

"Just fifteen years ago, Natah Otann, who was hardly twenty years of age, but already a renowned warrior, left his tribe, at the head of some fifty picked warriors, to attempt a *coup de main* on the Whites. At that period, the Kenhas did not live where they now are; the Fur Company had not advanced so far on the Missouri, and Fort Mackenzie did not exist. The Blood Indians hunted freely on the vast territories from which the Americans have since expelled them. Up to that moment, Natah Otann had never been the commander in chief of an expedition; like all young men of his age and circumstances, his brow shone with pride; he burned to distinguish himself, and prove to the sachems of his nation that he was worthy to command brave warriors. So soon as he entered on the war trail, he scattered his spies in every direction, and even forbade his men smoking, lest the light of their pipes might betray his presence. In short, he took, with extreme wisdom, all the precautions employed in similar cases. His expedition was brilliant; he surprised several caravans, and plundered and burned the clearings; his men returned laden with booty, and the bits of their horses garnished with scalps. Natah Otann only brought back, as his share, a weak creature of two or three years of age at the most, whom he bore tenderly in his arms, or laid on the front of his saddle. That child was the tall and lovely girl you saw today."

"Ah! Is she white or red, American or Spanish?"

"No one knows; no one will ever know. You are aware that many Indians are born white, thus colour is of no avail in finding her relations again. In short, the chief adopted her; but, strange to say, as she grew up, she gained such an ascendency over Natah Otann's mind, that the chief of the tribe grew alarmed; besides, the life led by Prairie-Flower—that is her name—"

"I knew it," the Count interrupted him.

"Good," the hunter continued, "I say, then, that this girl's life is extraordinary; instead of being sportive and laughing, like girls of her age, she is gloomy, dreamy, and wild, wandering ever alone on the prairie, flying over the dew-laden grass like a gazelle; or else, at night, dreaming in the moonlight, and muttering words no one hears. At times, from a distance (for no one ventures to approach her), another shadow may be traced by the side of her's, and moving for hours at her side: then she returns alone to the village; if questioned, only shakes her head, and begins crying."

"That is really strange."

"Is it not? so much so, that the chiefs assembled in council, and agreed that Prairie-Flower had cast a charm over her adopted father."

"The asses!" the Count muttered.

"Perhaps so," the hunter went on, turning his head; "at any rate, they agreed that she should be left alone to perish in the desert."

"Poor child! Well, what happened then?"

"Natah Otann and White Buffalo, who were not summoned to the council, went there on learning this decision, and succeeded by their deceitful words in so thoroughly altering the chiefs' sentiments, that they not only gave up all idea of deserting her, but she has since been regarded as the tutelary genius of the tribe."

"And Natah Otann?"

"His condition is still the same."

"Is that all?"

"It is."

"Well, then, Bright-eye, within two days I shall know whether that girl is the enchantress you fancy her, and what I am to think on the subject."

The hunter only answered by an unintelligible grunt, and, saying no more, lay down on his furs.

CHAPTER XV
THE WHITE BUFFALO

So soon as Natah Otann emerged from the cabin into which he had conducted the Count, he proceeded towards the hut inhabited by White Buffalo. The night was beginning to fall; the Kenhas, collected round fires kindled at the door of each wigwam, were conversing gaily while smoking their long calumets. The chief replied by a nod of the head, as a friendly sign to the affectionate salutations the warriors made him whom he met; but he did not stop to talk with anyone, and continued his walk with greater rapidity as the darkness grew denser. He at length reached a cabin, situated at the extremity of the village, on the banks of the Missouri. The chief, after taking a scrutinizing glance around, stopped before this hut, and prepared to enter. Still in the act of raising the buffalo curtain that served as a doorway, he hesitated for a few seconds, and appeared to be collecting his courage.

This dwelling, externally, had nothing to distinguish it from the others forming the village; it was round, with a roof shaped like a beehive, made of intertwined branches, with clay stuffed between them, and covered with matting. Still, after a moment's reflection, Natah Otann raised the curtain, walked in, and stopped at the threshold, saying in French—

"Good evening, my father."

"Good evening, child, I was awaiting you impatiently: come, sit down by my side, we have to talk."

These words were uttered in the same language, and in a gentle voice.

Natah Otann took a few steps forward, and let the curtain fall behind him. If, externally, the hut the Chief had just entered was not distinguished from the others, that was not the case with the interior. All that human industry can imagine, when reduced to its simplest expressions, that is to say, when deprived of tools and matters of primary necessity to express its thoughts, had been as it were invented by the master of this house. Hence the interior of this hut was a sort of strange pandemonium, in which were collected the most discordant articles, apparently least suited to be side by side. Differing from the other wigwams, this cabin had two windows, in which oiled paper was substituted for glass; in one corner was a bed, in the centre a table, a few scattered chairs, and armchair by the table, but all these articles carved with an axe, and clumsily. Such was the furniture of this singular room.

On shelves, some forty volumes, for the most part out of their binding; stuffed animals hanging by cords, insects, &c.; in a word, an infinite number of things without name, but classified, arranged, and labelled, completed this singular abode, which more resembled the cell of an anchorite, or the secret den of a mediaeval alchemist, than the abode of an Indian chief; and yet this hut belonged to White Buffalo, one of the first Kenha chiefs. But, as we have said, this chief was a European, and had, doubtlessly, kept up some reminiscences of his past life, the last rays of a lost existence.

At the moment when Natah Otann entered the hut, White Buffalo, seated in the easy chair at the table, with his head resting on his hands, was reading by the light of a lamp, whose smoky wick only spread a flickering and uncertain light around, from a large folio, with yellow and worn leaves. He raised his head, took off his spectacles, which he placed in the book, and, turning the chair half round, the old man smiled, and, pointing to a chair in a kindly way, said—

"Come, my child, sit down there."

The Chief took a chair, drew it to the table, and sat down, without any reply. The old man looked at him attentively for a few moments, and then said:—

"Hem! you appear to me very thoughtful for a man who, as I suppose, has just obtained a grand result so long expected. What can render you so gloomy? Would you hesitate, now you are on the point of success? or are you beginning to understand that the work which, in spite of me, you wished to undertake, is beyond the strength of a man left to himself, and who has only an old man to support him?"

"Perhaps so," the Chief answered, in a hollow voice. "Oh why, my father, did you let me taste the bitter fruit of that accursed civilization, which was not made for me? Why have your lessons made of me a man differing from those who surround me, and with whom I am compelled to live and die?"

"Blind man! when I showed you the sun, you allowed yourself to be dazzled by the beams; your weak eyes could not endure the light; in the place of that ignorance and brutalization in which you would have vegetated all the days of your life, I developed in you the only feeling which elevates man above the brute. I taught you to think, to judge, and this is the way in which you recompense me. This is the reward you give me for the pains I have taken, and the cares I have never ceased to bestow on you."

"My father!"

"Do not attempt to exculpate yourself, child," the old man said, with a shade of bitterness. "I should have expected what now happens, ingratitude and egotism are deposited in man's heart by Providence, as his safeguard. Without those two supreme virtues of humanity, no society would be possible. I am not angry with you; I have no right to be so; and, as the sage says, you are a man, and no human feeling must be alien to you."

"I make neither plaint nor recrimination, my father; I know that you have acted towards me with good intentions," the Chief replied, "but, unfortunately, your lessons have produced a very different result from what you awaited: in developing my ideas, you have, without your knowledge or mine, increased my wants; the life I lead preys upon me: the men who surround me are a burden to me, because they cannot understand me, and I can no longer understand them. As respects myself, my mind rushes towards an unknown horizon. I dream wide awake of strange and impossible things. I suffer from an incurable malady, and cannot define it. I hopelessly love a woman, of whom I am jealous, and who can never be mine, save by a crime. Oh, my father, I am very wretched!"

"Child!" the old man exclaimed, shrugging his shoulders in pity. "What, you are unhappy! Your grief inclines me to laughter. Man has in himself the germ of good and evil; if you suffer, you have only yourself to blame. You are young, intelligent, powerful, the first of your nation: what do you want for happiness? Nothing. If you wish to be so permanently, stifle in your heart that insensate passion which devours it, and follow, without looking to the right or left, the glorious mission you have traced for yourself. What can be more noble or grander than the deliverance and regeneration of a people?"

"Alas! can I do it?"

"What! you doubt?" the old man shouted, striking the table with his fist and looking him in the face; "then you are lost: renounce your plans, you will not succeed; on a road like that you follow, hesitation or stoppage is ruin."

"Father!"

"Silence," he said, with redoubled energy, "and listen to me; when you first revealed your plans to me, I tried by all arguments possible to make you abandon them. I proved to you that your resolves were premature. That the Indians, brutalized by a lengthened slavery, were only the shadow of their former selves; and that to attempt to arouse in them any noble or generous feeling was like galvanizing a corpse. You resisted; you would hear nothing;

you went Headlong into intrigues and plots of every description—is it not so?"

"It is true."

"Well! now it is too late to return; you must go on at all risks. You may fall, but you will do so with honour; and your name, cherished by all, will swell the martyrology of the chosen men who have devoted themselves to their country."

"Things are not yet sufficiently advanced, I think, for me——"

"Not to be able to withdraw—you mean?" he interrupted him.

"Yes."

"You are mistaken; while you were engaged in collecting your partisans, and preparing to take up arms, do you fancy I remained inactive?" "What do you mean?"

"I mean that your enemies suspect your plans; are watching you; and if you do not prevent them, will lay a trap, into, which you will fall."

"I?" the chief said, violently. "We shall see."

"Then redouble your activity; do not let yourself be taken unawares; and, above all, be prudent, for you are closely watched, I repeat."

"How do you know it?"

"That I know it, is sufficient, I imagine; trust to my prudence. I am on the watch. Let the spies and traitors fall asleep in a doubtful security; were we to unmask them, others would take their place, and we are better off with those we know; in that way none of their movements escape us, we know what they are doing and what they want, and while they flatter themselves with the idea of knowing our plans, and divulging them to their paymasters, we are their masters, and amuse them with false information, which conceals our real plans. Believe me, their confidence produces our security."

"You are always right, my father. I trust entirely to you. But may I not be permitted to know the names of the traitors?"

"For what end, since I know them? When the time arrives, I will tell you all."

"Be it so."

There was a lengthened silence; the two men, absorbed in thought, did not notice a grinning head over the curtain in the doorway, and which had for a long time been listening to their conversation. But the man, whoever he might be, who indulged in this espial, every now and then gave signs of ill temper and disappointment. In fact, while listening to the two chiefs, he had forgotten one thing, that he could not understand a word of what they said, for they spoke in French, and that was a sad disappointment to the spy. Still he did not despair, but continued to listen, in the hope that they might at any moment revert to his idiom.

"And now," the old man continued, "give me an account of your trip. When you went away, you were happy, and hoped, as you told me, to bring back with you the man you wanted to play the principal part in your conspiracy."

"Well, you saw him here today, my father. He is here. This evening he entered the village by my side."

"Oh! oh! explain that to me, my child," the old man said, with a gentle smile, and settling himself in the easy chair to listen at his ease. By an imperceptible movement, and while seeming to listen with the greatest attention, he drew towards him the heavy pistol that lay before him.

"Go on," he said; "I am listening."

"About six months ago, I do not know if I told you of it then, I succeeded in capturing a Canadian hunter, to whom I owe an old grudge."

"Wait a minute. I fancy I have a confused remembrance of it. A certain Bright-eye, I think, eh?"

"The very man. Well! I was furious with him, because he had mocked us so long, and killed my warriors with extraordinary skill. So soon as he was in my power I resolved he should die by violence."

"Although, as you know, I do not approve of that barbarous custom, you were in the right, and I cannot offer any opposition to it."

"He, too, made no objection; on the contrary, he derided us; in a word, he rendered us so mad with him, that I gave the order for the punishment. At the moment that he was about to die, a man, or rather a demon, appeared all at once, rushed among us, and careless as it seemed of the risk he ran, unfastened the prisoner."

"Hum! he was a brave man, do you know?"

"Yes, but his daring action would have cost him dear; when suddenly, at a signal from myself, all my warriors fell at his feet, with marks of the most profound respect."

"Oh! what are you telling me now?"

"The strictest truth: on looking this man in the face, I perceived on his face two extraordinary signs."

"What?"

"A scar over the right eyebrow, and a black mark under the eye, on the same side of the face."

"That is strange," the old man muttered, pensively.

"But what is still more so, this man exactly resembles the portrait which you drew, and which is in that book."

"What did you do then?"

"You know my coolness and rapidity of resolution. I let the man depart with the prisoner."

"Well! and afterwards?"

"I pretended as if I did not wish to meet him."

"Better and better still," the old man said, with a nod of his head, and with a movement swift as thought, he cocked the pistol he held in his hand, and fired. A cry of pain was heard from the door, and the head disappeared suddenly under the curtain. The two men jumped up, and rushed out, but saw nothing, except that a rather large pool of blood clearly indicated that the shot had told.

"What have you done, my father?" Natah Otann exclaimed, in astonishment.

"Nothing. I have merely given a lesson, rather a rough one, to one of those spies I mentioned to you just now."

And he went back coolly, and eat down again. Natah Otann wished to follow the bloody trail left by the fugitive, but the old man checked him.

"Stay! what I have done is sufficient; continue your story, which is deeply interesting. Still you can see you have no time to lose, if you wish to succeed."

"I will lose none, father, you may be assured," the Chief exclaimed, wrathfully, "but I swear that I will know the scoundrel."

"You would do wrong to seek him. Come, proceed with your narrative."

Natah Otann then described in full detail his meeting with the Count, and in what way he had made him consent to follow him to his village. This time no incident interrupted his story, and it seemed as if the lesson read by White Buffalo to the listener was sufficient for the present. The old man laughed heartily at the experiment with the matches, and the Count's surprise when he perceived that the man he had hitherto taken for a coarse and half-idiot savage was, on the contrary, a man endowed with an intellect and education at least equal to his own.

"And what shall I do now?" Natah Otann added, in conclusion. "He is here; but with him is Bright-eye, in whom he places the greatest confidence."

"Hum!" the old man answered, "all this is very serious. In the first place, my son, you did wrong to let him know you as you really are: you were much stronger than he, so long as he merely fancied you a stupid savage: you allowed your pride to carry you away through the desire to shine in the eyes of a European. It is a great fault, for now he doubts you, and keeps on his guard."

The young man looked down, and made no reply.

"However," the old man went on, "I will try to arrange matters; but I must first see this Bright-eye and have a talk with him."

"You will obtain nothing, my father; he is devoted to the Count."

"The greater reason, child. In which hut have you lodged them?"

"In the old council lodge."

"Good! they will be convenient there, and it will be easy to hear all they say."

"That is what I thought."

"Now, one last remark."

"What is it?"

"Why did you not kill the She-wolf of the Prairies?"

"I did not see her. I was not in the camp; but I would not have done so."

The old man laid his hand on his shoulder.

"Natah Otann, my son," he said to him, in a stern voice, "when a man like yourself is intrusted with the fortunes of a people, he must recoil before nothing. A dead enemy makes the living sleep quietly. The She-wolf of the Prairies is your enemy. You know it; and her influence is immense over the superstitious minds of the Redskins. Remember these words, uttered by an old, experienced man:—As you would not kill her, she will kill you."

Natah Otann smiled contemptuously.

"Oh!" he said, "a wretched, half-mad woman."

"Ah!" White Buffalo replied, with a shrug of his shoulders, "are you ignorant that a woman lurks behind every great event? They kill men of genius for futile interests, and paltry passions cause the finest and boldest prospects to fail."

"Yes; you are, perhaps, right," Natah Otann said; "but I feel I cannot stain my hands with that woman's blood."

"Scruples, poor child," White Buffalo said, with disdain; "well, I do not insist; but be assured that scruples will ruin you. The man who wishes to govern others must be made of marble, and have no feelings of humanity, else his prospects will be nipped in the bud, and his foes will ridicule him. That which has ever ruined the greatest geniuses is, that they would not comprehend this fact; but worked for their successors and not for themselves."

In speaking thus, the old man had involuntarily let himself be carried away by the tumultuous feelings that still agitated his mind. His eye sparkled; his brow was unwrinkled; his glance had an irresistible majesty; he had returned, in thought, to his old days of struggling and triumph. Natah Otann listened to him, yielding to the dominating ascendency of this prostrated giant, who was so great even after his fall.

"What am I saying? I am mad! pardon me, child," the old man continued, sinking in his chair despondingly. "Go, leave me; tomorrow, at sunrise, I may, perhaps, have some news for you."

And he dismissed the Chief with a sign. The latter, accustomed to these outbursts, bowed, and departed.

CHAPTER XVI
THE SPY

The pistol shot fired by the White Buffalo had not quite produced the result the latter expected from it. The man was wounded; but the haste with which the chief had been obliged to fire, injured the precision of his aim, and the listener escaped with a slight wound; the bullet grazed his skull, and only produced a copious hemorrhage. Still this hurt had been enough for the spy, who saw that he was unmasked, and that a longer stay at the spot would inevitably produce a catastrophe; hence he ran off at full speed. After running for several minutes, feeling certain that he had thrown off any persons inclined to follow him, he stopped to draw breath, and attend to his wound, which still bled profusely. In consequence, he looked anxiously around him; but all was silent and solitary. A dense snowstorm, which had been falling for many an hour, had compelled the Indians to seek shelter in their lodges The firing of the pistol had caused no panic, for the Redskins, accustomed to nocturnal disputes in their villages, had not stirred. No other noise could be heard but the barking of a few straying dogs, and the hoarse cries of the wild beasts that wandered over the prairie in search of prey. The spy, reassured by the calm prevailing in the village, set about bandaging the wound, in his heart thanking the snow for falling, as it effaced the traces of blood left in his flight.

"Come," he muttered, in a low voice, "I shall know nothing this night; the genius of evil protects those men; I will go into the cabin."

He turned a parting glance around, and prepared to start; but, at the same moment, a white shadow, gliding over the snow like a phantom, passed a short distance from him.

"What is that?" the Indian muttered, suddenly assailed by a superstitious terror. "Is the 'Virgin of the dark hours' wandering about the village? What terrible misfortune is menacing us then?"

The Indian bent forward, and, as if attracted by a superior power, followed with his eyes the strange apparition, whose white outline was already blending with the distant gloom.

"That creature is not walking," he said to himself, with terror; "she leaves no footfall on the snow. Is she a Genius hostile to the Blackfeet? There is a mystery about this which I must fathom."

The instinct of the spy heightening the curiosity of the Indian, the latter soon forgot his terror for a moment, and rushed boldly in pursuit of the phantom. After an interval of a few minutes, the shadow or spectre stopped, and looked around with evident indecision. The Indian, lest he might be discovered, had just time to hide himself behind the wall of a cabin; but a pale gleam of moonlight, emerging between two clouds, had, for a second, lighted up the face of the person he was pursuing.

"Prairie-Flower!" he muttered, suppressing with difficulty a cry of surprise.

In fact, that was the person thus wandering about in the darkness. After some hesitation, the maiden raised her head, and walked resolutely toward a cabin, the buffalo skin of which she lifted with a firm hand. She entered, and let the curtain fall behind her. The Indian bounded up to the cabin, walked round it, thrust his knife up to the hilt in the wall, turned it round twice or thrice, to enlarge the hole, and, placing his ear to it, listened. The most complete quiet continued to prevail in the village.

At the first step the young girl took in the lodge, a shadow suddenly rose before her, and a hand fell upon her shoulder; instinctively she recoiled.

"What do you want?" a menacing voice asked. This question was asked in French, which rendered it doubly unintelligible by the Indian girl.

"Answer! or I'll blow out your brains," the voice continued.

And the sharp sound produced by cocking a pistol could be heard.

"Wah!" the girl replied in her gentle, melodious voice, "I am a friend."

"It is evidently a woman," the first speaker growled, "but no matter, we must be prudent. What on earth does she want here?"

"Halloh!" Bright-eye suddenly shouted, aroused by this short altercation, "what's the matter there, what have you caught, Ivon?"

"My faith, I don't know; I believe it is a woman."

"Eh, eh," the hunter said, with a laugh, "let us have a look at that: don't let her escape."

"Don't be alarmed," the Breton replied, "I have hold of her."

Prairie-Flower remained motionless, not making the slightest effort to escape from the clutch of the man who held her. Bright-eye rose, felt his way to the fire, and began blowing it up. In a few minutes a bright flame burst forth, and illumined the interior of the lodge.

"Stay, stay," the hunter said, with surprise, "you are welcome, girl; what do you want here?"

The Indian maid blushed, and replied:—

"Prairie-Flower has come to visit her friends, the Palefaces."

"The hour is a strange one for a visit, my child," the Canadian continued, with an ironical smile; "but no matter," he added, turning to the Breton, "let her loose, Ivon; this enemy, if she is one, is not very dangerous."

The other obeyed with ill grace.

"Come to the fire, girl," the hunter said, "your limbs are frozen; when you have warmed yourself, you can tell us the cause of your presence here at this late hour."

Prairie-Flower smiled sadly, and sat down by the fire, Bright-eye taking a place by her side. The girl had with one glance surveyed the interior of the lodge, and perceived the Count sleeping tranquilly on a pile of furs. Bright-eye's whole life had been spent in the desert; he was thoroughly acquainted with the character of the Redskins, and knew that circumspection and prudence are their two guiding principles. That an Indian never attempts anything without having first calculated all the consequences, and that he never decides on doing a thing contrary to Indian habits, except from some pressing motive. The hunter, therefore, suspected that the object of the young girl's visit was important, though unable to read, beneath the mask of impassibility that covered her face, the motive that caused her to act.

The Redskins are not, like other men, easy to question; cunning and finesse obtain no advantage over these doubtful natives. The most skilful Old Bailey practitioner would get nothing out of them, but confess himself vanquished, after making an Indian undergo the closest cross-examination. If one of these shades of character were unknown to the hunter; hence he was careful not to let the girl suppose that he took any interest in her explanation.

With a nod of the head, Bright-eye soon gave Ivon the order to go to sleep again, which he did immediately. The girl was sitting by the fire, warming herself mechanically, while every now and then taking a side glance at the hunter. But the latter had lit his pipe, and, nearly concealed by the dense cloud of smoke that surrounded him, appeared completely absorbed in his agreeable occupation. The two remained thus face to face nearly half an hour, and did not exchange a word; at length Bright-eye shook out the ash on his left thumbnail, put his pipe in his belt, and rose. Prairie-Flower followed his every movement, without appearing to attach any importance to it; she saw him collect furs, carry them to a dark corner of the lodge, where he spread them so as to form a species of bed; then, when he fancied it was soft enough, he threw a coverlid over it, and returned to the fire.

"My Pale brother has prepared a bed," Prairie-Flower said, laying her hand on his arm, just as he was about to draw out his pipe again.

"Yes," he replied.

"Why four beds for three persons?"

Bright-eye looked at her with a perfectly natural amazement.

"Are we not four?" he said.

"I only see the two Pale hunters and my brother—for whom is the last bed?"

"For my sister, Prairie-Flower, I suppose; has she not come to ask hospitality of her Pale brothers?"

The girl shook her head.

"The women of my tribe," she said, with an accent of wounded pride, "have their cabins for sleeping, and do not pass the night in the lodges of the warriors."

Bright-eye bowed respectfully.

"I am mistaken," he said; "I did not wish to vex my sister; but on seeing her enter my lodge so late, I supposed she came to ask hospitality."

The girl smiled with finesse.

"My brother is a great warrior of the Palefaces," she said; "his head is grey; he is very cunning; why does he pretend not to know the reason that brings Prairie-Flower to his lodge?"

"Because I am really ignorant of it," he replied; "how should I know it?"

The Indian girl turned towards the place where the young man was sleeping, and said, with a charming pout—

"Glass-eye knows all: he would have told my brother the hunter."

"I cannot deny," the hunter said, boldly, "that Glass-eye knows many things, but in this matter he has been dumb."

"Is that true?" she asked, quickly.

"Why should I deny it? Prairie-Flower is not an enemy to us."

"No, I am a friend: let my brother open his ears."

"Speak."

"Glass-eye is powerful."

"So it is said," the hunter replied, evasively, too honest to stoop to a lie.

"The elders of the tribe regard him as a genius superior to other men, arranging events as he pleases, and able, if he will, to change the course of the future."

"Who says so?"

"Everybody."

The hunter shook his head, and pressing the girl's dainty hands in his own, he said, simply—

"You are deceived, child; Glass-eye is only a man like the others; the power you have been told of does not exist: I know not for what reason the chiefs of your nation have spread this absurd report; but it is a falsehood, which I must not allow to go further."

"No, White Buffalo is the wisest sachem of the Blackfeet; he possesses all the knowledge of his fathers on the other side of the Great Saltlake, he cannot err. Did he not announce, long ago, Glass-eye's arrival among us?"

"That is possible; although I cannot guess how he knew it, as only three days ago we were quite ignorant that we were coming to this village."

The maiden smiled triumphantly.

"White Buffalo knows all," she said; "besides, for many thousand moons the sorcerers of the nation have announced the coming of a man exactly like Glass-eye: his apparition was so truly predicted, that his arrival surprised nobody, as all expected him."

The hunter recognized the inutility of contending any longer against a conviction so deeply rooted in the young girl's heart.

"Good," he replied; "White Buffalo is a very wise sachem. What is there he does not know?"

"Nothing! Did he not predict that Glass-eye would place himself at the head of the Redskin warriors, and deliver them from the Palefaces of the East?"

"It is true," the hunter said, though he did not know a word of what the girl was revealing to him; but he now began to suspect a vast plot formed by the Indians, and he naturally desired to know more. Prairie-Flower looked at him with an expression of simple joy.

"My brother sees that I know all," she said.

"That is true," he answered; "my sister is better informed than I supposed; now she can explain to me, without fear, the service she desires from Glass-eye."

The girl took a long glance at the young man, who was still sleeping.

"Prairie-Flower is suffering," she said, in a low and trembling voice; "a cloud has passed over her mind and obscured it."

"Prairie-Flower is sixteen," the old hunter answered, with a smile; "a new feeling is awakened in her; a little bird is singing in her heart; she listens unconsciously to the harmonious notes of those strains which she does not yet understand."

"It is true," the maiden murmured, suddenly growing pensive; "my heart is sad. Is, then, love a suffering?"

"Child," the hunter answered, with a melancholy accent, "creatures are thus made by the Master of Life. All sensation is suffering. Joy, carried to an excess, becomes pain; you love without knowing it; loving is suffering."

"No," she said, with a gesture of terror, "no, I do not love, at least not; in the way you say. I have come, on the contrary, to seek your protection from a man who loves me, whose love frightens me, and for whom I shall never feel aught but gratitude."

"You are quite certain, poor child, that such is the feeling you experience for that man?"

She bowed assent. Without saying anything further, Bright-eye rose.

"Where are you going?" she asked, quickly.

The hunter turned to her.

"In all that you have told me, child," he answered, "there are things so important, that I must without delay arouse my friend, that he may listen to you in his turn, and, if it be possible, come to your aid."

"Do so," she said, mournfully, and let her head sink on her breast. The hunter went up to the young man, and bending over him, touched him gently on the shoulder. The Count awoke at once.

"What is it? What do you want?" he said, rising and seizing his weapons, with the promptness that a man constantly exposed to danger so soon acquires.

"Nothing that need frighten you, Mr. Edward. That young girl wishes to speak to you."

The Count followed the direction in which the hunter pointed, and his glance met that of the maiden. It was like an electric shock; she tottered, laid her hand on her heart, and blushed. The Frenchman rushed toward her.

"What is the matter? What can I do to help you?" he asked.

Just as she was about to reply, the curtain was lifted; a man bounded suddenly over Ivon, and reached the centre of the hut. It was the spy; the Breton suddenly aroused, flung himself on him, but the Indian held him back with a firm hand.

"Look out!" he said.

"Red Wolf!" the girl exclaimed, joyfully, as she stepped before him; "lower your weapons, it is a friend."

"Speak!" the Count said, as he returned the pistol to his belt.

The Indian had made no attempt to defend himself; he awaited stoically the moment to explain himself.

"Natah Otann is coming," he said to the maiden.

"Oh! I am lost if he find me here."

"What do I care for the fellow?" the Count said, haughtily.

"Prudence," Bright-eye interposed; "are you a friend, Redskin?"

"Ask Prairie-Flower," he answered, disdainfully.

"Good; then you have come to save her?"

"Yes."

"You have a way?"

"I have."

"I don't understand anything about it," Ivon said to himself, aside, quite confounded by all he saw; "what a night!"

"Make haste!" said the Count.

"Neither Prairie-Flower nor myself must be seen here," the Red Wolf continued; "Natah Otann is my enemy; there is deadly war between us. Throw all those furs on the girl."

Prairie-Flower, crouching in a corner, soon disappeared beneath the skins piled over her.

"Hum! it is a good idea," Bright-eye muttered: "and what are you going to do?"

"Look!"

Red Wolf leaned against the buffalo hides that acted as door, and concealed himself amid their folds. Hardly had all this been done, ere Natah Otann appeared on the threshold.

"What! up already?" he said, in surprise, turning a suspicious glance around him.

Red Wolf profited by this movement to go out unseen by the Chief.

"I am come to receive your orders for the hunt," Natah Otann resumed.

CHAPTER XVII
FORT MACKENZIE

Fort Mackenzie, built in 1832 by Major Mitchell, Chief Agent to the North American Fur Company, stands like a menacing sentry, about one hundred and twenty paces from the north bank of the Missouri, and seventy miles from the Rocky Mountains, in the midst of a level plain, protected by a chain of hills running from north to south. The fort is built on the system of all the outposts of civilization in the western provinces; it forms a perfect square, each side being about forty-five feet in length: a ditch, eight fathoms in depth and about the same in width; two substantial blockhouses; and twenty guns—such are the defensive elements of this fortress. The buildings contained in the enceinte are low, with narrow windows, in which parchment is substituted for glass. The roofs are flat, and covered with turf. The gateways of the fort are solid, and lined with iron. In the middle of a small square, in the centre of the fort, rises a mast, from which floats the star-spangled banner of the United States, while two guns are stationed at the foot of the mast. The plain surrounding Fort Mackenzie is covered with grass, rarely more than three feet high. This plain is almost constantly invaded by Indian tribes, that come to traffic with the Americans, especially the Blackfeet, Assiniboins, Mandans, Flatheads, Gros-ventres, Crows, and Koutnikés.

The Indians displayed a repugnance in allowing the white men to settle in their domains, and the first agent the Fur Company sent to them had a narrow escape with life. It was only by dint of patience and cunning that they succeeded in concluding with the tribes a treaty of peace and barter, which the latter were disposed, indeed, to break, through the slightest pretext. Thus the Americans were always on the watch, considering themselves in a perpetual state of siege. It still happened at times, in spite of the Indians' protestations of amity, that some *engagé* or trapper of the Company was brought to the fort scalped and murdered, and they were obliged, through policy, to refrain from taking vengeance for such murders, which, however, were becoming rare. The Indians, with their greedy instincts, at length understood that it was better to live in good intelligence with the Palefaces, who supplied them with abundant provisions, spirits, and money, in exchange for their furs.

In 1834, Fort Mackenzie was commanded by Major Melville, a man of great experience, who had spent nearly his whole life among the Indians, either fighting or trafficking with them, so that he was thoroughly versed in all their habits and tricks. General Jackson, in whose army he had served, put great reliance in his courage, skill, and experience. Major Melville combined with uncommon moral energy rare physical strength; he was the very man to keep in check the fierce tribes with which he had to deal, and to command the trappers and hunters in the Company's service, thorough ruffians, only understanding the logic of the rifle and the bowie knife; he based his authority on inflexible severity and an irreproachable justice, which had contributed greatly to maintain the good relations between the inhabitants of the fort and their crafty friends. Peace, with the exception of the mutual distrust that was its basis, appeared for some few years past to be solidly established between the Palefaces and the Redskins. The Indians camped annually before the fort, and generally exchanged their peltry for spirits, clothes, gunpowder, &c. The seventy men who formed the garrison had gradually relaxed their usual precautions, for they felt so confident of having induced the Indians to renounce their plundering inclinations by kind treatment and concessions. Such was the respective positions of the whites and the Redskins on the day when the exigencies of our story take us to Fort Mackenzie.

The scenery round the fort is exquisite and charmingly varied. On the day after that in which the events we have described took place in the Kenha village, a leather canoe, manned by only one rower, descended the Elk river, in the direction of the American fort. After following the numerous bends of the stream, the canoe at length entered the Missouri, and coasted the northern bank, studded with magnificent prairies at least thirty miles in depth, on which countless herds of buffaloes, antelopes, and bighorns were grazing, which, with ears erect and startled eyes, watched the silent boat pass with gloomy dissatisfaction. But the person, man or woman, in the boat seemed too anxious to reach the destination, to waste any time in firing at these animals, which it would have been easy to do.

With his eyes imperturbably fixed ahead, and bowed over the paddles, the rower redoubled his energy the nearer he approached the fort, uttering at times hoarse exclamations of anger and impatience, though never checking the speed of the boat. At length an "ah!" of satisfaction escaped his lips on turning one of the numberless bends of the river: a magnificent scene was suddenly displayed before him.

Gentle slopes, with varied summits, some rounded, others flat, of a pleasant green colour, occupied the centre of the picture. In the foreground were tall forests of poplars of a vivid green, and willow trees on the banks of the river, which meandered through a prairie to which the twilight had given a deep olive hue. A little further on, on the top of a grassy mound, stood Fort Mackenzie, where the handsome flag of the United States floated in the breeze, gilded by the parting beams of the setting sun; while on one side an Indian camp, on the other, herds of horses, tranquilly grazing, animated the majestic tranquillity of the scene.

The canoe drew nearer and nearer to the bank, and at last, when arrived under the protection of the guns, was run gently ashore. The individual occupying it then leaped on the sand, and it was easy to see that it was a woman. It was the mysterious being to whom the Indians gave the name of the She-wolf of the Prairies, and who has already appeared twice in this story. She had altered her dress. Although still resembling that of the Indians in texture, as it was composed of elk and buffalo skins sown together, it varied from it in shape; and if, at the first glance, it was difficult to recognize the sex of the person wearing it, it was easy to perceive that it was a white, through the simplicity, cleanliness, and, above all, the amplitude of the folds carefully draped round the strange being hidden in these garments.

After leaving the canoe, the She-wolf fastened it securely to a large stone, and without paying further attention to it, walked hastily in the direction of the fort. It was about six in the evening; the barter with the Indians was over, and they were returning, laughing and singing, to their tents of buffalo hide; while the *engagés*, after collecting the horses, led them back slowly to the fort. The sun was setting behind the snowy peaks of the Rocky Mountains, casting a purple gleam, over the heavens. Gradually, as the planet of day sank in the distant horizon, gloom took possession of the earth. The songs of the Indians, the shouts of the *engagés*, the neighing of the horses, and the barking of the dogs, formed one of those singular concerts which in these remote regions impress on the mind a feeling of melancholy reflection. The She-wolf reached the gate of the fort at the moment when the last *engagé* had entered, after driving in the laggards of his troop.

At these frontier posts, where momentary vigilance is necessary to foil the treachery constantly lurking in the shadows, sentinels especially appointed to survey the gloomy and solitary prairies, that stretch out for miles around their garrisons, stand watching day and night with their eyes fixed on space, ready to signalize the least unusual movement, either on the part of animals or of men, in the vast solitudes they survey. The She-wolf's canoe had been detected more than six hours before, all its movements carefully watched, and when the She-wolf, after fastening her boat up, presented herself at the gate of the fort, she found it closed and carefully bolted; not because she personally caused the garrison any alarm, but because the order was that no one should enter the fort after sunset, except for overpowering reasons.

The She-wolf repressed with difficulty a gesture of annoyance at finding herself thus exposed to spend the night in the open air; not that she feared the hardship, but because she knew the importance of her news, and desired no delay. She did not allow herself to be defeated, however, but stooped, picked up a stone, and struck the gate twice. A wicket immediately opened, and two eyes glistened through the opening it left.

"Who's there?" a rough voice asked.

"A friend," the She-wolf replied.

"Hum; that's very vague at this hour of the night," the voice continued, with a grin that augured ill for the success of the mediation the She-wolf had commenced.

"Who are you?"

"A woman, and a white woman too, as you can see by my dress and accent."

"It may be, but the night is dark, and it is impossible for me to see you: so if you have no better reasons to give, good night, and go your ways; tomorrow we will meet again at sunrise."

And the speaker prepared to close the wicket, but the She-wolf checked him with a firm hand.

"One moment," she said.

"What's up now?" the other remarked, ill-temperedly; "I cannot pass the night in listening to you."

"I only want to ask you one question, and one favour."

"Plague take it!" the man went on; "well, you are going on at a fine rate; that's nothing, eh? Well; let me hear it; that binds me to nothing."

"Is Major Melville in the fort at this moment?"

"Perhaps."

"Answer, yes or no."

"Well, yes; what then?"

The She-wolf gave a sigh of satisfaction, hurriedly drew a ring from her right hand, and passing it through the wicket to the unknown speaker, said —

"Carry that ring to the Major; I will wait for your answer here."

"Mind what you are about; the Commandant does not like to be disturbed for nothing."

"Do as I tell you. I answer for the rest."

"That's a poor bail," the other growled; "but no matter—I'll risk it. Wait."

The wicket closed. The She-wolf seated herself on the side of the moat, and with elbows resting on her knees, buried her head in her hands. By this time night had completely set in; in the distance, the fires lighted up by the Indians on the prairies shone like lighthouses through the gloom; the evening breeze soughed hoarsely through the tops of the trees, and the howls of the wild beasts were mingled at intervals with the strident laughter of the Indians. Not a star sparkled in the sky, which was black as ink; nature seemed covered with a cerecloth; all presaged an approaching storm. The She-wolf waited, motionless, as one of those patient sphynxes which have watched for thousands of years at the entrance of the Egyptian temples. A quarter of an hour elapsed, then a sound of bolts was heard, and the gates of the fort slightly opened. The She-wolf sprung up, as if moved by a spring.

"Come!" a voice said.

She entered, and the door was immediately closed after her. An *engagé*—the same who had spoken to her through the wicket—stood before her with a torch in his hand.

"Follow me," he said to her.

She walked after her guide, who crossed the entire length of the courtyard, and then turning to the She-wolf, said—

"The Major is waiting for you here."

"Rap," she said.

"No, do so yourself; you no longer need me; I will return to my post."

And, after bowing slightly, he withdrew carrying the torch with him. The She-wolf remained alone in the darkness; she passed her hand over her damp forehead, and making a supreme effort—

"I must," she muttered, hoarsely.

She then struck the door.

"Come in," a voice said from within.

She turned the key, pushed open the door, and found herself in the presence of an elderly man, dressed in uniform, and seated near a table, who gazed fixedly at her. This man, by the position he occupied, and the way in which the light was arranged, could see her perfectly; while, on the other hand, the She-wolf could not distinguish his features, hidden as they were by the gloom. The She-wolf walked resolutely into the room.

"Thanks for having received me," she said; "I was afraid you had utterly forgotten."

"If that is meant for a reproach, I do not understand you," the officer said, sternly; "and I should feel obliged by a clear explanation."

"Are you not Major Melville?"

"I am."

"The way in which I entered the fort proves to me that you recognised the ring I sent you."

"I recognized it; for it reminds me of a very dear person," he said, with a suppressed sigh; "but how is it in your hands?"

The She-wolf regarded the Major sadly for a moment, then walked up to him, gently took his hand, which she pressed in hers, and replied, with an accent full of tears—

"Harry, I must be changed by suffering, if you do not even recognise my voice."

At these words a livid pallor covered the officer's face; he rose with a movement quick as lightning; his body was agitated by a convulsive tremor, and seizing, in his turn, the woman's hands, he exclaimed madly—

"Margaret! Margaret! my sister! Have the dead come from the tomb? Do I find you again at last:"

"Ah!" she said, with an expression of joy impossible to render, as she sank in his arms, "I was certain he would recognise me."

But the shock she had received was too strong for the poor woman, whose organization was worn out by sorrow; accustomed to suffering, she could not endure joy, and fell fainting into her brother's arms. The Major carried her to a species of sofa that occupied one side of the room, and, without calling anyone to his aid, paid her all that attention her case required. The She-wolf remained for a long time insensible; but she gradually came to herself again, opened her eyes, and, after muttering a few incoherent words, burst into tears. Her brother did not leave her for a moment, following, with an anxious glance, the progress of her return to life. When he perceived that the height of the crisis was past, he took chair, sat down by his sister's side, and by gentle words sought to restore her courage. At length, the poor woman raised her head, dried her eyes—reddened by tears, and hollowed by fever—and turning to her brother, who watched her every movement, said in a hoarse voice—

"Brother, for sixteen years I have been suffering an atrocious martyrdom, which never ceased for an instant."

The Major shuddered at this fearful revelation.

"Poor sister!" he muttered. "What can I do for you?"

"All, if you will."

"Oh!" he exclaimed, with energy, as he struck the woodwork of the sofa with his fist, "could you doubt me, Margaret?"

"No, since I have come," she answered, smiling through her tears.

"You will avenge yourself, I think?" he went on.

"I will."

"Who are your enemies?"

"The Redskins."

"Ah! ah!" he said, with a bitter smile; "I, too, have an old account to settle with those demons. To what nation do your enemies belong?"

"To the Blackfeet. They are the Kenha tribe."

"Oh," the Major continued, "my old friends, the Blood Indians; I have long been seeking a pretext to give them an exemplary punishment."

"That pretext I now bring you, Harry," she answered, passionately; "and do not fancy it a vain pretext invented by hatred. No, no! 'tis the revelation of a plot formed by all the Missouri Indians against the whites, which must break out within a few days, perhaps tomorrow."

"Ah!" the Major observed, thoughtfully, "I do not know why, but, for the last few days, suspicions have invaded, my mind; my presentiments did not deceive me, then. Speak, sister, at once, I conjure you; and since you have come to me, in order to appease your hatred of these red devils, I promise you a vengeance, the memory of which will make their grandsons shudder."

"I thank you for your promise, brother, and will not forget it," she answered. "Listen to me, then."

"One word first."

"Speak, brother."

"Has the narrative of your sufferings any connexion with the conspiracy you are about to reveal to me?"

"An intimate one."

"Well, it is scarce ten o'clock, we have the night before us; tell me all that has happened to you since our separation."

"You wish it?"

"Yes, for it will be by your narrative that I shall regulate my treatment of the Indians."

"Listen, then, brother, and be indulgent to me, for I have suffered bitterly, as you are about to hear."

The Major pressed her hand; he took a chair, sat by her side, and after bolting the door, to prevent any interruption of the story, he said—

"Speak, Margaret, and tell me everything; I do not wish to be ignorant of any of the tortures you have endured during the long years that have elapsed since our parting."

CHAPTER XVIII
A MOTHER'S CONFESSION

"It is just seventeen years ago, you will remember, Harry; you had recently received your commission as lieutenant in the army; you were young, enthusiastic; the future appeared to you to be drawn in the brightest colours. One evening, during weather like the present, you came to my husband's clearing, to tell us the news, and bid us an affectionate farewell; for you hoped, like ourselves, not to be long away from us. The next morning, in spite of our entreaties, after embracing the children, pressing the hand of my poor husband, who loved you so, and giving me a parting kiss, you galloped off, and soon disappeared in a whirlwind of dust. Alas! who could have foretold that we should not meet again till today, after seventeen years' separation, upon Indian territory, and under terrible circumstances? However," she added, with a sigh, "God has willed it so, may His holy name be blessed! It has pleased Him to try His creatures, and let His hand fall heavily on them."

"It was with a strange contraction of the heart," the Major said, "that six months after that parting, when I returned among you with a joyous heart, I saw, on dismounting in front of your house, a stranger open your door, and answer, that the white family had emigrated three months before, and proceeded in a western direction, with the intention of founding a new settlement on the Indian frontier. It was in vain that I tried to gain any information about you from your neighbours; they had forgotten you; no one could or would, perhaps, give me the slightest news about you, and I was forced to retrace, heartbroken, the road I had ridden along so joyfully a few days before. Since then, despite all the efforts I have made, I never was able to learn anything about your fate, or lift the mysterious veil that covered the sinister events to which I was convinced you had fallen victims during your journey."

"You are only half deceived, my brother, in your supposition," she went on. "Two months after your visit, my husband, who had long desired to leave our clearing, where he said the land was worth nothing, had a grave dispute with one of his neighbours about the limits of a field of which he believed, or pretended to believe, that neighbour had cut off a corner: under any other circumstances, the difference would have been easily settled, but my husband sought an excuse to go away, and having found it, did not let it slip again. He would listen to nothing, but quietly made all his arrangements for the expedition he had so long meditated, and at length told us one day that he should start the next. When my husband had once said a thing, all I could do was to obey, for he never recalled a determination he had formed. On the appointed day at sunrise, we left the clearing, our neighbours accompanying us for the first day's journey, and at nightfall left us, after hearty wishes for the success of our expedition. It was with inexpressible sorrow I quitted the house where I was married, where my children were born, and where I had been happy for so many years. My husband tried in vain to console me, and restore me that courage which failed me; but nothing could efface from my mind the gentle and pious recollections I previously kept up: the deeper we buried ourselves in the desert, the greater my sorrow became. My husband, on the other hand saw everything in a bright light; the future belonged to him; he was about to be his own master, and act as he thought proper. He detailed to me all his plans, tried to interest me in them, and employed all the means in his power to draw me from my gloomy thoughts, but could not succeed. Still we went onwards without stopping. The distance became daily greater between ourselves and the last settlements of our countrymen. In vain did I show my husband how remote we were from all help in case of danger, and the isolation in which we should find ourselves; he only laughed at my apprehensions; repeated incessantly that the Indians were far from being so dangerous as they were represented, and that we had nothing to fear. My husband was so convinced of the truth of his assertions, that he neglected the most simple precautions to defend himself against a surprise, and said each morning, with a mocking air, at the moment of starting, 'You see how foolish you are, Margaret; be reasonable, the Indians will be careful not to insult us,' One night the camp was attacked by the Redskins, we were surprised during our sleep; my husband was flayed alive, while his children were burned at a slow fire before his face."

While uttering these words, the poor woman's voice became more and more choked. At the last sentences, her emotion grew so profound, that she could not continue.

"Courage!" the Major said, as much moved as herself, but more master of his feelings.

She made an effort, and continued in a harsh, unmodulated voice,—

"By a refinement of cruelty, the barbarism of which I did not at first understand, my youngest child, my daughter, was spared by the Pagans. On seeing the punishment of my husband and children, at which I was forced to be present, I felt such a laceration of the heart, that I imagined I was dying.

I uttered a shriek, and fell down. How long I remained in that state, I know not: but when I regained my senses, I was alone. The Indians, doubtlessly, fancied me dead, and left me where I lay. I rose, and not conscious of what I was doing, but impelled by a force superior to my will, I returned, tottering and falling almost at every step, to the spot where this mournful tragedy had been enacted. It took me three hours—how was I so far from the camp?—at length I arrived, and a fearful sight presented itself to my horror-struck eyes. I looked unconscious upon the disfigured and half carbonized bodies of my children—my despair, however, restored my failing strength. I dug a grave, and, half delirious with grief, buried in it husband and children, all that I loved on earth. This pious duty accomplished, I resolved to die at the spot where the beings so dear to me had perished. But there are hours during the long nights in which the shades of the dead address the living, and order them to take vengeance! That terrific voice from the tomb I heard on a sinister night, when the elements threatened to overthrow nature. From that moment my resolution was formed. I consented to live for revenge. From that hour I have walked firm and implacable on the path I traced, requiting the Pagans, on every opportunity that presents itself, for the evil they had done me. I have become the terror of the prairies. The Indians fear me as an evil genius. They have a superstitious invincible dread of me; in short, they have surnamed me the Lying She-wolf of the Prairies; for each time a catastrophe menaces them, or a frightful danger is hanging over their heads, they see me appear. For seventeen years I have been nursing my revenge, without ever growing discouraged, certain that the day will come when, in my turn, I shall plant my knee on the heart of my enemies, and inflict on them the atrocious torture they condemned me to suffer."

The woman's face, while uttering these words, had assumed such an expression of cruelty, that the Major brave as he was, felt himself shudder.

"And your enemies," he said, after a moment's delay, "do you know them, have you learned their names?"

"I know them all!" she said, in a piercing voice; "I have learned all their names!"

"And they are preparing to break the peace?" Mrs. Margaret smiled ironically.

"No, they will not break the peace, brother, but attack you suddenly. They have formed among themselves a formidable league, which—at least they fancy so—you will find it impossible to resist."

"Sister!" the Major exclaimed energetically, "give me the name of these wretched traitors, and I swear that, even were they concealed in the depths of Hades, I will seek them, to inflict an exemplary chastisement."

"I cannot give you these names yet, brother; but be at ease, you shall soon know them; you will not have to seek them far, for I will lead them under the guns of your soldiers and hunters."

"Take care, Margaret," the Major said, shaking his head, "hatred is a bad counsellor in an affair like this; he who grasps at too much, frequently risks the loss of all."

"Oh," she replied, "my precautions have been taken for a long time: I hold them, I can seize them whenever I please, or, to speak more correctly, when the moment has arrived."

"Do as you think proper, sister, and reckon on my devoted aid: this vengeance affects me too closely for me to allow it to escape."

"Thanks," she said.

"Pardon me," he continued, after a few minutes' reflection, "if I revert to the sad events you have just narrated; but you have, it strikes me, forgotten an important detail in your story."

"I do not understand you, Harry."

"I will explain: you said, I think, if my memory serves me, that your youngest daughter escaped from the frightful fate of her brothers, and was saved by an Indian."

"Yes, I did say so, brother," she replied in an oppressed voice.

"Well, what has become of the unhappy child? Does she still live? Have you any news of her? Have you seen her again?"

"She lives, and I have seen her."

"Ah!"

"Yes; the man who saved her educated her, even adopted her," she said, sarcastically. "Do you know what this wretch would do with the daughter of the man he murdered, whom he flayed alive before my eyes?"

"Speak; in Heaven's name!

"What I have to say is very dreadful! it is so frightful, indeed, that I hesitate to reveal it to you."

"Good God!" the Major ejaculated, recoiling involuntarily before his sister's flaming glance.

"Well," she continued, with a strident laugh, "this girl has grown up, the child has become a woman, as lovely as it is possible to be. This man, this monster, this demon, has felt his tiger heart soften at the sight of the angel; he loves her to distraction, he wishes to make her his wife."

"Horror!" the Major exclaimed.

"Is that not truly hideous?" she continued, still with that nervous, spasmodic laugh which it pains one to hear: "he has pardoned his victim's daughter. Yes, he is generous, he forgets the atrocious torture he inflicted on the father, and now covets the daughter."

"Oh, that is frightful, Margaret; so much infamy and cynicism is impossible, even among Indians!"

"Do you believe, then, that I am deceiving you?"

"Far from me be such a thought, sister; the man is a monster."

"Yes, yes, so he is."

"You have seen your daughter; you have talked with her?"

"Yes; well, what then?"

"You have, doubtless, turned her from this monstrous love?"

"I!" she replied, with a grin, "I did not say a word to her about it."

"What!" he said, in amazement.

"By what right could I have spoken?"

"How, by what right—Are you not her mother?"

"She does not know it!"

"Oh!"

"And my vengeance?" she said, coldly. This word which so thoroughly explained the character of the woman, had before struck the heart of the old soldier with terror.

"Unhappy woman!" he exclaimed.

A smile of disdain curled the She-wolf's lip.

"Yes, so you are," she said, with a bitter voice, "you men of cities, with natures worn out by civilization. To understand a passion, it must be kept within certain limits, traced beforehand. The grandeur of hatred, with all its fury and excesses, terrifies you; you only admit that legal and halting vengeance which the criminal code sanctions. Brother, he who wishes the end, wishes the means. To arrive at my object, what do I care, do you think, whether I walk over ruins or wade through blood? No, I go straight before me, with the fatal impetuosity of the torrent which breaks down and overthrows all the obstacles which rise in its passage. My object is vengeance! blood for blood, eye for eye; that is the law of the prairies. I have made it mine, and I will obtain that vengeance, if for it I—. But," she added, suddenly breaking off, "what need of this useless discussion between us, brother? Reassure yourself my daughter has been better warned by her instincts than all the advice I could have given her. She does not love this man. I know it, she told me so; she will never love him."

"Heaven be praised!" the Major exclaimed.

"I have only one desire; only one," she continued with a melancholy air; "it is after the accomplishment of my vengeance, to recover my daughter, press her to my heart, and cover her with kisses, while at length revealing to her that I am her mother."

The Major shook his head sorrowfully.

"Take care, sister," he said, in a stern voice; "God has said, 'Vengeance is mine!' take care, lest, after wishing to assume the office of Providence, you may be cruelly chastised by it in some of your dearest affections."

"Oh, say not so, Harry!" she exclaimed with a sign of terror; "you would turn me mad."

The Major let his head sink on hid breast. For a while brother and sister remained opposite each other, not uttering a word; they were both reflecting. The She-wolf was the first to renew the conversation.

"Now, brother," she said, "if you will permit me, we will leave this mournful subject for a moment, and allude to what concerns you more particularly, that is, the formidable conspiracy formed against you by the Indians."

"On my word," he replied, with a sigh of relief, "I confess, sister, that I ask nothing better; my head is confused, and I believe that if this went on much longer, I should be unable to re-collect my thoughts, so much am I affected by what you have told me."

"Thanks,"

"Night is drawing on, Margaret; indeed, it has almost entirely slipped away, we have not a moment to lose, so pray continue."

"Is the garrison complete?"

"Yes."

"How many men have you?"

"Seventy, without counting some fifteen hunters and trappers occupied without, but whom I will recall without delay."

"Very good: do you require the whole of the garrison for the defence of the fort?"

"That is according. Why?"

"Because I want to borrow twenty men of you."

"Hum I for what object?"

"You shall learn; you are alone here, without any hopes of help, and for this reason: while the Indians are burning the fort, they will intercept your communication with Fort Clarke, Fort Union, and the other posts scattered along the Missouri."

"I fear it, but what can I do?"

"I will tell you; you have doubtless heard of an American squatter, who settled hardly a week back about three or four leagues from you?"

"I have; a certain John Black, I think."

"That is the man; well, his clearing will naturally serve you as an advanced post?"

"Famously."

"Profit by the short time left you; under pretence of a buffalo hunt, send twenty men from the fort, and conceal them at John Black's, so that when the moment for action arrives, they may make a demonstration in your favour, which will place the enemies between two fires, and make them suppose that reinforcements have reached you from other posts."

"That is a good idea," the Major said. "You must choose men on whom you can count."

"They are all devoted to me; you shall see them at work."

"All the better; then that is settled!"

"It is."

"Now, as it is urgent that no one should know of our relations, as it might compromise the success of our scheme, I must ask you to open the gates of the fort for me.

"What, so soon, in this frightful weather?"

"I must, brother, it is of the utmost importance that I should start at once."

"You insist."

"I beg it of you, Harry, for our common benefit."

"Come, then, sister, I will detain you no longer."

Two minutes later, in spite of the storm which still howled with the same fury, the She-wolf was rowing from Fort Mackenzie at full speed.

CHAPTER XIX
THE CHASE

When Natah Otann entered the lodge inhabited by the white men, under pretext of warning them to prepare for the chase, his searching eye in a few seconds had explored every corner of the building. The Indian Chief was too clever to omit noticing the Count's constraint and embarrassment: but he understood that it would be impolitic to show the suspicions he had conceived. Hence he did not in the slightest degree affect to notice the annoyance caused by his presence, and continued the conversation with that politeness the Redskins can display when they choose to take the trouble. On their side the Count and Bright-eye at once regained their coolness.

"I did not hope to find my White brother already risen," Natah Otann said with a smile.

"Why not?" the young man replied; "a desert life accustoms one to little sleep."

"Then the Palefaces will go and hunt with their red friends?"

"Certainly, if you have no objection."

"Did I not myself propose to Glass-eye to procure them a true chase?"

"That is true," the young man said, with a laugh; "but take care, Chief, I have become uncommonly fastidious since I have been in the prairie; there is hardly any game I have not hunted, as it was the love of sport alone that brought me into these unknown countries; hence, I repeat, I shall expect choice game."

Natah Otann smiled proudly.

"My brother will be satisfied," he said.

"And what is the animal we are about to follow?" the young man asked.

"The ostrich."

The Count made a sign of amazement.

"What, the ostrich?" he exclaimed, "that is impossible, Chief—"

"Because?"

"Oh, simply because there are none."

"The ostrich, it is true, is disappearing; it fled before the white men, and becomes daily rare, but it is still numerous on the prairies; in a few hours my brother will have a proof of it."

"I desire nothing better."

"Good, that is settled: I will soon come and fetch my brother."

The Chief bowed courteously and retired, after taking a parting look around. The curtain had scarcely fallen behind the Chief ere the pile of furs that covered the young girl was thrown off, and Prairie-Flower ran up to the Count.

"Listen," she said to him, seizing his hand, which she pressed tenderly, "I cannot explain to you now, for time fails me; still, remember, you have a friend who watches over you."

And before the Count could reply, or even think of replying, she fled with the bound of an antelope. He passed his hand several times over his brow, his eye being fixed on the place where the Indian girl had disappeared.

"Ah!" he at length murmured, "have I at last met with a true woman?"

"She is an angel," the hunter said, replying to his thought. "Poor child! she has suffered greatly."

"Yes; but I am here now, and will protect her!" the Count exclaimed, with exaltation.

"Let us think of ourselves first, Mr. Edward, and try to get away from here with whole skins; it will not be an easy task, I assure you."

"What do you mean, my friend?"

"It is enough that I understand it all," the hunter said, shaking his head; "let us only think now of our preparations: our friends, the Redskins, will soon arrive," he added, with that derisive smile which caused the Count to feel increased embarrassment.

But the impression caused by the Canadian's ambiguous language was promptly dissipated, for love had suddenly nestled in this young, man's heart; he only dreamed of one thing, of seeing the woman again whom he adored with all his strength.

In a man like the Count, who was gifted with a fiery organization, every feeling must necessarily be carried to an excess; and it was the case in the present instance. Love is born by a word, a sign, a look, and scarcely born, suddenly becomes a giant. The Count was fated to learn this at his own expense.

Scarcely half an hour after Natah Otann's departure, the gallop of several horses was heard, and a troop of horsemen stopped in front of the cabin. The three men went out, and found Natah Otann awaiting them at the head of sixty warriors, all dressed in their grand costume, and armed to the teeth.

"Let us go," he said.

"Whenever you please," the Count answered.

The Chief made a signal, and three magnificent horses, superbly caparisoned in the Indian fashion, were led up by children. The whites mounted, and the band set out in the direction of the prairie.

It was about six in the morning, the night storm had completely swept the sky, which was of a pale blue; the sun, fully risen in the horizon, shot forth its warm beams, which drew out the sharp and odoriferous vapours from the ground, The atmosphere was wondrously transparent, a slight breeze refreshed the air, and flocks of birds, lustrous with a thousand hues, flew around, uttering joyous cries. The troop marched gaily through the tall prairie grass, raising a cloud of dust, and undulating like a long serpent in the endless turnings of the road.

The spot where the chase was to come off was nearly thirty miles distant from the village. In the desert all places are alike, tall grass, in the midst of which the horsemen entirely disappear; stunted shrubs, and here and there clumps of trees, whose imposing crowns rise to an enormous height;—such was the road the Indians had to follow up to the spot where they would find the animals they proposed chasing.

In the prairies of Arkansas and the Upper Missouri, at the time of our story, ostriches were still numerous, and their chase one of the numerous amusements of the Redskins and wood rangers. It is probable that the successive invasions of the white men, and the immense clearings effected by fire and the axe, have now compelled them to abandon this territory, and retire to the inaccessible desert of the Rocky Mountains, or the sands of the Far West.

We will say here, without any pretence at a scientific description, a few words about this singular animal, still but little known in Europe. The ostrich generally lives in small families of from eight to ten, scattered along the banks of marshes, pools, and streams. They live on fresh grass. Faithful to their native soil, they never quit the vicinity of the water, and in the month of November lay their eggs in the wildest part of the plain, fifty to sixty at a time, which are brooded, solely at night, by male and female in turn, with a touching tenderness. When the incubation is terminated, the ostrich breaks the barren eggs with its beak, which are at once covered with flies and insects, supplying nourishment to the young birds. The ostrich of the Western prairies differs slightly from the *Nandus* of the Patagonian prairies and the African species. It is about five feet high, and four and a half long, from the stomach to the end of the tail; its beak is very pointed, and measures a little over five inches.

A characteristic trait of the ostriches is their extreme curiosity. In the Indian villages, where they live in a tamed state, it is of frequent occurrence to see them stalking through groups of talkers, and regarding them with fixed attention. In the plain this curiosity is often fatal to them, for it leads them to look unhesitatingly at everything that seems strange or unusual to them. We will give a capital Indian story here in proof of this.

The jaguars are very fond of ostrich meat, but unfortunately, though their speed is so great, it is almost impossible for them to run the birds down; but the jaguars are cunning animals, and usually obtain by craft what they cannot manage by force. They, therefore, employ the following stratagem. They lie on the ground as if dead, and raise their tails in the air, where they wave them in every direction; the ostriches, attracted by this strange spectacle, approach with great simplicity—the rest may be guessed; they fall a prey to the cunning jaguars.

The hunters after a hurried march of three hours, reached a barren and sandy plain; during the journey, very few words were exchanged between Natah Otann and his white guests, for he rode at the head of the column, conversing in a low voice with White Buffalo. The Indians dismounted by the side of a stream, and exchanged their horses for racers, which the chief had sent to the spot during the night, and which were naturally rested and able to run for miles. Natah Otann divided the hunting party into two equal troops, keeping the command of the first himself, and courteously offering that of the second to the Count. As the Frenchman, however, had never been present at such a chase, and was quite ignorant how it was conducted, he courteously declined. Natah Otann reflected for a few moments, and then turned to Bright-eye:—

"My brother knows the ostriches?" he asked him. "Eh!" the Canadian replied, with a smile; "Natah Otann was not yet born when I hunted them on the prairie."

"Good," the chief said; "then my brother will command the second band?"

"Be it so," the hunter said, bowing: "I accept with pleasure."

On a given signal, the first band, under Natah Otann's command, advanced into the plain, describing a semicircle, so as to drive the game towards a ravine, situated between two moving downs. The second band, with which the Count and Ivon remained, was echelonned so as to form the other half of the circle. This circle, by the horsemen's advance, was gradually being contracted, when a dozen ostriches showed themselves; but the male bird, standing sentry, warned the family of the danger by a sharp cry like a boatswain's whistle. At once the ostriches fled in a straight line rapidly, and without looking back. All the hunters galloped off in pursuit.

The plain, till then silent and gloomy, grew animated, and offered the strangest appearance. The horsemen pursued the luckless animals at full speed, raising in their passage clouds of impalpable dust. Twelve to fifteen paces behind the game, the Indians, still galloping and burying their spurs in the flanks of their panting horses, bent forward, twisted their formidable clubs round their heads, and hurled them after the animals. If they missed their aim, they stooped down without checking their pace, and picked up the weapon, which they cast again.

Several flocks of ostriches had been put up, and the chase then assumed the proportions of a mad revel. Cries and hurrahs rent the air; the clubs hurtled through the space and struck the necks, wings, and legs of the ostriches, which, startled and mad with terror, made a thousand feints and zigzags to escape their implacable enemies, and buffeting their wings, tried to prick the horses with, the species of spike with which the end of their wings is armed. Several horses reared, and, embarrassed by the ostriches between their legs, fell with their riders. The ostriches, profiting by the disorder, fled on, and came within reach of the other hunters, who received them with a shower of clubs.

Each hunter leaped from his horse, killed the victim he had felled, cut off its wings as a sign of triumph, and renewed the chase with increased ardour. Ostriches and hunters rushed onwards like the *cordonazo*, that terrible wind of the Mexican deserts, and forty ostriches speedily encumbered the plain. Natah Otann looked round him, and then gave the signal for retreat; the birds which had not succumbed to this rude aggression, ran off to seek shelter. The dead birds were carefully collected, for the ostrich is, excellent eating, and the Indians prepare, chiefly from the meat on the breast, a dish renowned for its delicacy and exquisite savour. The warriors then proceeded to collect eggs, also highly esteemed, and secured an ample crop.

Although the chase had scarce lasted two hours, the horses panted and wanted rest before they could return to the village; hence Natah Otann gave orders to stop. The Count had never been present at so strange a hunt before, although ever since he had been on the prairie he had pursued the different animals that inhabit it; hence he entered into it with all the excitement of youth, rushing on the ostriches and felling them with childlike pleasure. When the signal for retreat was given by the Chief, he reluctantly left off the amusement, which at the moment caused him such delight, and returned slowly to his comrades. Suddenly a loud cry was raised by the Indians, and each ran to his weapons. The Count looked around him with surprise, and felt a slight tremor. The ostrich hunt was over; but, as frequently happens in these countries, a far more terrible one was about to begin—the chase of the cougar.[1]

Two of these animals had suddenly made their appearance. The Count recovered at once, and, cocking his rifle, prepared to follow this new species of game. Natah Otann had also noticed the wild beasts; he ordered a dozen warriors to surround Prairie-Flower, whom he had obliged to accompany him, or who had insisted on being present; then, certain that the girl was, temporarily at least, in safety, he turned to a warrior standing at his side.

"Uncouple the dogs," he said.

A dozen mastiffs were let loose, which howled in chorus on seeing the wild beasts. The Indians, accustomed to see the ostrich hunt disturbed in this way, never fail, when they go out for their favourite exercise, to take with them dogs trained to attack the lion. About two hundred yards from the spots where the Indians had halted, two cougars were now crouching, with their eyes fixed on the Redskin warriors. These animals, still young, were about the size of a calf; their heads bore a strong, likeness to a cat's, and their soft smooth hide of silvery yellow was dotted with black spots.

"After them!" Natah Otann shouted.

Horsemen and dogs rushed on the ferocious beasts with yells, cries, and barks, capable of terrifying lions unused to such a reception. The noble animals, motionless and amazed, lashed their flanks with their long tails, and drew in heavy draughts of air; for a moment they remained stationary, then suddenly bounded away. A party of hunters galloped in a straight line to intercept their retreat, while the others bent over their saddles, and guiding their horses with their knees, fired their arrows and rifles, without checking the cougars which turned furiously on the dogs, and hurled them ten yards from them, to howl with pain. Still the mastiffs, long habituated to this chase, watched for a favourable moment, leaped on the lions' backs, and dug their nails in their flesh; but the latter, with one stroke of their deadly claws, swept them off like flies, and continued their flight.

One of them, pierced by several arrows, and surrounded by the dogs, rolled on the ground, raising a cloud of dust under its claws, and uttering a fearful yell. This one the Canadian finished by putting a bullet through its eye, but the second lion remained still unwounded, and its leaps foiled the attack and skill of the hunters. The dogs, now wearied, did not dare assail it. Its flight had led it a few paces from the spot where Prairie-Flower stood: it suddenly turned at right angles, bounded among the Indians, two of whom it ripped up, and crouched before the young girl, ere making its leap. Prairie-Flower, pale as a corpse, clasped her hands instinctively, uttered a stifled cry, and fainted. New cries replied to hers, and at the moment the lion was about to leap on the maiden, two bullets were buried in its chest. It turned to face its new adversary; it was the Count de Beaulieu.

"Let no one stir!" he exclaimed, stopping by a sign Natah Otann and Bright-eye, who ran up, "this game is mine—no other than I shall kill it."

The Count had dismounted, and with his feet firmly planted, his rifle at his shoulder, and eyes fixed on the lion, he waited. The lion hesitated, cast a final glance at the prey lying a few paces from it, and then rushed on the young man with a roar. He fired again: the animal bit the dust, and the Count, hunting knife in hand, ran up to it. The man and the lion rolled together on the ground, but soon one of the combatants rose again—it was the man. Prairie-Flower was saved. The maiden opened her eyes again, looked timidly around her, and holding out her hand to the Frenchman.

"Thanks!" she exclaimed, and burst into tears.

Natah Otann walked up to her.

"Silence!" he said, harshly; "what the Paleface has done Natah Otann could have achieved."

The Count smiled contemptuously, but made no reply, for he had recognized a rival.

[1] The *felis discolor* of Linnæus, or American lion.

CHAPTER XX
INDIAN DIPLOMACY

Natah Otann feigned not to have perceived the Count's smile.

"Now that you have recovered," he said to Prairie-Flower, in a gentler tone than he at first assumed towards her, "mount your horse, and return to the village. Red Wolf will accompany you; perhaps," he added, with an Indian smile, "we may again come across cougars, and you are so frightened at them, that I believe I am doing you a service in begging you to withdraw."

The young girl, still trembling, bowed and mounted her horse. Red Wolf had involuntarily made a start of joy on hearing the order the chief gave him, but the latter, occupied with his thoughts, had not surprised it.

"One moment," Natah Otann went on, "if living lions frighten you, I know that in return you greatly value their furs; allow me to offer you these."

No one can equal the skill of Indians in flaying animals; in an instant the two lions, over which the vultures were already hovering and forming wide circles, were stripped of their rich hides, which were thrown across Red Wolfs horse. That animal, terrified by the smell that emanated from the skins, reared furiously, and almost unsaddled its rider, who had great difficulty in restraining it.

"Now go," the Chief said, drily, dismissing them with a haughty gesture.

Prairie-Flower and Red Wolf departed at a gallop; Natah Otann watched them for a long time, then let his head fall on his breast, as he uttered a deep sigh, and appeared plunged in gloomy thought. A moment later he felt a hand pressing heavily on his chest; he raised his head—White Buffalo was before him.

"What do you want with me?" he asked, angrily.

"Do you not know?" the old man said, looking at him fixedly.

Natah Otann quivered.

"It is true," he said, "the hour has arrived, you mean?"

"Yes."

"Are all precautions taken?"

"All."

"Come on then; but where are they?"

"Look at them."

While uttering these words, White Buffalo pointed to the Count and his comrades lying on the grass, at the skirt of a wood, about two hundred yards from the Indian encampment.

"Ah, they keep aloof," the Chief observed, bitterly.

"Is not that better for the conversation which we wish to have with them?"

"You are right."

The two men then walked up to the hunters without speaking again. The latter had really kept away, not through contempt for the Indians, but in order to be more at liberty. What had occurred after the death of the cougars, the brutal way in which the Chief spoke to Prairie-Flower, had vexed the Count, and it needed all the power he possessed over himself, and the entreaties of Bright-eye, to prevent him breaking out in reproaches of the Chief, whose conduct appeared to him unjustifiably coarse.

"Hum," he said, "this man is decidedly a ruffian: I am beginning to be of your opinion, Bright-eye."

"Bah! that is nothing yet," the latter replied, with a shrug of his shoulders; "we shall see plenty more, if we only remain a week with these demons."

While speaking, the Canadian had reloaded his rifle and pistols.

"Do as I do," he continued; "no one knows what may happen."

"What need of that precaution? are we not under the protection of the Indians, whose guests we are?"

"Possibly; but no matter, you had better follow my advice, for with Indians you can never answer for the future."

"There is considerable truth in what you say; what I have just seen does not at all inspire me with confidence."

The Count, therefore, began reloading his weapons; as for Ivon, he had not used his. The two Indian Chiefs came up at the moment the Count finished loading the last pistol.

"Oh, oh!" Natah Otann said, in French, saluting the young man with studied politeness, "have you scented any wild beast in the neighbourhood?"

"Perhaps so," the latter replied, as he returned his pistols to his belt.

"What do you mean, sir?"

"Nothing but what I say."

"Unfortunately for me, doubtlessly, that is so subtile, that I do not understand it."

"I am sorry for it, sir; but I can only reply to you by an old Latin proverb."

"Which is?"

"What need to repeat it, as you do not understand Latin?"

"Suppose I do understand it?"

"Well, then, as you insist upon it, here it is—*si vis pacem para bellum.*"

"Which means—" the Chief said, impertinently, while White Buffalo bit his lips.

"Which means—" the Count said.

"If you wish for peace, prepare for war," White Buffalo hurriedly interrupted.

"It was you who said it," the Count remarked, bowing with a mocking smile.

The three men stood face to face, like skilful duellists, who feel the adversary's sword before engaging, and who, having recognized themselves to be of equal strength, redouble their prudence before dealing a decisive thrust.

Bright-eye, though not understanding much of this skirmish of words, had still, through the distrust which was the basis of his character, given Ivon a side-glance, and both, though apparently inattentive, were ready for any event. After the Count's last remark there was a lengthened silence, which Natah Otann was the first to break.

"You believe yourself to be among enemies, then?" he asked, in a tone of wounded pride.

"I did not say so," he replied, "and such is not my thought; still, I confess that all I have seen during the last few days is so strange to me, that, in spite of all my attempts, I can form no settled opinion either about men or things, and that causes me deep reflection."

"Ah!" the Indian said, coldly, "and what is it so strange you see around you? Would you be kind enough to inform me?"

"I see no harm in doing so, if you wish it."

"You will cause me intense pleasure by explaining yourself."

"I am quite ready to do so; the more so, as I have ever been accustomed to express my thoughts freely, and I see no reason for disguising them today."

The two Chiefs bowed, and said nothing; the Count rested his hands on the muzzle of his gun, and continued, while regarding them fixedly—

"My faith, gentlemen, since you wish me to unveil my thoughts, you shall have them in their entirety: we are here in the wilds of the American prairies, that is, in the wildest countries of the new Continent; you are always on hostile terms with the whites; you Blackfeet are regarded as the most untameable, savage, and ferocious of the Indians; or, in other words, the most devoid of the civilization of all the aboriginal nations."

"Well," Natah Otann remarked, "what do you find strange in that? Is it our fault if our despoilers, since the discovery of the new world, have tracked us like wild beasts, driven us back in the desert, and regarded us as beings scarcely endowed with the instinct of the brute? You must blame them, and not us. By what right do you reproach us with a brutalization and barbarism, produced by our persecutors and not by ourselves?"

"You have not understood me, sir: if, instead of interrupting me, you had listened patiently a few minutes longer, you would have seen that I not merely do not reproach you for that brutalization, but pity it in my heart; for, although I have been only a few months in the desert, I have been on several occasions in a position to judge the unhappy race to which you belong, and appreciate the good qualities it still possesses, and which the odious tyranny of the whites has not succeeded in eradicating, despite all the means employed to attain that end."

The two Chiefs exchanged a glance of satisfaction; the generous words uttered by the young man gave them hopes as to the success of their negotiation.

"Pardon me, and pray continue," Natah Otann said, with a bow.

"I will do so:" the Count went on: "I repeat it, it was not that barbarism which astonished me, for I supposed it to be greater than it really is: what seemed strange to me was to find in the heart of the desert, where we now are, amid the ferocious Indians who surround us, two men, two Chiefs of these self-same Indians—I will not say civilized, for the word is not strong enough—but utterly conversant with all the secrets of the most advanced and refined civilization, speaking my maternal tongue with the most extreme purity, and seeming, in a word, to have nothing Indian about them, save the dress they wear. It seemed strange to me that two men, for an object

I know not, changing in turn their manners and fashions, are at one moment savage Indians, at another perfect gentlemen; but instead of trying to raise their countrymen from the barbarism in which they pine, they wallow in it with them, feigning to be as ignorant and cruel as themselves. I confess to you, gentlemen, that all this not only appeared strange to me, but even frightened me."

"Frightened!" the two Chiefs exclaimed, simultaneously.

"Yes, frightened!" the Count continued, quickly; "for a life of continual feints, such as you lead, must conceal some dark plot. Lastly, I am frightened, because your conduct towards me, the urgency with which you sought to attract me amongst you, causes involuntary suspicions to spring up in my heart as to your secret intentions."

"And what are those suspicions, sir?" Natah Otann asked, haughtily.

"I am afraid that you wish to make me your accomplice in some scandalous deed."

These words, pronounced vehemently, burst like a thunderbolt on the ears of the two strange Chiefs; they were terrified by the perspicuity of the young man, and for several moments knew not what to say, to disculpate themselves.

"Sir!" Natah Otann at length exclaimed, violently.

White Buffalo checked him by a majestic gesture.

"It is my duty," he said, "to reply to our guest's words: in his turn, after the frank and loyal explanation he has given us, he has a right to one equally frank on our side."

"I am listening to you," the young man said, coolly.

"Of the two men now standing before you, one is your fellow countryman."

"Ah!" the Count muttered.

"That countryman is myself."

The young man bowed coldly.

"I suspected it," he said, "and it is a further reason to heighten my suspicions."

Natah Otann made a gesture.

"Let him speak," White Buffalo said, holding him back.

"What I have to say will not be long, sir: it is my opinion that the man who consents to exchange the blessings of European civilization for a precarious life on the prairie; who breaks all the ties of family and friendship which attached him to his country, in order to adopt an Indian life—in my opinion that man must have many disgraceful actions to reproach himself with, and his remorse forces him to offer society expiation for them."

The old man's brow contracted, and a livid pallor covered his face.

"You are very young, sir," he said, "to have the right to bring such accusations against an old man whose actions, life, and even name are unknown to you."

"That is true, sir," the Count answered, nobly. "Pardon any insult my words may have conveyed."

"Why should I be angry with you?" he continued, in a sad voice; "a child born yesterday, whose eyes opened amid songs and fêtes, whose life, which counts but a few days, has been spent gently and calmly in the peace and prosperity of that beloved France which I weep for every day."

"Who are you, sir?" he asked.

"Who I am?" the old man said, bitterly. "I am one of those crushed Titans who sat in the Convention of 1793."

The Count fell back a pace, letting fall the hand he had taken.

"Oh!" he said.

The exile looked at him searchingly.

"Enough of this," he said, raising his head and assuming a firm and resolute tone; "you are in our hands, sir, any resistance will be useless; so listen to our propositions."

The Count shrugged his shoulders.

"You throw off the mask," he said, "and I prefer that; but allow me one remark before listening to you."

"What is it?"

"I am of noble birth, as you are aware, and hence we are old enemies; on whatever ground we may meet, we can only stand face to face, never side by side."

"They are ever the same," the other muttered; "this haughty race may be broken, but not bent."

The Count bowed, and folded his arms on his breast.

"I am waiting," he said.

"Time presses," the exile continued; "any discussion between us would be superfluous, as we cannot agree."

"At least, that is clear," the Count remarked, with a smile; "now for the rest."

"It is this: in two days, all the Indian nations will rise as one man to crush the American tyranny."

"What do I care for that? Have I come so far to dabble in politics?"

The exile repressed a movement of anger.

"Unfortunately, your will is not free; you are here to obey our conditions, and not to impose your own: you must accept or die."

"Oh, oh, always your old means, as it seems, but I will be patient: come, what is it you expect from me?"

"We demand," he went on, laying a stress on every word, "that you should take the command of all the warriors, and direct the expedition in person."

"Why I, rather than anyone else?"

"Because you alone can play the part we give you."

"Nonsense—you are mad."

"You must be so, if, since your stay among the Indians, you have not seen that you would have been killed long ago, had we not been careful to spread reports about you, which gained you general respect, in spite of your rashness and blind confidence in yourself."

"Eh, then, this has been prepared a long time?"

"For centuries."

"Hang it!" the Count went on, still sarcastically, "what have I to do in all this?"

"Oh, sir, not much," the White Buffalo answered, with a sneer; "and anyone else would have suited us just as well; unfortunately for you, you have an extraordinary likeness to the man who can alone march at our head; and as this man died long ago, it is not probable that he will come from his grave expressly to guide us to battle; hence you must take his place."

"Very well; and would there be any indiscretion in asking you the name of the man to whom I bear so wonderful a likeness?"

"Not the slightest," the old man replied, coldly; "the more so, because you have doubtlessly already heard his name; it is Motecuhzoma."

The Count burst into a laugh.

"Come!" he said, "it is a capital joke; but I find it a little too long. Now, a word in my turn."

"Speak."

"Whatever you may do, whatever means you may employ, I will never consent to serve you in any way. Now, as I am your guest, placed under the guarantee of your honour, I request you to let me pass."

"That resolution is decided."

"Yes."

"You will not change it."

"Whatever happens."

"We shall see that," the old man remarked, coldly.

The Count looked at him contemptuously.

"Make way there," he said, resolutely.

The two Chiefs shrugged their shoulders.

"We are savages," Natah Otann said, gibingly.

"Make way!" the Count repeated, as he cocked his rifle.

Natah Otann whistled; in an instant, some fifteen Indians rushed from the wood, and fell on the white men, who, however, though surprised, endured the shock bravely. Standing instinctively back to back, with shoulder supported against shoulder, they suddenly formed a tremendous triangle, before which the Redskins were constrained to halt.

"Oh, oh," Bright-eye said, "I fancy we are going to have some fun."

"Yes," Ivon muttered, crossing himself piously; "but we shall be killed."

"Probably," the Canadian said.

"Fall back!" the Count ordered.

The three men then began to retire slowly toward the wood, the only shelter that offered, without separating, and still pointing their rifles at the Indians. The Redskins are brave, even rash; that question cannot be disguised or doubted; but with them courage is calculated; they never fight save to gain an object, and are not fond of risking their lives unprofitably. They hesitated.

"I fancy we did well to reload our arms," the Count said, ironically, but with perfect calmness.

"By Jove!" Bright-eye said, with a grin.

"No matter, I am very frightened," Ivon groaned his eyes sparkling and his lips quivering.

"*Eha*, sons of blood!" Natah Otann shouted, as he cocked his gun. "Do three Palefaces frighten you? Forward! Forward!"

The Indians uttered their war yell, and rushed on the hunters. The other Indians, warned of what was happening by the shouts of their comrades, ran up hurriedly to take part in the fight.

CHAPTER XXI
MOTHER AND DAUGHTER

We must leave our three valiant champions for a few moments in their present critical position, to speak of one of the important persons of this story, whom we have neglected too long.

Immediately after the departure of the Indians, John Black, with that American activity equalled in no other country, set to work, beginning his clearing. The peril he had incurred, and which he had only escaped by a miracle incomprehensible to him, had caused him to make very earnest reflections. He understood that in the isolated spot where he was, he could not expect assistance from anyone; that he must alone confront the danger that would doubtlessly menace him; and that, consequently, he must, before all else, think about defending the settlement against a *coup de main*, Major Melville had heard, through his *engagés* and trappers, of the colonist; but the latter was perfectly ignorant that he was only ten miles from Fort Mackenzie. His resolution once formed, John Black carried it out immediately.

To those people who have not seen American clearings, the processes employed by the squatters, and the skill with which they cut down the largest trees in a few moments, would appear as prodigies. Black considered that he had not a moment to lose, and, aided by his son and servants, set to work. The temporary camp, as we have seen, was situated on a rather high mound, which commanded the plain for a long distance. It was here that the colonist determined to build his house. He began by planting all round the platform of the hill a row of enormous stakes, twelve feet high, and fastened together by large bolts. This first enceinte finished, he dug behind it a trench about eight feet wide and fifteen deep, throwing up the earth on the edge, so as to form a second line of defence. Then, in the interior of this improvised fortress, which, if defended by a resolute garrison, was impregnable, unless cannon were brought up to form a breach—for the abrupt slope of the hill rendered any assault impossible—he laid the foundation of his family's future abode. The temporary arrangements he had made allowed him to continue his further labours less hastily; through his prodigious activity, he could defy the attacks of all the prowlers on the prairie.

His wife and daughter had actively helped him, for they understood, better than the rest of the family, the utility of these defensive works. The poor ladies, little used to the rude toil they had been engaged in, needed rest. Black had not spared himself more than the rest. He understood the justice of his wife and daughter's entreaties, and as he had nothing to fear for the present, he generously granted a whole day's rest to the little colony.

The events that marked the squatter's arrival in the province had left a profound impression on the hearts of Mrs. Black and her daughter. Diana, especially, had maintained a recollection of the Count, which time, far from weakening, rendered only the more vivid. The Count's chivalrous character, the noble way in which he had acted, and—let us speak the truth—his physical qualities, all combined to render him dear to the young girl, whose life had hitherto passed away calmly, nothing happening to cast a cloud over her heart. Many times since the young man's departure she stopped in her work, raised her head, looked anxiously around her, and then resumed her toil, while stifling a sigh.

Mothers are quick-sighted, especially those who, like Mrs. Black, really love their daughters. What her husband and son did not suspect, then, she guessed merely by looking for a few minutes at the poor girl's pale face, her eyes surrounded by a dark ring, her pensive look, and inattention.

Diana was in love.

Mrs. Black looked around her. No one could be the object of that love. So far back as she could remember, she called to mind no one her daughter had appeared to distinguish before their departure from the clearing, where she had passed her youth. Besides, when the little party set out in search of a fresh home, Diana seemed joyful, she prattled gaily as a bird, and appeared to trouble herself about none of those she left behind.

After these reflections, the mother sighed in her turn; for, if she had divined her daughter's love, she had been unable to discover the man who was the object of that love. Mrs. Black resolved to cross-question her daughter as soon as she happened to be alone with her; till then she feigned to be in perfect ignorance. The day of rest granted by John Black to his family would probably offer her the favourable opportunity she awaited so impatiently. Hence she joyfully received the news which her husband gave her in the evening after prayers, which, according to the custom of the family, were said in common before going to bed.

The next morning, at sunrise, according to their daily habit, the two ladies prepared the breakfast, while the servants led the cattle down to the river.

"Wife," the squatter said, at breakfast, "William and I intend, as work is suspended for today, to mount our horses, and go and visit the neighbourhood, which we have not seen yet."

"Do not go too far, my friend, and be well armed; you know that in the desert dangerous meetings are not rare."

"Yes; so be at ease. Although I believe that we have nothing to fear for the present, I will be prudent. Would you not feel inclined to accompany us, as well as Diana, and take a look at your new domain?"

The girl's eyes glistened with joy at this proposition; she opened her lips to reply; but her mother laid her hand on her mouth, and spoke instead of her.

"You must excuse us, my dear," she said, with a certain degree of vivacity, "but women, as you know, have always something to do. Diana and I will put everything in order during your absence, which our busy labours of the last few days have prevented us doing."

"As you please, wife."

"Besides," she continued, with a smile; "as we shall probably remain a long time here—"

"I fancy so," the squatter interrupted.

"Well, I shall not lack opportunity of visiting our domains, as you call them, another day."

"Excellently argued, ma'am, and I am quite of your opinion; William and I will therefore take our ride alone; I would ask you not to feel alarmed if we do not come home till rather late."

"No; but on condition that you return before night."

"Agreed."

They spoke of something else; still, towards the end of the meal, Sam, without suspecting it, brought the conversation back nearly to the same subject.

"I am certain, James," he said to his comrade, "that the young man was not a Canadian, as you fancy, but a Frenchman."

"Who are you talking about?" the squatter asked.

"The gentleman who accompanied the Redskins, and made them give us back our cattle."

"Yes, without counting the other obligations we are under to him, for if I am now the owner of a clearing, it was through him."

"He is a worthy gentleman," Mrs. Black said, with a purpose.

"Yes, yes," Diana murmured, in an indistinct voice.

"He is a Frenchman," Black asserted. "There cannot be a doubt of that: those Canadian scoundrels are incapable of acting in the way he did to us."

Like all the North Americans, Black heartily detested the Canadians; why he did so, he could not have said, but this hatred was innate in his heart.

"Bah!" William said, "what matter his country, he has a fine heart, and is a true gentleman. For my part, father, I know a certain William Black, who is ready to die for him."

"By heaven!" the squatter exclaimed, as he struck the table with his fist, "you would be only doing your duty, and discharging a sacred debt: I would give anything to see him again, and prove to him that I am not ungrateful."

"Well spoken, father," William said joyously; "honest men are too rare in the world for us not to cling to those we know; if we should meet again, I will show him what sort of man I am."

During this rapid interchange of words, Diana said nothing; she listened, with outstretched neck, beaming face, and a smile on her lips, happy to hear a man thus spoken of, whom she unconsciously loved since she first saw him. Mrs. Black thought it prudent to turn the conversation.

"There is another person to whom we owe great obligations; for if Heaven had not sent her at the right moment to our help, we should have been pitilessly massacred by the Indians; have you already forgotten that person?"

"God forbid!" the squatter exclaimed, quickly, "the poor creature did me too great a service for me to forget her."

"But who on earth can she be?" William said.

"I should be much puzzled to say; I believe even that the Indians and trappers, who cross the prairies, could give us no information about her."

"She only appeared and disappeared," James observed.

"Yes, but her passage, so rapid as it was, left deep traces," Mrs. Black said.

"Her mere presence was enough to terrify the Indians. That woman I shall always regard as a good genius, whatever opinion may be expressed about her in my presence."

"We owe it to her that we did not suffer atrocious torture."

"May God bless the worthy creature!" the squatter exclaimed; "if ever she have need of us, she can come in all certainty; I and all I possess are at her disposal."

The meal was over, and they rose from the table. Sam had saddled two horses. John Black and his son took their pistols, bowie knives, and rifles, mounted their horses, and after promising once again not to be late, they cautiously descended the winding path leading into the plain.

Diana and her mother then began putting things to rights, as had been arranged. When Mrs. Black had watched the couple out of sight on the prairie, and assured herself that the two servants were engaged outside in mending some harness, she took her needlework, and requested her daughter to come and sit by her side. Diana obeyed with a certain inward apprehension, for never had her mother behaved to her so mysteriously. For a few minutes the two ladies worked silently opposite each other. At length Mrs. Black stopped her needle, and looked at her daughter; the latter continued her sewing, without appearing to notice this intermission.

"Diana," she asked her, "have you nothing to say to me?"

"I, mother?" the young girl said, raising her head with amazement.

"Yes, you, my child."

"Pardon me, mother," she went on, with a certain tremor in her voice, "but I do not understand you."

Mrs. Black sighed.

"Yes," she murmured, "and so it ever must be; a moment arrives when young girls have unconsciously a secret from their mothers."

The poor lady wiped away a tear; Diana rose quickly, and throwing her arms tenderly round her mother—

"A secret? I, a secret from you, mother? Oh, how could you suppose such a thing?"

"Child!" Mrs. Black replied, with a smile of ineffable kindness, "a mother's eye cannot be deceived;" and putting her finger on her daughter's palpitating heart, she said, "your secret is there."

Diana blushed, and drew back, confused.

"Alas!" the good lady continued, "I do not address reproaches to you, poor dear and well-beloved child. You unconsciously submit to the laws of nature; I too, at your age, was as you are at this moment, and when my mother asked my secret, like you, I replied that I had none, for I was myself ignorant of that secret."

The girl hid her face, all bathed in tears, in her mother's breast. The latter gently moved the flowing locks of light hair which covered her daughter's brow, and giving her a kiss, said, with that accent which mothers alone possess —

"Come, my dear Diana, dry your tears, do not trouble yourself so; only tell me your feelings during the last few days."

"Alas! my kind mother," the girl replied, smiling through her tears, "I understand nothing myself, and suffer without knowing why; I am restless, languid; everything disgusts and wearies me, and yet I fancy there has been no change in my life."

"You are mistaken, child," Mrs. Black answered, gravely, "your heart has spoken without your knowledge; thus, instead of the careless, laughing girl you were, you have become a woman, you have thought, your forehead has turned pale, and you suffer."

"Alas!" Diana murmured.

"Come, how long have you been so sad?"

"I know not, mother."

"Think again."

"I fancy it is—."

Mrs. Black, understanding her daughter's hesitation, finished the sentence for her.

"Since the day after our arrival here, is it not?"

Diana raised to her mother her large blue eyes, in which profound amazement could be read.

"It is true," she murmured.

"Your sorrow began at the moment when the strangers, who so nobly aided us, took their leave?"

"Yes," the girl said, in a low voice, with downcast eyes and blushing forehead.

Mrs. Black continued smilingly her interesting interrogatory.

"On seeing them depart, your heart was contracted, your cheeks turned pale, you shuddered involuntarily, and, if I had not held you—I who watched you carefully, poor darling—you would have fallen. Is not all this true?"

"It is true, mother," the girl said, with a more assured voice.

"Good; and the man from whom you regret being separated—he who causes your present sorrow and suffering, is—?"

"Mother!" she exclaimed, throwing herself into her arms, and hiding her shamed face in her bosom.

"It is—?" she continued.

"Edward!" the girl said, in an inarticulate voice, and melting into tears.

Mrs. Black directed on her daughter a glance of supreme pity, embraced her ardently several times, and said, in a soft voice,—

"You see that you had a secret, my child, since you love him."

"Alas!" she murmured, naively, "I do not know it, mother."

The good lady nodded her head with satisfaction, led her daughter back to her chair, and herself sitting down, said to her,—

"And now that we have had a thorough explanation, and there is no longer a secret between us, suppose we have a little talk, Diana."

"I am quite willing, mother."

"Listen to me, then; my age and experience, leaving out of sight the position in which I stand to you, authorize me in giving you advice. Will you hear it?"

"Oh, mother! you know I respect and love you."

"I know it, dear child; I know too, as I have never left you since your birth, and have incessantly watched over you, how generous your mind is, how noble your heart, and how capable of self-devotion. I must cause you great pain, poor girl; but it is better to attend to the green wound, than allow time to render the evil incurable."

"Alas!"

"This raging love, which has unconsciously entered your heart, cannot be very great; it is rather the awakening of the mind to those gentle feelings and noble instincts, which embellish existence and characterize the woman, than a passion; your love is only in reality a momentary exaltation of the brain's feverish imagination; like all young girls, you aspire to the unknown, you seek an ideal, the reality of which does not exist for you; but you do not love. Nay, more, you cannot love; the feeling you experience at the moment is entirely in the head, and the heart goes for nothing."

"Mother!" the young girl interrupted.

"Dear Diana," she continued, taking her hand, and pressing it, "let me make you suffer a little now, to spare you at a later date the horrible pangs which would produce the despair of your whole existence. The man you fancy you love you will probably never see again; he is ignorant of your attachment, and does not share it. I am speaking cold and implacable reason; it is logical, and spares us much grief, while passion is never so, and always produces pain; but supposing for a moment that this young man loved you, you could never be his."

"But if he love me, mother," she said, timidly.

"Poor babe!" the mother continued, with an accent of sublime pity. "Do you know even whether he be free? Who has told you that he is not married? But I will allow it for a moment: this young man is noble; he belongs to one of the oldest and proudest families in Europe; his fortune is immense. Do you believe that he will ever consent to abandon all the social advantages his position guarantees him?—that he will bow his family pride to give his hand to the daughter of a poor American squatter?"

"It is true," she murmured, letting her head fall in her hands.

"And even if he did so, though it is impossible, would you consent to follow him, and leave in the desert a father and mother, who have only you, and who would die of despair ere your departure? Come, Diana, answer, would you consent?"

"Oh, never, never, mother!" she exclaimed, madly "Oh, I love you most of all!"

"Good, my darling; that is how I wished to see you. I am happy that my words have found the road to your heart. This man is kind; he has done us immense service; we owe him gratitude, but nothing more."

"Yes, yes, mother," she murmured, with a sob.

"You must only see in him a friend, a brother," she continued, firmly.

"I will try, mother."

"You promise it me?"

The girl hesitated for a moment. Suddenly she raised her head, and said, bravely,—

"I thank you, mother. I swear to you not to forget him, that would be impossible, but so thoroughly to conceal my love, that, with the exception of yourself, no one shall suspect it."

"Come to my arms, my child; you understand your duty; you are noble and good."

At this moment James entered.

"Mistress," he said, "the master is coming back, but there are several persons with him."

"Wipe your eyes, and follow me, dear; let us go and see what has happened."

And, stooping down to her daughter's ear, she whispered, —

"When we are alone, we will speak of him."

"Yes, mother," Diana said, almost joyfully, "Oh, how good you are, and how I love you."

They went out, and looked in the direction of the plain. At a considerable distance from the fort, they noticed a party of four or five persons, at the head of whom were John Black and his son William.

"What is the meaning of this?" Mrs. Black said, anxiously.

"We shall soon know, mother; calm yourself; they seem to be riding too gently for us to feel any alarm."

CHAPTER XXII
IVON

The Count and his two companions, as we have seen, bravely awaited the attack of the Indians; it was terrible. For an instant there was a horrible mêlée hand to hand; then the Indians fell back to draw breath, and begin again. Ten corpses lay at the feet of the three men, who were motionless and firm as a block of granite.

"By heavens!" the Count said, as he wiped away, with the back of his hand, the perspiration mingled with blood that stood in large beads on his forehead, "it is a glorious fight."

"Yes," Bright-eye replied, carelessly; "but it is mortal."

"What matter, if we die like men?"

"Hum! I am not of that opinion. As long as there is a chance, we must seize it."

"But none is left us!"

"Perhaps there is; but let me act."

"I ask no better. Still I confess to you that I find this fight glorious."

"It is really very agreeable; but it would be much more so, if we lived to recount it."

"On my word, that is true. I did not think of that."

"Yes, but I did."

The Canadian stooped down to Ivon, and whispered some words in his ear.

"Yes," the Breton replied, "provided I am not afraid."

"Bravo!" the hunter said, with a smile; "you will do what you can. That is agreed?"

"Agreed."

"Look out, comrades," the Count shouted; "here are the enemy!"

In truth, the Indians were ready to renew the attack. Natah Otann and White Buffalo were resolved on taking the Count alive, and without a wound; they had consequently given their warriors orders not to employ their firearms, content themselves with parrying the blows dealt them, but take him at every risk. During the few moments' respite which the Indians had allowed the white men, the other Indians had run up to take part in the fight; so that the hunters, surrounded on all sides, had to make head against at least forty Redskins. It would have been madness or blind temerity to attempt opposing such a mass of enemies; and yet the white men did not appear to dream of asking quarter. At the moment Natah Otann was going to give the signal for attack, White Buffalo, who had hitherto stood aloof, gloomy and thoughtful, interposed, —

"A moment!" he said.

"For what good?" the Chief remarked.

"Let me make the attempt. Perhaps they will recognize that a struggle is impossible, and consent to accept our propositions."

"I doubt it," Natah Otann muttered, shaking his head; "they appear very resolute."

"Let me try it. You know how necessary it is for the success of our plans that we should seize this man?"

"Unfortunately; if we do not take care, he will be killed."

"That is what I wish to avoid."

"Try it then; but I am convinced you will fail."

"Who knows? I can try, at any rate."

White Buffalo walked a few paces in advance, and was then about six yards from the Count.

"What do you want?" the young man said. "If I did not involuntarily know that you are a Frenchman, I should have long ago put a bullet into your chest."

"Fire!—what stops you?" the exile replied, in a sad voice. "Do you believe that I fear death?"

"Enough talking. Retire! or I will fire."

And he levelled his rifle at him.

"I wish to say one word to you."

"Speak quickly, and be off."

"I offer you and your comrades your lives, if you will surrender."

The Count burst into a laugh.

"Nonsense," he said, with a shrug of his shoulders; "do you take us for fools? We were the guests of your companions, and they have impudently violated the law of nations."

"That is your last word, then?"

"The last, by Jove! You must have lived a long time among the Indians to have forgotten that Frenchmen would sooner die than be cowards."

"Your blood be on your own heads, then."

"So be it, odious renegade, who fight with savages against your brothers."

This insult struck the old man to the heart; he bent a fearful glance on the young man, turned pale as death and withdrew, tottering like a drunkard, and muttering, in a low voice,—

"Oh, these nobles!"

"Well?" Natah Otann asked him.

"He refuses," he answered quickly.

"I was sure of it. Now it is our turn."

Raising to his lips his war whistle, he produced a shrill and lengthened sound, to which the Indians responded with a frightful yell, and rushed like a legion of demons on the three men, who received them without yielding an inch. The mêlée recommenced in all its fury; the three men clubbed their rifles, and dealt crushing blows around. Ivon performed prodigies of valour, rising and sinking his rifle with the regularity of a pendulum, smashing a man at every blow, and muttering,—

"Ouf, there's another: holy Virgin, I feel my terror coming upon me."

Still the circle drew closer round the three men; others took the places of the Indians who fell, and were in their turn pushed onward by those behind. The hunters were weary of striking. Their arms did not fall with the same vigour; their blows failed in regularity; the blood rose to their heads; their eyes were injected with blood, and they had a dizziness in their ears.

"We are lost!" the Count muttered.

"Courage!" Bright-eye yelled, as he smashed in the skull of an Indian.

"It is not courage that fails me, but strength," the young man answered, in a fainting voice.

"Forward, forward!" Natah Otann repeated, bounding like a demon round the three men.

"Now, Ivon, now!" Bright-eye cried out.

"Good bye," the Breton replied.

And turning his terrible weapon round his head, he rushed into the densest throng of the Indians.

"Follow me, Count," Bright-eye went on.

"Come on then," the latter shouted.

The two men executed on the opposite side the manoeuvre attempted by the Breton. Ivon, the coward you know, seemed to have at the moment entirely forgotten his fear of being speared; he appeared, like Briareus, to have a hundred arms to level the numerous assailants who incessantly rose before him, and cleft his way through the throng. Fortunately for the Breton, most of the Indians had rushed in pursuit of game more valuable to them, that is, the Count and the Canadian, who had redoubled their efforts, though already so prodigious.

While still fighting, Ivon had reached the skirt of the wood, about three or four yards from the spot where the horses were tied. This was probably what the Breton wished for. So soon as he found himself in a straight line with the horses, instead of pushing forward as he had hitherto done, he began to fall back step to step, so as to arrive close to them. Still, he always fought with that cold resolution which distinguishes the Bretons, and renders them such terrible foemen.

Suddenly, when he found himself near enough to the horses, Ivon gave a parting blow to the nearest Indian, sent him staggering backwards with a dashed-in skull, took a panther leap, and reached the Count's horse. In a second he had mounted, dug his spurs into the flanks of the noble animal, and galloped off, after knocking down two Indians who tried to stop him.

"Hurrah! saved! saved!" he shouted, in a voice of thunder, as he disappeared in the forest, where the Blackfeet did not dare to follow him.

The Redskins stood stupefied by such a prodigious flight. The cry uttered by Ivon was doubtlessly a signal agreed on between him and Bright-eye; for, so soon as he heard it, the hunter, by a hurried movement, seized the Count's arm as he was in the act of striking.

"What on earth are you about?" the latter said, turning to him angrily.

"I am saving you," the hunter replied, coolly; "throw down your weapon!—We surrender," he then exclaimed.

"You will explain your conduct, I presume?" the Count continued.

"Be of good cheer; you will approve it."

"Be it so."

And he threw the gun down. The Indians, whom the hunters' heroic defence kept at a distance, rushed upon them so soon as they saw they were disarmed, Natah Otann and White Buffalo hurried up; the two men already were thrown down on the sand, when the Chief interposed.

"Sir," he said, "you are my prisoner; and you too, Bright-eye."

The young man shrugged his shoulders with contempt.

"Reckon up what your victory has already cost you," the hunter replied, with a sardonic smile, and pointing to the numerous corpses that lay on the plain. Natah Otann, however, pretended not to hear this remark.

"If you will give me your word of honour not to escape, gentlemen," White Buffalo said, "you will be unloosed, and your weapons restored to you."

"Is this another trap you are laying for us?" the Count asked, haughtily.

"Bah!" Bright-eye said, with a significant glance at his comrade, "we will give our word for four-and-twenty hours; after that, we will see."

"You hear, gentlemen," the young man said; "this hunter and myself pledge our words for four-and-twenty hours. Does that suit you? Of course, at the end of that time, we are free to recall it."

"Or to pledge it again," the Canadian added, with a smile; "what do we risk by doing so?"

The two Chiefs exchanged a few whispered words.

"We accept," Natah Otann at length said.

At a sign from him, the prisoners' bonds were cut, and they rose.

"Hum!" Bright-eye said, stretching himself with delight, "it does one good to have the use of his limbs. Bah! I knew they would not kill me this time, either."

"Here are your horses and arms, gentlemen," the Chief said.

"Permit me," the Count remarked coolly, drawing his watch from his pocket, "it is now half-after seven; you have our parole till the same time tomorrow evening."

"Very good," White Buffalo said, with a bow.

"And now, where are you going to take us, if you please?" the hunter asked, with a crafty look.

"To the village!"

"Thank you."

The two men jumped into their saddles, and followed the Indians, who only waited for them to start. Ten minutes later, this place, on which so many events had occurred during the day, became again calm and silent.

We will leave the Count and the hunter returning to the village under good escort, to follow the track of Ivon.

After leaving the battlefield, the latter rode straight ahead, not caring to lose precious time in looking for a path; for the moment all were good, provided that they bore him from the enemies he had so providentially escaped. Still, after galloping for about an hour across the wood, reassured by the perfect silence that prevailed around him, he gradually checked his horse's speed. It was high time for this idea to occur to him, as the poor horse, so harshly treated, was beginning to break down. The Breton profited by this slight truce to reload his weapons.

"I am not brave," he said in a low voice, "but by Jove! as my poor master says, the first scamp that attempts to bar my way, I will blow out his brains, so surely as my name is Ivon."

And the worthy man would have done as he said, we feel assured. After advancing a few hundred yards, Ivon looked around, stopped his horse, and dismounted.

"What is the use of going any farther?" he said, resuming his soliloquy; "my horse wants rest, and I shall not be the worse for a halt. As well here as elsewhere."

On this, he took off his horse's saddle, carried his master's portmanteau to the foot of a tree, and began lighting a fire.

"How quickly night comes on in this confounded country," he muttered; "it is hardly eight o'clock, and it is as black as in an oven."

While discoursing thus all alone, he had collected a considerable quantity of dry wood; he returned to the spot he had selected for camping, piled up the wood, struck a light, knelt, and began blowing with all the strength of his lungs to make it catch. In a moment he raised his head to breathe; but uttered a yell of terror, and almost fell backwards. He had seen, about three paces from the fire, two persons silently watching him. The first moment of surprise past, the Breton bounded on his feet, and cocked his pistols.

"Confuse you," he shouted, "you gave me a pretty fright; but no matter, we will see."

"My brother may be at rest," a soft voice replied, in bad English, "we do not wish to do him any harm."

As a Breton, Ivon spoke nearly as good English as he did French. On hearing these words, he bent forward, and looked. "Oh!" he said, "the Indian girl."

"Yes, it is I," Prairie-Flower answered, as she stepped forward.

Her companion followed her, and Ivon recognized Red Wolf.

"You are welcome," he remarked, "to my poor encampment."

"Thanks," she answered.

"How is it that you are here?"

"And you?" she said, answering one question by another.

"Oh, I!" he said, shaking his head, "that is a sad story."

"What does my brother mean?" Red Wolf asked.

"Good, good," the Breton said, turning his head; "that is my business, and not yours. First, tell me what brings you to me, and I will then see if I may confide to you what has happened to my master and myself."

"My brother is prudent," Prairie-Flower answered, "he is right: prudence is good on the prairie."

"Hum! I wish my master had heard you make that remark, perhaps he would not be where he now is."

Prairie-Flower gave a start of terror.

"Wah! has any misfortune happened to him?" she said, in an agonized voice.

Ivon looked at her.

"You appear to take an interest in him?"

"He is brave," she exclaimed, passionately; "this morning he killed the cougars that threatened Prairie-Flower; she has a heart — she will remember."

"That is true; quite true, young lady," he said; "he saved your life. Tell me first, though, how it is we should have met in this forest."

"Listen, then, as you insist."

The Breton bowed. To all his other qualities Ivon added that of being as obstinate as an Andalusian mule. Once the worthy man had taken a theory into his head, nothing could turn him from it. We must grant, however, that he had at present excellent reason to distrust the Indians.

Prairie-Flower continued: —

"After Glass-eye had so bravely killed the cougars," she said, with considerable emotion, "the great Chief, Natah Otann, was angry with Prairie-Flower, and ordered her to return to the village with Red Wolf."

"I know all that," Ivon interrupted, "I was there; and that is why it seems to me so extraordinary to meet you here when you should have been on the road to the village."

The Indian girl gave one of those little pouts peculiar to her, and which rendered her so seductive.

"The pale man is as curious as an old squaw," she said, with an accent of ill-humour; "why does he wish to know Prairie-Flower's secret? She has in her heart a little bird which sings pleasant songs to her, and attracts her in the footsteps of the Paleface who saved her."

"Ah!" said the Breton, partly catching the girl's meaning; "that is different."

"Instead of returning to the village," Red Wolf interposed, "Prairie-Flower wished to return to the side of Glass-eye."

The Breton reflected for a long time; the two Indians watched him silently, patiently waiting till he thought proper to explain himself. Presently, he raised his head, and, fixing his cunning grey eye on the girl, he asked her distinctly, —

"You love him, then?"

"Yes," she answered, looking down on the ground.

"Very good. Now listen attentively to what I am about to tell you; it will interest you prodigiously, or I am greatly mistaken."

The two hearers bent down toward him, and listened attentively. Ivon then related most copiously his master's conversation with the two Chiefs; the dispute that arose between them; the combat that ensued from it, and the way in which he had escaped.

"If I did run away," he said, in conclusion, "heaven is my witness that it was not for the purpose of saving my life. Though I am a desperate coward, I would never hesitate to sacrifice my life for him; but Bright-eye advised me to act in this way, so that I may try and find assistance for them both."

"Good," the girl said, quickly; "the Paleface is brave. What does he intend to do?"

"I mean to save my master, by Jove!" the Breton said, resolutely. "The only thing is, that I do not know how to set about it."

"Prairie-Flower knows. She will help the Paleface."

"Is what you promise really true, young girl?"

The Indian maid smiled.

"The Paleface will follow Prairie-Flower and Red Wolf," she said; "they will lead him to a spot where he will find friends."

"Good; and when will you do it, my good girl?" he asked, his heart palpitating with joy.

"So soon as the Paleface is ready to start."

"At once, then, at once!" the Breton exclaimed, hurriedly rising, and hurrying to his horse.

Prairie-Flower and Red Wolf had concealed their steeds in the centre of a clump of trees. Ten minutes later, and Ivon and his guides quitted the clearing where they had met; it was about midnight when they started.

"My poor master!" the Breton muttered. "Shall I be permitted to save him?"

CHAPTER XXIII
THE PLAN OF THE CAMPAIGN

The night was black, gloomy, and storm-laden. The wind howled with a mournful murmur through the branches; at each gust the trees shook their damp crowns, and sent down showers, which pattered on the shrubs. The sky was of a leaden hue; so great was the silence in the desert, that the fall of a withered leaf, or the rustling of a branch touched in its passage by some invisible animal, could be distinctly heard.

Ivon and his guides advanced cautiously through the forest, seeking their road in the darkness, half lying on their horses, so as to avoid the branches that lashed their faces at every moment. Owing to the endless turns they were compelled to take, nearly two hours elapsed ere they left the forest. At length they debouched on the plain, and found themselves almost simultaneously on the banks of the Missouri. The river, swollen by rain and snow, rolled along its yellowish waters noisily. The fugitives followed the bank in a south-western direction. Now that they had struck the river, all uncertainty had ceased for them; their road was so distinctly traced that they had no fear of losing it.

On arriving at a spot where a point of sand jutted out for several yards into the bed of the river, and formed a species of cape, from the end of which objects could be seen for some distance, owing to the transparency of the water, Red Wolf made a sign to his companions to halt, and himself dismounted. Prairie-Flower and Ivon imitated him. Ivon was not sorry to take a few moments' rest, and, above all, make some inquiries before proceeding further. At the first blush, carried away by an unreflecting movement of the heart, which impelled him to save his master by any means that offered, he had not hesitated to follow his two strange guides; but, with reflection, distrust had returned still more powerfully, and the Breton was unwilling to go further with the persons he had met, until he possessed undoubted proofs of their honesty.

So soon as he had dismounted then, and taken off his horse's bridle, so that it should crop the tender shoots, Ivon walked up boldly to the Redskin, and struck him on the shoulder. The Indian, whose eyes were eagerly fixed on the rider, turned to him.

"What does the Paleface want?" he asked him.

"To talk a little with you, Chief."

"The moment is not good for talking," the Indian answered, sententiously; "the Palefaces are like the mockingbird; their tongues must be ever in motion; let my brother wait."

Ivon did not understand the epigram.

"No," he said, "we must talk at once."

The Indian suppressed an impatient gesture.

"The Red Wolf's ears are open," he said; "*the Chattering Jay* can explain himself."

The Redskins, finding some difficulty in pronouncing the names of people with whom the accidents of the chase or of trade bring them into relation, are accustomed to substitute for these names others, derived from the character or physical aspect of the individual they wish to designate. Ivon was called by the Blackfoot Indians the Chattering Jay, a name whose justice we will refrain from discussing. The Breton did not seem annoyed by what Red Wolf said to him; absorbed by the thought that troubled him, every other consideration was a matter of indifference to him.

"You promised me to save Glass-eye," he said.

"Yes," the Chief answered, laconically.

"I accepted your propositions without discussion; for three hours I have followed you without saying anything; but, before going further, I should not be sorry to know the means you intend to employ to take him out of the hands of the enemy."

"Is my brother deaf?" the Indian asked.

"I do not think so," Ivon answered, rather wounded by the question.

"Then let him listen."

"I am doing so."

"My brother hears nothing?"

"Not the least, I am free to confess."

Red Wolf shrugged his shoulders.

"The Palefaces are foxes without tails," he said, with disdain; "weaker than children in the desert. Let my brother look," he added, pointing to the river.

Ivon followed the direction indicated, winking, and placing his hands over his eyes, to concentrate the visual rays.

"Well," the Indian asked, after a moment, "has my brother seen?"

"Nothing at all," the Breton said, violently. "May the evil one twist my neck, if it is possible for me to distinguish anything."

"Then my brother will wait a few minutes," the Indian said, perfectly calm; "he will then see and hear."

"Hum!" the Breton went on, but slightly satisfied with this explanation. "What shall I see and hear?"

"My brother will know."

Ivon would have insisted, but the Chief took him by the arm, pushed him back, and hid with him behind a clump of trees, where Prairie-Flower was already ensconced.

"Silence!" the Redskin muttered, in such an imperative tone that the Breton, convinced of the gravity of the situation, deferred to a more favourable moment the string of questions he proposed asking the Chief.

A few minutes elapsed. Redskin and Prairie-Flower, with their bodies bent forward, and carefully parting the leaves, looked eagerly in the direction of the river, while holding their breath. Ivon, bothered in spite of himself by this sort of conduct, imitated their example. A sound soon struck on his ears, but so slight and weak, that at first he fancied himself mistaken. Still the noise grew gradually louder, resembling that of paddles cautiously dipped in the water; next, a black dot, at first nearly imperceptible, but which grew larger by degrees, appeared on the river.

There was soon no doubt in the Breton's mind. The black dot was a canoe. On arriving within a certain distance, the sound could be no longer heard, and the canoe remained motionless about halfway between the two banks. At this moment the cry of the jay broke the silence, repeated thrice, with such perfection, that Ivon instinctively raised his head to the upper branches of the tree that sheltered them. Upon this signal, the canoe began drawing nearer the cape, where it soon ran ashore; but upon landing, the person in it raised the paddle twice in the air. The cry of the jay was heard again, thrice repeated.

Upon this, the rower, perfectly reassured, as it seemed, leaped on the sand, drew the canoe half out of the water, and walked boldly in the direction of the clump of trees that served Ivon and his comrades as an observatory. The latter, deeming it useless to wait longer, quitted their shelter, and walked toward the newcomer, after recommending the Breton not to show himself without their authority. This order he obeyed; but, with that prudence which distinguished him, he cocked his pistols, took one in each hand, and, reassured by this precaution, waited what was about to happen.

The new actor who had entered on the scene, and in whom the reader will have recognised Mrs. Margaret, had left Major Melville only about an hour previously, after having that conversation we have repeated. Although she did not expect to meet Prairie-Flower at this spot, she did not appear at all astonished at seeing her, and gave her a friendly nod, to which the girl responded with a smile.

"What is there new?" she asked the Indian.

"Much," he replied.

"Speak."

The Red Wolf thereupon told her all that had happened during the chase; in what way he had learned it, and how Ivon had escaped in order to seek help for his master. Margaret listened to the long story without letting a sign of emotion to be seen on her wrinkled, grief-worn face. When Red Wolf had ceased speaking, she reflected for a few moments; then raising her head, asked—

"Where is the Paleface?"

"Here," the Indian answered, pointing to the clump of trees.

"Let him come."

The Chief turned to fetch him, but the Breton, who had heard the last word spoken in English, and judged that it was intended for him, left his hiding place, after returning the pistols to his belt, and joined the party. At this moment the first gleam of day began to appear, the darkness was rapidly dissipated, and a reddish hue, which formed on the extreme limit of the horizon, indicated that the sun would speedily rise. The She-wolf fixed on the Breton her cunning eye, as if desirous to read the depths of his heart. Ivon had nothing to reproach himself with, and hence he bravely withstood the glance. The She-wolf, satisfied with the dumb interrogatory to which she had subjected the Breton, softened down the harsh expression of her face, and at length addressed him in a voice she attempted to render conciliatory.

"Listen attentively," she said to him.

"I am listening."

"You are devoted to your master?"

"To the death," Ivon answered, firmly.

"Good: then I can reckon on you?"

"Yes."

"You understand, I suppose, that we four cannot save your master?"

"That appears to me difficult, I allow."

"But we wish to revenge ourselves on Natah Otann."

"Very good."

"For a long time our measures have been taken to gain this end at a given moment; that moment has arrived; but we have allies we must warn."

"It is true."

She drew a ring from her finger.

"Take this ring; you know how to use a paddle, I suppose?"

"I am a Breton, that is to say, a sailor."

"Get into the canoe lying there, and without losing a moment, go down the river till you reach a fort."

"Hum! is it far?"

"You will reach it in less than an hour if you are diligent."

"You may be sure of that."

"So soon as you have arrived at the fort, you will ask speech with Major Melville; give him that ring, and tell him all the events of which you have been witness."

"Is that all?"

"No; the Major will give you a detachment of soldiers, with whom you will join us at Black's clearing: can you find your way there again?"

"I think so; especially as it is on the river bank."

"Yes; and you will have to pass it before reaching the fort."

"What shall I do with the canoe?"

"Abandon it."

"When must I start?"

"At once; the sun has risen, we must make haste."

"And what are you going to do?"

"I told you we were going to Black's clearing, where we shall wait for you."

The Breton reflected for a minute.

"Listen, in your turn," he said; "I am not in the habit of discussing orders, when I think those given us are just; I do not think that you intend, under such grave circumstances, to mock a poor devil, whom grief renders half mad, and who would joyfully sacrifice his life to save his master's."

"You are right."

"I am therefore going to obey you."

"You should have done so already."

"Maybe; but I have a last word to say."

"I am listening."

"If you deceive me, if you do not really help me, as you pledge yourself, in saving my master—I am, a coward, that is notorious; but on my word as a man, I will blow out your brains: even were you hidden in the bowels of the earth, I would go and seek you to fulfil my oath. You hear me?"

"Perfectly! and now have you finished?"

"Yes."

"Then be off."

"I am doing so."

"Good-bye, till we meet again."

The Breton bowed once more, pulled the boat into the water, jumped in, and hurried off at a rate which showed he would soon reach his destination. His ex-companions looked after him till he was hidden by a bend in the river.

"And now what are we going to do?" Prairie-Flower asked.

"Go to the clearing, to arrange with John Black."

Margaret mounted Ivon's horse, Prairie-Flower and Red Wolf each took their own, and the three started at a gallop. By a fortunate coincidence, it was a day chosen by the squatter to give his family a rest, and, as we have said, he had gone out with William to take a look at his property. After a long ride, during which the squatter had burst into ecstasies only known to landed proprietors, they were preparing to return to their fortress, when William pointed out to his father the three mounted persons coming towards them at full gallop.

"Hum!" Black said, "Indians, that is an unpleasant meeting! let us hide behind this clump, and try to find out what they want."

"Stay, father," the young man said, "I believe that precaution unnecessary."

"Why so, boy?"

"Because of the party two are women."

"That is no reason," the squatter said, who, since the attack, had become excessively prudent; "you know that in these bad tribes the women fight as well as the men."

"That is true; but stay, they are unfolding a buffalo robe in sign of peace."

In fact, one of the riders at this moment fluttered a robe in the breeze.

"You are right, boy," the squatter observed, presently; "let us await them; the more so, as, if I am not mistaken, I can recognize an old acquaintance among them."

"The woman who saved us, I believe."

"Right; by Jove! the meeting is a strange one. Poor woman, I am delighted to see her again."

Ten minutes later the parties joined; after the first salutations, the She-wolf took the word.

"Do you recognize me, John Black?"

"Of course I do, my worthy woman," he replied, with emotion; "although I only saw you for a few moments, and under terrible circumstances, the remembrance of you has never left my heart and mind; I have only one wish, and that is, that you will give me the opportunity to prove it."

A flash of joy shot from the She-wolfs eye.

"Are you speaking seriously?" she asked, quickly.

"Try me."

"Good; I was not deceived in you. I am glad of what I did. I see that the service I rendered you has not fallen on ungrateful soil."

"Speak."

"Not here: what I have to tell you is too lengthy and serious for us to be able to discuss it properly at this place."

"Will you come to my house? There you need not be afraid of being disturbed."

"If you permit it."

"What, my good creature, permit it? Why, the house, all it contains, and the owner in the bargain, all are yours, and you know it."

Margaret smiled sadly.

"Thanks!" she said, offering him her hand, which Black pressed gladly.

"Come," he said, "as we have nothing more to do here, let us be off."

They started in the direction of the house; but the return was silent; each, absorbed in thought, rode on without thinking of addressing a word to the other. They were but a short distance from the house, when they suddenly saw some twenty horsemen debouch from a wood on the right, dressed, as far as could be distinguished, as wood rangers.

"What is this?" Black said, with astonishment, as he pulled his horse up.

"Eh!" the She-wolf said, not replying to the squatter. "The Frenchman has been diligent."

"What do you mean?"

"I will explain all that presently; for the present you need only offer your hospitality to these good people."

"Hum!" Black said, doubtingly. "I shall be glad to do it, but must know who they are, and what they want of me."

"They are Americans; like yourself. I asked the commandant of the fort where they are stationed to send them here."

"What fort and what garrison are you talking of, my good woman? On my soul! I do not know what you mean."

"What! have you not learned to know your neighbours since you have been here?"

"What! have I neighbours?" he said, in an angry tone.

"About ten miles off is Fort Mackenzie, commanded by a brave officer, Major Melville."

At this explanation the squatter's face was unwrinkled; it was not a rival, but a defender he had as neighbour, hence all was for the best.

"Oh, I will go and pay him my respects," he said; "the acquaintance of a fort commandant is not to be neglected in the desert."

Major Melville sent off at once the detachment asked by his sister; but reflecting that soldiers could not execute so well as hunters the meditated *coup de main*, he chose twenty hardened and resolute trappers and *engagés* under the command of an officer who had been a long time in the Fur

Company's service, and was versed in all the tricks of the crafty enemies he would have to fight.

At the foot of the hill the two parties combined. Black, though still ignorant for what purpose the detachment had come, received most affably the reinforcement sent to him. Ivon was radiant; the worthy Breton, now that he could dispose of such a number of good rifles, believed in the certainty of saving his master; all his suspicions had disappeared, and he burst forth into apologies and thanks to the She-wolf and her two Indian friends. So soon as all were comfortably lodged in the building, Black returned to his guests, and, after offering them refreshments, said—

"Now, I am waiting for your explanation."

As we shall soon see the development of the plans formed at this meeting, it is useless to describe them.

CHAPTER XXIV
THE CAMP OF THE BLACKFEET

Two days have elapsed since the events of our last chapter. It is evening in the Kenhas' village. The tumult is great; all are preparing for an expedition. The night is clear and starlit; great fires, kindled before each cabin, spread around immense reddish gleams, which light up the whole village. There is something strange and striking in the scene presented by the village, crowded with a motley population. The Count de Beaulieu and Bright-eye, apparently free, are conversing in a low tone, sitting on the bare ground, and leaning against the wall of a cabin.

The time fixed by the Count for his parole has long passed, still the Indian Chiefs have satisfied themselves with taking away his weapons and the hunter's, and pay no more attention to them.

On the large village square two immense fires have been kindled. Round the first, placed in front of the Council Lodge, are seated White Buffalo, Natah Otann, Red Wolf, and three or four other chiefs of the tribe; round the second some twenty warriors are silently smoking the calumet. Such was the appearance offered by the Kenhas' village at about nine in the evening of the day we return to it.

"Why allow the Palefaces thus to wander about the village?" Red Wolf asked.

Natah Otann smiled.

"Have the white men the eyes of the eagle and the feet of the gazelle, to find again their trail lost in the desert?"

"My father is right, if he speaks of Glass-eye," Red Wolf urged; "but Bright-eye has a Redskin heart."

"Yes; if he was alone he would try to escape, but he will not abandon his friend."

"The latter can follow him."

"Glass-eye has a brave heart, but his feet are weak; he cannot walk in the desert."

Red Wolf looked down, with an air of conviction, and made no reply.

"The hour has arrived to set out; the allied nations are proceeding to the rendezvous," White Buffalo said, in a sombre voice. "It is nine o'clock; the owl has twice given the signal, and the moon is rising."

"Good," Natah Otann said, "we will have the horses smoked, so as to set out immediately after."

Red Wolf gave a shrill whistle. At this signal some twenty horsemen galloped into the square, and went up to the second fire, round which an equal number of warriors, naked to the waist, were crouching and smoking silently. These men were warriors of the tribe who were dismounted, either by accident or in action; the horsemen, at this moment prancing round them, were their friends, and came up to make each a present of a horse prior to the departure of the expedition. While cantering round, the horsemen drew gradually nearer to the smokers, who did not appear to notice them. Each horseman chose out the man to whom he intended to give a horse, and a shower of lashes fell on the naked shoulders of these stoical warriors. At each blow they struck, the warrior shouted, each calling his friend by name.

"So and so, you are a beggar and wretched man. You desire my horse, I give it to you; but you will bear on your shoulders the bloody marks of my whip."

This performance lasted about a quarter of an hour, during which the sufferers, although the blood ran down their backs, did not utter a cry or a groan, but remained calm and motionless, as if they had been metamorphosed into bronze statues. At length the Red Wolf gave a second whistle, and the horsemen disappeared as rapidly as they came. The patients then rose as if nothing had happened to them, and went with radiant forehead and firm step, each to take possession of a magnificent steed, held by the ex-scourgers, now become their friends once more. This is what the Blackfeet call *smoking horses*.

When the tumult occasioned by this semi-serious episode was appeased, an *hachesto*, or public crier, mounted the roof of the council lodge. All the population of the village was drawn up silently on the square.

"The hour has struck! The hour has struck! The hour has struck!" the hachesto cried. "Warriors, to your lances and guns! The horses are neighing with impatience! Your chiefs are awaiting you, and your enemies sleep. To arms! To arms! To arms!"

"To arms!" all the warriors shouted simultaneously.

Natah Otann, followed by his warriors, mounted like himself on impetuous steeds, then appeared in the square, and uttered, in a terrible voice, the war yell of the Blackfeet. At this cry every man rushed on his weapons, mounted, and ranged under the respective chiefs, who, within scarce ten minutes, found themselves at the head of five hundred warriors, perfectly armed and equipped.

Natah Otann cast a triumphant glance around him; his eye fell immediately on the two prisoners, who had remained quietly seated, talking together, and apparently indifferent to all that happened. At the sight of them the Chiefs thick eyebrows were contracted, he leant over to the White Buffalo, who rode by his side, and muttered a few words in his ear. The old man gave a sign of assent, and walked towards the prisoners, while Natah Otann, taking the head of the war party, gave the signal for departure, and went off, only leaving ten warriors on the square to aid White Buffalo, if required.

"Gentlemen," the latter said, sharply, but courteously; "be good enough to mount and follow me, if you please."

"Is this an order you give us, sir?" the Count asked, haughtily.

"What does that, question mean?"

"Because I am not in the habit of obeying anybody."

"Sir," the Chief answered, "any resistance would be insensate, and rather injurious than useful to your interests: so to horse without further delay."

"The Chief is right," Bright-eye said, with a significant look at the Count; "why any obstinacy? we cannot be the stronger."

"But—" the young man remarked.

"Here is your horse," the hunter interrupted him, sharply.

"We obey the Chief," he added, aloud; then he added in a whisper,—

"Are you mad, Mr. Edward? Who knows the chances luck has in store for us during the accursed expedition?"

"Still—"

"Mount! Mount!"

At length the young man, partly convinced, obeyed the hunter. When the prisoners had mounted, the warriors surrounded them, and led them off at a gallop, till they caught up the column, of which they took the lead.

Despite the Count's resistance, Natah Otann and White Buffalo had not given up their plan of making him pass for Motecuhzoma, and placing him at the head of the Allied Nations. Still this plan had been modified, in this sense, that, as the young Count refused his help, they would force him to give it in spite of himself. The following is the way in which they intended to act. They had succeeded in persuading the Indians who accompanied them during the ostrich hunt, that the struggle sustained by the Count, and which had struck them with stupor, owing to the energetic resistance the two men had so long offered to fifty warriors, was a ruse invented by them to display their strength and power in the sight of all.

The Redskins, owing to their ignorance, are stupidly credulous. Natah Otann's clumsy falsehood, which any man but slightly civilized would have regarded with contempt, obtained the greatest success with these brutalized beings, and enhanced, in their eyes, the personal value of the men whom they saw continuing to live on good terms with their Chiefs, and remaining apparently free in the village.

Matters were too far advanced, the day chosen for the outbreak of the plot was too near, for the Chiefs to give counterorders to their allies, and concoct some other scheme to replace the prophet they had announced to the Missouri nations. If, on arriving at the rendezvous, the man they had expected was not presented to them, it was evident they would retire with their contingents, and that all would be broken off with no hope of recombination; but a catastrophe must be guarded against at all risks.

The resolution formed by the two Chiefs, desperate as it was, they were compelled to adopt through the suspicious nature of the circumstances, and they trusted to chance to make it succeed. The Count and his companion would march, so long as the expedition lasted, at the head of the attacking columns, without weapons it is true, but apparently free, while guarded by ten picked warriors, who would never leave them, and kill them on the slightest suspicious gesture. The plan was absurd, and, with other men than Indians, the impossibility would have been recognized in less than an hour; but, through its very impracticability, it offered chances of success, and this was chiefly owing to the belief the Indians held that the Count had no friends to attempt his rescue.

Ivon's flight had troubled Natah Otann for a few moments: but the discovery made in the forest, where he had sought shelter, of the body of a man clothed in the servant's dress, and half devoured by wild beasts, restored him all his serenity, by proving to him that he had nought to fear from the poor fellow's devotion.

Three hours prior to the departure of the column, the Chief had, on White Buffalo's revelations, had five spies secretly strangled. Red Wolf, on whom Natah Otann and White Buffalo placed unbounded confidence, and whose courage could not be doubted, was appointed head of the detachment to watch over the prisoners. Hence matters were in the best possible state. The two Chiefs marched about fifty paces ahead of their warriors, conversing in a low voice, and definitely arranging their final plans. White Buffalo described in a few words the position and their hopes.

"Our prospect is desperate," he said, "chance may make it fail or succeed: all depends upon the first attack. If, as I believe, we surprise the American garrison, and seize Fort Mackenzie, we shall have no further need of this Count, whose disappearance we can easily account for, by saying that he has reascended to heaven, because we are victors. However, we shall see; all will be decided in a few hours. Till then, courage and prudence."

Natah Otann made no reply; but cast a glance at Prairie-Flower, who cantered along in apparent carelessness on the flank of the column, which she had asked leave to accompany, and the Chief had gladly granted it. The warriors advanced in a long line, silently following one of those winding paths formed on the desert for centuries by the feet of wild beasts. The night was transparent and calm; the sky, embroidered with millions of stars, shed down on the landscape floods of melancholy light, harmonizing with the grand and primitive nature of the desert. About four in the morning, Natah Otann halted on the top of a wooded dell, in the centre of an immense clearing, where the entire detachment disappeared, without leaving a trace.

Fort Mackenzie rose gloomy and majestic at about a gunshot off. The Indians had effected their march with such prudence, that the American garrison had given no sign of alarm. Natah Otann had a tent put up, into which he courteously begged his prisoners to enter, and they obeyed.

"Why so much politeness?" the Count said.

"Are you not my guests?" the Chief replied, with an ironical smile, and then withdrew.

The Count and his comrade, when left alone, lay down on a pile of furs intended for their bed.

"What is to be done?" the Count muttered, greatly discouraged.

"Sleep," the hunter said, carelessly. "Unless I am mistaken, we shall soon have some news."

"Heaven grant it!"

"Amen," Bright-eye continued, with a laugh. "Bah! we shall not die this time either."

"I hope so," the Count repeated, to say something.

"And I am sure of it. It would be curious, on my word," the hunter said, with a laugh, "were I, who have traversed the desert so long, to be killed by these red brutes."

The young man could not refrain from admiring, in his heart, the cool certainty with which the Canadian uttered so monstrous an opinion; but at this moment the prisoners heard a gentle sound near them.

"Silence!" Bright-eye commanded.

They listened attentively. A harmonious voice then sang to a melody, full of gentleness and melancholy, the exquisite Blackfoot song beginning with the verses:—

"I confide to you my heart, in the name of the Master of Life; I am unhappy, and no one takes pity on me, yet the Master of Life is great in my sight."

"Oh!" the Count muttered joyously, "I recognise that voice, my friend."

"And I too, by Jupiter! It is Prairie-Flower's."

"What does she say?"

"It is a warning she gives us."

"Do you believe so?"

"Prairie-Flower loves you, Mr. Edward."

"Poor child! and I love her too; but alas!—"

"Bah! after the storm comes fine weather."

"If I could but see her."

"For what good? She will contrive to make herself visible when it is necessary. Come, wild or tame, all women are alike. But, look out, here is somebody."

They threw themselves on the furs, and pretended to be asleep. A man had quietly lifted the curtain of the tent. By the moon's ray, that passed through the opening, the prisoners recognized Red Wolf. The Indian looked outside for a moment; then, probably reassured by the calmness that prevailed around, he let the curtain of the tent fall, and took a few paces in the interior.

"The jaguar is strong and courageous," he said, in a loud voice, as if talking to himself; "the fox is cunning; but the man whose heart is big is stronger than the jaguar, and more cunning than the fox, when he has in his hand weapons to defend himself. Who says that Glass-eye and Bright-eye will allow their throats to be cut like tamed gazelles?"

"And not looking at the prisoners, the Chief laid at their feet two guns, from which hung powder flasks, bullet bags, and long knives; then he left the tent again, as calmly as if he had done the simplest matter in the world. The prisoners looked at each other in amazement.

"What do you think of that?" Bright-eye muttered in stupefaction.

"It is a trap," the Count answered.

"Hum! trap or no, the weapons are there, and I shall take them."

The hunter seized the guns and the knives, which he immediately hid under the furs. The arms were hardly in security, ere the curtain of the tent was again raised, and Natah Otann walked in. He bore in his hand a branch of ocote, or candlewood, which lit up his thoughtful face, and gave it a sinister expression. The Chief dug up the ground with his knife, planted his torch in the ground, and walked toward the prisoners, who looked on without giving any sign.

"Gentlemen," the Chief then said, "I have come to ask for a moment's interview with you."

"Speak, sir; we are your prisoners, and as such compelled to hear you, if not to listen to you," the Count said, drily, as he sat up on the furs, while Bright-eye rose carelessly, and lit his pipe at the candlewood torch.

"Since you have been my prisoners, gentlemen," the Chief continued, "you have not had, to my knowledge, any reason to complain of the way in which I have treated you."

"That depends. In the first place, I do not admit that I am legally your prisoner."

"Oh, sir," the Chief said, with a smile of mockery, "do you speak of legality to a poor Indian? You know well that we are ignorant of that word."

"That is true; go on."

"I have come to see you—"

"Why?" the Count interrupted him, impatiently. "Explain!"

"I have a bargain to propose to you."

"Well, I will frankly confess that your way of bargaining does not impress me with great confidence."

The Indian made a move.

"No matter," the Count continued, "let us hear it."

"I should not like to be obliged, sir, to tie you again, as you were when you were captured."

"I am extremely obliged to you."

"But; at this moment I absolutely need all my warriors, and I cannot leave anybody to guard you two gentlemen."

"Which means?"

"That I ask your parole not to escape for the next twenty-four hours."

"But that is not a bargain."

"Wait; I am coming to it."

"Good; I am waiting."

"In return, I pledge myself—"

"Ah!" the Count said, contemptuously, "let us see to what you pledge yourself; that must be curious."

"I pledge myself," the Chief continued, still cold and calm, "to give you your liberty in twenty-four hours."

"And my comrade?"

The Indian bowed his head in affirmation; the Count burst into a loud laugh.

"And suppose we did not accept?" he asked.

"But you will do so," he said, with an ironical smile.

"Possibly; but suppose the contrary for a moment."

"At daybreak you will both be attached to the stake, and tortured until sunset."

"Oh, oh! Is that your final word?"

"The last; in half an hour I will come for your answer."

And he turned to go out. The Count bounded like a jaguar, and stood before the Chief, his gun in one hand, his knife in the other.

"A moment," he shouted.

"Wah!" the Chief said, crossing his hands on his wide chest, and gazing at them sarcastically. "You had taken your precautions, it appears."

"By Jove!" Bright-eye said, with a grin; "I rather fancy it is our turn to make conditions."

"Perhaps so," Natah Otann replied, coolly; "but I have no time to lose in vain words; let me pass, gentlemen."

Bright-eye threw himself quickly before the door.

"Come, Chief," he said, "things cannot end like that; we are not old women to be frightened. Before we are fastened to the stake, we will kill you."

The Chief shrugged his shoulders disdainfully,

"You are mad; let me pass, old hunter, and do not oblige me to use force."

"No, no, Chief," Bright-eye added, with an ironical laugh; "we shall not part like that; all the worse for you; you should not have put your head in the wolf's throat."

Natah Otann made an impatient gesture.

"You wish it; well, then, see!"

Raising to his lips his war-whistle, made of a human thigh bone, he produced a shrill sound. All at once, before the two Europeans could comprehend what was happening, the sides of the tent were cut open, and the Blackfeet bounded into the interior. The Count and Bright-eye were seized and disarmed. The Sachem, with his arms still crossed on his chest, looked like a stoic, while the Kenhas, with their eyes fixed on the Chief, and uplifted tomahawks, seemed to await from him a final signal.

There was a moment of intense anxiety; though the two white men were so brave, the attack had been so rapid and unexpected, that they could not refrain from an inward shudder. For a few seconds the Chief enjoyed his triumph; then, raising his hand, with a gesture of supreme authority, he said, —

"Enough! Restore their weapons to these warriors. Are they not the guests of Natah Otann?"

The Blackfeet retired as suddenly as they had appeared.

"Well," the Chief asked, with slight irony, "do you understand me at last? Do you still fancy me in your power?"

"Very good, sir," the Count replied, coldly, still suffering from the struggle he had gone through; "I am forced to recognize the advantage that chance gives you over me; any resistance would be useless. I consent to submit for the present to your will; but only on two conditions."

"They are accepted beforehand, sir," Natah Otann said, with a bow.

"Do not be too certain, sir; for you do not yet know what I mean to ask from you."

"I am awaiting your explanation."

"As it must be so, I will march at the head of your tribes; but alone, unarmed, and on condition, that under no pretext you impose on me any other character in the gloomy tragedy you are preparing to act."

The Chief frowned.

"And supposing that I refuse?" he said, in a hoarse voice.

"If you refuse," the young man answered, with his calmest air, "I will employ sure means to compel you to assent."

"They are?"

"I will blow out my brains, sir, in the sight of all your warriors."

The Chief cast a viper's glance at him.

"Very good," he said, presently. "I accept; now let us have the other condition."

"It is simply this: conqueror or conquered; and I hope sincerely that the latter may be the case—"

"Thank you," the Chief interrupted him, with an ironical bow.

"After the battle, whatever its issue may be," the Count continued, "you will fight me honourably with equal weapons."

"Why, Sir Count, you are proposing to me what white men call a duel!"

"Yes. Does that displease you?"

"Me? certainly not, and I accept gladly; the more so, as we Blood Indians are accustomed to have such fights to settle our own personal quarrels."

"Then you accept my conditions?"

"I do so."

"But who will guarantee your good faith?" the young man asked.

"I, Sir," a powerful voice said.

The three men turned. White Buffalo was standing motionless in the doorway of the tent. At the unexpected appearance of this strange man, whose features revealed at the moment an imposing majesty, the young Count felt subdued, and bowed respectfully.

"Gentlemen," Natah Otann continued, "you are free within the limits of the camp."

"Thanks," Bright-eye said coarsely; "but I have made no promise."

"You!" the Chief said carelessly; "go or stay, I care very little."

And after bowing ceremoniously to the Count, the two Chiefs withdrew.

CHAPTER XXV
BEFORE THE ATTACK

After leaving the tent, the two Chiefs walked for some moments side by side, and did not exchange a word; both seemed plunged in deep thought, doubtlessly caused by the serious events that were preparing—events whose success would decide the fate of the Indian tribes of this part of the continent. While walking along, they reached a point on the hillock, whence a most extensive view could be enjoyed in every direction.

The night was calm and balmy, there was not a breath in the air, not a cloud on the sky, whose deep azure was enamelled with a profusion of twinkling stars; an imposing silence reigned over this desert, where, however, several thousand men were ambushed, only waiting a word or a signal to out each other's throats. Mechanically the two men stopped, and gazed at the grand landscape extended at their feet, in the immediate foreground of which frowned Fort Mackenzie, throwing its gloomy shadow far across the prairie.

"By sunrise," Natah Otann muttered, answering his own thoughts, rather than addressing his companion, "that haughty fortress will be mine. The Redskins will command at the spot where their oppressors are still reigning."

"Yes," White Buffalo repeated, mechanically, "tomorrow you will be master of the fort, but will you manage to keep it? Conquering is nothing; the white men have been several times defeated by the Redskins, and yet they have enslaved, decimated, and dispersed them like the leaves the autumn breeze bears away."

"That is only too true," the Chief said, with a sigh; "it has ever been so, since the first day the white men set foot in this unhappy land. What is the mysterious influence that has constantly predicted them against us?"

"Yourselves, my child," White Buffalo said, mournfully shaking his head; "you are your own greatest enemies. You can only impute to yourselves your continued defeats, for you are so obstinate for internecine warfare; the whites have taken care to foster strongly your headstrong passions, by which they have skilfully profited to conquer you in detail."

"Yes, you have told me that often, my father, so you see I have profited by your advice; all the Missouri Indians are now united, they obey the same chief, and march under one totem; thus, believe me, this union will be fertile in good results, we shall drive these plundering wolves from our frontiers, we shall send them back to the villages of stone; and henceforth only the moccasin of the Redskins will tread our native prairies, and the echoes will only be aroused by the joyous laughter of the Redskins, or repeat the war cry of the Blackfeet."

"No one will be happier than I at such a result; my most ardent desire is to see men free, from whom I have received such paternal hospitality; but, alas, who can foresee the future? These Sachems, whom you have succeeded in combining by attention and patience, are agitating darkly; they fear to obey you; they are jealous of the power themselves gave you, so there is a chance they will abandon you."

"I will not; give them the time, my father; for the last few days I have known all their designs, and followed their plans; up to the present, prudence has closed my mouth. I did not wish to risk the success of my enterprise; but so soon as I am master of this fortress below us, believe me, I shall speak loudly, for my voice will have exercised an authority, my power a strength, which the most turbulent will be compelled to recognize. Victory will render me great and terrible: will trample under foot those who now conspire in the darkness, and who would not hesitate to turn against me, if I experienced a defeat. Go, my father, let all be ready for the attack so soon as I give the signal, visit the outposts, watch the movements of the enemy, for in two hours I shall utter my war cry."

White Buffalo regarded him for a moment with a singular expression, in which friendship, fear, and admiration struggled in turn; then laying his hand on his shoulder he said, with much emotion, —

"Child, you are mad; but it is a sublime madness: the work of reformation you meditate is impossible—but, whether you triumph or succumb, your attempt will not be useless. Your passage on earth will leave a long, luminous trace, which may one day serve as a beacon to those who succeed in accomplishing the liberation of your race."

After a few seconds of silence, more eloquent than vain words, the two men fell into each other's arms, and held each other in a firm embrace; they then separated, and Natah Otann remained alone.

The young Chief did not conceal from himself in any way the difficulties of his position. He recognized the justice of his adopted father's observations; but now it was too late to recoil, he must push onward at all risks. Now that the moment had arrived to descend into the arena, all hesitation had ceased, all fear had died out in the young Chief's bosom, to give way to a cold and invincible resolution, that imparted to him the lucidity of mind required to play skilfully the great part on which the fate of his race would depend.

When White Buffalo left him alone, Natah Otann sat down on a rock, and, resting his head on his hand, fixed his eyes on the place, and fell into a serious contemplation. For a long time he had been dreaming, with a vague consciousness of external objects, when a hand was gently laid on his shoulder. The Chief quivered, as if he had received an electric shock, and quickly raised his head.

"*Ochtl?*" he said, with an emotion he could not master. "Prairie-Flower here at this hour?"

The young girl smiled sweetly.

"Why is my brother astonished?" she replied, in her gentle and melodious voice; "does not the Chief know that Prairie-Flower loves to wander about at night, when nature is slumbering, and the voice of the Great Spirit can be more easily heard? We girls love to dream at night, by the melancholy light that comes from the stars, and seems to give reality to our thoughts, at times, in the mist."

The Chief sighed in reply.

"You are suffering?" Prairie-Flower asked him, gently; "You, the first Sachem of our nation, the most renowned warrior of our tribes—what reason can be powerful enough to draw a sigh from you?"

The Chief seised the dainty hand the girl yielded to him, and pressed it gently between his own.

"Prairie-Flower," he said at length, "you are ignorant why I suffer when I am by your side?"

"How should I know it? Although my brothers call me the *Virgin of Sweet Love*, and suppose me to be in relation with the spirits of air and water, alas! I am only an ignorant young girl. I should like to know the cause of your grief; perhaps I could succeed in curing you."

"No," the Chief answered, shaking his head, "it is not in your power, child; to do that the beating of your heart ought to respond to mine, and the little bird, which sings so melodiously in the hearts of maidens, and murmurs such gentle words in their ears, should have flown near you."

The girl blushed and smiled; she let her eyes fall, and, making an effort to disengage her hand, which Natah Otann still held in his,—

"The little bird, of which my brother speaks, I have seen: its song has already been chanted near me."

The Chief sprung up, and fixed a flashing glance on the maiden.

"What!" he exclaimed, with agitation, "you love? Has one of the young warriors of our tribe known how to touch your heart, and fill it with love?"

Prairie-Flower shook her charming head petulantly, while a sweet smile parted her coral lips.

"I know not if what I experience is what you call love," she said.

Natah Otann had, by a painful effort, checked the emotion which made his limbs tremble.

"Why should it not be so?" he continued, thoughtfully. "The laws of nature are immutable, no one can prevent it; the child's hour was destined to arrive. By what right can I quarrel with what has happened? Have I not in my heart a sacred feeling, which fills it, and before which every other must be extinguished? A man in my position is too far above vulgar passions; the object he proposes to himself is too great for him to allow himself to be ruled by love of a woman. The man who lays claim to become the saviour and regenerator of a people, no longer belongs to humanity. Let me be worthy of the task I have taken on myself, and forget, if possible, the mad and hopeless passion that devours me. That girl can never be mine; everything separates us. I will be to her what I ought never to have ceased to be—a father."

He let his head hang despairingly on his chest, and remained for a few moments absorbed in gloomy meditation. Prairie-Flower regarded him with an expression of tender pity; she had only imperfectly caught the words the Chief muttered, and understood but little of them. Still she felt a deep friendship for him; she suffered in seeing him, and sought vainly some consolation to afford. She waited anxiously till he should remember her presence, and speak to her again. At length he raised his head.

"My sister has not told me which of our young warriors she prefers to all the rest."

"Has not the Sachem guessed it?" she asked, timidly.

"Natah Otann is a chief. If he is the father of his warriors, he is no spy on their deeds or thoughts."

"The man of whom I speak to my brother is not a Kenha warrior," she continued.

"Ah!" he said in surprise, and looking scrutinizingly at her, "Can it be one of the Palefaces who are Natah Otann's guests?"

"My brother would say his prisoners," she murmured.

"What mean these words, girl? Have you, born but yesterday, any right to try and explain my actions? Ah!" he added, with a frown, "now I understand how the Palefaced Chiefs had weapons when I visited them an hour ago. It is useless for my daughter to tell me now the name of him she loves, for I know it."

The girl hung her head, with a blush.

"*Achtsett*—it is good," he continued, in a rough voice, "my sister is free to place her affections where she pleases; but her love must not lead her to betray her friends for the Palefaces. She is a daughter of the Kenhas. Was it to give me this news that Prairie-Flower came to me?"

"No," she answered timidly; "another person ordered me to come here, where she will also come herself, as she has an important secret to reveal to me in the presence of the Sachem."

"An important secret?" Natah Otann repeated. "What do you mean? Of what woman is my sister speaking?"

"I am speaking of her who is called the She-wolf of the prairies; she has ever been gentle, good, and affectionate to me, in spite of the hatred she bears to the Indians."

"That is strange," the Chief muttered. "So you are waiting for her?"

"I am."

"But that woman is mad," the Chief exclaimed. "Do you not know it, my poor child?"

"Those whom the Great Spirit wishes to protect he deprives of reason, that they may not feel grief," she replied, softly.

For some minutes an almost imperceptible rustling had been going on in the bushes; this sound, though so slight, the Chiefs practised ear would have detected, had he not been entirely absorbed by his conversation with the girl. All at once the branches were violently torn asunder; several men, led by the She-wolf of the prairies, rushed toward the Chief, and, before he had recovered from the surprise caused by this sudden attack, he was thrown down, and securely pinioned.

"The mad woman!" he exclaimed.

"Yes, yes, the mad woman," she repeated, in a hoarse voice. "At length I hold my vengeance! Thanks," she added, addressing the three men who accompanied her; "I will now take his guard on myself, he shall not escape."

The men withdrew without replying. Although they wore the Indian dress, a panther skin drawn over their faces rendered them perfectly secure from detection. Only three persons remained on the top of the hill—Prairie-Flower, Margaret, and Natah Otann, who tried to break his bonds, while uttering hoarse and inarticulate sounds. The She-wolf surveyed her enemy, prostrated at her feet, with a joy impossible to describe, while Prairie-Flower, standing motionless by the Chief, gazed on him sorrowfully and thoughtfully.

"Yes," the She-wolf said, with a glance of satiated vengeance, "howl, panther; bend the bonds you cannot break. I hold you at last; it is my turn to torture you, to repay you all the suffering you lavished on me. Oh! I can never be sufficiently avenged on you, the assassin of my whole family. God is just: tooth for tooth, eye for eye, wretch!"

She picked up a dagger that had fallen on the ground near her, and began to prick him all over.

"Answer me—do you not feel the cold steel piercing your flesh?" she asked him. "Oh! I should like to make you suffer death a thousand times, were it possible."

A smile of contempt played over the Chief's lips. The She-wolf, exasperated, raised the dagger to strike him; but Prairie-Flower held her arm. Margaret turned like a tiger; but, recognizing the girl, she let the weapon fall from her trembling hand, and her face assumed an expression of infinite gentleness and tenderness.

"You here?" she exclaimed. "Then you did not forget the meeting I arranged with you? It is Heaven that sends you!"

"Yes," the young girl replied, "the Great Spirit sees all. My mother is good; Prairie-Flower loves her. Why thus torture the man who acted as father to the abandoned child? The Chief has ever been kind to Prairie-Flower; my mother will pardon him."

Margaret gazed at the girl with an expression of mad stupor; then her features were suddenly distorted, and she burst into a strident laugh.

"What!" she exclaimed, in a piercing voice, "you, Prairie-Flower, intercede for this man?"

"He was a father to Prairie-Flower," the girl answered, simply.

"But you do not know him then?"

"He has been kind to me."

"Silence, child! do not implore the She-wolf," the Chief said, in a gloomy voice. "Natah Otann is a warrior; he knows how to die."

"No, the Chief must not die," the Indian girl said, resolutely.

Natah Otann laughed.

"It is I who am avenged," he said.

"Dog!" the She-wolf yelled, stamping her heel on his face, "silence! or I will tear out your viper's tongue."

The Indian smiled with contempt.

"My mother will follow me," the girl said: "I will unfasten the Chief, in order that he may rejoin his warriors, who are about to fight."

She picked up the dagger, and knelt down near the prisoner; but the She-wolf checked her.

"Before cutting his bonds, listen to me, child," she said.

"Afterwards," the girl objected. "A Chief must be with his warriors in battle."

"Listen to me for a few minutes," She-wolf continued, earnestly; "I implore it of you, Prairie-Flower, by all I may have done for you; then, when I have ceased speaking, if you still wish it, you shall deliver that man. I swear to you that I will not prevent it."

The girl looked at her fixedly.

"Speak," she said, in her gentle and sympathizing voice. "Prairie-Flower is listening."

A sigh of relief escaped from the She-wolf's oppressed chest. There was a moment's silence: nothing could be heard, save the panting of the prisoner.

"You are right, girl," the She-wolf at length said, in a mournful voice, "that man took care of your infancy, was kind to you, and brought you up tenderly; you see that I do him justice! But he never told you how you fell into his hands."

"Never," the maiden said, in a melancholy voice.

"Well," the She-wolf continued, "that secret, which he has not dared to reveal to you, I will tell you. On just such a night as this, at the head of his ferocious warriors, the man you call your father attacked your real father, and while your two brothers, by that monster's orders, were burned alive, your father fastened to a tree, and there was flayed alive."

"Horror!" the young girl shrieked, as she sprang up.

"And if you do not believe me," she continued, in a shrill voice, "tear from your neck that bag made of your unhappy father's skin, and you will find in it all that remains of him."

With a feverish movement the young girl drew out the bag, which she squeezed convulsively.

"Oh!" she exclaimed, "no! no! it is impossible; such atrocities could not be committed."

Suddenly her tears ceased, she looked fixedly at the She-wolf, and said, in a harsh voice —

"How do you know all this? The man who told it you lied."

"I was present," the She-wolf said, coldly,

"You were present? You witnessed this horrible scene?"

"Yes, I did."

"Why?" she asked, madly. "Answer, why?

"Why?" she said, with an accent of supreme majesty; "because I am your mother, child."

At this unexpected revelation the girl's features were convulsed, her voice failed her, her eyes seemed ready to start from their sockets, her body was agitated by a convulsive tremor; for an instant she tried to utter a shriek, but then suddenly broke into sobs, and fell into Margaret's arms, exclaiming, with a piercing accent, —

"My mother! My mother!"

"At last," the She-wolf said, deliriously, "I have found you again, and you are really mine."

For some moments mother and daughter, yielding to their tenderness, forgot the whole world. Natah Otann tried to profit by the opportunity, and seize the chance of safety which accident offered him. He noiselessly began rolling over to gain the top of the enclosure; but the young girl suddenly noticed him, and sprang up as if a serpent had stung her.

"Stop, Natah Otann!" she said to him.

The chief remained motionless: he imagined, from the girl's accent, that he was lost, and he resigned himself to his fate with that fatalism which forms the base of the Indian character.

Still he was mistaken.

Prairie-Flower, with burning eyes and pallid brow, turned a haggard glance from her mother on the man extended at her feet, asking her heart if she had a right, after all the kindness he had shown her, to avenge her father's death upon him. She felt that her arm was too weak, her heart too tender for such a deed. For several seconds the three actors of this terrible scene remained plunged in a gloomy silence, which was only interrupted by the dull and mysterious noises of the night.

Natah Otann did not fear death; but he trembled at leaving uncompleted the glorious task he had taken on himself; he was ashamed at having fallen into so clumsy a snare, set by a half insane woman. With his head stretched out, and frowning brow, he anxiously read on the girl's face the feelings in turn reflected on it as in a mirror, in order to calculate the chances of saving a life so precious to those he wished to render free. Though resigned to his fate, like all great men, he did not despair, but struggled to the last moment. Prairie-Flower at length raised her head; her lovely face had assumed a strange expression her brow glistened, her gentle blue eyes seemed to flash forth flames.

"Mother," she said, in her melodious voice, "give me those pistols you have in your hand."

"What will you do with them?" the She-wolf asked.

"Avenge my father! Was it not for that you summoned me here?"

Without replying, the She-wolf gave her the weapons. The girl, at first, threatened Natah Otann, and then, with a gesture as rapid as thought, threw them down the hill.

"Unhappy girl," Margaret yelled, "what have you done?"

"I avenge my father," she answered, with an accent of supreme dignity.

"Unhappy child, he is the assassin of your father."

"I know it; you have told me so. This man, in spite of his crimes, has been kind to me—he watched over my childhood. Although he obeyed the feeling of hatred his race entertains for the Palefaces by murdering my father, he took his place with me as far as was possible, and almost changed his Indian nature to protect and support me. The Great Spirit will judge us, He whose eye is eternally fixed on earth."

"Woe is me! Woe is me!" the She-wolf yelled, wringing her hands in despair.

The girl bent over the Chief, and cut the bonds that fettered him. Natah Otann sprang to his feet with the bound of a jaguar. The She-wolf made a movement, as if to rush upon him, but she checked herself.

"All is not over yet," she shrieked, "yes! yes! I will have my revenge, no matter at what cost."

And she rushed into the thicket, where she disappeared.

"Natah Otann," the maiden continued, turning to the Chief, who stood by her side, calmly and stoically, as if nothing extraordinary had happened; "I leave vengeance to the Great Spirit—a woman can only weep. Farewell! I loved you as that father you deprived me of. I do not feel the strength to hate you, I will try to forget you."

"Poor child," the Sachem replied, with much emotion; "I must appear to you very culpable. Alas! it is only today that I understand the atrocity of the deed of which I allowed myself to be guilty: perhaps, I may succeed one day in obtaining your pardon."

Prairie-Flower smiled sorrowfully.

"Your pardon does not depend from me," she said, "Wacondah alone can absolve you."

And, after giving him a parting glance of sadness, she withdrew slowly, and thoughtfully entered the wood.

Natah Otann looked after her for a long while.

"Can the Christians be right?" he muttered, when done; "do angels really exist?"

He shook his head several times, and, after attentively looking at the sky, in which the stars were beginning to shine,—

"The hour has arrived," he said, hoarsely; "shall I be the victor?"

CHAPTER XXVI
RED WOLF

To understand the facts we are now about to narrate, we must retrace our steps a short distance, and return to the tent which served as a temporary abode to the Count and Bright-eye.

The two white men were somewhat discontented by the way in which the interview had terminated. Still the Count was too thorough a gentleman not to allow, honourably, that on this occasion the Chief had been the victor in magnanimity. As for Bright-eye, however, he could not see so far. Furious at the check he had sustained, and especially at the slight value the Chief appeared to set on his capture, he revolved the most terrible schemes of vengeance while biting his nails savagely.

The Count amused himself for a few minutes in watching his comrade's manoeuvres, as he walked up and down the tent, growling, clenching his fists, dashing the butt of his rifle on the ground, and looking up to heaven with comic despair. At last the young man could stand it no longer, but burst into a hearty laugh. The hunter stopped in amazement, and looked around the tent, to discover the cause for such untimely gaiety.

"What has happened, Mr. Edward?" he at length asked, "Why do you laugh so?"

Naturally this question, asked with a startled air, had no other result than to augment the Count's hilarity.

"My good fellow," he said, "I am laughing at the singular faces you cut, and the strange manoeuvres you have been indulging in during the last twenty minutes."

"Oh, Mr. Edward!" Bright-eye said, reproachfully; "how can you jest so?"

"Why, my boy, you seem to take the affair seriously to heart, and to have lost that magnificent confidence which made you despise all dangers."

"No, no, Mr. Edward! you are mistaken. My opinion has been formed a long time. Look you, I am certain these red devils will never succeed in killing me; but I am furious at having been so thoroughly duped by them.

It is humiliating, and I am now racking my brains to discover a way to play them a trick."

"Do so, my friend, and I would help you, were it possible; but, for the present, at least, I am forced to remain neutral—my hands are tied."

"What?" Bright-eye said, with astonishment; "you mean to remain here, and serve their diabolical jugglery?"

"I must, my good fellow; have I not pledged my word?"

"You certainly pledged it, and I do not know why. Still, a pledge given to an Indian counts for nothing. The Redskins are tribes who understand nothing about honour; and, in a similar case, I am certain that Natah Otann would consider himself in no way bound to you."

"That is possible, although I am not of your opinion. The Chief is no ordinary man. He is gifted with a great intellect."

"What good is it to him? None. Except to be more cunning and treacherous than his countrymen. Take my advice, and do not stand on any ceremony with him. Take French leave, as they say in the South, and leave them in the lurch. The Redskins will be the first to applaud your conduct."

"My good fellow," the Count said, seriously, "it is useless to discuss the point; when a gentleman has once given his word, he is a slave to it, no matter the person to whom he has given it, or the colour of his skin."

"Very good, then, Mr. Edward, pray act as you think proper. I have no right to thrust my advice on you. You are a better judge than myself of how you are bound to act. So, be easy. I will not mention it again."

"Thank you."

"All that is very good, but what are we going to do now?"

"What we are going to do? I suppose you mean what are you going to do?"

"No, Mr. Edward, I said exactly what I meant; you understand that I am not going to leave you alone in this nest of serpents, I hope!"

"On the contrary, you will do so directly."

"I?" the hunter said, with a loud laugh.

"Yes, you, my friend; you must."

"Bah! why so, pray, if you remain?"

"That is the very reason."

The hunter reflected for a moment.

"You know that I do not understand you at all," he said.

"Yet it is very clear," the Count answered.

"Hum! that is possible, but not to me."

"What, you do not understand that we must avenge ourselves?"

"Oh, of course, I understand that, Mr. Edward."

"How can we hope to succeed, if you insist on remaining here?"

"Because you remain," the hunter said, obstinately.

"With me it is very different, my good fellow. I remain, because I have given my word; while you are free to go and come, and must therefore profit by it to leave the camp. Once in the prairie, nothing can be easier for you than to join some of our friends. It is evident that my worthy Ivon, coward as he fancies himself, is working actively at this moment for my deliverance; so see him, come to an understanding with him, for though it is true I cannot leave this place, I cannot, on the other hand, prevent my friends liberating me; if they succeed, my parole will be suspended, and nothing will hinder my following them. Do you understand me now?"

"Yes, Mr. Edward; but I confess that I cannot make up my mind to leave you alone, among these red devils."

"Do not trouble yourself about that, Bright-eye; I run no danger by remaining with them; they have too much respect for me; besides, Natah Otann well knows how to defend me, should it be needful. So, my friend, start at once. You will serve me better by going, than by insisting on remaining here, where your presence, in the event of danger, would be more injurious than useful to me."

"You are a better judge than I in such a matter, sir; as you insist on it, I will go," the hunter said, with a mournful shake of his head.

"Above all, be prudent, do not expose yourself to risk in quitting the camp."

The hunter smiled disdainfully.

"You know," he said, "that the Redskins cannot harm me."

"That is true; I forgot it," the young man said, laughingly; "so, good-bye, my friend, stay no longer, but go, and joy be with you."

"Good-bye, Mr. Edward; will you not give me a shake of the hand before we part, not knowing whether we shall ever meet again?"

"Most gladly, for are we not brothers?"

"That is famous," the hunter said, joyfully, as he pressed the Count's offered hand.

The two men presently separated. The Count fell back on the pile of furs that served as his bed, while the hunter, after assuring himself that his arms were in good condition, quitted the tent. With his rifle under his arm, and head erect, he crossed the camp. The Indians did not seem at all to trouble themselves at the hunter's presence among them, and allowed him to depart unimpeded.

Bright-eye, when he had gone about two musket shots from the camp, stopped, and began reflecting on what was best to be done to liberate the Count; after a few moments' reflection, his mind was made up, and he proceeded toward the squatter's settlement with that long trot peculiar to the hunters.

When he reached the clearing, the squatter was holding a conference with Ivon and the party sent by Major Melville. His arrival was greeted with a hurrah of delight.

The North Americans were considerably embarrassed. Mrs. Margaret, in spite of the exclusive details she had obtained about Natah Otann's plans, and the movements of the Indians, had only made an incomplete report to the Major, from the simple reason, that the old Sachems of the Allied Nations kept their deliberations so secret, that Red Wolf, despite all his cleverness and craft, had himself picked up but a slight part of the plan the Chiefs proposed to follow. The scouts, sent out in all directions, had brought in startling reports about the movements of the Blackfeet; the Indians appeared resolved to strike a grand blow this time; all the Missouri nations had responded to Natah Otann's appeal; the tribes arrived one after the other, to join the coalition, so that their number now attained four thousand, and threatened not to stop then.

Fort Mackenzie was surrounded on all sides by invisible enemies, who had completely cut off the communication with the other settlements of the Fur Company, and rendered the Major's position extremely critical. Thus the hunters were greatly perplexed; and during the many hours they had been deliberating, they had only hit on insufficient or impracticable means to relieve the fortress.

The White men have only succeeded in holding their own in Western America by the divisions they have managed to sow among the aborigines of the continent; whenever the latter have remained united, the Europeans have failed, as witness the Araucanos of Chili, whose small but valiant republic has maintained its independence to the present day; or the Seminoles of

Louisiana, who have only lately been conquered after a desperate contest, carried on with all the rules of modern warfare, and many other Indian nations, whose names we could easily quote, if necessary, in support of our arguments.

This time the Indians seemed to have understood the importance of open and energetic action. The several Chiefs had, ostensibly at least, forgotten all their hatred and jealousies, to destroy the common enemy. Thus the Americans, in spite of their approved bravery, trembled at the mere thought of the war of extermination they would have to sustain against enemies exasperated by a long series of vexations, when they counted their numbers, and saw how weak they were, compared to the warriors preparing to crush them. The council, interrupted for a moment by Bright-eye's arrival, immediately assembled again, and the debate was continued.

"By heaven!" John Black exclaimed, angrily, as he smote his thigh with his fist, "I confess that I have no luck, everything turns against me; hardly have I settled here, whither everything made me forebode a prosperous future, than I am dragged, in spite of myself, into a war with these vagabond savages. Who knows how it will end? It is plain to me that we shall all lose our scalps. That is a pleasant prospect for a man who is anxious to raise his family honourably by his labour."

"That is not the question at this moment," Ivon said; "we have to save my master at all risks. What! you are all afraid to fight when it is almost your trade? and you have done hardly anything else during your lives; while I, who am known to be a remarkable coward, do not hesitate to risk my scalp to save my master."

"You do not understand me, Master Ivon; I do not say that I am afraid to fight the Indians; heaven guard me from fearing these Pagans, whom I despise. Still, I believe that an honest and laborious man, like myself, may be permitted to deplore the consequences of a war with these demons. I know too well all I and my family owe to the Count, to hesitate in hurrying to his help, whatever the result may be. The little I possess was his gift, I have not forgotten it, and even were I to fall, I would do my duty."

"Bravo! that is what I call speaking," Ivon replied, joyously; "I was certain you would not hang back."

"Unfortunately," Bright-eye objected, "all this does not advance matters much. I do not see how we can serve our friends. These red devils fall upon us more numerous than locusts in June. We may kill many of them, but in the end they will crush us by their weight."

This sad truth, perfectly understood by the auditors, plunged them into dull grief, A material impossibility cannot be discussed; it must be submitted to. The Americans felt an imminent catastrophe coming on, and their despair was augmented by the consciousness of their impotence. Suddenly the cry "To arms!" several times repeated outside, made them bound on their seats. Each seized his weapons, and ran out. The cry, which had broken up the conference, was raised by William, the squatter's son.

All eyes were turned on the prairie, and the hunters perceived, with secret terror, that William was not mistaken. A large band of Indian warriors, dressed in their grand war paint, was galloping over the plain, and rapidly approaching the clearing.

"Hang it!" Bright-eye muttered, "matters are getting worse. I must confess that these most accursed Pagans have made enormous progress in military tactics. If they continue, they will soon give us a lesson."

"Do you think so?" Black asked, anxiously.

"Confound it!" the hunter replied, "it is evident to me that we are about to be attacked, I now know the plan of the Redskins as thoroughly as if they had explained it to me themselves."

"Ah!" Ivon said, curiously.

"Judge for yourselves," the hunter continued; "the Indians intend to attack simultaneously all the posts occupied by white men, in order to render it impossible for them to help one another. That is excessively logical on their parts. In that way they will have a cheap bargain of us, and massacre us in detail. Hum! the man who commands them is a rough adversary for us. My lads, we must make up our minds gaily. We are lost, that is as plain to me as if the scalping knife was already in our hair. All left to us is to fall bravely."

These words, pronounced in the cool and placid tone usual with the wood ranger, caused all who heard them to shudder.

"I alone, perhaps," Bright-eye added, carelessly, "shall escape the common fate."

"Bah!" Ivon said; "you, old hunter, why so?"

"Why?" he said, with a sarcastic smile, "because, as you are perfectly aware, the Indians cannot kill me."

"Ah!" Ivon remarked, stupefied by this reason, and gazing on his friend with admiration.

"That is the state of the case," Bright-eye ended his address, and stamped his rifle on the ground.

In the meanwhile the Redskins advanced rapidly. The band was composed of one hundred and fifty warriors at least, the majority armed with guns, which proved they were picked men. At the head of the band, and about ten yards in advance, galloped two horsemen, probably Chiefs. The Indians stopped just out of range of the entrenchments; then, after consulting together for a few minutes, a horseman left the group, and, riding within pistol shot of the palisades, he waved a buffalo robe.

"Eh! eh! Master Black," Bright-eye said, with a cunning smile, "that is addressed to you as the chief of the garrison. The Redskins wish to parley."

"Ah!" the-American said, "I have a great mind to send a bullet after that rascal parading down, as my sole answer," and he raised his rifle.

"Mind what you are about," the hunter said, "you do not know the Redskins. So long as the first shot is not fired, there is a chance of treating with them."

"Suppose, old hunter," Ivon said, "you were to do something?"

"What is it, my prudent friend?" the Canadian asked.

"Why, as you are not afraid of being killed by the Redskins, suppose you go to them. Perhaps you could arrange matters with them."

"Stay! that is a good idea. No one can say what may happen. I will go. That will be the best, after all. Will you accompany me, Ivon?"

"Why not?" the latter answered; "with you, I am not afraid."

"Well, that is settled, then. Open the gate for us, Master Black; but keep a good lookout during our absence, and, on the first suspicious movement, fire on these heathens."

"Do not alarm yourself, old hunter," the latter said, squeezing his hand cordially; "I should not like any harm to happen to you, for you are a man."

"I believe so," the Canadian said, with a laugh; "but what I say to you is more for this worthy fellow's sake than mine, for I assure you I am quite easy on my own account."

"No matter, I will watch these demons carefully."

"That can do no harm."

The gate was opened. Bright-eye and Ivon went down the hill, and went toward the horseman, who was patiently awaiting them.

"Ah! ah!" Bright-eye muttered, as soon as he drew near enough to recognize the rider; "I fancy that our affairs are not quite so well as I suspected."

"Why so?" Ivon asked.

"Look at that warrior. Do you not see it is Red Wolf?"

"That is true. Well?"

"Well, I have reasons for believing that he is not so great an enemy as he appears to be."

"Are you sure of it?"

"Silence! we shall soon see."

The three men saluted each other courteously in the Indian fashion, by laying the right hand on the heart, and holding out the other open, with the fingers apart and the palm turned outwards.

"My brother is welcome among his Paleface brothers," Bright-eye said; "does he come to sit at the council fire, and smoke the calumet in my wigwam?"

"The hunter will decide. Red Wolf comes as a friend," the Indian answered.

"Good," the Canadian remarked; "did Red Wolf then fear treachery from his friend, that he brought so large a body of warriors with him?"

The Blackfoot smiled cunningly.

"Red Wolf is a chief among the Kenhas," he said, "his tongue is not forked. The words that pass his lips come from his heart. The Chief wishes to serve his Pale friends."

"Wah!" Bright-eye said, "the Chief has spoken well. His words have sounded pleasantly in my ears. What does my brother desire?"

"To sit at the council fire of the Palefaces, and explain to them the reasons that bring him here."

"Good. Will my brother go alone among the white men?"

"No! another person will accompany the Chief."

"And who is this person in whom so great a Chief as my brother places confidence?"

"The She-Wolf of the prairies."

Bright-eye suppressed a movement of joy.

"Good," he went on, "my brother can come with the She-Wolf. The Palefaces will receive them kindly."

"My brother, the hunter, will announce the visit of his friends."

"Yes, Chief, I will go at once and do so."

The conference was over. The three men separated, after again saluting, and Bright-eye and Ivon hurried back to the entrenchments.

"Victory!" the hunter said, on arriving, "we are saved!"

All pressed round him, greedy to learn the details of the conference, and Bright-eye satisfied the general curiosity without a moment's delay.

"Ah!" Black said, "if the old lady is with them we are, indeed, saved," and he rubbed his hands joyfully.

After having failed so unluckily in the snare she had laid for Natah Otann, Mrs. Margaret, far from being discouraged, felt her desire of revenge increased; and, without losing time in regretting the check she had undergone, she immediately drew up her plans, for she had reached that pitch of rage when a person is completely blinded by hatred, and goes onward regardless of consequences. Ten minutes after leaving the Sachem, she quitted the camp, accompanied by Red Wolf, who, by her orders, led off the warriors he commanded and started for the clearing.

Bright-eye had scarce given his friends the information they desired, ere Margaret and Red Wolf entered the stockade, where they were received with the greatest affability by the trappers, and especially by Black, who was delighted to find that his clearing was not menaced, and that the storm was turning from him to burst elsewhere.

Let us now return to Fort Mackenzie, where, at this very moment, events of the utmost importance were occurring.

CHAPTER XXVII
THE ATTACK

White Buffalo and Natah Otann had drawn up their strategic arrangements with remarkable skill. The two Chiefs had scarce formed their camp in the clearing, ere they assembled the Sachems of the other tribes camped not far from them, in order to combine their movement, so as to attack the Americans simultaneously from all points.

Though the Redskins are excessively cunning, the Americans had succeeded in thoroughly deceiving them, in the gloom and silence that prevailed through the fort, for not a single bayonet could be seen glistening behind its parapets. Leaving their horses concealed in the forest, the Indians lay down on the ground, and, crawling through the tall grass like reptiles, began crossing the space that separated them from the ramparts.

All was still apparently gloomy and silent, and yet two thousand intrepid warriors were crawling up in the shadow to attack a fortress behind which forty resolute men only waited for the signal to be given, and commence the attack. When all the orders had been given, and the last warriors had quitted the hill, Natah Otann, whose perspicuous eye had discovered a certain hesitation of evil omen in the minds of the allied chiefs, resolved to make that final appeal to the Count to secure his co-operation. We have already seen the result. When left alone, Natah Otann gave the signal for attack; the Indians rushed like a hurricane down the sides of the hill, and ran towards the fort, brandishing their arms, and uttering their war yell. Suddenly a heavy discharge was heard, and Fort Mackenzie was begirt with smoke and dazzling flashes. The battle had commenced.

The plain was invaded, as far as eye could trace, by powerful detachments of Indian warriors, who, converging on one point, marched resolutely toward the fort, incessantly discharging their bullets at it; while new bands could be seen constantly arriving from the place where the chain of hills abuts on the Missouri. They came up at a gallop, in parties of from three to twenty men; their horses were covered with foam, which led to the presumption that they had come a long distance. The Blackfeet were in their war attire, loaded with all sorts of ornaments and arms, with bow and quiver on their backs, and musket in hand, while their heads were crowned with feathers, some of which were the magnificent black and white eagle plumes. They were seated on handsome saddle cloths of panther skin, lined with red; the upper part of the body was naked, with the exception of a long strip of wolf skin passing over the shoulder as a cross belt, while their bucklers were adorned with feathers and cloth of various colours.

These men, thus accoutred, had something imposing and majestic about them, which affected the imagination, and inspired terror.

The struggle seemed most obstinate in the environs of the fort, and on the hill. The Blackfeet, sheltered by tall palisades planted during the night, replied to the Americans' fire with an equally rapid fire, exciting each other, with wild cries, courageously to resist the attack of their implacable foes. The defence was, however, as vigorous as the assault, and the combat did not appear destined to terminate so soon. Already many corpses lay on the ground, startled horses galloped in every direction, and the shrieks of the wounded mingled at intervals with the defiant shouts of the assailants.

Natah Otann, so soon as the signal had been given, ran off to the tent where his prisoner was.

"The moment has arrived," he said to him.

"I am ready," the Count answered, "go on. I will keep constantly at your side."

"Come on, then!"

They went out, and at once rushed into the thickest fight. The Count, as he had said, was unarmed, raising his head fiercely at each bullet that whistled past his ear, and smiling at the death which he, perhaps, invoked in his heart. In spite of his contempt for the white race, the Indian could not refrain from admiring this courage, which was so frankly and nobly stoical.

"You are a man," he said to the Count.

"Did you ever doubt it?" the latter remarked, simply.

Still the combat became, with each moment, more obstinate. The Indians rushed forward, roaring like lions, against the palisades of the fort, and were killed without flinching; their bodies almost filled up the moat. The Americans, compelled to make a front on all sides, defended themselves with the methodical and resolute impassiveness of men who know they have no help to expect, and who have made up their minds to sell their lives dearly.

From the beginning of the fight, White Buffalo had, with a picked body of men, held the hill that commanded Fort Mackenzie, which rendered the position of the garrison still more precarious, for they were thus exposed to a terrible and well-sustained fire, which caused them irreparable loss, regard being had to the smallness of their numbers. Major Melville, standing at the foot of the flagstaff, with his arms crossed on his breast, a pallid brow and compressed lips, saw his men fall one after the other, and he stamped his foot with rage at his impotence to save them.

Suddenly, a terrific shriek of agony rose from the interior of the buildings, and the wives of the soldiers and *engagés* rushed simultaneously into the square, flying, half mad with terror, from an enemy still invisible. The Indians, guided by White Buffalo, had turned the fortress, and discovered a secret entrance which the Major fancied known to himself alone, and which, in case of a serious attack and impossibility of defence, would serve the garrison in effecting its retreat. From this moment the Americans saw that they were lost; it was no longer a battle, but a massacre. The Major, followed by a few resolute men, rushed into the buildings, and the Indians scaled on all sides the palisades, now deprived of protection.

The few surviving Americans collected round the flagstaff, from the top of which floated the starry banner of the United States, and strove to sell their lives as dearly as possible, for they feared most falling alive into the bands of their implacable enemies. The Indians replied to the hurrahs of their foes by their terrific war cry, and bounded on them like coyotes, brandishing over their heads the blood-stained weapons.

"Down with your arms!" Natah Otann shouted, on reaching the scene of action.

"Never!" the Major replied, rushing on him at the head of the few soldiers still left him.

The mêlée recommenced, more ardently and implacable than before. The Indians rushed about in every direction, throwing torches on the roofs, which immediately caught fire. The Major saw that victory was hopeless, and tried to effect his retreat. But that was not so easy; there was no chance of climbing over the palisades; the only prospect was the gate; but before that gate, the Blackfeet, skilfully posted, repulsed with their lances those who tried to escape by it. Still there was no alternative. The Major rallied his men for a final effort, and rushed with incredible fury on the enemy, with the hope of cutting his way through.

The collision was horrible—it was not a battle, but a butchery; foot to foot, chest against chest—in which the men seized each other round the waist, killed each other with knives, or tore the foe with teeth and nails: those who fell did not rise again—the wounded were finished at once. This frightful carnage lasted about a quarter of an hour; two-thirds of the

Americans succumbed; the rest managed to force a passage and fled, closely pursued by the Indians, who then commenced a horrible manhunt. Never, until this day, had the Redskins fought the Whites with such fury and tenacity. The presence among them of the Count, disarmed and smiling, who, although rushing into the thickest of the contest by the side of the Chief, appeared invulnerable, electrified them, and they really believed that Natah Otann had told them the truth—and that the Count was that Motecuhzoma they had waited so long, and whose presence would restore them for ever that liberty which the White men had torn from them. Thus they had kept their eyes constantly fixed on the young man, saluting him with noisy shouts of joy, and redoubling their efforts to secure the victory. Natah Otann rushed toward the American flag, tore it down, and wound it over his head.

"Victory—victory!" he shouted, joyfully.

The Blackfeet responded to this cry with yells, and spread in every direction to begin plundering. A few men still remained in the fort, among them being the Major, who did not wish to survive his defeat. The Indians, rushed upon him with loud yells, to massacre him, but the veteran remained calm, and did not offer to defend himself.

"Stay!" the Count shouted; and turning to Natah Otann, said,—"Will you let this brave soldier be assassinated in cold blood?"

"No," the Sachem answered, "if he consents to surrender his sword to me."

"Never!" the old gentleman said, with energy, as he broke across his knee his weapon, blood-stained to the hilt, threw the pieces at the Chief's feet, and, crossing his arms, he regarded his victor with supreme contempt, as he said—

"Kill me now; I can no longer defend myself."

"Bravo!" the Count exclaimed; and, not calculating the consequences of the deed, he went up to the Major, and cordially pressed his hand. Natah Otann regarded the two for an instant with an indefinable expression.

"Oh!" he muttered to himself, with sorrow; "we may beat them, but we shall never conquer them: these men are stronger than we; they are born to be our masters."

Then raising his hand above his head.

"Enough!" he said, in a loud voice.

"Enough!" the Count repeated, "respect the conquered."

That which the Sachem could not have obtained, in spite of the respect the Indians had for him, the Count obtained instantaneously, through the superstitious veneration he inspired them with; they stopped, and the carnage finally ceased; the Americans were disarmed in a second, and the Redskins remained masters of the fort.

Natah Otann then took his totem from the hands of the warrior who bore it, and, after swinging it several times in the air, hoisted it in the place of the American flag, in the midst of the frenzied shouts of the Indians, who, intoxicated with joy, could hardly yet believe in their victory.

White Buffalo had not lost a moment in assuring himself of the peaceful possession of a conquest which had cost the confederates so much blood and toil. When the Sachems had restored some little order among their warriors; when the fire, that threatened the destruction of the fort, had been extinguished; and all precautions taken against any renewal of the attack by the Americans—though that was very improbable—Natah Otann and White Buffalo withdrew to the apartment hitherto occupied by the Major, and the Count followed them.

"At length," the young Count exclaimed, with delight, "we have proved to these haughty Americans that they are not invincible."

"Your weakness caused their strength," White Buffalo replied. "You have made a good beginning, and now you must go on; it is not enough to conquer; you must know how to profit by that victory."

"Pardon my interrupting you, gentlemen," the Count said; "but I fancy the hour has arrived to settle our accounts."

"What do you mean, sir?" White Buffalo asked, haughtily.

"I will explain myself, sir," the Count continued, and, turning to Natah Otann, "you will do me the justice to allow that I have scrupulously kept the promise I made you; in spite of the grief and disgust I felt, I did not fail once; you ever found me cold and calm at your side. Is this not so?—answer, sir."

"It is true," Natah Otann replied, coldly.

"Very good, sir; it is now my turn to ask from you the fulfilment of the promises you made me."

"Be a little more explicit, sir," the Chief said. "During the last few hours I have been actor in and witness of so many extraordinary things, that I may possibly have forgotten what I did promise you."

The Count smiled with disdain.

"I expected such trickery," he said, drily.

"You misinterpret my words. I may have forgotten, but I do not refuse to satisfy your just claims."

"Very good; I admit that, so I will remind you of the stipulations made between us."

"I shall be glad to hear them."

"I pledged myself to remain by yourself unarmed during the action, to follow you everywhere, and ever to go in the first rank of the combatants."

"That is true, and it is my duty to allow that you have nobly performed that perilous task."

"Very well; but in doing so I only acted as my honour dictated; you, on your part, pledged yourself whatever the issue of the battle might be, to grant me my liberty, and give me an honourable satisfaction, in reparation for the unworthy treachery of which you rendered me the victim, and the odious part you forced me unconsciously to play."

"Oh, oh!" White Buffalo said, frowning, and striking the table with his fists. "Did you really make such a promise as that, child?"

The Count turned to the old man with a gesture sovereign contempt.

"I believe, sir," he said, "that you are doubting the honour of a gentleman."

"Nonsense, sir," the republican said, with a grin "How can you talk to us of honour and nobility? You forget that we are in the desert, and that you are addressing savage Indians, as you call us. Do we recognize your foolish caste distinctions here? Have we adopted your laws and absurd prejudices?"

"What you treat so cavalierly," the Count sharply retorted, "has hitherto been the safeguard of civilization, and the cause of intellectual progress; but I have nothing to discuss with you; I am addressing myself to your adopted son; let him answer me, yes or no, and I shall then know what remains for me to do."

"Be it so, sir," White Buffalo said, with a shrug of his shoulders. "Let my son answer, and, according to his reply, I shall then know what remains for me to do."

"As this affair concerns me alone," Natah Otann interposed, "I should feel mortally offended, my friend, if you interfered in any way in it."

The White Buffalo smiled with contempt, but made no reply. Natah Otann continued—

"I will employ no subterfuges with you, sir; you have spoken the truth; I promised you liberty and satisfaction, and I am prepared to keep my word."

"Oh, oh!" White Buffalo said.

"Silence!" the Chief ordered, peremptorily. "Listen, my friend; prove to these Europeans, so vain and so proud of their so-called civilization, that the Redskins are not the ferocious brutes they imagine them, and that the code of honour is the same among nations who are regarded as the most barbarous. You are free, sir, from this moment, and, if you please, I will myself lead you in safety outside the lines. As for the duel you desire, I am equally ready to satisfy you in any way you may indicate."

"Thank you, sir," the Count answered, with a bow, "I am happy to hear your determination."

"Now that affair is arranged between us, allow me to add a few words."

"I am listening to you, sir."

"Am I in the way?" White Buffalo asked, ironically.

"On the contrary," Natah Otann said, with emphasis, "your presence is at this moment more necessary than ever."

"Ah, ah! what is going to happen?" the old man went on, in a sarcastic tone.

"You will learn," the Chief said, still cold and impassive; "if you will take the trouble to listen to me for five minutes."

"Be it so; speak."

Natah Otann seemed to be collecting himself for a few moments, and said, in a voice which, spite of all his efforts to conceal it, trembled slightly, through some hidden emotion, —

"Owing to events too long to narrate here, and which I would probably possess but slight interest for you, I became the guardian of a child, who is now a charming maiden. This girl, to whom I have ever paid the greatest attention, and whom I love as a father, is known to you; her name is Prairie-Flower."

The Count quivered, and made a gesture in affirmation, but no other reply. Natah Otann continued, —

"As I am entering now on a hazardous expedition, in which I may meet my death, it is impossible for me to watch longer over this girl; it would be painful to me to leave her alone, and without support, among my tribe, if destiny were to cause my plans to fail. I know that she loves you, I entrust her to you frankly and honestly; I have full faith in your honour—will you give to her protection? I know that you will never abuse the trust I offer you; I am only a brutalized Indian, a monster, perhaps, to your civilization; but, believe me, sir, the lessons a great man has consented to give me have not been all lost, and my heart is not so dead, as might be supposed, to finer feelings."

"Good, Natah Otann," White Buffalo said, joyfully; "good, my son. Now I recognize my pupil, and I am proud of you; the man who succeeds in each a victory over self is really born to command others."

"You are satisfied," the Chief answered; "all the better. And you, sir? I await your answer."

"I accept the sacred trust you offer me, sir. I will be worthy of your confidence," the Count answered, with much emotion. "I have no right to judge your actions; but, believe, sir, that whatever may happen, there will be always one man to defend your memory, and proclaim aloud the nobility of your heart."

The Chief clapped his hands, the door opened, and Prairie-Flower appeared, led by an Indian woman.

"Child," Natah Otann said to her, nothing evincing the violence he did to his feelings, "your presence among us is henceforth impossible; this Chief of the Palefaces consents to watch over you for the future; follow him, and if at times you are reminded of your stay with the tribe of the Kenhas, do not curse them or their Chief, for all have been kind to you."

The maiden blushed, the tears rose to her eyes, a nervous tremor agitated her limbs, and, without uttering a word, she took her place by the Count's side. Natah Otann smiled sorrowfully.

"Follow me," he said, "I will escort you out of the camp."

And he went out, accompanied by the two young people.

"We shall soon meet again, I presume, noble Count?" White Buffalo called out, after his countryman.

"I hope so," the latter answered, simply.

Guided by Natah Otann, the Count and his companion left the fort, and entered the prairie, passing through groups of Redskins, who stood back respectfully to make room for them. Their walk was silent; it lasted about half an hour, until the Chief stopped.

"Here you have nothing more to fear," he said; and going to a dense thicket, and pulling back the branches, "Here are two horses I had prepared for you; take also these weapons, perhaps you will need them; and now, if you wish to fight with me, I am ready."

"No," the Count answered, nobly, "any combat is henceforth impossible between us; I can no longer be the enemy of a man whom honour orders me to esteem; here is my hand, I will never lift it against you; I offer it you frankly, and without any afterthought; unfortunately, too deep a hatred divides our two races to prevent us being ere long opposed to each other, but if I fight your brothers, I shall not the less remain personally your friend."

"I ask no more of you," the Chief replied, as he pressed the hand offered him; "farewell! be happy!"

And without adding a word, he turned away, and hurried back by the road he had come; he soon disappeared in the darkness.

"Let us go," the Count said to the maiden, who was pensively watching the departure of the man she had so long loved as a father, and whom now she did not feel strong enough to hate. They mounted and went off, after a parting glance at the scattered fire of the Blackfoot camp.

CHAPTER XXVIII
CONCLUSION

The night was gloomy, cold, and mournful; not a star shone in the sky, and the young people only forced their way with extreme difficulty through the shrubs and creepers, in which their horses' feet were continually caught. They advanced very slowly, for both were too absorbed by the strange situation in which they found themselves, and the extraordinary events of which they had been actors or witnesses, to break the silence they had maintained since leaving the fort. They went on thus for about an hour, when a great noise was suddenly heard in the bushes. Two men rushed to the horses' heads, and, seizing the bridles, compelled them to stop. Prairie-Flower gave a shriek of terror.

"Halloh, brigands!" the Count shouted, as he cocked his pistols, "back, or I fire."

"Do not do so, for goodness sake, sir, for you would run the risk of killing a friend," a voice at once answered, which the Count recognized as the hunter's.

"Bright-eye?" he said, in amazement.

"By Jove!" the latter said, "did you fancy, pray, that I had deserted you?"

"My master, my kind master!" the Breton shouted, leaving hold of Prairie-Flower's bridle, and rushing toward the young man.

"Halloh!" the Count continued, after the emotion caused by the first surprise was slightly calmed, "what on earth are you doing here in ambush, like pirates of the prairie?"

"Come to our encampment, Mr. Edward, and we will tell you."

"Very good; but lead the way."

They soon reached the entrance of a natural cavern, where, by the uncertain light of an expiring fire, they perceived a large number of white and half-bred hunters, among whom the Count recognized John Black, his son, his wife, and daughter. The worthy squatter had left the clearing under the charge of his two servants, and fearing lest his wife and daughter might not be in safety during his absence, he asked them to accompany him; and though this offer was somewhat singular, they gladly accepted it. Prairie-Flower immediately took her place by the side of the two ladies.

Bright-eye, the squatter, and above all Ivon, were impatient to learn what had happened to the Count, and how he had succeeded in escaping from the Redskin camp. The Count made no difficulty in satisfying their curiosity; the more so, as he was eager to learn for what reason his friends were ambuscaded so near the camp.

What the hunter had foreseen had really happened; scarce victors over the Americans, and masters of the fort, disunion had set in among the Redskins. Several Chiefs had been dissatisfied at seeing, to their prejudice, Natah Otann, one of the youngest Sachems of the Confederates, claim the profits of the victory, by installing himself, with his tribe, in the fort, which all had captured at such an effusion of blood; a dull discontentment had begun to prevail among them; five or six of the most powerful even spoke, hardly two hours after the victory, of withdrawing with their warriors, and leaving Natah Otann to continue the war as he thought proper with the Whites.

Red Wolf had found but slight difficulty in commencing the work of defection he meditated; thus, at nightfall, he entered the camp with his warriors, and began fanning the flame which at present only smouldered, but which must soon be a burning and devouring fire, owing to the means of corruption the Chief had at his disposal. Of all the destructive agents introduced by Europeans in America, the most effective and terrible is, indubitably, spirits. With the exception of the Comanches, whose sobriety is proverbial, and who have constantly refused to drink anything but the water of their streams, all the Indians are mad for strong liquors. Drunkenness among their primitive race is terrible, and attains the proportions of a furious mania.

Red Wolf, who burned to avenge himself on Natah Otann, and who, besides, blindly obeyed the insinuations of Mrs. Margaret, had conceived an atrocious plan, which only an Indian born was capable of forming. John Black had brought with him into the desert a considerable stock of whiskey. Red Wolf had asked for this, placed it on sledges, and thus entered the camp. The Indians, when they knew the species of merchandize he brought with him, did not hesitate to give him a hearty reception.

The Chief, while indoctrinating them, and representing Natah Otann to them as a man who had only acted from personal motives, and with the intention of satiating his own wild ambition, generously abandoned to them the spirits he had brought with him. The Indians eagerly accepted the present Red Wolf made them, and, without the loss of a moment, took hearty draughts. When Red Wolf saw that the Indians had reached that state of intoxication he desired, he hastened to warn his allies, so that they might attempt a bold *coup de main* on the spot.

The hunters at once mounted their horses, and proceeded toward the fortress, concealing themselves about two hundred paces from it, so as to be ready for the first signal.

Natah Otann, in crossing the camp after escorting the two young people, perceived the effervescence prevailing among his allies, and several unpleasant epithets struck his ear. Although he did not suppose that the Americans, after the rude defeat they had suffered during the day, were in a condition to assume the offensive immediately, still, his thorough knowledge of his countrymen's character made him suspect treachery, and he resolved to redouble his prudence, in order to avoid a conflict, whose disastrous results would be incalculable for the success of his career. Agitated by a gloomy foreboding, the young Chief hurried on to reach the fort; but at the moment he prepared to enter, after opening the gate, a heavy hand was laid on his shoulder, while a rough voice hissed in his ear—

"Natah Otann is a traitor."

The Chief turned, as if a serpent had stung him, and wheeling his heavy axe round his head, dealt a terrible blow at this bold speaker; but the latter avoided the stroke by springing on one side, and raising his axe in his turn, he directed a blow, which the Sachem parried with the handle of his weapon, and then the two men rushed on each other. There was something singularly startling in this desperate combat between two men dumb as shadows, and in whom their fury was only revealed by the hissing of their breath.

"Die, dog!" Natah Otann suddenly said, his axe crashing through the skull of his adversary, who rolled on the ground, with a yell of agony. The Chief bent over him.

"Red Wolf," he shouted, "I suspected it."

Suddenly an almost imperceptible sound in the grass reminded him of the critical situation in which he was; he made a prodigious bound back, entered the fort, and bolted the gate after him. It was high time; he had scarce disappeared, ere some twenty warriors, rushing in pursuit of him, ran their heads against the gate, stifling cries of rage and deception. But the alarm had been given, the general combat was evidently about to begin.

Natah Otann, immediately on entering the fort, perceived, with a groan, that this victory, which he had so dearly bought, was on the point of slipping from him. The Kenhas had done within the fort what the other Blackfeet, incited by Red Wolf, had effected on the prairie.

After the capture of the fortress they spread in every direction, and the spirits did not long escape their search; they had rolled the barrels into the square, and tapped them, availing themselves of the White Buffalo being asleep, and the absence of Natah Otann, the only two men whose influence would have been great enough to have kept them in subordination. A frightful orgy had then commenced—an Indian orgy, with all its incidents of murder and massacre. As we have said, drunkenness in the Redskins is madness carried to the last paroxysm of fury and rage; there had been a frightful scene of carnage, at the end of which the Indians had fallen on the top of one another, and gone to sleep in the midst of the confusion.

"Oh!" the Chief muttered, in despair. "What is to be done with such men?"

Natah Otann rushed, into the room where he had left White Buffalo; the old Chief was quietly sleeping in an easy chair.

"Woe! woe!" the young man yelled, as he rushed toward him, and shook him vigorously, to rouse him.

"What is the matter?" the old man asked, opening his eyes, and sitting up. "What news have you?"

"That we are lost!" the Chief replied.

"Lost!" the White Buffalo said, "what is happening then?"

"The six hundred men we had here are drunk, the rest of our confederates are turning against us, and the only thing left to us is to die."

"Let us die then, but as brave men," the old man said, rising.

He asked Natah Otann for details, which he soon gave him.

"The situation is grave, but all is not lost, I hope," he said; "let us collect the few men still capable of fighting, and make head against the storm."

At this moment a tremendous fusillade was heard, mingled with war cries and shouts of defiance.

"The final struggle has commenced!" Natah Otann exclaimed.

"Forwards!" the old Chief said.

They rushed out. The situation was most critical. Major Melville, taking advantage of the intoxication of his keepers, had broken out of his prison at the head of some twenty Americans, and boldly charged the Redskins, while the hunters outside tried to scale the barricades.

The Indians of the prairie, ignorant of Red Wolf's death, and believing they were carrying out his plans, advanced, in a compact body, on the fort, with the intention of carrying it. Natah Otann had to contend against the enemies without and those within; but he did not despair; his energy seemed to increase with peril; he was everywhere at once; encouraging some, rebuking others, and imparting some of his own nerve to all. At his voice, many of his warriors sprang up, and joined him; then the battle was organized, and became regular.

Still the hunters, excited by the Count and Bright-eye, redoubled their efforts; climbing on each other's backs, they reached the top of the palisades, which they wished to scale. The Americans, though themselves surprised, when they expected to surprise their enemies, fought with indescribable fury, returning instantly to the attack in spite of the bullets that decimated them, and seemed resolved to fall to the last man, rather than give way an inch.

During the two hours that night still lasted, the fight was maintained without any decided advantage on either side; but when the sun appeared on the horizon, matters changed at once. In the darkness it was impossible for the Indians to recognize the enemies against whom they were fighting; but so soon as the gloom was dissipated, they saw, combating in the first rank of their enemies, and pitilessly cutting down the Redskins, the man on whom they counted most, whom their chiefs and medicine men had announced to them as their leader to victory, who would render them invincible. Then they hesitated, disorder broke out among them, and, in spite of the efforts made by Chiefs, they gave way.

The Count, having at his side Bright-eye, the squatter and his son, and Ivon, made a frightful butchery of the Indians; he was avenging himself for the treachery of which they had made him their victim, and, at each stroke, cut them down like corn ripe for the sickle. The Count at length reached the gate of the fort; but there he came in contact with a band of picked warriors, commanded by White Buffalo, who was effecting his retreat in good order, and without turning his back, closely pursued by Major Melville, who was already almost master of the interior of the fortress. There was a moment, we will not say of hesitation, but of truce between the hostile bands; each of them understood that the fate of the battle depended on the defeat of the other.

Suddenly Natah Otann made his appearance, mad with grief and rage; brandishing in one hand his totem, he guided with his knees a magnificent steed, with which he had already ridden several times into the thickest of the enemies' ranks, in the vain hope of reanimating the courage of his men, and turning the current of the action. Horse and rider were bathed in blood and perspiration; the shadow of death already brooded over the Chiefs contracted face; but his forehead still shone with enthusiasm. His eyes seemed to flash forth lightning, and his hand wielded an axe, the very handle of which dripped gore. Some twenty devoted warriors followed him, wounded like himself, but resolved, like him, not to survive defeat.

On reaching the front of the American line, Natah Otann stopped; his eyebrows were contracted, a nervous smile played round his lips; and, rising in his stirrups, he bent a fascinating glance around.

"Blackfeet, my brothers," he shouted, in a strident voice, "as you know not how to conquer, learn at least from me how to die!"

And burying his spurs in the flanks of his steed, which shrieked with pain, he rushed on the Americans, followed by a few warriors who had sworn not to abandon him. This weak band, devoted to death, was engulfed in the ranks of the hunters, when it entirely disappeared; for a few minutes there was a sullen contest, a horrible butchery, an ebb and flow of courage impossible to describe, a Titanic struggle of fifteen half naked men against three hundred; gradually the agitation ceased, the calm returned, and the ranks of the hunters were reformed. The Blackfeet heroes were dead, but they had a sanguinary funeral, for one hundred and twenty Americans had fallen, burying their enemies under their corpses.

White Buffalo's band alone resisted; but, attacked in the rear by Major Melville, and in front by the Count, its last hour had struck: still the collision was rude, the Indians resisted obstinately, and made the whites purchase their victory dearly; but, attacked on all sides at once, and falling helplessly under the unerring bullets of the white men, disorder entered their ranks, they disbanded, and the rout commenced.

One man alone remained calm and impassive on the field of battle. It was White Buffalo, leaning on his long sword; with pallid brow and haughty look, he still defied the enemies he could no longer combat.

"Surrender!" Bright-eye shouted, as he rushed upon him; "surrender, or I will shoot you like a dog."

The Chief smiled disdainfully, and made no reply. The implacable hunter seized his rifle by the barrel, and whirled it round his head. The Count seized him sharply by the arm.

"Stay, Bright-eye," he said.

"Let the man alone," White Buffalo said, coldly.

"I do not wish him to kill you," the young man replied.

"I suppose you wish to kill me yourself, noble Count of Beaulieu," he said, in a cutting voice.

"No, sir," the young man said, with disdain; "throw down your weapons; I spare your life."

The exile gave him a withering glance. "Instead of telling me to throw down my weapons," he said, ironically, "why do you not try to take them from me."

"Because I pity your age and your grey hair,"

"Pity? confess rather, O noble Count, that you are afraid."

At this insult the young man trembled, and his face became livid. The Americans formed a circle round the two men, and anxiously awaited what was going to happen.

"Put an end to this!" Major Melville exclaimed, "kill that mad brute."

"One moment, sir, I beg; let me settle this affair,"

"As you wish it, air, act as you think proper."

"You desire a duel then?" the Count said, addressing White Buffalo, who still stood perfectly calm.

"Yes," he answered, through his clenched teeth, "a duel to the death! two principles, and not two men, will contend here. I hate your race, and you hate mine."

"Be it so."

The Count took two sabres from the hands of the men nearest him, and threw one at the exile's feet. The latter stooped to pick it up, but as he rose again, Ivon aimed a pistol at him, and blew out his brains.

The young man turned furiously on his servant.

"Wretched fellow," he shouted, "what have you done?"

"Kill me, if you will, sir," the Breton replied, simply, "but indeed it was stronger than myself, I was so frightened."

"Come, come," the Major said, interposing, "you must not be angry with the poor fellow, he fancied he was acting for the best, and for my part I think he was."

The incident had no other result; the exile died on the spot, taking with him the secret of his name.

While this scene was taking place in the courtyard of the fort, John Black, who was anxious to reassure his wife and daughter, went to look for them; but though he went through all the rooms and outbuildings of the fort, where he had concealed them for a few minutes previously, he could not possibly find them anywhere.

The poor squatter returned, with lengthened face and despair in his soul, to announce to the Major the disappearance of his wife and daughter, probably carried off by the Indians. Without losing a moment, the Major ordered a dozen hunters to go in search of the ladies; but just as the band was about to start, they arrived, accompanied by Bright-eye and two American hunters. Margaret and her daughter were with them. So soon as Prairie-Flower perceived the Count, she uttered a cry of joy, and rushed toward him.

"Saved!" she exclaimed.

But all at once she blushed, trembled, and went in confusion to seek refuge by her mother's side. The Count went up, took her hand, and pressed it tenderly.

"Prairie-Flower," he said to her, softly, "do you no longer love me now that I am free?"

The maiden raised her head, and looked at him for a moment with tear-laden eyes.

"Oh! ever, ever!" she answered.

"Look, daughter," Mrs. Black said to poor Diana.

"Mother," she replied, in a firm voice, "did I not tell you that I should forget him?"

The squatter's wife shook her head, but made no further remark. The Indians had fled without leaving a man, and a few hours later the fort returned to its old condition.

The winter passed away without any fresh incident, for the rude lesson given the Indians had done them good. Prairie-Flower, recognized by her uncle, remained at Fort Mackenzie. The girl was sorrowful and pensive; she often spent long hours leaning over the parapets, with her eyes fixed on the prairie and the forests, which were beginning to reassume their green dress. Her mother and the Major, who were so fond of her, could not at all understand the gloomy melancholy that preyed upon her. When pressed to explain what she suffered from, she replied, invariably, that there was nothing the matter with her.

One day, however, her face brightened up, and her joyous smile reappeared. Three travellers arrived at the fort. They were the Count, Bright-eye, and Ivon; they were returning from a long excursion in the

Rocky Mountains. As soon as he arrived, the Count went up to the maiden, and took her hand, as he had done three months before.

"Prairie-Flower," he asked her once again, "do you no longer love me?"

"Oh! yes, and for ever!" the poor child answered, gently, for she had grown timid since she gave up her desert life.

"Thank you," he said to her; and, turning to the Major and his sister, who were looking at each other anxiously, he added, without loosing the hand he held,—"Major Melville, and you, Madam, I ask you for this lady's hand."

A week later the marriage was solemnized; the squatter and his family were present. And a month previously, Diana had married James. Still, when the "yes" was uttered, she could not suppress a sigh.

"You see, Ivon, that you are never killed by the Indians—and here is a proof of it," Bright-eye said to the Breton, on leaving the chapel.

"I am beginning to believe it," the latter made answer, "but no matter, my friend, I shall never get accustomed to this frightful country; it makes me so afraid."

"The old humbug!" the Canadian muttered; "he will never alter."